THE
Death
LAW

D^{THE}eath LAW

For Sally —

CLAIRE COLE CURCIO

Claire Cole Curcio
January 9, 2016

ARCHWAY
PUBLISHING

Archway Publishing books may be ordered through booksellers or by contacting:

Archway Publishing
1663 Liberty Drive
Bloomington, IN 47403
www.archwaypublishing.com
1 (888) 242-5904

Because of the dynamic nature of the Internet, any web addresses or
links contained in this book may have changed since publication and
may no longer be valid. The views expressed in this work are solely those
of the author and do not necessarily reflect the views of the publisher,
and the publisher hereby disclaims any responsibility for them.

Any people depicted in stock imagery provided by Thinkstock are models,
and such images are being used for illustrative purposes only.
Certain stock imagery © Thinkstock.

ISBN: 978-1-4808-2234-4 (sc)
ISBN: 978-1-4808-2233-7 (hc)
ISBN: 978-1-4808-2235-1 (e)

Library of Congress Control Number: 2015916870

Print information available on the last page.

Archway Publishing rev. date: 10/14/2015

DEDICATION

For my family, for their on-going belief that I could do this,

and

For my sweet Selby, who rekindled my
zest for life so I could write again.

I was inspired to write this book through knowing
the "shaking Quaker", Byron Sandford, Executive
Director of The William Penn House in Washington,
DC, and the dedicated and caring staff and the residents
of Spring Hills Mount Vernon in Alexandria, VA.

ACKNOWLEDGEMENTS AND THANKS

Two people were integral to this novel's completion. My partner Selby McCash taught me the intricacies, trials and tribulations of journalism and Congressional work. To the extent that this book is accurate, Selby gets the credit. Inaccuracies are probably where I didn't ask him for help. When I was really bogged down, he'd leave his own writing and read a section to help me get started again. Dr. June McCash, my fictive sister-in-law and a well-published author herself, helped with both the publication process and the content of this book. I learned how to write something other than a textbook from June.

I thank family members for listening to progress reports far more than they were interested in and for believing in me: Lt. Col. (ret.) Scott Cole for helping shape the characters early on in the book; Dr. Jane Roberts for giving me numerous sources and suggestions on how to do the gerontology parts of the book, as well as vetting some of the content; Patrick Cole for continuing encouragement and interest; Robin Lacy and family for building confidence by giving me a fancy book-signing pen for Christmas; and Steve Cole for being the first person actually to read the manuscript all the way through, with encouragement and helpful suggestions.

Friends were very important in the shaping and writing of this book. Dr. Karen Scanlon reminded me that bad guys in Congress are not party- or ideologically-specific. Ronda Worcester offered enthusiasm for the work and corrections that many other eyes had missed. Lisa Vittoria gave me a whole new idea to include. Ann Bernardi, LCSW, offered validation and wrote a heartfelt review of the work. Carole Klumb dared to tell me some things that just didn't work in an early version, but offered encouragement as well. The Rev. Pam Webb helped me get the priest parts right (rite?).

My wonderful editor, Emily Carmain, offered much more than simply getting the words correct. Michelle Brantley is a very positive and most efficient detail-oriented personal assistant.

Two groups were particularly important. The Trinity Episcopal Church (Fredericksburg, VA) Women's Book Group, the most awesome group of women anywhere, had faith all the way. The Water Street Studio Writers' Group in Fredericksburg, VA, critiqued, corrected and cheered both the writing and the publication process.

Thanks are never enough – but thanks, everybody! And love to you all.

PART ONE
The Beginning

CHAPTER 1

Kill old people to save money? Is that what she'd just heard on the radio?

Julia Sanchez threaded her way through the morning gridlock into the District of Columbia. Vivaldi on the radio had made a soothing counterpoint to the traffic until she heard the news bulletin. In the car's mirror, Julia was checking the streaks of gray in her short glossy black hair when the announcer interrupted the music. At fifty-eight, she was aging gracefully, but should she listen to the television ads and cover up that gray?

She was startled to hear the radio newscaster say, "A bill has just been signed into law. People seventy years or older unable to care for themselves are subject to euthanasia by the government, according to a law signed by the President last night. Americans are expressing shock, anger and disbelief at this new death law. We couldn't find a legislator willing to comment. Stay tuned for further details on this breaking news."

What legislation? As chief of staff for veteran Congressman Marcus Simms of Florida, Julia kept up with current and proposed legislation. She hadn't heard anything about this.

She hated her morning commute. The traffic had always

been awful but now it was even worse with abandoned construction projects clogging every roadway. Since the budget crisis of the past several months, there was no money to continue the work. Abandoned road-repair machines obstructed traffic on major highways while potholes and out-of-repair stoplights and signs impeded progress on minor roads. The only good part was there was considerably less traffic with much of the government closed down because of the budget situation.

She wheeled into her parking space in the underground caverns of the Sam Rayburn House Office Building and rushed upstairs to her office. Other staffers hurried by, heads down. She wondered if they, too, had heard the news.

Most of Julia's staff had not yet arrived. Closing the door to her office, she called her most trusted fellow congressional staffer.

Max answered immediately. "Hi, Julia."

"Did you hear the news this morning?"

"I just did. Do you know what they're talking about?"

"No," said Julia. "I can't think of anything waiting for a signature, other than that big budget and defense bill."

"Yeah, everyone was so eager to vote, to end the government shutdown," said Max. "That's the first true bi-partisan agreement we've had in years."

"Oh, God, do you suppose the death language was buried in there somewhere? We were so engrossed with re-election, we probably didn't read it as well as we should've."

"You might be right. Uh-oh, remember that line in a rider about choosing death if you're sick?"

"Oh, no, Max, remember that human trafficking bill that got through awhile back with the abortion language in it we didn't notice? I thought we'd learned our lesson after that one. Is this the same thing? How'd they sneak it through both the House and the Senate? That took a lot of conniving!"

A few more phone calls convinced Julia they'd all been caught flat-footed. Nobody knew anything, other than that line about physician-assisted suicide.

Max called back and said, "Oh, hell, what do we do now, Julia?"

The death law, as it was soon called by everyone, had been secretly conceived by politicians colluding in both the House and the Senate to reduce the alarming budget deficit and was so well camouflaged that it surprised almost everyone. The wily politicos inserted a sentence into a budget bill to curtail skyrocketing costs of Medicare, Medicaid, and Social Security. They buried it deep in legislation heavy on defense spending and measures to avoid government shutdown, and the sentence somehow escaped everyone's notice. The complicit President had signed it into law immediately.

Congressmen not in the know on the death law were horrified at the Monday morning news. Thus began chaos.

Following the Biblical measure of three score and ten, the death law targeted people seventy and older incapable of caring for themselves. The language was convoluted and softened so that people assumed it to be a humanitarian measure intended to alleviate human suffering. The timeline required the death law to take effect in six months.

However, on closer reading, it *mandated* curtailment of life for those with a disability or afflicted with a terminal or debilitating disease. The growing population of Americans with Alzheimer's and other dementias was a particular target.

The political climate was a perfect storm for passage of the bill. Slipped into the dense language of another bill, timed around ending a government shut-down, slated for a vote when incumbents needed to go home to campaign, the death law went unexamined until too late. No legislator debated end-of-life issues in the well of the House or Senate but plenty advocated the reopening of the government. However, deep down, especially to younger legislators, the death law made logical, albeit gruesome, economic sense.

The government shutdown had been devastating to the economy. A twenty-first-century version of bread lines formed at soup kitchens and food pantries. Schools and senior centers ran out of money feeding both ends of the age spectrum. Garbage piled up on the streets and hungry people, some quite well-dressed from their former lives, furtively poked through it trying to find something, anything, still edible.

Crime skyrocketed, especially shoplifting, as desperate adults tried to feed their families. Cutbacks in spending for public safety had dramatically reduced police forces and security guards, and those remaining operated almost as SWAT teams trying to keep order in the chaotic marketplace. Mental health and social service agencies had virtually ceased to exist due to loss of funds, and churches struggled to feed the homeless and poor. Illegal aliens thought about going back home but trains, planes, and buses weren't running dependably anymore.

In short, the country was a mess. Everybody was mad at the government, all parts, all branches, all parties, all legislators, all employees. In retrospect, no wonder Congress had voted hastily late at night on a package that included the death law. The government had to reopen, and a few legislators had been clever enough to slip in some devastating legislation.

In theory, it couldn't happen. In fact, it had. The battle to save the senior citizens was on.

Julia put her head in her hands, thinking of her own parents. Her mother, seventy-four, had mid-stage Alzheimer's. Her step-father, though mentally competent at seventy-five, was mostly wheelchair-bound with Parkinson's disease. A black wave broke over her as she realized what this legislation portended. She remembered her own father's last year – unable to walk or speak intelligibly after a stroke, young man though he was. She recalled her relief when her father died. Even though only a small child herself, she had understood her mother's despair over finding him care in a health system largely inaccessible to undocumented residents. Julia was joyous many years later when her mother, by then an American citizen, married Henry Horton. Julia also welcomed no longer being fully responsible for Beatriz, her aging mother.

Lately she'd begun to worry anew about taking care of her mother and stepfather in coming years. *What if the death law is really a good thing?* The enormity of the moral, financial, and legal questions flooded her mind and Julia couldn't decide if this death law was good, bad, or somewhere in between, or what it portended for her family. But she did know they were all in deep trouble as the belated debate commenced, carried out in the public eye of C-SPAN and other media.

Julia had fought for her every success. Born to a young illegal immigrant mother, she herself was an American citizen by virtue of her birth in the United States. Julia had loved school and her mother made sure she did her homework every night.

She quickly became the star of every class she ever attended. Her teachers paid special attention to the bright, attentive, diligent little girl.

She'd done her homework in the kitchens of big houses where her mother worked. With no other entertainment, Julia either studied or read quietly. Her mother wouldn't work for women who wouldn't allow Julia in their houses after school. Scholarships had put her through college and graduate school and hard work had guided her to her current prestigious position. Because the death law required ending her sick mother's life, Julia felt betrayed by her own government.

Right now the family did okay, all living together with excellent daytime and on-call evening assistance, costly but workable. Julia worried that the time neared when she would be unable to do enough for her parents. She hated to admit it, but the law could actually make the next several years of her own life much simpler. She would grieve their deaths, but would be relieved of their care.

What if she had to stay home with them? Could they all get along on her parents' pensions – a teacher's annuity and Social Security? She was in the prime of her career, never married because she'd not found the right person. What of her own future if she sacrificed her career to take care of them?

Analogous to a single parent, Julia was a single child with needy parents. Would it be more humane to give her parents the best possible care for the next several months and then have them exit their lives, and hers? The enormity of the moral issues involved overwhelmed her.

Deep in thought, Julia responded in perfunctory manner when her phone rang: "Simms' office, Julia speaking."

"Jake Jordan here, with the Kidd-Ruddman news service. We

met a month or two ago at a reception. Would you have time for a few questions?"

Julia remembered Jake, a journalist she'd noticed because he was older and more congenial. She'd enjoyed a few minutes' conversation with him before heading home to relieve her parents' caregiver. His alert blue eyes had engaged hers as they chatted and she'd been sorry to leave. She'd felt listened to, not interviewed, unusual when sharing a glass of wine with the media.

She debated. Should she refer him elsewhere? See what he knew about the death law? She knew that was what this call concerned. Her need to know about the legislation outweighed her usual caution. "How can I help you?" she asked.

"How do you think the death law will affect Representative Simms' constituents? Is he in favor of killing old people?"

"Representative Simms believes that we urgently need to have a conversation on end-of-life decisions. He voted for the bill so that medical personnel who help ailing elders carry out their decisions will not become criminals or pariahs of society."

Julia realized she had no idea why Simms had voted for this. This call was probably the beginning of an onslaught. She needed to call a staff meeting immediately and figure out damage control, before every constituent in the state of Florida dialed the DC office.

"Look, Jake, I'm glad to hear from you but I'm really tied up right now. Could we have lunch tomorrow?"

"I have a deadline on this," he persisted. "Can't you take a few minutes now?"

"No, I have a meeting."

"Breakfast?" ventured Jake.

"Okay, seven-thirty at Grady's in the morning," said Julia, desperate to get off the phone and rally her staff.

"Fine," he said.

Julia sent out an all-hands-on-deck memo for an immediate meeting. Mystified, staff began trickling into the conference room. It took a very few minutes for the bewildered staff to realize that something monumental had escaped all of them. It couldn't have happened to such a diligent staff ... but it had. Such meetings were repeated in most offices in the building.

CHAPTER 2

Tuesday, November 8

Jake took his morning meds and pondered what the death law might mean for him personally. At the age of sixty-four, he was still vigorous and active in his career as a journalist. But he was aware that the heart disease he'd fought for years would eventually catch up with him. As with many other men his age, he'd faced down prostate cancer but knew it could recur.

Widowed when his wife died in a head-on collision with a drunk driver many years ago, and childless, Jake was not particularly concerned with longevity. However, he still enjoyed life and did not believe the government should dictate his life span.

He dressed with a little more care than usual, since he was meeting an influential, attractive woman. He still had his wits, some of his hair and a reasonable girth. He got out his clippers to tidy up his short gray beard and thought his blue-striped tie looked pretty good with his blue eyes.

Jake saw Julia immediately when he entered Grady's. She was even more punctual than he, and he was early. Her booth was against a wall strewn with photos of legislators shaking hands with almost everyone in the world. He greeted her, ordered coffee, and mentally girded himself for a verbal sparring match.

The waiter said, "Yeah, we got coffee and hot food today. We were worried when they threatened to shut down electricity with the budget cuts, but now that Congress got us out of the mess, everything's working. Too bad about the old people, though."

Julia and Jake exchanged a glance at the departing waiter's words. She surprised him with, "I hope you know something about this death law, because we've been caught flat-footed."

"It caught us journalists by surprise, too. I'm researching an in-depth story on what it means for seniors."

"If you can tell us that, you're our hero," said Julia. "We were swamped by phone calls from Floridians yesterday. Nobody else seems to know anything about this, either."

Their breakfast conversation led both Julia and Jake privately to the same two conclusions: neither knew anything about the death law, and they'd enjoyed each other's company. Both intended to find out more about the new law.

In his office Jake pondered what the death law meant to various segments of the population. A reporter on every street corner, interviewing passers-by, covered the surface aspects of the story, so he intended to investigate more deeply. He planned a series of stories and columns, maybe even a book later. He'd interview people over seventy who were in the searchlight of the death law, as well as their caregivers. He could also talk to those who were apparently not affected at present. Dreams of a Pulitzer flitted through his brain.

Julia walked briskly back to her office, her mind a clutter of organizational details. She now knew that neither other staff in her immediate circle nor well-informed journalists knew much about the death law. She began planning strategy, first to circle the wagons and brief their legislator as well as they could. The most empathic staffers in her office could handle the phones as outraged queries from the home district in Florida poured in.

They needed to use the press to their office's best advantage. Julia speculated that Jake would be her best contact, plus she'd get to see him again. She was getting tired of her single life, all work and worry and no play. Jake looked interesting.

She immediately sensed tension as she entered her office area. Staffers were bent over their computers while Representative Simms screamed at the top of his voice, "What the Sam hell is going on here and why doesn't anyone know? Where's Julia?" Julia noted Simms' use of his trademark expletive, a deliberate malapropism, and herded him into his private office.

Thankful Simms had been out of the office yesterday, she began, "Marcus, it might not be as bad as you think."

He yelled, "No, missy, it's probably a zillion times worse. What the Sam hell!" From years of working together, she knew his roaring would calm down. However, this time she felt like roaring herself, or at least whimpering a little.

"Marcus, we were blind-sided. Didn't you hear anything about it yourself?"

She regretted her words as he snarled, "Would I be asking you if I had? I thought staff was for keeping me informed!" Twenty minutes later, Julia exited his office ready to marshal the staff to action, more than a little shaken herself.

In his many years of covering Congress, Jake couldn't think of any bill that had been pushed through as covertly as the death law. Questions streamed furiously through his mind. His notes gradually emerged as the outline of a story, a series of stories, even a book. The chaos had overtones of a farcical television show, but there wasn't anything funny about what was happening.

His thoughts racing, he wrote, "Effect on economy – spending habits of senior citizens? Health care costs – diminished senior care – economy gets better or worse??? Independent living and assisted care? The homeless and poor? Senior communities? Take care of yourself – financially, physically, mentally? Tourism industry with no senior travelers? Religious leaders' views? Illicit drug traffic to ease the fear of death? A new subset of Dr. Deaths? A Disneyland of Death explaining what death is and where'd Grandma go? Medicare, Social Security, Medicaid – effect?" The more he wrote, the more he wondered. Would a smart lawyer contend that the death law itself constituted elder abuse?

Putting aside his growing feeling of doom, Jake considered his idea of interviewing people potentially affected by the mandate. Some internet research and a call to a professor or two would help him shape the backstory.

But where to begin? At breakfast, Julia had said her parents were in precarious health. Maybe that was a starting place. At the very least, he'd get to talk to her again.

Surprised but pleased to hear from Jake again so soon, Julia hesitated. "Well, I don't know... I guess. Morning's the best time to interview my stepdad, and he'll be the one talking. If he agrees, of course." As she hung up the phone, she recalled her boss's words earlier in the day, "This is one g-d effing mess, isn't it?!"

Little did they know how profanely prophetic those words were.

CHAPTER 3

Wednesday, November 9

Henry had readily agreed to the interview. Jake arrived at Julia's house and admired the neighborhood in the DC suburb of Falls Church, near a Metro station, on a tree-lined street of moderately sized houses. Jake knew even a modest home in this area was still a high-priced property. The people he saw getting into their cars and walking dogs were fashionably dressed apparent professionals of different ethnic groups. One man wore a turban and a suit as he walked his tiny brown dog. The lawns were well kept and the houses tidy and individual in style. The driveways featured Mercedes, Saabs and an occasional SmartCar.

Jake never liked interviews on sad subjects, though Lord knows, he'd done too many of them in his journalistic career. He gathered his small digital recorder, pen and notebook and rang the doorbell.

An elderly man in a wheelchair opened the door. "Hello, I'm Henry Horton – you must be Jake," he said, offering a palsied hand in greeting.

"Thank you for meeting with me," Jake said. He saw a smiling, well-groomed older woman seated on a couch, holding a crossword puzzle. "I really appreciate your taking the time to talk."

"Time – that's all we got! Or at least, that's what I thought until they passed this law," said Henry. "Julia's in the kitchen fixing coffee. Then I told her to go to work." He confided, "I might say things I don't want her to hear. Can I say some stuff that might not go in your article?"

"Yes, we can go off the record. I'm hoping you'll let me use some of your thoughts on the death law."

As they sat down, Jake could see the woman staring at the crossword puzzle. He held out his hand to her and said, "You must be Beatriz." She gazed at the outstretched hand, looked vacantly at Jake for several seconds, and returned to her crossword puzzle, her smile never changing.

The living room was brightly decorated in a Latin American theme with rugs, paintings and small artifacts. Dark leather furniture made a pleasant backdrop for the colorful objects. Julia entered the room bearing a tray of coffee and cups, one of which resembled a child's sippy cup. Jake stood up, unsure of how to greet her. He wanted to hug her but the tray was between them and the moment was lost.

"Let me help you with that tray," he offered.

"Thanks. I see you've met my parents."

"Thanks for the coffee, honey," said Henry. "You go on to work. Your place will be a busy mess today. Jake and I will be just fine here. Right, Jake?"

"Uh, right, Henry," Jake said, hoping Julia wouldn't leave quite this quickly.

"I can use the time today," said Julia. "Mom shouldn't need anything before Hattie comes in a little while. Call me later today, Jake, and we can fill in any blanks after the interview." She gave him her cell phone number and said ruefully, "You won't be able to get me on the office number. I always have my cell phone, in case of emergency at home." With a parting kiss for Henry and for Beatriz, still smiling vacantly, Julia left.

Jake realized he was the only one of the three who could pour coffee. Henry sat waiting and Beatriz peered intently at the crossword puzzle, which was from a Friday *New York Times*. Jake couldn't do that puzzle, either.

As Jake handed the special cup to Beatriz, Henry said, "No, that's mine. Like a kid, I spill. Beatriz gets a regular cup."

When everyone had coffee, Jake said, "Could we begin with you describing your current situation? Mind if I record the interview while I take notes?"

"Not if you'll turn it off if I ask."

"Sure, you can hold it and punch the off button yourself."

Henry awkwardly accepted the little recorder and settled himself more comfortably in his wheelchair. "Where to start... at the beginning of Beatriz and me? We met several years ago at a lecture on birds, at the library. I was a widower. Beatriz hadn't married Julia's father because they weren't legal. When we met, he'd been dead for many years, since Julia was little, so we were both widowed."

"You're a bird watcher?" asked Jake.

"I love birds. I taught high school biology before I retired. Beatriz was a domestic worker, the smartest woman I've ever met. She loved birds and found it an inexpensive hobby where she didn't have to engage much with other people."

"So Beatriz isn't a citizen?"

"She is now," replied Henry. "She's been legal now for many years, but old habits die hard. We talked at the bird watchers' meeting and went for coffee afterwards. That was our beginning, and we've never looked back. She has just the one child, Julia, and my late wife and I never had children."

"How long have you and Julia lived together?" asked Jake.

"When our health problems surfaced several years ago, after we'd retired, Julia persuaded us to move so we could all live together. She said we could look out for her, but we knew who'd need the help. We are so lucky she's our daughter."

"And I'm sure you save money this way," commented Jake.

"When we pool our money plus Julia's salary, we live quite comfortably. We all do better than we would on our own. At least, that's been the case up until now."

"What's changed?"

"About five years ago Beatriz began to have trouble speaking her thoughts. Words came out as gibberish. We took her to doctors – neurologists, internists, speech therapists, even psychiatrists – and couldn't get a diagnosis. Then she began to forget things."

"Did you get help?"

Henry shook his head sadly. "We got caught in a maze. The mental health people said she had dementia and they couldn't help her. The medical folks said she had mental problems, not their domain. We felt we were on our own with nobody offering any assistance."

"That must have been tough," said Jake.

"Devastating. Now she's not able to recognize anyone except me most of the time, and Julia sometimes. It's really sad and I miss her so much. My biggest worry is if she outlives me, or I can't help her anymore." Henry's voice quavered and he wiped his eyes.

Jake glanced at Beatriz and saw she had become agitated, picking at the cloth on her slacks and rocking back and forth, apparently sensing Henry's agitation. Henry pulled himself together and patted her hand. She immediately smiled and resumed gazing at the crossword puzzle.

"So do you have an accurate diagnosis now?" asked Jake. "A prognosis?"

"Yes, mid- to late-stage Alzheimer's. The prognosis? She could live six months or six years, longer or less. One thing's for sure, she's not going to get any better.

"I fear the day when I can't watch over her anymore. I have a functioning brain and lousy body but I can still guard her from harm and call 911. What if I fell or dropped dead and our caregiver wasn't here?"

Jake said, "So what's your own situation? Can you talk about yourself a bit?"

"I'll talk but I'm gonna punch this recorder off." His palsied hands finally turned it off. "I've lost much of my mobility due to Parkinson's and my shakiness keeps me from doing things. I fall sometimes, so I usually just stay in my chair. Sometimes I use a walker to feel more independent."

"You seem alert and sensible," observed Jake.

"So far my mind is clear and the medication I take has slowed the disease. However, I may become a blithering idiot. Then what happens to Beatriz? What have we saddled Julia with? I don't know if we could afford a nursing home or around-the-clock help and we make too much money for Medicaid. It's a catch-twenty-two with no way out."

Henry leaned forward, and said, "Actually, there is a way out now, the death law. Everyone's saying how bad it is, but for us, it may be a Godsend. I care very much that I not leave Beatriz uncared for and that I not bankrupt Julia."

"She seems pretty devoted to you and her mother."

"She's got her career but pretty much has her life on hold otherwise," explained Henry. "We don't talk about it, but I know she worries herself to sleep – or to insomnia – every night about the future. I'm ready to die and I bet Beatriz would say the same thing if she could."

Henry continued, "We've had a good life. It's only going to go downhill from here. I've already lost my wife. One of these days, I'll lose myself, too. So why hang around and wait? My life is over but I'm not dead yet. Don't put that in your article, it'd just upset Julia."

Jake recognized a new viewpoint, someone elderly actually welcoming the relief of the death law. "You've given me a different perspective than I expected to find. May I use some of the ideas you've presented, if no one knows who said them?"

Henry studied Jake a moment and sighed. "Yeah, whatever, it won't make any difference. I've got to talk to Julia soon, anyway. Just don't use my name for that last part."

Jake agreed. "May I call you if I have more questions?"

"Certainly. Actually, it's been a relief to talk this morning. These things have been on my mind, and I didn't want to burden Julia. Plus it's nice to have company. We don't exactly have a booming social life here. But Julia's everything to us."

"Yes, I can see what a special person she is," replied Jake.

"I bet you do," Henry said, with a twinkle in his eye.

Knowing he might have revealed his burgeoning interest inadvertently, Jake said, "I'll see myself out. Is there anything I can do for you or Beatriz before I go? Should I wait for the caregiver to get here?"

"Let's see, how about a new brain for Beatriz and a new body for me?" joked Henry. "Thanks again for hearing me out. We'll be fine until Hattie gets here."

With a final handshake for Henry and a wave for Beatriz, Jake headed to his car. His first thought was to call Julia, but he wanted to think over the interview first. While he hadn't exactly promised Henry confidentiality, he surely had implied it. He decided to organize his notes and plan other interviews before he talked to Julia.

As he headed into Blackwood Coffee Shop, he felt his cell phone vibrate. He'd forgotten to turn it back on after the interview. He saw Julia's name and should have anticipated she'd be on the phone to him first. He was pretty sure she moved faster than he did.

"Hello, Julia."

"Oh, hey, just wondered how things went," said Julia. "I have to admit, I'm more than a little anxious about my parents."

Jake noted that she called Henry her parent, not her step-parent.

"We just finished, and I haven't had a chance to sort out my notes or my thoughts," replied Jake. "The topic made it a hard interview. Your ... uh... Henry is a charmer, though, and a clear thinker."

"Unlike my mother," Julia said ruefully. "I assume she sat there since she usually stays near Henry. I'm betting you observed her, too."

"You guessed it. I did watch her while I was listening to him. Look, I really need to organize my thoughts. Could we have dinner tonight?" *Uh-oh, too much too soon,* he thought.

To his relieved surprise, Julia replied, "Sounds good. It needs to be short and early, though, because I'll need to relieve the caregiver. Would that work for you?"

Jake suggested a time and place convenient to both of them. They each quickly returned to work, and he hoped she had the same warm feeling that he had from talking with her.

CHAPTER 4

Wednesday, November 9

The phones rang constantly. Listening intently for a few minutes, Julia concluded that all calls were variations on a theme: the death law. Constituents were realizing the effect the law would have on themselves and their families. She knew the staff had to get their act together quickly. And they needed to get the congressman on the air ASAP.

Her first job was to assist the communications director to compose a speech distancing Simms from the death law. Her second task was to explain his having voted for it without looking too stupid. Her third, biggest task was to persuade her boss actually to give the speech to the American public. Her hunch was networks would be looking for congressional opinions. Time was of the essence. She quickly typed out a few paragraphs on her computer.

"What the Sam hell are we going to do about this, missy?" greeted her as she entered Marcus Simms' office.

Julia said, "Marcus, we're going to get this thing under control. Properly played, you're going to be a hero. First thing, you denounce the death law publicly, admitting that you didn't realize the full implications and you promise to help overturn it. The second thing, we need to get with other legislators and decide how to replace this with what you thought you were voting for, physician-assisted suicide. It shouldn't be hard to get everyone's support on that, except maybe the radicals who hold that even a mercy killing is wrong. See what you think of this."

"Let me see," growled Simms, as he grabbed the paper. The denouncement earned a nod, the admission of fault a frown, and the idea of a rectifying resolution, a ghost of a smile. He mentally savored the votes he could get being a hero on this thing. Maybe his secret ambition of being governor of Florida wasn't lost yet. They could spin this crisis with him as savior for the senior population of Florida, maybe the whole country. Seniors were the most reliable voters in the nation.

Julia guessed at his thoughts as she watched him read. His secret ambitions were not so secret from her. "Okay, get me on wherever you can, ASAP. I'd prefer CNN, the Today show, or something like that, maybe Larry King or 60 Minutes."

As Julia had suspected, the Today show schedulers were already seeking legislators for interviews. Most were lying low, trying to figure out politically correct positions. Praying this bold interview was the way to go, Julia scheduled a time for two days hence, giving her team little time to prepare a position that would be applauded by their Florida constituents. That meant one day to research the issue and develop their position and one day to coach Marcus Simms on his interview – indeed, on his beliefs and his future.

Julia called yet another staff meeting to tackle the issue. With Simms at a committee meeting, they could meet in the relative privacy of his larger office. Julia had a hunch they were a step ahead of other staffs and she wanted to keep it that way.

Calming the staff came first. They jabbered over each other to explain why they were not responsible for the fiasco. Some felt guilty and some feared for their jobs. Others were in a panic over what might be about to happen to their parents, grandparents and the nice old guy next door in the wheelchair.

"Look," said Julia, "this is a real mess but we have a plan. First of all, we've still got jobs. We all messed up, so I want to hear no blaming or finger-pointing. He can't get rid of all of us at once and we're all equally culpable. So get that part out of your head." The glances among staff confirmed that was the most immediate concern of everyone.

"As far as what happens in the future for our families and constituents, let's cross that bridge when we have more information. As you know, I have elderly parents in poor health, and I'm trying to ignore that, so I know how hard it is. But we've got a job to do here and a window of opportunity. Okay?"

Seeing a few nods and more relaxed body posture, she continued, "Marcus has an interview scheduled in two days on the Today show." At their collective gasp, she admitted, "Yeah, a bold move. But there's nothing to lose getting out ahead on this thing. Others are burying their heads, hoping it'll blow over. Our guy is in good position to make a statement and he's known for being bold, fair, well informed and willing to take a stand."

As people glanced at each other, she conceded, "Well, most of those things most of the time. He could emerge a leader on this thing." She saw some nods, people sitting up straighter and a few jotting notes.

"Okay, this is what we'll do. Carla and Juan, you handle the telephones. Sid, monitor e-mail and Facebook, other social media. Georgia, you're our researcher. Get with those other three and do a quick-and-dirty tally sheet of the concern, the opinion, any suggested solutions, and make a guess at the emotional state of each caller. Get the same data from both phone and internet responses. If you can, discreetly guess at the ethnic background. Juan, you take the Spanish-speakers. Try to answer as quickly as you can but give constituents a good listening-to, too. Signal us if you're swamped and we'll add more people to the phones. Georgia, make sure we're getting data to translate into sound bites. Jump online and see what's on blogs, see how different regions of the country are responding.

"Jeff, read every sentence of that bill several times and do a one-page analysis. Sandy, use your best Southern charm on whoever comes into the office so it looks like a normal day. But stonewall anyone who actually wants an appointment. Roberta, read everything you can find on euthanasia, physician-assisted suicide, the Kevorkian stuff, any positions from groups like AMA and the Alzheimer's association."

Now everybody was scribbling notes. The staff was relieved to have something concrete to do, a plan, and some leadership.

Julia hoped to God she was providing the last two. "And me – I'll be sniffing around to see what everybody else is doing."

"And keepin' our boss calm," said Sandy.

"Yes, reassuring him that we'll have a viable position and facts to him by noon tomorrow. We can do that, right?" Staffers gulped but nodded, now visibly eager to get to work, some already reaching for their cell phones to tell their families they wouldn't be home on time today. "We'll meet here at eight a.m. tomorrow and see where we are," said Julia. She hoped her dinner date with Jake would tell her what was going on with the press.

As everyone filed out carrying their chairs back to their cubicles, Julia said to a grizzled veteran, "Walter, stay a minute, please."

Walter grinned and said, "I didn't get an assignment so I figured I'd be staying." Simms' communications director, an observer of many congressional crises, Walter Akers was perhaps the calmest member of the staff. "Julia, I've never seen this big a mess before. I've got a hunch the nitwits that pushed this bill through don't even understand what they've done."

"I agree, Walter, and I'm glad you can view this drama with some perspective. My own take is skewed, with my parents in the bull's-eye. What interview questions do you think the Today people will ask? The scheduler didn't know who the interviewer'll be but it's in the DC studio of NBC. Also, draft a speech and we'll see if the Congressman can squeeze some good sound bites in."

"I'm on it," said Walter. "And I'll find out if other legislators are agreeing to interviews. You got this one nailed down, right?"

"Yes, it's a firm commitment from the network – unless some bigger fish comes along, of course!"

"Do you want me in on the briefing?"

"Yes, the briefing, the coaching, the rehearsing, the soothing and reassuring, whatever else we have to do to get him ready. Make sure he's dressed right, too."

"Okay, I'm on it," Walter repeated. "It's good to be retirement age. If this screws up, everyone'll be looking for jobs. I hope I have enough money put away by then for a condo in our Florida home district, near our grandkids."

Julia spent the day putting out fires, soothing, reassuring, and lighting a fire under one staff member who hadn't grasped the urgency.

Mid-afternoon, Hattie, her parents' caregiver, called to say Henry had fallen, but he didn't seem hurt and hadn't wanted her to call Julia. Following Julia's instructions, Hattie had called anyway. The aide assured her Henry was fine, just upset with himself.

A few minutes' conversation with Henry calmed everyone at home down somewhat. Julia verified that Hattie could stay as late as needed, though Henry protested that he and Beatriz did not need a "babysitter" once they were in bed. Julia ignored him and managed not to think about the cost of overtime for Hattie. As she hung up, she mused, *Dear God, what's next?* as she mentally shifted back to the task at hand.

Late that afternoon, Julia walked to meet Jake for dinner, enjoying the few minutes of peace in the brisk air. At Antonio's she saw Jake already seated at a table, flipping through what were probably his notes of the morning's interview. He did not have a drink in front of him, mirroring her alcohol-free plan for the evening since her work was far from over.

Jake rose, gave her a quick hug, took her jacket and helped her get seated. *Old-school manners,* she thought. *That's refreshing.*

"I'm glad to see you. I know you really don't have time to be here," said Jake.

"I'm glad to see you, too. You're right. I can't stay long. I need to get home. We can talk business and enjoy some dinner, though." *And each other's company,* she added silently.

"And each other's company," said Jake. "Let's order dinner and then get this interview business over with, shall we?"

"Good idea. I'll have the antipasto platter as an entree, water to drink," Julia told the waiter standing nearby.

"And I'll have the penne vodka, house dressing on the salad.

And iced tea." He told Julia, "I think I remember you drink wine, but I figure we're both working tonight."

"I love a glass of wine, especially with the right companion, but it's not on tonight's agenda."

"I'd like to schedule that soon," ventured Jake.

"I'd definitely like that but, as you know, I've got a whole lot on my plate right now. I'd like to hear about your meeting with Henry."

He hedged. "I have to be honest and tell you he didn't want me to let you know everything he said. I will comply with that request and hope you understand."

Julia smiled. "I'd expect no less from you. Let me tell you what he doesn't want me to know. He thinks his, my mother's and my lives would all be simplified if he and my mother died. While I respect his belief, I do not agree with him. I love the two of them despite their infirmities, and they are not a burden."

As Jake began to interrupt, she held up her hand. "Wait. I don't want you to comment on that. Henry thinks I don't know what he feels. So don't think you need to protect me from the truth."

Jake laughed. "I'm pretty sure there's not much I need to protect you from. Okay, let me give you my impressions. Henry showed me there are two sides to this issue. I hadn't looked at it from the viewpoint of the elder. Much less had I considered the viewpoint of those who wish to die, if they could still speak for themselves. It gives me pause as I consider the whole issue. We assume everyone wants to live but that's not always true."

"I'm going to be candid here, too," said Julia. "It would be an enormous relief for the caretaker emotionally and financially. But that's balanced against the feeling of duty and the wish to prolong a loved one's life if there's any quality at all. I'm ashamed even to think this, but I understand that my life would be infinitely simpler if my first thoughts weren't always worries about my parents."

Jake nodded as he crunched a breadstick.

"I'd like to be freer in my own personal life," she said, hoping he'd get the nuance of her interest in him but limitations on her availability.

"Okay, I get it," said Jake, reaching for her hand. "I hope I'm not mishearing what you're saying, but I'm looking forward to time with you in the future. Not rushing into anything, but I'm not running away, either."

Julia smiled and squeezed his hand back, then began to eat her antipasto. She suddenly realized she hadn't eaten since early morning and she was starving, especially since her life had just taken a more optimistic turn. "Back to the interview. What was your impression of Henry and my mother?"

"Henry is one sharp fella, well aware of what's going on around him," said Jake as he forked in his pasta. "He seems a clear thinker, although obviously unable to care for himself physically. In some ways your parents are opposites: one physically able and one mentally able. Their situation points up some of the difficulty of the death law. What constitutes being unable to take care of yourself? If you can hire someone, are you capable? I know families where the children or spouse would be unwilling to care for a family member, but I know others where it would be unthinkable not to."

"You've hit that right, Jake. One of the things I've been thinking about is the response already from our Latino constituents. They don't like to even think about death, much less talk about it. Taking care of their elders is what they're brought up to do. The death law may create an underground society where disabilities remain hidden from the authorities."

"Kind of like hiding your crazy aunt in the attic?"

"Exactly. Maybe a reverse people-smuggling system where the 'coyotes' turn into 'storks' and deliver seniors to safety over the border. Latinos know how to run people across borders. But tell me more about your impressions, especially of my mother," prompted Julia.

"I really didn't have the opportunity to form much of an impression because I was so attentive to Henry. She looked and acted normal until I noticed that her facial expressions rarely changed and she seemed unaware of what was going on around her. She held a crossword puzzle but didn't write anything down while I was there. However, once when Henry became a bit emotional, your mother also became agitated. I'm guessing she was reacting to his feelings rather than his words."

"I think you're right. It's hard for me to tell what she's thinking, if anything. That's one of the most frustrating things, not knowing what's going on inside her head. That's a confounding factor in knowing how the death law plays into our own family. Henry's quite clear on the choice he would make, but my mother, I'm not so sure."

She leaned forward. "I do believe in euthanasia or physician-assisted suicide or whatever is the right term. We put down our pets humanely when they're in a hopeless situation. I don't believe in the state making that decision, but I think an individual should be able to decide, to write an advanced directive to make it legal. Why should we suffer through a downhill end to life?"

"I just thought of something that could maybe help us both," said Jake. "What if I took Henry to some of his appointments and listen to the conversations with people who take care of him? He said he had a doctor's appointment tomorrow."

"Wow, what a boon that would be to me – hate to sound so selfish! I'm guessing Henry would love helping you research this. Let's see, in the next few days he's also scheduled to see his lawyer. And we were going to visit an assisted living place, just to have a back-up plan."

"How about your mom?"

"She can stay home with Hattie, who usually drives them both, then manages Mom in the waiting room. Mom gets very uncomfortable if Henry is out of her sight. If you drove Henry, he'd have a little outing and relief of responsibility for my mom. I think we're onto something here, and it's going to be hell around my office for the next several days. I couldn't thank you enough."

"It'd be a help to me, too. My editor has given me free rein to work on this for a little while. I'll hold you to that promise of a glass of wine together as my thank-you," said Jake.

"Excuse me for using my cell phone at the table," Julia said, "and I'll call Henry right now."

A few minutes later, all was set. Julia also learned that the media seemed to be disorganized in its reporting, unable to isolate the issues. Reporters were in a kind of feeding frenzy to report the developments, if they could just figure out what they were.

After a satisfying hug, Julia headed home, reflecting that their plan got them on-air near the head of the pack. Both Jake's company and the good food had refreshed her sufficiently to feel and look confident and purposeful as she went home to an evening of work.

CHAPTER 5

Thursday, November 10

Beatriz stared intently through the glass doors leading to the patio that adjoined a wooded area behind the house.

Following her gaze, Henry exclaimed, "It's a kitten!"

Jake had arrived early enough to hug Julia on her way out. He'd served her parents coffee and they were chatting.

He slid open the patio door and a little black kitten straggled in, limping and holding up one back leg. Beatriz became animated, stroking the kitten's head and cooing to him. The kitten rubbed against her legs and let her pick him up.

Motioning to her mouth, Beatriz let out a jumble of words that he figured probably meant the kitty's hungry.

Jake had read about this symptom of dementia called "word salad," but had not observed it in Beatriz previously. He watched her infatuation with the little cat.

"Beatriz always loved cats," Henry said. "This little fellow looks just like our cat that died. She may think this is our old Calvin-cat come back to life. Who knows, maybe she's right!"

"If we all believed in reincarnation, the death law wouldn't be so alarming," commented Jake.

"Could you look around to see if there's anything to feed a

cat? There was some cat chow left over when Calvin died a few months ago."

Jake rummaged around, hoping he'd not incur Julia's wrath for inviting a cat in. Nobody could have resisted opening the door to that poor little beast. And Beatriz clearly would not abandon her new friend.

He poured a dish of cat food and reached to take the kitten from Beatriz, earning a vicious scratch from the cat and a malevolent glare from the woman. She set the cat next to the food and crouched beside him, crooning as he chomped the chow. She pantomimed drinking and Jake filled a small bowl with water. He had to wash off his profusely bleeding scratch, anyway.

Great, thought Jake, *now I'll get some kind of exotic cat fever from this mangy animal.* Henry returned with first aid supplies and he and Jake patched the wound while Beatriz and the cat communed. Fascinated by her obvious rapport with the kitten, Jake continued to observe her.

"Sometimes I see the old Beatriz but those times happen less and less often," said Henry. "I think she's totally gone from us, then my lovely wife returns for a few minutes."

"Must be really tough to watch her come and go like that."

"It is, and that's what makes me unsure about the death law, despite what I said yesterday. Just when I think we're totally useless, a burden to Julia, something like this happens."

Henry shook his head. "But I know Beatriz didn't want to live as she is now. My own life isn't so bad at the moment. But am I willing to just sit in my wheelchair and wait for things to get worse? I'm not so sure."

He looked at the cat. "That poor little thing needs to get to a vet with that leg. I don't suppose you... No, you're already taking me to the doctor this morning. Hattie can drive us this afternoon. The vet knows Beatriz and won't mind if she accompanies the cat to the office."

Jake was already a step ahead and had decided he wanted to know more about this family. He said, "We'll go this afternoon."

He had led a pretty solitary life lately. His relatives were either dead or living far away. Sometimes he went with other reporters to a bar or a golf course. He dated occasionally but hadn't met anyone he was really interested in. Now he was being drawn into a family and it felt good, though a little risky. It would undoubtedly be psychologically safer to remain isolated in his own cocoon.

"We could see your doctor, maybe get lunch, and then see the vet in the early afternoon. Is that too much for you?"

Henry beamed at the idea. "Much as I love Beatriz, some time away would be most welcome. Lunch sounds great, Jake. I'll call the vet."

The front door opened as the caregiver, Hattie, arrived.

"Let me talk to Hattie and we'll be underway. It's about time to get to the doctor's, anyway. Can you fold the wheelchair and stow it in your trunk?"

"Yes, ready when you are." Jake's mind was whirling with all the things he was learning about aging in the past few days. His family had tended to die young from heart attacks so he had little experience with aging – other than himself, and he was trying to ignore that.

Jake held out his hand to the thin, wiry, middle-aged dark-skinned woman. "Hey, I'm Jake Jordan. I'm taking Henry to his doctor's appointment this morning."

"Pleased to meet you, Mist' Jake," she said. "I'm Hattie and I take care of these folks. It's good for Mist' Henry to be out awhile. But don't tire him out and y'all don't forget his pills."

Hattie's Southern accent and diction reminded Jake of his childhood in Georgia.

Henry rolled into the living room saying, "Hattie, we'll be gone until after lunch. Then we'll–"

Beatriz entered holding the cat and Hattie interrupted with, "Law, Mist' Henry, where'd that cat come from? Does Miss Julia know? Y'all in big trouble if she don't."

"We'll be home after lunch and take the poor little cat to the vet."

"To have him put down? Uh-uh, I'll take him home if that's what y'all thinkin'."

"No, Hattie, to patch him up. Julia doesn't know yet. The cat just wandered in a little bit ago. If she calls, don't tell her. We'll do that later, okay?"

"'Deed I'll not tell her," agreed Hattie. "This is y'all's doins'. I don't want Miss Julia mad at me!"

With Beatriz engrossed in the cat, Jake and Henry made their way to the car, where Jake learned the intricacies of loading a wheelchair into a Prius.

During the ride to the doctor's office, Henry kept up a running commentary on new construction and window displays, showing his pleasure at being outside. Henry obviously appreciated an outing, if only to the doctor's office.

"Do you have an idea for lunch afterward?" Jake asked.

"Could we go to that Taco Factory? I'm paying, of course. A nice young man owns it and we used to go there even after Beatriz started acting different, back when I could still drive."

"Do you go out much now?"

"No, things have sure changed," said Henry pensively. "Julia doesn't have much time and we never know how Beatriz is going to act. Sometimes I'm pretty sloppy when I eat, if it's a bad day. A friend who had a stroke calls it 'flinging meatballs.'"

"The Taco Factory sounds like a good place to me," said Jake. "Would you be willing to tell your doctor why I'm with you, and maybe I'll ask him some questions?"

"That's what I planned," Henry said.

Jake found a parking place, easy with Henry's handicapped vehicle tag. He unloaded the wheelchair and clumsily helped Henry transfer into it.

The receptionist greeted Henry warmly. "Where's your girlfriend today?"

"She's at home," responded Henry. "I brought another friend with me."

"Dr. Singh's free soon," said the receptionist. Soon the doctor himself opened the door and called Henry's name.

Jake and Henry rolled down the hall as Henry introduced Jake as "my new friend."

"Glad to meet you," said Dr. Singh. "I can take Henry from here."

"No, I want him with me," said Henry. "I'll explain in a minute."

"As you wish," said Dr. Singh with a slight bow.

When the examining room door closed, Henry explained, "Jake is a journalist doing an article on the death law. Have you heard of the death law?"

Warily Dr. Singh said, "Of course. Who hasn't? But why talk to me?"

Recognizing an opportunity, Jake said, "The death law baffles everyone. I'm trying to understand what it means by interviewing people directly affected by it. Would you be willing to answer a few questions?"

"I'm very busy and I do not want my name in the newspapers," said Dr. Singh.

"I wouldn't need to use your name," said Jake.

"If you're a friend of Henry's, I guess I could do that. If there's anything I don't want to answer, I will say that," the physician said with a sigh. "This is one big mess and I am glad someone is trying to figure it out. But do not use my name."

"Agreed."

"But first, I tend my patient," said Dr. Singh. "How are you doing, Henry? Where's Beatriz today?"

"I'm doing okay, taking my meds, walking some, only falling a little. I'm helping Jake with this project so I need to live a little longer," joked Henry. "Beatriz is about the same. She's having fewer outbursts and that helps."

"That is not surprising. As patients enter dementia more deeply, they become less frightened about what's happening to them. Therefore, we often see less acting out and anger and sadness."

"Well, she's happy this morning because a little stray kitty wandered in. She's acting more like her old self. Do you think it's possible she's coming back?"

Dr. Singh shook his head sadly. "Henry, we've already been over this. Your Beatriz will not be returning to you."

Henry remembered all too well the appointment a few years ago when Beatriz had so miserably failed her mental status exam. He had become upset, though Beatriz had remained unaware of her intellectual lapses.

Dr. Singh had turned to Henry that day and said, "Henry, get a grip. You are going to lose her, you know. Your emotional outburst will not help things. We will help you with your grief. But right now, you need to hold yourself together while we make plans."

Since then Henry had had many private moments of anguish but had mostly maintained his equilibrium when he was with Beatriz. He understood she was not going to get better, but it was hard to give up hope.

Today, Dr. Singh pronounced Henry in as good health as could be expected for an elderly man with Parkinson's and heavy responsibility. The doctor turned to Jake and said, "What do you want to ask me?"

Jake decided to cut to the chase with this busy doctor. "How will the death law affect your practice of medicine?"

Dr. Singh virtually erupted into words: "This is worrying me. Most of my patients are seniors with chronic conditions. Will I be the one to decide when they can no longer care for themselves? How will I tell someone they have terminal cancer, knowing it is an immediate death sentence, even though medicine might prolong their lives for a few years? Will people stop coming to the doctor because they fear the diagnosis? That's already a problem."

He shook his head and waved his pen and patient folder in the air. "Do I lie about what disease a patient has, to keep him off the government's list? The legal system will not permit that. Will I, Allah forbid, be required to terminate a life? My beliefs will not permit that. Must I decide to refuse patients who cannot continue to live under the death law?" Gesturing to documents on the wall, he said, "My medical ethics and the Hippocratic Oath will not permit that. Will the government request a list of my patients who cannot care for themselves? I am too moral a man to make that list."

Dr. Singh spread his hands toward Henry. "I love my patients. But I am wondering if I can continue my work." He sat rigidly, eyes glistening with emotion. Then he reached for Henry's hand and said, "My friend, I will not abandon you." To Jake, he said, "I have nothing more to say."

There's really nothing else to say, anyway, Jake thought. "Dr. Singh, thank you for giving me your honest thoughts on this. I will not use your name." Looking at Henry, who seemed not at all perturbed by the doctor's speech, Jake said, "Ready, Henry?"

Shaking hands all around, the pair exited the waiting room and Henry joked his way past the receptionist. Almost immediately his cell phone rang. "That'll be Julia," he predicted.

"Dad, how was your appointment? I thought you were going to call me."

"Julia, I just now came out of the doctor's office. Why are you worrying so much? I got a very good check-up for an old, sick geezer. Now we're going to lunch, and we'll have a little outing with your mother for this afternoon."

"What kind of outing? To lunch where? Can you manage?" rushed Julia.

"We'll tell you about the outing later, we're going to the Taco Factory, and yes, I can manage. Now quit fussing! Here, here's Jake, he wants to talk to you."

I do? thought Jake. *Well, yes,* but he wasn't sure he wanted to while Julia was ranting at Henry. No choice; he was holding the phone now. "I can't talk, Julia, I'm driving and that's illegal. I'll call you back later."

"What kind of outing? Where are you taking my mother?"

"Can't talk now, traffic and policemen, look forward to later." He switched off the phone and handed it back to Henry. No way was he explaining a new cat to Julia. Let Henry do that in his own sweet time.

This was Jake's first visit to the Taco Factory and he liked the bright walls in Southwestern colors, the masks and large photographs of Mexican scenes. The small garden of peppers growing in front of the restaurant made him anticipate good food.

The smiling owner, Carlos, greeted them and seated them with Henry's back to the other patrons, allowing him to dribble privately as he dug into the warm tortilla chips and spicy salsa. Jake asked Henry what he recommended.

"Black beans and rice, that's all I ever get. The portions are huge, so I can take some home to Beatriz."

Jake ordered the taco salad with grilled chicken. Halfway through their chips a new basket arrived at their table, deftly delivered by a young woman. "Complimentary guacamole from the *patron*," she said, smiling.

Henry said, "Hey, Rosa, how's your dad?" Her elderly ailing father lived in San Salvador.

"I am very worried about him. He is so far away and my country is very poor. But I will not bring him here, where the government may kill him!" Rosa bustled off to take care of other customers.

"Well, that's another view of the death law," Jake said. Rosa's comments suggested an area of investigation: How would immigrants, legal and illegal, be affected by the death law?

"Best restaurant in the area with the best waiters," proclaimed Henry, totally absorbed in his chips and guacamole.

After they'd gorged on chips and Henry had cleaned himself up from spilled salsa, Jake asked, "So what did you make of Dr. Singh's comments?"

"It made me look at the death law from a different perspective," Henry said. "I've thought about it from my own and Beatriz's perspective, and tried to visualize it from Julia's. I never thought about what it might mean to a doctor to have to pronounce a death sentence for a person still alive. Like me, for instance. And even Beatriz. What did you think?"

"Journalists aren't supposed to think, just collect and report data."

"But you're my friend, Jake, not just a journalist. I'm not asking what you think I should do, just what you thought of the doctor's comments."

"The issue clearly touched him personally. I wonder if he's had first-hand experience in his own life, not just his professional practice."

Jake hadn't ever given much thought to the issue of death and he suspected most Americans were in the same boat. If pressed, he'd probably say life is sacred and no one should deprive another person of life. He'd always been against capital punishment, though at first he'd have liked to see the drunk driver who'd killed his wife tried and fried.

But Henry's situation was entirely different, the perspective of someone who wanted to die. Jake considered himself somewhat religious but had never thought very deeply about heaven and hell. An afterlife someone might be eager to get to – that wasn't in Jake's own worldview.

After lunch Henry said, "I'll call and ask Hattie to get Beatriz ready for a car ride and find the cat carrier. We'll be ready in just a few minutes. I hate to take any more of your time this afternoon."

"I'm good, don't worry about me. I've really enjoyed talking to you today and interviewing the doctor. Lunch felt like two friends talking," Jake said, wondering what had happened to his journalist's objectivity. Shot to hell, apparently.

Henry called for the check and fumbled his credit card out of his wallet. He calculated the tip and managed to sign the credit slip without assistance.

Impressed that Henry was still able to perform this small everyday task, Jake said, "Thanks for lunch, Henry. This was a great place."

CHAPTER 6

Thursday afternoon, November 10

Hattie had Beatriz ready to go when they got home and, as Henry confirmed, toileted. "Beatriz wears an 'adult undergarment.' as they euphemistically call it. But it upsets her if she uses it so we try to keep her on a bathroom schedule," confided Henry.

Jake raised his eyebrows. *Did I really need to know that?* He turned to the task of getting two disabled adults, one disabled cat, and one caregiver into his small car. The kitten was quite vocal about the cat-carrier, but willing to stay in Beatriz's arms. Everyone stayed out of paw's length and no one got scratched this time.

Henry said to Hattie, "I think we can manage. Why don't you stay here while we go to the vet's?"

"Okay, Mist' Henry, if you sure," she replied. "I can get the wash done and start dinner for Miss Julia. Y'all have a whole lot to talk about cat-wise this evening."

"You got that right," he said. This cat thing might not be a slam dunk. "I'm hoping Jake can persuade her it's a good idea. Be sure to set him a place at the table."

"Me?" said Jake. "How'd I get into this?" *Oh, well, in for a penny...* and he'd get to see Julia. "Okay. Maybe we can map out some more interviews after we get home from the vet's."

At the office, a vet tech reached for the kitten. Beatriz swatted the young man and began to shriek. *Oops,* thought Jake, *here's a behavior I haven't seen, and it's not pretty.*

Henry said to the techie, "Beatriz will carry the cat and we'll stay with her."

The technician said dubiously, "There's not a lot of space in the examining room. You'd better let me help." He reached for the cat, Beatriz swatted and shrieked again, and the technician said, "Sure, good idea."

They all squeezed into the little room. The technician hastily backed out, saying, "Dr. Jenner will be right in."

Jake wondered if Henry was nervous about keeping Beatriz on an even keel. She was smiling and crooning to the cat, but Jake had just learned how fast her mood could change.

"Dr. Jenner understands Beatriz's problems because her grandmother had Alzheimer's. She tended our old cat Calvin and she had to deal with both Beatriz and the cat when she put Calvin down. It was really hard on all of us."

Jake noticed that Dr. Jenner's diploma was from the Virginia Tech School of Veterinary Medicine, explaining the orange-and-maroon décor in the waiting room.

Dr. Jenner walked in, greeting Henry and Beatriz by name and holding out her hand to Jake. "I'm Dr. Jenner and you are..?"

"He's our friend Jake who's brought us here today with this little stray kitten. He's also a journalist doing interviews on the death law and a good friend of Julia's," explained Henry.

"Don't get me started on that law!" said Dr. Jenner.

"Actually, I'd like to hear your views, if you've got time," said Jake.

"Let's take care of the little guy and then maybe I'll say a word or two." She turned to Henry. "Fill me in on the details." She'd been stroking the cat's head all the time she'd been talking, but hadn't tried to separate him from Beatriz. To Beatriz, she said, "Let's put him here so I can get a better look," and guided the bundle of fur and hands to the examining table.

"He just wandered out of the woods, hungry and hurt, this morning," said Henry. "Beatriz loves him."

"Yes, I can see that. He probably reminds her of the late Calvin." As she spoke, she gently probed the kitten who stayed calm until she touched his leg. Then he let out a howl. Beatriz shrieked and snatched the cat off the table, cradling him as she backed into a corner. "I can tell this exam is over," laughed Dr. Jenner. "Has he eaten?"

"Yes, and had some water. Don't know if he's used his litter box. Other than that, I don't think he's left Beatriz's lap."

"He's probably a fairly recent stray, but he hasn't eaten much for awhile. He wasn't born feral, the way he's reacting to Beatriz, but he's a little beat up around the edges."

She shook her head. "Probably someone just dropped him off. I just hate it when that happens. At least people could take their pets to the animal shelter.

"Looks like he's about six weeks old and that leg's definitely broken. It's already mending, so we'll leave it alone. No telling what parasites he's picked up in the wild and he may have health problems in the future. We'll give him flea medicine and take some blood, if Beatriz will let us, and we'll know more then."

Shooting a glance at Beatriz, happily swaying with the cat

in the corner of the room, she continued, "You may have to put him down if he's got feline AIDS or something similar. Or we can put him down right now, since he's not your responsibility and he may have picked up something while he was in the woods."

"Oh, no," said Henry, "we'll deal with that in the future. We can't deprive Beatriz of this little bit of pleasure. I'm sure Julia will agree, once she gets over the shock."

Jake exhaled, grateful that he was not going to be party to a cat-lynching.

"Okay, let me see if I can get some blood out and some meds in without upsetting either the cat or your wife too much."

As she worked, the vet said to Jake, "If it's unthinkable to us to zap a cat, how much harder will it be under the death law for a person, even an old sick one? I believe in euthanasia for animals when they are in pain, and I think people should make their own decisions to end their lives with assistance.

"But the government deciding? No way! That's so wrong. We have grief counselors who work with pet owners, ministers to do pet burials or accompany the owner to the vet's. If it's that hard to put down a pet, how much harder would it be to make that decision for Grandma?"

When they got home, Henry said, "I need to take a rest. Could you make yourself comfortable for an hour or so? You could work in the den."

Jake nodded. "I'd welcome an hour to get my notes organized, maybe make some phone calls. Would that disturb you?"

"Not at all. Our wi-fi password is Calvin, the name of our old cat. I guess that'll be the name of our new cat, too, assuming we can talk Julia into keeping him. I feel like a kid asking permission from his parent, which can be hard sometimes on both Julia and me."

"Thanks," said Jake, as he punched in the password. "I'm online. It's been a busy day, hasn't it?"

"Yes, and it's not over yet. It's going to take some fast talking to get Julia to accept this kitten. But I think she will be okay when she sees how attached her mother is to him," Henry said optimistically.

CHAPTER 7

Thursday afternoon, November 10

Julia convened her staff meeting at three. "Let the phones go to voice mail," she directed as everyone assembled.

"Jeff, what did you find re-reading the bill?" she asked.

"There are very few details contained in the wording. The outcome is clear – euthanasia of those seventy and over who cannot care for themselves. What's missing is definition of what constitutes self-care. If you've got the bucks, can you stick around, sans government money? Will insurance companies pay medical and long-term care for their insured parties if the death law lets them drop people or procedures, no pun intended?"

Jeff got an uneasy staff laugh with his gallows humor. "It's also unclear whether a temporary illness fits the definition. There's no mention of mental health. Clearly the originators want to dump Medicaid and Medicare bills of seniors who are terminally ill. In ICUs and CCUs the bills are astronomical. Everyone over seventy would essentially have a standing government-issued Do Not Resuscitate order."

Julia asked, "Are there guidelines for any of this?"

"No, that's the other missing piece. Who makes the decisions?

Who does the killing? Firing squad? Electric chair? Your doctor with a syringe?"

"How can this ever be implemented, given the lack of specificity?" asked Julia.

"The one clear part is it takes effect July 1 of next year. The Department of Health and Human Services, National Institute of Health, the surgeon general and the CDC will figure out how to do it."

"Why CDC?"

"A new study says the national rate of Alzheimer's and other dementia is at epidemic level. Almost as many people die annually from Alzheimer's and similar diseases as from heart disease and cancer. So that puts CDC into the picture. Bottom line, this thing looks hit or miss to me."

"Thanks, Jeff. Carla, Juan, Georgia, what've you got from the phones?"

Georgia began, "I consulted my research textbooks for the best protocol—"

Julia interrupted, "Georgia, I'd love to hear that later, but right now, we need a quick and dirty on what's coming in on the phones."

"Okay, sorry, I forget I'm not a grad student anymore. We're tallying gender, age if they'll give it, reason for call, suggestions, ethnic identifiers we can surmise, and a guess at emotional state, categorized as sad, angry, unhappy, puzzled, derisive, anxious, and other. We had to add thankful."

"Really?" asked Julia. "I wouldn't have predicted *thankful*."

Georgia continued, "Carla and Juan ask no personal questions, just check off the demographics they can surmise. Many people start with something like 'I'm seventy-five and...'

"So far we have calls from both genders, mostly *angry* and

unhappy. Most callers are late sixties or older or caretakers of older people. We estimate about fifty percent of the callers so far sound white, about thirty percent black, and twenty percent or so Latino, but that's pure guesswork. Would you agree with that, Carla, Juan?"

Both nodded and Carla confirmed, "Most are just mad and tell us we are fools. It's been a little hard to get each caller off the phone. So far no one has really offered a suggestion, except a new congressman. I didn't think you'd want a tally on that."

"You're so right. No notes on that!"

"Gracias," Juan put in. Discussing the subject of death and dying, a traditional taboo in his culture, was stretching his tolerance. He said that his talks with callers consisted mostly of soothing histrionic Latinas. He'd taken the approach of just assuming he was speaking to someone like his own mother on the phone. He was pretty sure she'd be calling soon, as well as his grandmother and aunts and neighbors in Florida.

Georgia said, "For blogs, we never know who is writing or why. The blogs are almost universally vitriolic about the death law, the most unified subject response I've ever seen."

"Okay, thanks, Georgia, Carla, and Juan. Very useful data. What's on e-mail, Facebook, and Twitter, Sid?"

"About the same, only worse language. Some are thoughtful messages, mostly begging Congress to repeal, but most are just cuss words. We've had a few e-mails from assisted-suicide advocates, remnants of the Hemlock Society, people like that, thanking Congress for standing up for what's right. They ignore the fact that the suicides might be euthanasia unsought by the victims."

"Well, that's the minority viewpoint," said Julia. "Print off any comments we could stick into a sound bite. Thanks for the update. Roberta, what have you found?"

"Not as much as I would have expected. Maybe it's still too soon. There's an anti-death law message on some religious web sites, condemning it in Biblical terms. Ditto the capital punishment people, minus the Bible. There's nothing on sites of large health and mental health organizations. Maybe it takes awhile for those quasi-political organizations to get a statement together."

"Okay," said Julia. "Anything else?"

"I also checked on hospice groups. I didn't see anything specific to the death law, but the statements already on their web sites pretty much cover their views.

"However, I did find some specific responses on web sites such as American Civil Liberties Union and Southern Law Poverty Center. They fear the weak, poor, and persons of color may be targeted by the death law. ACLU also mentions the rights of those who want to die legally but may be younger than the death law designates.

"I did a little research and learned that historically suicide has been a crime in the United States, mostly decriminalized now. In most states it's still a felony to assist with a suicide, other than Oregon. They passed the Oregon Death With Dignity Act in 1994. Washington State has a similar law and other states are considering such legislation."

"Really," said Julia. "That's interesting."

Roberta continued, "The biggest response is from organizations like AARP that represent older Americans. They have taken a strong stand against 'mandated euthanasia' and 'legalized slaughter of the elderly.' There are many negative responses to the death law but also a few positive ones on their member blogs."

Julia shook her head wearily. "I wonder how many of these

viewpoints the authors of that bill considered. Did they just see it as a budget measure, forget the emotional and moral considerations? Sandy, what have you picked up?" she asked.

Sandy waved her hands in the air and said in her Southern drawl, "Everyone's runnin' around like the proverbial chicken here in the buildin'. I learned in the ladies' room that everyone's pretty panicked about losin' their jobs and every legislator is blamin' the staff."

Sandy looked at Julia and added, "Most people have a family member they're worried about. Lots of finger-pointin' going on. Other than handlin' constituents already scheduled this week, everyone's lyin' low and scurrying around tryin' to get a handle on this thing."

"Thanks, Sandy. Sounds like we're right in with everyone else – is that a comfort or not? Okay, everyone, same assignments, and let Walter or me know immediately if there's anything different or alarming to report. Thanks, everyone. Let's meet in the morning after the TV interview is over and see where we are then," said Julia.

"You mean, figure out damage control in the morning, right?" said Jeff with a pessimistic shake of his head.

"Let's help the Congressman put the best possible spin on this," said Julia. "After all, he just got a mandate from the district, so we have our whole two years solid in front of us."

As the other staff members filed out, Julia and Walter got to work on preparations for the TV interview. Their guy – charismatic, believable, popular and smart – could pull it off if anyone could.

Walter began, "I have some more information. Jackson Smith, their current news rock star, is in DC this week and will interview. He's a hard-baller but also fair, so that's in our favor.

If Simms says the right things, it'll be more credible because of the host.

"There are several points he has to get in and I've begun a briefing guide. First, we dropped the ball just like everybody else, budget bill, government shutdown, defense needs, re-election pressure, late at night, bad weather, yadda, yadda."

Julia interrupted, "I like the first part but leave out re-election. That sounds too self-serving, even if it may have been a huge factor with everybody trying to get home for last-minute campaigning. Can we have the admission of error but keep it very general and issues-focused?"

"You're the boss," Walter shrugged, "but I'd be surprised if Jackson doesn't zing in to bring other points out. I think it might be better to get them on the table ourselves."

"You may be right. Let's see what Marcus thinks. What else?"

"This part's tricky. Should Simms give his own view on assisted suicide as legalized and humane when a person so chooses? Could he make the distinction between self-determined and government-mandated?"

"I think that's the only way to go. That's what they all thought they were voting for. He'll lose a few constituents over that but he'll pick up others. Anything else will look like he's just evading the question."

Walter asked, "What would he propose to clean up this mess?"

"Repeal, of course. But maybe he needs to be a little indefinite," said Julia. "After all, there's a six-month time period for the details to be worked out, so it's not like the death law goes into effect on Monday. We know six months will go by in a flash. But he could point that out on camera and hopefully look like the voice of reason in a chaotic time."

"I like that. Okay, let me work on something he can carry in with him. Will we release a statement to the press ourselves after the TV interview?"

"I think that's a great idea. This is the biggest issue he's ever dealt with, and how he handles it affects his future." To herself she added, and hers... and she needed this job, or she might be forced to favor the death law.

"Oh, good, here he is now. Let me start briefing him and you come in as soon as you have a statement ready," said Julia, hearing conversation become subdued in the main office as Simms neared his inner sanctum where she and Walter were meeting.

"What've you got? I'm tired of sounding like the village idiot," said Simms. "Really, we are *all* a village of idiots right now. I've never before been embarrassed by how I voted but I sure the Sam hell am right now!"

Walter hurried from Simms' office, leaving Julia, as usual, to soothe the raging beast. "Did you eat lunch? Want some coffee?" she asked.

"Missy, I don't look hungry, I look stupid! Make me look smart!" bit off Simms.

She went over the details of the interview for the next day and both the congressman and his chief of staff relaxed just a bit. Julia was grateful for the basic trust they'd developed through their years of working together. It would doubtless carry them through this crisis as it had others in the past. As they talked, they saw how this interview could just possibly, with a little luck, catapult him into Florida-wide or even national attention in a very positive way.

Satisfied the circus was under the tent for the moment, Julia wrapped up with her staff and decided to go home and get some peace and quiet and rest. She needed to be at the TV station at five the next morning to help Marcus figure out last-minute details.

CHAPTER 8

Thursday evening, November 10

Jake spent an hour organizing his notes and devising an interview plan. He wandered back into the living room as Hattie emerged from the kitchen.

Dressed in blue surgical scrubs and white sneakers, she looked informal but professional. She sported a short Afro and a warm smile. Jake thought she probably contributed as much to Henry's and Beatriz's mental well-being as to their physical care.

"Cup of coffee?" asked Hattie. "I generally have one while I wait for Mist' Henry and Miz Beatriz to rise from their naps."

"Sounds good," said Jake. "Would you happen to have decaf?"

"That's all we do have," Hattie said, chuckling. "I bring my own regular in a bottle. My agency says we bring our own food to the job."

"Really? Seems like when you're fixing their food, you'd just eat, too. Um, good coffee," he said as he sipped.

"Most times I sit down with them at lunch and eat my sandwich. Sometimes I have a nibble of their food 'cause Mist' Henry insists. My cooking's pretty good, if I do say so myself. Mostly he likes the talking. It gets pretty quiet around here, what with Miz Beatriz not saying much and what she does say, you can't understand. Mist' Henry says you a newspaper man working on a story about the death law, Mist' Jordan."

"Call me Jake. Do you have thoughts on that?"

"You just bet I do. Government got no right to tell people who lives and who dies, least not unless they're a criminal. Not so sure it's right even then. The Good Book says, 'Thou shalt not kill,' and I believe every word in that book."

"Have you helped many people who can't take care of themselves?"

"You best believe it. I've taken care of some in my family and in my job, lots more. Ain't no one nicer than this family, though. Miss Julia trying to do right by them and love them, no matter how they are."

Jake nodded and sipped his coffee.

"Another thing: How poor folks like me gonna make a living if people like Mist' Henry don't hire us? I didn't get no good education. When I was little in the South, schools weren't no good, least for us black kids. This the best job I ever had. I do know how to care for sick folks. When the people's as nice as these folks, it's a pure pleasure to go to work each day."

"They really rely on you," said Jake.

"I worry about them on my day off, they're like family to me. Most of my neighbors have jobs like this. What we gonna do, these jobs go away? Then we be living off the welfare and maybe the government kill the welfare people next. All the folks in jail and the homeless people – where will it end? Anybody the government have to pay for, they just zap them instead? No, sir, not in the US of A."

Jake pondered this slippery slope theory as he ate the delicious scone Hattie had served him. As they sat there, a bleat sounded down the hall. "Excuse me, Mist' Jake, that's Miz

Beatriz. I'll go help her up. Thanks for listening. This thing's really eating on me."

"Thank you for giving me your viewpoint. And also for this great scone," added Jake.

A key in the front door heralded Julia's arrival. Hanging up her briefcase, purse, and jacket on the hall tree, she called, "Whose Prius in the driveway? Is that you, Jake?"

"That'd be me. I forgot you didn't know I was still here," said Jake, as he walked into the hall. "Henry invited me to dinner and I decided to stay after I ate one of Hattie's scones. I hope that's okay."

"Good with me as long as we declare ourselves off duty," joked Julia half-heartedly.

Jake could see how tired she was. She had few stress-free days, between her office and home life, moving from crisis to crisis. He reached out to rub her back and she relaxed into his hands. Then Calvin II ambled out and rubbed against Julia's legs.

"Is that a cat?" she shrieked.

Jake admired her volume. She was a first-class shrieker.

Pointing a finger at Jake, she snapped, "Is this why you're here? Did you bring this cat into the house?"

Jake suspected Henry and Beatriz were lingering in their room until Julia's opening volleys were spent, on him. "Well, uh, technically I did bring the cat into the house–"

"Well, you can just take him right back out," yelled Julia, shaking her finger in Jake's face. "The last thing we need around here is another dependent creature!"

"Just calm down, Julia, and–"

"Don't you tell me to calm down. I've been calming everyone else down all day. I don't need that from you in my own house!"

Jake thought maybe she did need that but said, "Julia, please let me explain," talking fast while she took a breath. "The cat wandered out of the woods, obviously hurt. Your mother spied him and we took him in, fed him, and took him to the vet this afternoon. We couldn't have ignored him. And wait until you see your mother with him."

Recognizing a cue, Henry shuffled Beatriz out of their room saying, "Hi, daughter."

"Don't you 'daughter' me," yelled Julia. "That cat can't stay!"

"Before you issue edicts, look at your mother," said Henry. Calvin II had immediately limped to Beatriz, who was sitting on the floor crooning to him, stroking his fur. Beatriz was in her own little world with Calvin and it was a happy place.

"Oh, Lord," Julia said, sinking to the couch. "Let's talk about this, Henry."

"I'll be going now," said Jake.

"Oh, no, you don't, mister. You're part of this, too."

"Yes, help me explain," implored Henry. "Your reward will be Hattie's supper."

While Beatriz and Calvin II enjoyed each other's company, the other three settled in the living room. Hattie stepped in, hat, coat and gloves on, and said, "I'm going now. Miss Julia, that kitty won't be no trouble and that's the happiest Miz' Beatriz been since I been working here." She opened the door and slipped quickly into the evening.

"Okay," Julia said with a sigh. "What if you trip over the cat and fall, Henry?"

"I'm falling, anyway," he reminded her. "My most recent fall was pre-cat. I'd rather trip over a cat that makes your mother happy than over my own feet."

"What'd the vet say about his health? Who'll clean up the cat box?"

"We'll use the old Calvin's box – we call this cat Calvin II. Your mother probably thinks it's the old Calvin come back. I can still scoop poop and Hattie'll change the pad in the litter box when she empties the trash."

"What about the bills? And who'll take a sick cat to the vet?" asked Julia plaintively, losing this battle fast.

"I paid today's bill and I'll pay the rest. And Jake will take us to the vet."

"I will?" asked Jake. "I mean, yeah, I will. I admire your father for looking out for your mother's needs."

"It's called love," Julia said, as if Henry were not seated beside her. "Why do I feel like I'm being manipulated by this cat thing?"

"Not by me," said Jake. "I truly am an unwitting accomplice." Gesturing at Beatriz and the cat, he added, "I do think she loves the cat, but don't bite my head off for saying so."

"Okay," Julia said reluctantly. "I suppose so. I know when I've lost a vote. Let's have dinner – no wine tonight. I have a very early morning at the TV station. Henry, can you manage tomorrow until Hattie arrives?"

"Of course," said Henry, brushing off her concern. "Let's eat. I think Hattie made chicken and dumplings, my favorite."

"I'll set the table," offered Jake, "if you'll tell me where everything is."

"I'm surprised you don't know. You seem to have become a family member today," said Julia tartly.

Jake thought no answer was prudent.

Over chicken and dumplings with pie and ice cream for dessert, Jake commented, "This is the best meal I've eaten in a long time. I mostly live on scrambled eggs and grilled cheese sandwiches."

Henry laughed. "And bar food, I'll bet."

"Well, some of that," admitted Jake. "But I don't drink much anymore and I don't miss it. The noise and smoke in a bar are just tiresome these days."

"I know what you mean," replied Julia. "Sometimes I need to go out with a group or meet a lobbyist in a restaurant. But mostly I enjoy being a homebody."

"I'm not even in this conversation anymore," said Henry sadly. "But I was never a boozer. Just seemed wrong when I taught high school kids about the evils of alcohol and drugs. But I did like a beer with a ball game. As far as I know, your mom never tasted anything alcoholic other than communion wine."

The conversation drifted to each person's memories of younger days. Jake learned that Julia had been a brilliant student, putting herself through impressive university degrees through academic scholarships and part-time jobs. Julia discovered that Jake had spent a couple of years in Europe and North Africa after he'd saved some money from his first few jobs, traveling around absorbing information as only a journalist could. Henry just listened, observing what he hoped might be a budding romance. Beatriz played with the cat and Calvin II purred contentedly. It was the best domestic scene any of them had experienced in quite some time – maybe better than their future. According to the death law, two of them might not have much future left.

"I'll help clean up and be on my way," said Jake. "You have a very early morning tomorrow, Julia."

"I can still load the dishwasher, if you carry dishes in," said Henry. "Julia, can you get your mother ready for bed if we clean up?"

"You mean, get Mom and Calvin II ready for bed, right?"

Jake said to Henry, "Could we plan a few more interviews, if you're willing?"

"Willing? I'm loving it!" exclaimed Henry. "It's giving me new purpose in life and gets me out of the house. I love Beatriz, but our current life is either boring or in crisis. Who else would you like to interview? There's our accountant, a friend who's a hospice social worker, my lawyer, and I'd like to visit a memory care facility, in case we have to move Beatriz. Would you want to go with me and ask some questions there?"

"Thanks. Those are exactly the people I'd like to visit."

"Call us after eight-thirty in the morning. I'll go see how things are with Beatriz and send Julia out to say goodbye to you. See you tomorrow, my friend," said Henry, wheeling off toward the bedroom.

Jake was packing up his computer when Julia returned.

"Sorry for my outburst earlier," she said. "I can see how good Calvin II is for my mother. It's just, he's one more damn thing to worry about."

"I can see how all this would multiply," said Jake.

"No, you really can't, unless you live it daily. I freak out over something as simple as not charging my cell phone because I expect it to ring any minute. And the tragedy is, there are so many people in much worse shape than we are.

"We're coping for the moment," she continued. "I thank you for making my father's days brighter. When you take him to an appointment, that really helps me, too."

"I'm glad to do it. And I'm glad to have the chance to see you again, too," answered Jake. Julia moved closer and laid her head on his chest. His arms went around her for a long embrace and he felt their unspoken intimacy. Dropping a kiss on her head, he gave her an extra squeeze and headed out because neither of them knew what to say next.

CHAPTER 9

Thursday night, November 10

As Jake parked under his apartment building, his neighbor George Lafont wheeled his new Jaguar into the adjacent space. George was a realtor dealing in high-end residential properties in Washington. George and his partner, Jeff – a local minor celebrity, Jeff the Chef – were good neighbors and Jake enjoyed their company.

"Want to grab a beer at the pub across the street?" invited George. "Jeff will be working late and I've had a crazy day."

"Sure, why not?" About all Jake had to look forward to were quiz shows and Vanna and Alex could wait. "I'll be there in ten minutes."

Inside the bar, Jake saw no one he knew. He was becoming kind of a hermit these days. Maybe that's why being with Julia and her family was so enjoyable.

George seated himself, saying, "It's a crazy world out there these days!"

"What's happening?" asked Jake. "Reporters focus on the crazy so sometimes I lose perspective."

"It's this death law thing. Everybody approaching seventy

has decided to sell so they can have a fling with their money before they die. I've never seen anything like it."

"Why would they sell now?" puzzled Jake. "That doesn't seem to make sense. The death law isn't taking effect yet."

"Well, it actually does make sense," explained George. "If lots of people are going to die about the same time, that'll be a lot of property on the market. Some of the fine property here is still held by old people who inherited it. They've decided to get rid of it now rather than wait for the market to devalue in six months. It's a realtor's dream come true!"

"I thought the housing market was down," remarked Jake.

"It's come back some and it never was that bad in DC. These people are either making astute financial decisions or they just say what the hell and plan to spend while they're still here."

"Kinda makes you think," said Jake. "The Bible's got that thing about not knowing the appointed hour. My late wife died in that car crash with no warning at all."

"Well, a lot of people will soon know the appointed hour, and they have to think about it. Our phones are ringing off the hook. It's insane."

"Sounds like a good problem."

"It's way better than waiting for the phones to ring. Some savvy buyers are looking for property to snap up while people are selling in a panic. It'll probably turn into a gold mine for us if we can survive it. Uh-oh, didn't mean to imply death. Realtors have to be politically correct.

"Oh, hey, Dreama," George said, greeting another neighbor who'd just walked in. "Join us?"

"Sure," Dreama said as she slid onto a seat. Jake didn't know Dreama Conn well, though he saw her occasionally in the elevator. She was a middle-aged travel agent who lived alone, a sharp dresser and a pleasant person, but he hadn't ever really talked with her.

"It's been one of those days at the office. I don't usually wander into bars alone, but I'm out of wine and it was easier to come in here than to go buy a bottle. Glass of chardonnay, please," she told the bartender.

"I was just telling Jake about my crazy week," said George. "What's new with you?"

After a sip of the cold wine, Dreama said, "Everybody in DC over the age of sixty-five wants to go on a trip, right now, far away. That stupid death law has every old person in the city either running scared or looking to celebrate, depending on their mind-set."

"Running away?" asked George.

"Some want open-ended tickets, makes me think they don't plan to come back. For others, the death law is a wake-up call that they'd better get on with it. Everybody is planning travel within the next six months. Isn't that when it's supposed to take effect?"

Both Jake and George were shaking their heads in disbelief. "Better travel through legislation?" quipped George.

"We can't even get through to resorts and cruise companies using our private numbers. I guess every other travel professional is the same, busy."

"Why so many new travelers?" asked Jake. "I thought seniors were the backbone of the travel industry already."

"That's true, but not all at once and not all out of the US. Most senior citizens who travel take a trip or two a year, spaced out over the non-summer months. Today everyone wants to go right now."

"Where are they going?" asked Jake.

"Unusual requests: Canada, Iceland, Scandinavia, places people don't go in the winter months. But those are countries with good health care and a benevolent attitude toward elders. A lot of the open-ended tickets are for Mexico, the Caribbean islands, Spain, other places with large ex-pat communities. Boy, this wine hits the spot tonight!"

"Wow," replied Jake, "who'd have ever thought the death law could boost tourism? I've been investigating this with the help of a congressional staffer."

"And what does he think?" asked George.

"It's a 'she.' I mean Julia's a 'she.'" Jake realized he might be blushing and hoped the low light in the bar hid his red face.

"And who might this 'she' be? A new girlfriend?" teased George.

"She's Julia Sanchez, works for Congressman Marcus Simms. Not sure yet if it's a romance, but I'm really enjoying her company."

Returning to the topic, George said, "The fools who pushed this through will be ecstatic. Want more profit? Kill the old people! Next thing we know, they'll be selling euthanasia packages."

"Hmmm," mused Dreama, "not a bad idea. Just kidding, just kidding," she hastily added, seeing her friends' faces. "But think of it – older people go off on a cruise, have the time of their lives, and just don't come back. For those without relatives, it could be a blessing."

"But what cruise line would want to be the equivalent of railroad cars taking people to Auschwitz? That would kill, oops, hurt business," said George.

"It'd actually be just the opposite. It'd be all old people, voluntary, and very enjoyable, just choosing the time, place and method of their deaths. They'd be cheating the government of the pleasure of executing them."

Jake and George were recoiling in disbelief, but Dreama continued, lost in her own vision. "Imagine working on such a boat. You'd have to be some kind of humanitarian, kind of a cross between a cabin attendant and a hospice worker, I guess. Maybe cruise lines could hire veterinarians' assistants? They're used to putting creatures down."

By now both Jake and George were trying to hide in their beer glasses.

"Think of the tips – you'd have old people with some cash and nothing to save it for," continued Dreama, caught up in her macabre fantasy. "You'd have to offload the bodies somewhere, unless you buried them at sea... maybe retrofit the ships with morgues..." Noting that her audience was actually inching backward, she realized she'd better shut up and drink her wine.

Jake was appalled that he actually saw some merit in the idea. He was relieved when George verbalized the same thoughts. "It sounds awful but maybe better than some other avenues. I hate to think we profit from death, but that's not new. I've seen plenty of greedy relatives trying to get a senior to sell her house, or heirs divvying up the spoils even before someone's died. I guess the funeral homes will make a killing – oops, I mean, big profits. Better buy some stock in coffin companies, I guess."

Draining his Newcastle, Jake said, "I've got a busy day tomorrow and I can't take any more of this speculation tonight. You're helping me shape my thoughts on some investigative reporting I'm doing on the death law. Thanks for the perspectives, friends."

As he walked from the bar, Jake noted that he was probably the oldest patron there. Were older people already hiding, or had he just never noticed who frequented bars before? If nothing else, the death law was surely sharpening people's perceptions of age. Would it soon no longer be a crime if you murdered someone over seventy, saving the government the expense?

CHAPTER 10

Friday, November 11

Julia entered the Channel 4 studio and found Congressman Simms in the make-up chair being readied for the interview.

"'Bout time you got here, missy. Where the Sam hell you been?"

"Good morning to you, too, Marcus. What shall we go over?" asked Julia, thankful she'd had a decent night's sleep. Her mother was happy with the kitten and Henry was absorbed in helping with the interviews. Jake would be with them part of the day, relieving her of the full responsibility. She cautioned herself not to begin counting on him, though.

"Here's what I'm thinking. I've got all the facts you put together. It's only a short interview so I need to get in a lot, fast. I'll explain how legislators didn't read the fine print. I won't criticize anybody because we'll need a bipartisan fix to repeal."

"You're right," agreed Julia. "Okay, a few more facts. According to a study from Morgan University's Center on Aging, the number of people over sixty-five in the United States will double in about the next thirty years. In fifteen years, about twenty percent of the American population will be sixty-five or older, the current Medicare age. Some think older people are bankrupting the country. Others think it's health care costs in general, not just Medicare."

"We know we have to do something economically, if not morally," said Simms. "I'll mention people who don't want to live anymore, demented, disabled, imprisoned, or just plain tired of living. They have some rights, too."

He continued, "I'll quote some from constituent e-mails and phone calls. Most believe that assisted death is not wrong but government-mandated death is, that about right?"

"Yes, and that's what I've been hearing from my own father," said Julia. "You can use him as an example if you want to."

"Good, I might. And I might mention the stress I see that causing you," said Simms, with out-of-character compassion toward his chief. Julia hadn't known he even noticed her stress. She tried not to bring her worries to the office but obviously he was aware. "No names, of course," he added.

Someone came to take Marcus to the interview area before Julia could respond. "You look good and you always sound good. Stick to the facts, speak from the heart, and don't swear," advised Julia.

"Don't you leave, missy. You'll be the first person I want to talk to afterward."

Julia settled down in front of the monitor, enjoying the cup of coffee an assistant brought her. As Simms came on camera, he really did look good – conservatively fashionable with a pleasant, serious demeanor. He looked the part he played. She savored her few moments of quiet and coffee while she waited for the interview to begin.

Jackson Smith, known for his courteous manner while asking contentious questions, quickly led Simms through the elements of the death law and then asked his first zinger: "How in the world could this happen? Was everyone asleep at the switch?"

Julia tensed, glad they'd rehearsed that answer, which Simms delivered in a straightforward manner. He admitted yes, they'd all missed it, and enumerated the conditions under which that portion of the bill slipped through.

Simms said, "Some scholars think Judas kissed Jesus Christ and didn't mean for it to lead to the crucifixion, just light a fire under Jesus to get on with it. I suspect something like that happened with the death law. Maybe my esteemed colleagues meant to light a fire under us to work on the budget and the entitlement programs for the elderly, and it just got out of hand. A controlled burn led to a forest fire, and we in Florida know that happens sometimes, with disastrous results." He added some of the facts about aging Julia had just given him. So far he had not glanced at his notes.

The interviewer let him have the floor for a minute or two, then interrupted with, "What are you going to do about this?"

Marcus Simms looked straight into the camera and said, "I'm going to lead the movement to repeal this law right away. My fellow Americans, especially senior citizens, Floridians and your families all over the country, I will not let you down. I will see that the death warrant hanging over your heads is lifted. You can count on me. Veterans, this is your day today, November 11. I pledge that we will continue to take care of you in return for all you have done for us. And thank you for your service."

Taken by surprise at the forthright answer, knowing when someone had had the last word, the interviewer thanked the congressman for coming and signaled to his producer to cut to a commercial. Simms had already trumped any further questions he could ask.

Watching the interview on camera a few rooms away, Julia was so astonished at Simms' bold and unrehearsed pledge, she jumped up and spilled coffee all over herself. *Oh, my God, I'd better start looking for a job*, she thought. *If he fails after this, we're all done. What was that idiot thinking to be so bold? Nice touch on Veterans Day, though.*

Simms entered the room, ready to have his make-up removed, smiling like the Cheshire cat, and asked innocently, "Well, missy, what did you think?"

She snapped, "Geez, couldn't you have thought of this yesterday? I knew we'd be on the bandwagon for repeal but I didn't know you'd be the bus driver!"

"Why didn't *you* think of this yesterday?" countered Simms. "It's really the only position now. Everybody on the Hill is screwing around trying to figure out how to avoid blame. It's time to stop this nonsense before somebody gets hurt."

He rubbed his hand across his face, smearing his stage make-up, and said, "Now calm down and let's figure out what to do next. I'll admit, I didn't think it through, it just came to me. We're all dead meat anyway, for voting for this, so why not step into leadership and see what happens?

"Wait till I get cleaned up and we'll go get some breakfast someplace where nobody'll ask us questions while we get together a plan. Your blouse is a mess. What'd you do, spill your coffee?"

The office was abuzz when Julia walked in after leaving Marcus at his scheduled committee meeting on Foreign Affairs. *Oh, God, what now?* she thought. Several staff members waved paper at her with, "Have you seen this, boss?"

"No, what's going on?"

They all jabbered at once and she held up her hand like a policeman. "Wait, I can't understand. Georgia, what's happening?" Georgia began giving a pedantic chapter-and-verse description of the morning's message.

Holding up her hand again, Julia said, "Georgia, give me this in one sentence."

Georgia replied, "Preliminary guidelines came out today for implementation of the death law."

"Holy shit," said Julia. "That compresses the timeline. You saw Representative Simms' interview this morning?" All staff members nodded. "Then you know what direction we're going. Okay, same assignments as before. Sandy, give me a copy of those guidelines ASAP."

"They're sittin' on your desk, as well as on your computer, which you might check more often in this distressin' time, darlin'," drawled Sandy as she returned to her receptionist's desk to guard the sanctuary.

Julia began to scan the document, the product of a committee from the four agencies tasked with operationalizing the death law. She skipped to the meat:

> To be considered healthy and self-sustaining, an individual aged seventy or greater must be able to:

> - Perform six basic self-care tasks of toileting, feeding, dressing, grooming, physical ambulation, and bathing.
> - Perform the instrumental tasks of using the telephone, shopping, preparing food, housekeeping, doing laundry, using some mode of

transportation alone, being responsible for medication, and handling finances.

- Demonstrate intellectual capacity, cogency and orientation to time and place.
- Support self financially.
- Show lack of potentially fatal contagious or otherwise debilitating disease.
- Desire to continue living a viable life.
- Be a productive, contributing member of society.

Julia shook her head in disbelief, wondering what junior staff members had composed such ambiguous garbage. She didn't know many people of any age who could do all of the tasks all the time.

She hardly knew where to start, it was so vague. She'd assign their intern to request clarification of this confused jargon. Who was that prominent gerontologist in their home district at University of South Florida in Sarasota? Robinson, that was her name.

"Sandy, see if you can get me Doctor Robinson at USF," she spoke into her phone.

"Okay, boss, I'll have her in a minute." Sandy was already on the computer seeking a faculty directory.

Dr. Janet Robinson was in her office. The professor was pondering what to write first for a quick publication on the death law. Personally, she saw good parts and bad, though the idea of government intervention was abhorrent to her, especially as she entered her sixties with a chronic ailment or two. On the other hand, she'd watched her brother's wife decimate the family's finances and cause terrible stress as she'd descended into dementia for many years.

Also there was the Florida court case a few years ago that involved terminating life support for a young woman who'd been brain-dead for many years. When life should end was a thorny ethical debate and no one was more aware of that than this leading gerontologist surrounded by the elderly in Florida.

"Thanks for talking with me, Dr. Robinson," said Julia. "I need to know more about the issues in the first draft of the regulations surrounding the death law. You seemed the ideal person to ask."

"Sure, always glad to help," responded the professor. "Congressman Simms has worked on important elder legislation in the past. But, good grief, how did this law ever pass?"

"Wish I knew," replied Julia. "What's your take on this whole thing, anyway?"

Robinson replied, "It's mind-boggling. Getting rid of elders isn't new, you know. What's new is that so many of us are living longer and a potential drain on society. However, some see seniors as a boon for the economy as older people have more discretionary income. The facts aren't as clear as we'd like to pretend."

"What do you mean, it's happened before?" queried Julia.

"Well, not carried out very often," explained the professor, "but it's been theorized and sometimes done. For example, it's believed that some Native American tribes practiced senilicide – assisted suicide of elders – by moving the tribe and leaving the elderly and infirm behind to fend for themselves, or leaving them alone in the wilderness. Usually it occurred during famine, when the existence of the whole tribe was at stake without desperate measures."

"Didn't Eskimos do that?" asked Julia.

"There's a misconception that Eskimos set their elders on an ice floe to float off into never-never land, but that's not substantiated, especially after Christian missionaries arrived."

"The Bible says 'Honor thy father and thy mother,'" returned Julia. "That hardly speaks to a solo journey on an ice floe."

Robinson agreed, adding, "Some speculate that the origin of the Old Testament commandment to 'Honor thy father and thy mother' is based on the notion old people shouldn't be abandoned. Maybe Moses just didn't want to be left behind.

"In some cultures wives threw themselves – or were thrown – onto their husband's funeral pyre, a practice called *sati* in Hinduism. Widows were thought to be drains on society, thus the many injunctions in the Christian Bible to care for orphans and widows.

"I'll send you a draft of a paper I'm working on," said the professor. "Alexander Tille, a follower of Nietzsche, advocated 'helping nature' by purging society of what he called 'unproductive elements.' This philosophy became embedded in Hitler's Nazism and large numbers of so-called 'unproductive elements' were brutally purged."

"What was that name again?" asked Julia.

"T-I-L-L-E. Hitler instituted a eugenics policy to cleanse the Aryan nation, known as the T-4 Euthanasia Program. You can learn more about this at the Holocaust Museum right there in DC. Of the six million Jews exterminated, many were elderly because they weren't useful workers. Or they died because they couldn't withstand the hardships of the concentration camps."

"I never thought about this law reflecting Hitler's actions," Julia said.

"Hitler sent doctors to exterminate the elderly and disabled, not soldiers, because the doctors knew where the victims lived.

However, other than Hitler and the current US Congress, as far as I know, no other political bodies have actually established policy on it!"

Ooh, thought Julia, *sound bite!* "Have you seen the guidelines? They came just this morning and they weren't marked restricted. I'm guessing the committee is sending this up as a trial balloon."

"No. Can you send them to me?"

"Hang on, let me try. Okay, check your computer and see if that came through," said Julia.

"Yes, I see it. The first two sets of tasks are standard measures in the field for a person to be considered physically and mentally able. Do you read these as requiring a person to be able to perform all of the tasks? So if you can't shop for yourself, you can't live? That's absurd! The assisted living and home health people are going to have a cow over this. This piece of paper wipes out that whole section of health care.

"And what about time limits? Say I'm seventy and I break my foot so I can't use public transportation or drive for six weeks. Does that put me out forever? The loopholes are larger than life, if you'll pardon the expression. Practically everyone seventy and older would be euthanized. Surely that's not the intent of the legislation," exclaimed Robinson.

Julia fervently hoped the professor was correct.

"Look at the rest of this garbage," continued Robinson. "'Potentially fatal disease' – so everybody with the flu gets exterminated? Seniors might fear the government more than they fear illness. That's like many undocumented workers today.

"What's a 'productive, contributing member of society'? People not on welfare? People who still hold a job? Volunteers? This is ludicrous. It reads like a spoof on a law. The only one that makes any sense to me is 'desire to continue living a viable life.' Although semantically – what would constitute a non-viable life?"

Robinson continued, "I do personally think physician-assisted suicide should be legal in this country. And what does 'support self financially' mean? I swear, this looks like it was written by a bunch of smart fifth-graders or dumb undergraduates. Does the committee need to be reminded that people paid Social Security and Medicare tax when they were employed? I'm well aware that the numbers won't work for many more years, but that's not the fault of those that paid in.

"What if my children take care of me – is that self-supporting? And what if I have no children; is my old age in jeopardy more than if I'd produced offspring? I hate to keep using the word 'absurd.' The problem is, it's deadly absurd. Sorry, I have to get to class now."

"Dr. Robinson, this is so helpful to us. I hope we can repay the favor later," said Julia.

"I've got this conference coming up next year, and I need a keynote speaker. My crystal ball tells me Congressman Simms may emerge a national hero. Do you suppose he would consider keynoting my conference?" asked the professor.

"Send me the information and I'll put the date on his calendar. I'm willing to bet he'd be very interested." She thought, *This might be the perfect platform to announce bigger political aspirations.*

CHAPTER 11

Friday, November 11

The last few bright leaves were beautiful against the slate sky in the autumn storm. As he drove to pick up Henry, Jake wondered how wind affected Henry's mobility. He had learned a lot about disabilities from Henry and Beatriz this week.

Hattie was helping Henry into his coat when Jake arrived. "Y'all have a fine day. I'll give Miz Beatriz a good lunch and settle her for a nap." Turning to Jake, she warned, "Don't tire him out too bad." To Henry she said, "Y'all got your pills and know when to take them? Y'all know what happens when you miss. And don't get wet and chilled."

"Yes, thanks. I have my pills and I can still tell time," responded Henry tartly.

Jake figured Henry would tell him about the medicine if he wanted to. However, he wondered what to be prepared for if Henry missed a dose.

When they were in the car, Henry grumbled, "I know Hattie just takes care of us, but sometimes she's worse than a naggy wife. Not that I wouldn't be happy with a naggy wife these days."

"She's very serious about your care," agreed Jake.

"About the pill thing. Parkinson's patients follow a rigid

dosing schedule or we lose muscle control very quickly. My medication currently works well and I do have it with me. Feel free to remind me to take one at lunchtime, though, or we might both be sorry."

"Sorry how?"

"Let's not find out," said Henry. "I wish they'd legalize medical marijuana. That helps all kinds of ailments. I don't suppose you could get me a little pot?"

"Nope, no pot from me, sorry."

As they headed down the street, Henry asked, "Is that sleet? We don't need winter this early. Can we warm the car a little?"

Jake glanced over and saw Henry wet and shivering a little. "Sure, sorry. Are you okay? Julia and Hattie'll be mad at me if you get sick."

Henry said, "I'm ready to be out of the house. Plus I want to go to lunch. And we've got the accountant after lunch. The lawyer is meeting with us pro bono because he's interested in the work you're doing."

"That's good. What can you tell me about him?"

"He's a good friend," said Henry. "He's considered an outstanding eldercare lawyer. Gerard is tireless in his efforts to help us. He knows the eldercare system inside and out and he's also a financial wizard."

"So he helps with your finances?"

"Yes, we've discussed how things may be if Beatriz goes to a memory care place. I think we'll be financially okay. God knows we've paid him enough the last few years, but he's been worth every penny."

They pulled into the attorney's parking lot and Jake made sure Henry had on hat, gloves and buttoned-up coat. Henry pretended not to notice but smiled a little as though pleased that

Jake cared. He leaned back against the seat for a minute, looking tired today. Jake resolved to keep this interview short.

The receptionist greeted them warmly and helped Henry take off his wet coat and hat. "Thanks, Lily, good to see you again."

Gerard Hotchkiss stepped from his inner office. "Henry, so good to see you. And this is your journalist friend, Mr. ..."

Jake shook hands saying, "Jake Jordan, Kidd-Ruddman news. Thanks for taking the time to talk to me." Jake was surprised that Hotchkiss was only in his early forties and looked like a vegetarian runner with his slight, wiry build. Dressed impeccably in a starched shirt with impressive cuff links, striped tie and no jacket, Hotchkiss could pass for an ascetic don at Oxford if he wore an academic gown.

"I'm really interested to talk with you about this travesty of a death law," said the attorney. He was so hyper in speech and movement, it seemed he might have had too much coffee. "Call me Gerard. Henry's a very special guy with a whole lot on his plate right now. He doesn't need the government adding to his already considerable woes. Henry, I assume that since you brought Jake, it's okay to discuss generalities about your situation? Please stop me if I'm saying anything you don't want me to."

Henry nodded. "I've already told Jake all my secrets. I don't mind if he knows about finances. That's a very important part of this law thing, if the impetus is to cut costs of caring for us old guys."

Jake thought, *Good, we've clarified the ground rules.* "Do you have general impressions about the impact of the death law?"

"Can you imagine the legal challenges that are going to arise? It'll be an unfortunate gold mine for lawyers. Clients will spend whatever they have to stay alive. Plus there'll be families trying to prove incompetence even stronger, now there's a legal way to get rid of an elderly family nuisance. The death law is wrong, but it'll be a pot of gold for attorneys."

"Will we be seeing some injunctions soon?" asked Jake.

"I'm working on my first request right now. My clients all want to know what to do next. I can see you this morning only because someone canceled. I thought this issue was important enough to take the time with you."

"What do you see as the most important legal issues?"

"I'll answer that three ways," Gerard responded. "First, everyone wants to be sure their wills, powers of attorney and advanced medical directives are all in order, although no one knows if advanced directives will carry any weight anymore.

"Second, some people want to change their wills. Family feuds become either more or less significant. If you're going to die in six months, you may want to spread your estate around a little through endowments and be wined and dined by non-profits in your remaining time."

Gerard continued at some length about the implications and intricacies of endowments and legacies. Jake made a mental note to check over his own will.

"Third, some clients call with really perplexing questions for which we have no answers. How do I prove I'm competent? How do I set up offshore accounts and book an airline ticket? How do I pay a caregiver under the table? Should I buy a beach condo, take ski lessons, go to the moon, marry a young cutie, and, by the way, what happens to my debts when I die?

"This thing is wide open for challenge and I cannot imagine the Supreme Court upholding this." The lawyer cited chapter and verse on some previous Supreme Court decisions.

"A case is going to have to get through the state courts fast, though. Henry, you interested?" asked Hotchkiss.

"Uh, interested in what? Sorry, I drifted," said Henry.

Jake looked at Henry and realized they had overspent their time. "I think we'd better get going," he said. "I believe I have what I need. Can I call you if I have questions?"

"Sure, if you can get through on the phones. This thing's going to really heat up," predicted Gerard. The gleam in his eyes indicated his relish of a good legal fight.

"Thanks again for your time. Henry, let's roll," said Jake.

"Yeah, Gerard, thanks. Jake, I'm ready for lunch."

Jake eased them into traffic. "Where to for lunch? Same place or try something new?"

"Do you like Indian food? A great restaurant is nearby, and I can scoop up the food with the *naan*, makes it neater for me to eat in public." The elderly man perked up at the discussion about lunch.

"I love Indian food," replied Jake. "Heckuva good choice. Remember, it's my check today. Is it the place a couple of streets over from here?"

"Yes, the Taj. Beatriz and I used to go there when she was more herself."

"Sounds great. Okay, we're here, and thank goodness there's a parking place. It's raining like crazy."

"Jake, this is the best time I've had in the past few years," said Henry.

A smiling gentleman in a starched white apron held the door open for them. "Thank you for coming today. Where will you sit? A table might be easiest if you wish to remain in your chair, sir. Or a booth if you want to transfer out."

"You obviously know something about wheelchairs," remarked Jake.

"Yes, my dear late mother was chair-bound for several years and I determined that my restaurant would become easier for those in such circumstances."

"Booth okay with you, Jake?" asked Henry. "I'd rather be at the side of the room rather than in the middle when I eat. I think I'll have shrimp curry, some of that spinach *paneer*, and lots of *naan*. Oh, and *samosas*. Water to drink, with a straw, please."

"Sounds good to me, I'll have the same," said Jake.

"Very good, gentleman," said the waiter-owner as he bowed away from the table.

"Your pills, Henry?"

"Got 'em, thanks," said Henry as he shook his medicine out of a bottle and sipped some water through the straw.

"Did you realize today is the traditional Veterans Day?" mused Henry.

"I hadn't thought of it until Representative Simms mentioned it this morning on TV. Are you a veteran?" asked Jake.

"You bet I am, Semper Fi," replied Henry proudly. "I fought in the most useless war there ever was. Once a Marine, always a Marine. We don't have ex-Marines, only live ones and dead ones. Were you in the military?"

"Yes, got drafted into the Army near the end of Vietnam. I wasn't doing well in college, was thinking of quitting anyway, and thought why not? I didn't even try to get deferred. When I got my draft notice, I went shopping at all the services. The Air Force needed communication specialists and I'd always enjoyed writing and scored well on my aptitude test. I actually didn't end up in Vietnam but at Thule in Greenland and Elmendorf in Alaska. Other people went to the jungle while I went to the Arctic, but that was fine with me," said Jake. "I wrote lots of weather reports."

"Pretty much the same with me," said Henry. "I enlisted in the Marine Corps straight out of college, before Vietnam. I had a degree in biology and no idea what to do with it. I thought I'd be drafted so I enlisted first. I went to Parris Island for basic, then Officer's Basic School at Quantico, just like every other Marine officer. I loved the Corps – still do. I hope I'll always be able to stand up when the flag passes."

Jake asked, "So you did go to Vietnam?"

A look of pain twisted Henry's features and he looked around the room for a moment before he answered. "Yes, mine was one of the early units to go. I remember my buddies that were lost and it all seems so senseless.

"I mentioned pot the other day? It's a wonder we didn't all come back drug addicts. When a friend mentioned a non-standard Parkinson's treatment a few months ago, I wasn't any stranger to the remedy. We all smoked whatever we could get and drank too much. It was an awful place."

"But you survived, obviously."

"That war took a toll many of us didn't expect to pay. I was one of the lucky ones. I went back to school and got a master's degree on the GI Bill, and became a high school teacher."

"Were you married when you were in the Corps?" asked Jake.

"No, I met my first wife when we were both teachers. We had a pretty good marriage but no kids. I couldn't forget what had been done to kids in Vietnam – not by my unit, thank goodness – and she didn't really want children, either. But now that I'm a stepfather, I wonder if we didn't make the wrong decision all those years ago."

"How did your wife die?" asked Jake, hoping he wasn't crossing an invisible line.

Henry paused another minute, wiped his hand over his face and sighed. "She killed herself. She suffered from depression but kept it under control with medication. She was a fabulous teacher. She was fun to be with and vivacious most of the time, but had periods of darkness when nothing seemed to help. The last time, she took an overdose of some medication I didn't even know she had or I'd have thrown it out. Her death was ruled accidental, but I believe she just gave up on life."

"Oh, Henry, I'm sorry."

"It was devastating to me and to her friends. But that was a long time ago and here's our food, let's eat," he said, ending that conversation. "These *samosas* look awesome!"

As they finished eating, Henry said, "We're not in any hurry, are we? I'm cold and I'd like a cup of tea, if you don't mind watching me drink it through a straw. I'd like to know a little more about you."

"Sure. I've led a pretty ordinary life. Went back to school after writing my way through the Air Force. I decided to study journalism so I went to the University of Missouri. I'd never even been to Missouri but I figured anywhere was better than the Arctic Circle. I had good professors, and the kids in my classes were fairly hard-working. I got to write columns and stories and then was editor of the student newspaper. I had grown up in the Air Force so I appreciated the chances to learn a lot. Turned out to make some super contacts that I'm glad to have today."

"I'm guessing you've won awards? Any Pulitzers?" joked Henry.

"A few awards, one I'm proud of – it was for investigating government over-spending. No, no Pulitzer, been nominated twice."

"Oh, I thought I was joking on that. Maybe a Pulitzer if you write a book on the death law?" asked Henry. "You are prominent in your field, aren't you?"

"I guess you could call me respected. I've always moved on to a better job when I wanted. Newspapers are dying out, so I'm glad I'm old enough to retire whenever I want. I hosted a public television show for awhile and that was okay, but I like print better. I've had some fun times – sneaked into the Master's golf tournament on press credentials when I was a college kid, stuff like that. I've met a lot of politicians in the job I have now. Some are salt of the earth but a few are pure scum."

"Yes, I've noticed. And you don't have any children, either?"

"No," Jake said. "I met my wife after I got out of college. We were both big on careers and just never did see ourselves with children. We really weren't all that happy with each other. I wonder if we didn't subconsciously avoid having children. When she was killed in an automobile accident, I was glad I didn't end up a single father."

"I marvel at how well Beatriz raised Julia. She had no help or family around and very little money. Look at the exceptional woman Julia is. I'm sure you've noticed that," Henry added dryly. "And you never remarried?"

"No, I've had a few girlfriends through the years. Every time it looked like getting serious, one of us backed out. I've pretty much just been committed to my career. Yes, I think Julia's a very special person. This isn't an interview to determine my worthiness, is it?" joked Jake.

"Of course not," retorted Henry. "Julia makes her own decisions. I was just curious. Julia would kill me if she thought I was intervening. She's a better judge of character, anyway. I'd probably sell my soul right now for car rides and *samosas* more often."

A shared laugh broke the tension of the moment. Jake left

money for the bill with a generous tip for the gracious host. They headed for the exit and the proprietor again held the door for them with a cheerful, "I hope to see you gentlemen again soon."

Jake hustled Henry to the car in the chilly wind and rain, ready to head for the accountant's office. Henry looked exhausted.

"Say, can we crank up the heat?" asked Henry. Jake saw that Henry was wet and shivering as the older man emitted a prolonged cough.

"Sure, it'll take just a minute to warm up. Sorry, we stayed out too long."

"No, it's my fault. I was enjoying myself. Sometimes I just run out of steam all at once."

"Maybe we'd better leave the accountant for another day," offered Jake.

Laying his head back against the seat, his eyes closed, Henry agreed weakly, "Good idea. Let's go home." He coughed deeply and managed to get out, "I'll call him from there."

They pulled into the driveway at home and Hattie opened the door.

"It's about time you boys got home. This is a long time for Mist' Henry to be out, and on such a day, too," she scolded. "And you got company here. Lemme have that wet coat. And Mist' Jake, you set a spell, too."

Jake replied, "Thanks, but I need to get going."

He wheeled Henry into the living room and Henry said between coughs, "Well, look who's here, it's our neighbor Francine. Francine, this is my friend Jake."

"I kept seeing a strange car in your driveway so I decided I'd better come check on things. I've been having a good chat with Beatriz and admiring the cat, which she won't let me touch," said

Francine. "That is, I've been talking to Hattie, can't tell if Beatriz is hearing me or not. She sure is wrapped up in that cat."

Henry coughed again and gasped for breath. Francine got up to pat him on the back. As she rose, she stumbled sideways and almost fell on Beatriz and the cat. Hattie reached out and steadied Francine and shot a worried look at the coughing man. Francine put her hand on her head and sank back on the couch beside Beatriz.

"Francine?" asked Henry. "Are you feeling ill?"

"No, no, everything's all right. Just give me a minute," replied Francine faintly.

Where am I, a nursing home? thought Jake. *Three old sick people?* He reflected that his life was simpler when he was holed up in his own apartment watching mindless television.

"Have you been to the doctor?" asked Henry.

"No, I'm not going to any doctor, not anymore," said Francine.

"Why not?" persisted Henry. "You have a good doctor and insurance. Why wouldn't you go?"

"Because he might have to kill me, under this death law thing, that's why," wailed Francine. "I'm scared to find out what's wrong. I'm not ready to die yet. I have a headache all the time and I'm unsteady on my feet, but it's not that bad, really, it isn't." She began sobbing, Henry started coughing, Beatriz patted the cat, and Hattie headed for the telephone. Jake felt absolutely helpless.

"Let me get y'all some coffee and I'm calling Miss Julia. Y'all need to go to the doctor, Mist' Henry, and y'all do, too, Miz Francine," declared Hattie over her shoulder. "Can you stay a minute, Mist' Jake, while I call?"

"Don't you call anyone," growled Henry, going into another coughing fit.

"Yes, I'm not going anywhere," Jake said. "I'll get the coffee, you call Julia."

"I'm the caregiver and I know when to call Miss Julia," said Hattie firmly.

Jake served the coffee, assuming the role of family host once again. He asked Francine, "Do you have a way to get to the doctor?" *Oh geez, now I'm a social worker.*

"I said I'm not going and I'm not going!" reiterated Francine firmly. "I don't want to be put to death, or be on any government hit list."

Both Henry and Jake assured her the death law hadn't taken effect yet and she had nothing to worry about. But both wondered privately if their words of assurance were correct.

Hattie returned to the living room, saying, "Miss Julia wants to talk to y'all, Mist' Jake."

Uh-oh, thought Jake. *She's mad at me for making her dad sick.* "Hey, Julia."

"Jake, I hate to ask you this, but Hattie says Henry's really sick. Could you possibly drop him off at Patient First on your way home? They know us well there. I'm at least forty-five minutes away in traffic and Hattie thinks he needs to go right away."

"Of course, but I'll wait with him until you get there. What about taking Francine, too?"

"I'd be so grateful. Dad probably stayed out too long, though I'm sure it was his idea. He's not always sensible about his own stamina. Hattie said Francine's sick, too. I doubt she'll go with you but you can try. I'll call her daughter this weekend, if she won't go today."

"Oh, could you check if Dad took his meds?"

"He took them," said Jake. "I saw him." *At least I did something right.* He told her they were on their way to the clinic immediately.

Hattie was already helping Henry into a dry, warmer coat.

Henry looked beat and was not protesting either the trip to the clinic or the assistance. Turning to Francine, Jake said, "Want to ride along and help me get Henry where he needs to be?"

"No, sir, you know how to manage Henry. You dragged him around all day in the wet and cold. And you're not getting me to the doctor. I recognize a ploy, and I told you, I'm not going!"

Henry said to her, "Well, would you at least stay for a bite of supper and keep Beatriz company? You don't eat right these days. Maybe that's why you're dizzy. You don't mind to cook dinner and feed the cat, Hattie?"

"No, sir, Mist' Henry, as easy to cook for two as for one."

"Cook for three, Hattie. I want you to eat dinner, too," emphasized Henry.

"Yes, Mist' Henry, I expect I'll jus' do that." She'd wondered if she'd have to go supper-less since she hadn't brought extra food with her. And she might be spending the night with Beatriz if Henry had to go to the hospital.

Good thing she didn't have anyone depending on her at home anymore. She usually had her grandchildren over the weekend but decided her trifling daughter could just look after her own kids for a change. These people needed her tonight.

Jake got to the Patient First clinic in good time, glad the place wasn't overrun with patients on this early Friday evening. Inside the clinic, Henry said, "Could you help me with the computer check-in?"

"Sure," said Jake. "What do I do? Oh, I see, we punch in answers to questions. Okay, you're Henry Horton; birth date? street address, 104 Elm Street, Falls Church; ZIP code? Insurance? You have your insurance cards and ID?"

As he wheeled Henry toward the waiting room chairs, a medical worker called, "Mr. Horton?"

Jake started to hand over the wheelchair when Henry said, "Would you go with me, Jake? Just until Julia gets here?"

Jake had a sudden glimpse into how frightening this illness must be and how well Henry had kept the proverbial stiff upper lip until now. Right now he looked like a scared sick old man. Jake nodded, patted Henry's shoulder, and guided the chair into the examining area.

On Capitol Hill, Julia hastily assembled her staff, verified their assignments, and explained her home situation. She told everyone to get some rest because things were going to get worse before they got better, although she knew many staff would be in the office all weekend. However, she was pretty sure she herself wouldn't be, with Henry sick. She debated taking public transportation to be faster, but Jake was with Henry, so there was not as much urgency as sometimes. She thanked God for Jake's temporary help with the burden of care.

She finally got through the Friday afternoon traffic and pulled into the parking lot at Patient First, relieved to see Jake's little blue car still there. She entered and didn't see them in the waiting room. Henry must already have been called and Jake must be with him.

She checked with the receptionist, entered through the double doors, and found Jake and Henry in a small cubicle. She gave Jake a brief hug and did her own quick assessment of Henry's condition. She believed he'd be all right but would be glad to hear that from the doctor. Turning to Jake, she said, "I can't thank you enough. When we get through this crisis, I'd like to take you to dinner to make it up to you."

"No need, though I'd like us to have dinner soon. Call me later tonight and tell me how things are going?"

"I will. It may be a little late, ok?" asked Julia, feeling some tension drain at the thought of talking with Jake later.

"Yes, whenever, but please do call," said Jake as he shrugged into his wet coat. "You hang in there, Henry." He squeezed the older man's shoulder. "Talk to you later, Julia."

Henry gave a weak smile and a strong cough.

About nine-thirty Jake's phone rang. He'd nodded off on the couch over the new biography of Nixon. "Hello," he said, shaking himself mentally awake. "Oh, hey, Julia, thanks for calling. How's Henry?"

"Is this too late? You sounded asleep when you answered," apologized Julia.

"No, no, I'm very glad to hear from you."

"Henry's a little better. He got something for his cough and a sedative to help him sleep. The doctor said it's not pneumonia, just bronchitis. Turns out he's been feeling puny for a couple of days but hid it because he wanted to do the interviews with you."

"Oh, no, I did make him sick."

"No, you didn't. I hadn't realized how housebound he was feeling, and I'm so grateful to you for involving him in your project. I get so focused on their physical needs, I don't pay enough attention to what he's feeling sometimes."

"Oh, Julia, you're wonderful to them, keeping body and soul together under such circumstances. Your job isn't exactly nine to five, either," said Jake. "I've read about eldercare problems, but it's another thing to see them first-hand."

"You're doing more than observing. You're participating. You've been so helpful to us this week. Handling the cat thing, getting Henry to the doctor twice, taking him to lunch. It's been a load off my mind, just knowing there's someone else involved. Not that I expect you to continue that," she added hastily. "But this week especially, it's allowed me to focus on the mess in the office."

Jake surprised himself at his spontaneous response: "I do hope I'll continue to be involved. I really like and respect Henry. He's a very good companion. I'd like to make your life a little easier, too, if I can. I feel like I'm getting to know you through talking to Henry, as well as from our own conversations. I know our acquaintance is new, but it feels very special to me."

After a slight pause during which Jake mentally chided himself for saying too much too soon, Julia responded softly, "It feels that way to me, too. I've been on my own for so long and I haven't allowed myself to get close to anyone. Virtually all my time is taken up with Mom, Henry, and my job and that leaves very little band-width in my brain for anything – or anyone – else.

"It just hasn't seemed worth the trouble to get involved if I can't fully participate in a relationship. The stress takes a toll on me and I'm not sure how much of me's left for anybody else right now." *Oops*, thought Julia, *too far too fast. That's not what he said at all.*

"Then I'm the lucky one," Jake responded, "if you aren't already involved with anyone. Our lives have been kind of opposite. I've dated some since my wife died many years ago, but haven't really been interested in anyone. I'd feel like I was using the woman when she would get involved and I was emotionally distant. So I just started staying to myself and having a beer now and then with my buddies, male and female. Your life might be over-full and mine, under-full. Maybe together we'd be more of a happy medium."

Julia said, "Right now, with Mom and Henry asleep, Calvin II purring on my lap, things seem pretty under control. But I know how fast that can change. We live from crisis to crisis, both here and in the office. I have to say, though, having this phone conversation with you is a welcome end to this long day."

"Me, too," echoed Jake.

"My life is so much better than it could be. We have Hattie and Henry is mentally very able. We can pay our bills and we own our house. But being around you these past few days has reminded me of how closed off I've been and what's missing. And thank you for that – I guess!" she added ruefully.

"That's how I feel, too. Shall we leave it at that tonight and I'll call you tomorrow?"

"That'd be good. I have a lot to think about tonight – I suspect we both do. But for a change, it's good stuff instead of how to solve a problem," answered Julia. "Good night, and thanks again. Talk to you tomorrow."

Jake went to sleep with a smile on his face, his book falling neglected onto his chest.

CHAPTER 12

Saturday, November 12

Jake felt great when he woke up Saturday morning. His productive week and new friends – especially his new lady friend – had enabled him to have a good night's sleep. He puttered around, went out for a newspaper and coffee, paid a few bills, vacuumed, and realized it was only mid-morning. *Good grief, what's happening to me?* He felt aimless without Julia and her family around.

He decided to review his notes from his interviews and begin a first draft of what would become a series of stories. Monday morning he'd meet with his editor to nail down the scope and timeline. He thought he saw the beginning of a book but first had to fulfill his newspaper writing obligations. The editor had given him relatively free rein, but Jake knew he needed to clarify the boss' expectations.

Deep into his work, he was startled into the present by his telephone. His heart lifted to see Julia's name displayed. "Good morning. How's everyone?"

"Hello – we're doing much better." She sounded considerably more chipper than the evening before. "Mom's as usual and Henry's coughing much less. He's not as well as he thinks he is, but he's surely better."

From the background, Jake heard Henry say, "I'm fine. You tell him what I said for you to say."

Laughing, Julia said, "Henry insists I ask you to dinner tonight. I'm not doing that – we've been burden enough to you lately – but would you by chance be free to come tomorrow night? That'll give Henry another day to recover and me time to buy something to cook. It's been a hectic week."

"Tell him the rest," yelled Henry from the background. "Or I'll call him back myself."

"What does he want you to tell me?" asked Jake.

"Well, I'm embarrassed, but I think there's some matchmaking going on here. He says he and Mom go to bed early and you should plan to stay late," Julia said, laughing.

"That's not what I said!" howled Henry in the background.

"That's all I'm saying and you're not calling him back," retorted Julia to Henry. "Look, Jake, I don't want you to feel obligated, but we'd love to have you for dinner."

"Sure, I'd like to come. I was feeling at loose ends after this week and it'll give me something to look forward to. Maybe I can get some work done between now and then. I'm missing you," he added softly.

"Me, too, you. If Henry calls, don't answer the phone, okay?" she added teasingly for Henry's benefit.

"Could I bring dessert?" asked Jake.

"That'd be great. No seeds, Henry can't handle seeds anymore. Would five be okay? They do go to bed early – no hidden message though!"

"Don't tell him my secrets!" Jake heard Henry in the background. Jake realized this romance might be a family affair, no pun intended, conducted in something of a fishbowl. But he supposed that was part of being in a family.

"See you tomorrow. And take it a little easy yourself, if you can," he suggested. "Next week will probably be even rougher at the office."

"You're right, good advice. Oh, damn, I just stepped on the cat! Calvin's squalling and he bit me, and Mom's hitting me, gotta go! See you tomorrow."

Jake felt one hundred percent better and more focused than he had before the phone conversation. *Calm down, boy, early days yet. Let it play out and see where this goes.*

He considered the possibilities for dessert and decided cooking anything decent was out of the question. He'd better hunt up a bakery while it was open on Saturday.

Should I take flowers? he wondered. *No, too much; yes, flowers are always good; no, Henry will laugh at me; yes, just do it, as Nike says.* He thought about wine. Take it or not? Red? White? Pink? No, definitely not pink. A bottle each of red and white? Which red? Which white? Were dessert, wine and flowers all together too much? And what would he wear? Jeans? Tie? Jeans and tie? *Get a grip! It's just dinner with friends.*

But in his heart he knew it was more.

Julia ended her call and grabbed the kitten, since no amount of soothing calmed her mother. Picking up both the kitten and a few scratches, she restored Calvin to Beatriz's lap, stopping both Calvin's and Beatriz's howling and attacks. Julia couldn't decide whether to laugh or cry. The cat bite hurt but the situation was really ludicrous, a metaphor for their lives at present.

"Let me tend those, honey," said Henry. "You don't need cat scratch fever." They found antibiotic ointment and antibiotic bandages in the bathroom medicine cabinet. Henry doctored the wounds, saying, "Holding this cat is the only real pleasure your mother has shown in months."

"I know," replied Julia. "But I can't say I'm a big fan right now. Do we have any claw clippers? Why do I have a purple Band-Aid? Oh, I bought the children's by mistake, sorry. I've got to figure out dinner tomorrow night, since you invited Jake. Can you hold the fort together here while I run errands this morning? I hate to ask Hattie; she's already done enough extra this week."

"Sure, if you'll get a clean Depend on your mom. I'll call you if anything unforeseen happens."

As if there's anything foreseen at this point, grumped Julia mentally. "Any suggestions for dinner tomorrow?" She glimpsed herself in the mirror. "I'll see if I can get a haircut appointment, come home and fix lunch, then get groceries this afternoon, okay?"

"Fine," said Henry. "You need to primp up for that man of yours."

"He's not my man!" rejoined Julia. "I just need a haircut." She had worn her hair short for years and didn't disguise the gray that was taking over. She thought it gave her a little authority in the office. She liked what a friend called her "no-nonsense hair."

Kissing Henry goodbye on the cheek and verifying that they both had charged cell phones, she drove to the nearby salon. She paid a fortune for hair care in this shop, but that was about all the pampering she got these days. She always enjoyed conversation with her stylist. Today Kenya's hair was a bright purple, a shade more commonly seen on Easter eggs. She had a new tattoo to match, so Julia was distracted from her own woes as she observed Kenya. She admired the woman for being so individualistic in style.

"Hey, Kenya, what's new? Thanks so much for squeezing me in this morning."

"You do need a trim, that's for sure," said Kenya. "Cool purple Band-Aid! Where you been keeping yourself?"

"Busy at work and crises at home," said Julia. "Things are pretty calm this morning so I got away for a few minutes." If the Band-Aids suited Kenya's taste, she needed to get rid of them. "What's new with you?

"I'm taking burlesque dancing lessons. Hey, we've got a show coming up soon. Want some tickets?"

"I'm pretty busy right now," hedged Julia. "And I don't leave Mom and Henry alone at night. But thanks anyway."

When Julia asked Henry for dinner suggestions, he answered, "Something I can pick up and eat with my fingers."

"Okay, let's do oven-baked chicken and roasted asparagus. You can eat both with your fingers. And a salad plate of cherry tomatoes, olives, red and yellow pepper rings. You won't need a fork until dessert. We'll do those little taco thingies from Costco Mom likes for appetizer, and wine. Do you know what Jake likes? You've had lunch with him twice. Come to think of it, I've had breakfast and dinner with Jake, too. What a whirlwind week!"

"I really didn't notice what he ordered. We had Indian once and Mexican. Your menu sounds good."

"Easy to cook, too," said Julia. "I need to work some tomorrow afternoon while you and Mom nap. I'll run the rest of the errands while you rest for awhile. There's golf on TV, can you watch that while Mom and Calvin catnap? You got your meds, right?"

"Yes, dear. Julia, I hope you know how grateful I am to you, and your mom is, too, even though she can't say so," said Henry, patting Julia's hand. "Come on, Honey-Bea, let's go take a snooze," extending his hand to his wife who gave him a big smile as she followed him to their room, cat in tow.

As Julia headed out, she pondered what to wear. *Should I dress up? No, he's used to seeing me like that. Maybe that new pair of Chico's jeans with the sequins on the pockets that Henry calls "sparkly butt." Wine, or will Jake bring that? Flowers, or is that too much? Red wine? White wine? No pink, that's for sure. Oh, hell, I'm definitely overthinking this. Technically he's Henry's guest, anyway.*

But she knew Jake was really coming for her, not Henry. With a lighter heart than she'd had in many a month, she pulled into Wegman's, confident she could find everything she needed for a casual-chic dinner. Plus she could pick up Henry's prescription and their senior vitamins. And cat food, and maybe even a toy for the little bugger.

Sunday afternoon, Jake showered, put on his best jeans, chose a blue button-down shirt and fashionably rolled up the sleeves to his elbows. No, that wouldn't work. He rolled the sleeves back down and added a navy v-neck sweater to complement his blue eyes. He pondered his shoes: running shoes? Slip-on loafers? He settled on a pair of Topsiders, adding socks in deference to the November weather. He brushed his graying, flyaway hair and realized a haircut might have been a good idea. Oh, well, he at least trimmed his beard, remembering to take off his sweater first so he didn't look like a dog shedding fur.

Then he assembled his items to take along: cheesecake with

cherry topping (no seeds in these cherries); flowers; a bottle of Ingleside merlot and a Barboursville chardonnay. Jeez, how was he going to carry all that? Rummaging in the closet, he came up with a partitioned bag designed to carry wine and stuck the flowers down into one of the bottle sections, too. He placed the cheesecake in another bag. *Great, now I look like a delivery boy. Well, not boy, exactly...*

Julia did a similar wardrobe dance, donning and discarding several outfits before deciding on that pair of jeans, a light blue sweater and flats. She barely recognized herself in the mirror, compared to her usual glossy office look. She really didn't look like herself when she tied on an apron. She soon had little chicken-cheese tacos in the toaster oven, chicken pieces dusted with crumbs cooking in the main oven and a colorful platter of salad stuff arranged. She sprayed the asparagus with cooking spray, sprinkled it liberally with Italian seasoning, squirted a little lemon juice on top and set it aside to roast later in the toaster oven. She hoped Jake wasn't too attached to salt. Henry had to watch his blood pressure and they ate very little salt these days.

The table was set with colorful Fiesta ware – Henry had managed that task himself. Wine glasses and cocktail napkins were on the sideboard. The bread, Wegman's finest olive loaf, lay sliced and wrapped in a napkin in a basket. Everything looked ready to Julia, though she thought, *Damn, wish I'd remembered flowers for the table.*

The doorbell rang and the show was on.

"We need to give you a key, you spend so much time with us," joked Julia as she opened the door to Jake. She tried to hug him but he was so laden with flowers, wine and dessert, she could hardly reach around him. He leaned over and gave her a kiss on the cheek.

She exclaimed at what he'd brought. "Flowers – I can't remember the last time anyone brought me flowers! And the wine – I love Virginia wines! Thanks for the cheesecake. It's a favorite of everyone."

"I thought that might be the case. Wow, you look great. First time I've seen you without your office costume."

"Thanks. I like your casual look, too. Can we agree not to talk about work tonight? Or at least, not talk about issues? I'd like to hear more about your job, actually," said Julia as she found a clear blown-glass vase and arranged the bouquet of bronze chrysanthemums.

Jake nodded. "Deal. I'd like to hear more about your job, too. Journalists and congressional staffers are often antagonists but the last thing I feel toward you is antagonism."

"We're in here, Jake," said Henry loudly from the family room. "Come on in."

Jake and Julia both rolled their eyes and shared a laugh. "Here, carry in your wine and I'll be right behind you with the appetizers."

"Actually, the red may be a little cold, after sitting in the car," replied Jake.

"I'd prefer white, myself, and Henry gets only a half glass of white, regardless of what he tells you. We don't need any red-wine headaches around here," Julia explained. "There are glasses and an opener in there. Don't let Henry open the bottle, he'll spill, and that Barboursville's much too good a wine to waste."

Balancing wine, opener and wine glasses, he followed her into the living room where Henry, Beatriz and Calvin were sitting on the leather couch in front of the fireplace. "Don't get up," said Jake as Henry struggled to rise from the sofa. "Let me set the wine bottle down and I'll shake your hand."

"Shake my shaky hand, you mean?" joked Henry. "Unfortunately, it shakes itself these days."

Jake gave him a warm handshake and a man-pat on the shoulder. As Jake reached out to greet Beatriz, Calvin took a good swipe with his claws.

"Ow," snarled Jake, "that hurt. And I'm bleeding." Recovering himself, he said, "Just a little scratch, though, it'll be okay."

"Oh, no," cried Julia, "not you, too! That pesky cat got me good yesterday. Come on, let's fix that up."

"No, no, I'm fine," said Jake, embarrassed by his first reaction, when he was trying to be on his best behavior.

"No need for cat infections. Let me patch you up," insisted Julia, taking his arm and leading him toward the bathroom.

"Yes, Jake, go with her," urged Henry. "I'd put Calvin in the other room but we'd have to sequester Beatriz, too, or they'd both squall. Plus, Julia can hold your hand."

"Okay, Henry, that's enough. No more, or we'll put you three in your room and lock the door!" said Julia firmly. "Come on, Jake, it's quieter in the bathroom, anyway."

Doctoring Jake's hand, she asked, "Purple or green Band-Aid? That's all we have, sorry. And please ignore Henry with his adolescent remarks."

Jake laughed. "I'll take green. It's been a long time since anyone cared enough to bandage me. Thank you." Looking at her, Jake realized the moment was too good to pass up and drew her closer to him. They shared a brief but intimate kiss that held much promise.

Pulling away, slightly breathless, they gazed at each other, then shared a second, longer kiss. "We'd better get back in the other room before the chaperones catch us, I guess," said Jake.

Julia virtually giggled. "Yes, this does feel a bit adolescent, hiding in the bathroom." A brief hand-squeeze promised a replay later when the chaperones departed to their own room.

Dinner was fun as Jake again enjoyed fitting into family life. Henry sprayed crumbs as he punctuated conversation with his baked drumstick. Beatriz ate little but made sure the kitty in her lap was well fed, although he declined the asparagus. Henry urged his wife to eat but she ignored his efforts, focusing solely on the Calvin-cat.

Jake and Julia enjoyed the food but kept glancing at each other, a connection not lost on Henry. He'd keep the conversation going until he and Beatriz could gracefully retire to their own room.

Henry hoped what he thought he was observing was indeed happening. He'd long worried about Julia's lack of male companionship. He was concerned about her life after they died, which he thought wasn't too far in the future, law or no law. He'd feel easier about passing if Julia was attached to someone else. However, he knew he had to keep his mouth shut and hope nature and Cupid would suffice.

Finally the cheesecake was served and eaten. Henry was glad they hadn't excused themselves from the table before he got his share. He was a little messy but not too bad, as it stuck to his fork pretty well.

He noted that Beatriz was not even eating the cheesecake she normally loved. He wondered if she was entering a new phase of decline. He knew that people with dementia often stopped eating in the latter phase of their illness.

He and Beatriz had long since signed Do Not Resuscitate orders. He needed to hunt out those papers and put them in a prominent place, should Julia require them soon.

Pushing back his chair, Henry said, "Julia, if you could get your mother ready for bed, we'll let you enjoy the rest of the evening. Good night, Jake. I hope we'll do some more interviews next week."

"We already are enjoying the evening," protested Jake. "You don't need to leave so early. We'll do some interviewing, but I need to visit the office and catch up some tomorrow. You may need another day to recover from your bronchitis. Are you going to stick me with the clean-up of this great dinner all by myself?"

"You bet I am," said Henry, chuckling. "You can do it alone much faster than if I helped. My best assistance tonight is moving Beatriz and the cat and me into our own room. I'll talk to you tomorrow."

Jake couldn't argue with that, as it echoed his own thoughts. He put away food, scraped off the remains, rinsed dishes and loaded the dishwasher.

Soon Julia was beside him helping finish the task. "More wine?" she asked. "There's a little left in the bottle and it's really too good to leave. I vote we finish it." At Jake's nod, she poured them each a second glass.

"I'm feeling a bit awkward," said Jake.

Julia laughed. "That was my opening line. How dare you steal my conversation starter!"

Jake laughed with her, easing the tension between them a bit.

"Let's go sit by the fire," said Julia, "sip our wine, and talk about life. It feels like it's time for some serious conversation. For instance, I don't know anything about your childhood."

"Good idea," said Jake, "but you go first. You know guys don't know how to talk about stuff."

"Bull," rejoined Julia. "Guys just don't want to be bothered. But not you – you're a professional wordsmith."

They sank into the leather couch. "So tell me about when you were a boy," began Julia.

"Not a whole lot to tell. I grew up in a small town in Georgia, Wrightsburg, where everybody knew everybody else. My sister was five years younger than me, so we ran in different circles. I had friends, my parents took us to church and made us behave, we swam in the creek, ran barefoot, had a paper route, that was about it. I wouldn't call our family all that close, but we got along and helped each other. It was a very ordinary childhood."

"What did your dad do?"

"He ran the hardware store and my mom stayed home and took care of us. We weren't poor, but we sure weren't rich, either. I had an allowance so I could go to the movies on Saturday afternoon and watch the cowboy movie. And a little candy at the corner grocery, of course."

"Were you a good student?"

"I was okay," Jake said, shrugging. "Nothing special. I played a little baseball and football, but the thing I really liked was working on the school paper. That's how I got where I am now. After high school I went to college but didn't much like it. The draft was on for Vietnam and I got called up so I joined the Air Force, matured a lot, and went back to college for a journalism degree after that. How about you?"

"My childhood was very different. My dad died when I was little so it's just been my mom and me. I studied hard to get good grades. I went to Catholic school. Even before she was a legal resident, Mom'd go to school and talk to the sisters, make sure everything was the best. I don't remember much playtime and we sure didn't have much money. I helped her with her housecleaning jobs.

"I had a wonderful school counselor who helped me get into a few activities for my college applications and I sang in the school chorus. Sister helped me find scholarships. Being a Latina helped, but I'll be eternally grateful to Sister Daphnia. Without her help, I'd be cleaning houses, too."

"I don't even know where you went to college," said Jake.

"Georgetown University, just a few miles from here," said Julia. "I thought about going to law school. But I was very interested in politics, did my bachelor's in political economy and stayed on for a master's in public policy. My internships eventually led me to the job I have now."

"How did you get to the DC area?"

"My mom knew someone here and moved us here from Texas when I was little, after my dad died. She came from Jalisco in Mexico, near Guadalajara. I've often thought I'd like to go there and see where my parents grew up. I've never met any of my relatives."

"So you were born here? That made you a US citizen, right?"

"Mom got smuggled into the US with my dad when they were very young, before she was pregnant with me. I often think how courageous she was to come here, then get legal when she was a young widow. If she hadn't been the person she is, I would never have had the wonderful opportunities in my life. You can see why I'm so committed to her care now."

Julia drew up her knees on the couch and turned to face Jake. Taking a sip of her wine, she began, "Okay, here goes the serious part. I wasn't looking for any kind of entanglement right now. My plate is over-full with caring for Henry and Beatriz and trying to keep the circus under the tent at the office. At the moment, everything's reasonably under control and I'm comfortable financially."

"That all sounds good."

"However," Julia continued, "that could change in a literal heartbeat if Henry or Beatriz gets worse. I just don't know how much of me is left over to be involved with another person – with you. And I don't think it's fair to saddle you with my burdens."

"Do I get to vote on that?"

"You've seen how tenuous a grip we have on things," Julia said. "One small glitch puts everything else in jeopardy. If Hattie quits or Henry isn't able to keep watch or we can't keep Mom at home, who knows? Our whole house of cards can collapse very abruptly. I just don't know if there's anything of me left over after worrying about all that."

"Is there a *but* to that?" asked Jake.

With a smile, Julia nodded. "*But*... I really enjoy your company, this is the best week I've spent in years, and I think a relationship between us is worth investing in. No, that sounds too calculating. I like you and I want to be with you. It's that simple."

"That makes me feel better," said Jake, drawing her head onto his shoulder. "For a minute there, I thought you were handing me my hat. I've been living a pretty aimless life, not really getting involved with anyone except superficially with people at work.

"I would say I've been coasting along, living on the surface. I'm no hermit or anything, but the only family I have are my niece and nephew, and I rarely see them. I treasure the moments you and I have together," he said.

"Are you sure you want to be drawn into this family drama? And the death law just heightens all of that. I'm not talking about work, I'm talking about real life here in my own home," said Julia.

Her voice trembled. "I know how to live alone. I did that

just fine before Mom and Henry and I moved in together. I don't know how I'd be as part of a couple. I don't want to mess this up." Looking up at Jake, she added, "And I won't be trifled with. If you're not serious about this, then tell me now."

Taking a deep breath, he replied, "If I weren't serious, I wouldn't be sitting here. I'm too old to trifle, and I wouldn't do that, anyway. Being with you just feels right to me. And it's made me realize how lonely I've been. I'll help you any way I can with your family. I won't let you down and I won't be false with you."

They came together in a long kiss, which led to another and another. Sighing, Julia said, "You know what Henry wanted me to say to you yesterday on the phone?"

"I can't imagine," said Jake, wondering why Julia would break the mood.

"'Tell him to bring his toothbrush.'"

Jake laughed ruefully. "I wish I had!"

Snuggling further against him, she replied, "I have an extra one. Shall we move into my bedroom?"

And so began their private lives.

CHAPTER 13

Monday, November 14

When they woke up, Jake had no other clothes so Julia scrounged him socks and underwear from Henry's clean laundry.

"You need to bring some things here, if this will be a habit," teased Julia. "Seriously, when we're together, it'll mostly have to be here."

"I don't care where, as long as it's 'we,'" he said. "I want this to be a habit."

"Me, too," responded Julia softly. "Okay, let's go face Henry and get this over with."

Henry was already in the living room reading the paper.

"Good morning," he said, as if seeing them together was a usual thing. "Your mother's still asleep, so she can get up when Hattie gets here. What're we doing today, Jake?"

"Guess who's feeling better," said Julia. "That's wonderful. Are you sure you're up to going out with Jake?"

"Of course, Julia. Otherwise would I be up this early, dressed and ready?"

"I understand limits now," said Jake. "I won't tire him out again. Any ideas for today, Henry?"

"I've been putting off visiting memory care places. I've found a place online that looks good that I think we can afford if we're careful with our money. Would that fit your plan?"

"Yes, I was thinking that was lacking in my story. Where is it?"

"Not far, between here and DC, called Dale Meadows. It looked good when we passed it one time. Their ratings on a website are high. I'd like to help choose my next home."

"Henry. Would I do that without consulting you?" huffed Julia.

"No, honey, that's not what I meant. Later I might not be competent to have a vote. Your mother's sleeping more and seems to respond less. I'm afraid we're going to be more than you can handle before long."

Julia was near tears. Jake squeezed her hand and said, "Sounds like this would be a good visit. Will you trust me to take better care of Henry?"

Wiping her eyes, she said, "You didn't bargain for all this, did you?"

"So far there's nothing I didn't anticipate, except falling in love with you," he said. Then he remembered Henry was there, too, and saw the older man's eyes glistening. "Okay," said Jake, "let's get this show on the road. We've all got jobs to do. Henry, could you make an appointment for us?"

"Well, ah, actually, I already did. We meet them at ten o'clock, after Hattie gets here. I hope that wasn't presumptuous."

"Let's discuss things like that, but thanks, this works well. No other appointments, right?"

"Well, ah, actually, we do meet a hospice social worker tomorrow."

Jake shook his head laughing. "You're a better reporter than I am, Henry."

"I know more than I want to about the care of the elderly. I did a little work online, too, if that would help."

"Sure, thanks." Jake had underestimated Henry. The man had physical impairments, but no lack of brainpower.

"While you two reporters work, I've got to go," said Julia. "God knows what the congressman has dreamed up over the weekend." She turned to Jake, "About this evening…"

"Can I bring some take-out for dinner? Maybe my toothbrush?" he hazarded.

Both Julia and Henry laughed. "See you about seven," said Julia to Henry as she left, depositing a quick kiss on Henry with a longer one for Jake.

After she left, Jake said, "I need to leave, too, and clean up. I'll be back to get you."

"Maybe you should bring a few clothes to leave here?" suggested Henry.

Julia's morning commute flew by as she thought about last night. Her problems remained the same, but she had someone to share them with. Or maybe it was just the sex, she laughed. But she knew it was much more than that. She just hoped her parents' health problems wouldn't scare Jake off.

As she entered her office, the noise level was lower than usual. Congressman Simms must be here early.

As if on cue, he exited his office saying, "'Bout time you got here, missy. We got lots to do on this death law thing." Feeling a small leak in her happiness, Julia stowed her things, grabbed her iPad for notes, and followed him into his office. "Shut the door. How's your dad?" he asked, the first time she could remember he'd ever asked about her personal life.

"Much better, thanks. No crisis at the moment," she replied, uncomfortable at the shift in their roles. "How would you like to proceed with this repeal process?"

"I've already started a draft of a bill and I want to see what you think of it," he replied.

Wow, thought Julia, *when's the last time he asked for my opinion instead of giving me his?*

"I've been thinking all weekend. This is between you and me, understand? If we play this right, I can end up with a lot of credibility. The Senate seat in Florida opens up in two years and the incumbent will retire. I'd a lot rather run for the Senate every six years than the House every two. But if I don't do this right, we'll all be looking for a job in two years, Julia."

Wow again. He never calls me anything but "missy." I wasn't sure he even remembered my name.

"No, sir, not good for any of us. So you want to right a wrong and get the death law repealed?"

"The truth, missy? I do want this law repealed. But in some ways, I think it's a good thing. Old people are a lot of trouble and they damn sure cost the government a lot of money. But I don't think the government should decide. I want a seat in the Senate and I think this is the ticket. You figure out my position fast so I can stay ahead of everybody else. Do it right; we'll only get one chance. Tell me what to say and keep it simple so I can remember it. There'll be a lot of media here pretty soon. And I don't want others on the Hill to know what we're up to, so do it without squealing the beans."

Squealing the beans? Oh, spilling the beans. Gotta keep those mal-apropisms out of his speeches.

"Yes, sir, we're on it," she assured him more confidently than she felt. She understood the assignment but wasn't sure how to proceed. She disagreed with some of the congressman's views, but she had to admit, he was right in some ways.

She called Walter to prepare a few remarks for the media barrage soon to ensue.

"This is what I've got so far," began Walter as he closed Julia's office door, "a few fast sound bites for when reporters stop the congressman in the hallways. If he's going to be a Senatorial candidate, he needs to be consistent, careful, and available right now."

"Where'd you get the idea he might run for Senate?" asked Julia.

"Come on, Julia, I've been around here longer than you have. That's a no-brainer, a question he'll have to answer. We who know him already know the answer."

"You didn't hear it from me," Julia said.

"Nope, didn't hear it from anybody. I know the man. He neither confirms nor denies the Senatorial thing but says something like, 'We've got bigger things to worry about. Let's talk about the present, not the future.'"

"I like that. He needs to be very clear on his position on the death law."

"Yes, and he must admit that he voted for it in error. No 'yes but's.'"

"He'll go along with that," agreed Julia. "His position on the death law is that he is dead set against it – no, don't use that word! Totally against it. He believes physician-assisted suicide is acceptable but let's just go for repealing the death law and let somebody else bring up that issue."

"You're absolutely right," said Walter. "Three positions are enough for now: no answer on Senatorial run, error in voting for the death law, and the death law has got to go. We can later introduce the idea of physician-assisted suicide or voluntary euthanasia or homicide or whatever the hell you want to call it."

"Simms is good at sticking to a script. We'll feed him facts and figures later on. Right now the media will be after positions, not facts. I'll talk to him this afternoon."

"Not to contradict you, boss, but he'll be hit as soon as he steps out that door. I think he needs to be briefed right now."

"I guess the reporters will be after anyone they can get to talk," agreed Julia. "Let's go brief him."

As he drove into the city to his apartment, the traffic seemed lighter than usual, but it was actually Jake's mood that was lighter. He could see some signs that construction work was starting again, hopefully a harbinger of economic recovery.

Several inconsequential messages on his home telephone offered to sell him a home security system or a personal alert around his neck. He might take out the landline since he was hoping he wouldn't spend many nights at home. *Slow down, too soon to make changes,* he cautioned himself.

He felt a sense of well-being that was long-lost, though, he chuckled to himself, surely not the result of extra sleep. The allure of each other and the strangeness of the situation, plus the need to experience each other and talk intimately, had put sleep way down the priority list. At his age Jake knew he couldn't keep that up, but for one night, it was a heck of a high.

He returned a few phone calls, threw some clothes and

toiletries into a suitcase and, oh yes, his medications, and plunged into the world again. A call to Henry verified that Hattie was at the house and Henry was ready to go.

Jake saw Henry peering out the window. They would not stay out long today. He wasn't about to risk Henry's health or Julia's wrath.

Hattie fussed – was Henry's coat warm enough and could the car be warmer and other caretaker concerns as they settled Henry in the car. Jake said he'd have him home by naptime, sounding like a divorced father taking his toddler out for the morning. He resolved to quit infantilizing Henry and treat him respectfully as a competent thinker. They'd showed bad judgment by overdoing previous outings, but that wouldn't happen again.

On the drive to Dale Meadows, Jake said, "What can you tell me about this place? And who are we meeting with?"

"It's an assisted living facility – they call it an ALF – specializing in what's euphemistically called 'memory care.' That's a locked ward for dementia patients and hopefully a staff that understands the illness. I found this place at a website called Caring for Mother. This ALF is for-profit and costs a lot but looks very good. It's about ten years old and the photos look bright and cheerful. We're meeting with the director of admissions – sounds like a college, doesn't it? But instead of beginning your life, you're basically ending it. I hope Beatriz and I don't end up in an ALF, but we probably will."

"And it costs what, a few thousand dollars a month, paid for by Medicare?"

Henry snorted. "That's what most people think. No, it costs more like ten thousand a month and Medicare doesn't pay a dime. Nor will anybody's health insurance, either, unless they're among the few that have long-term care insurance."

"You're kidding me," said Jake incredulously. "That's over one hundred thousand dollars a year. Who could pay that?"

"Let's hope we don't have to answer that question. I do have long-term care insurance, but Beatriz doesn't."

"So you'd be taken care of financially?"

"I'm covered for much of the cost, but we'd pay out of pocket for Beatriz and some for my care, too. It's really a worry for me and I know it is for Julia, too."

"Wow," said Jake. "I had no idea. Maybe I'd better look into that for myself. But what if you don't have any money? Just sleep on the street?"

"You hope for a spot in a facility that takes Medicaid. I've heard some of those are places you'd rather not be. Where we're visiting doesn't accept Medicaid. So everyone in the place we'll be seeing is well enough off to pay for their own care."

"I had no idea," repeated Jake.

"You hear about someone old or crazy locked up at home for years. Sometimes their families just can't make other arrangements. We are so lucky we can pay Hattie and even better, we all enjoy living together."

Jake agreed. "Your family seems exceptionally caring for one another."

"It's been just the three of us for some years now. I've worried about Julia not having any social life so I'm glad you're with her now. Not," Henry added hastily, "that you have any responsibility here. I'm not implying that."

"I hear you," said Jake. "We'll see how life unfolds."

Their first impression of Dale Meadows was very positive – well tended grounds, a spiffy little green bus sporting the Dale

Meadows logo, and a bright, welcoming foyer. Despite the chill, one resident stumped around the grounds on a walker, a couple of people sat in an outdoor smoking area, and a woman lurched along behind a small white dog on a leash. An aide in a colorful set of scrubs pushed a wheelchair along the sidewalk. The bundled-up, belted-in occupant of the chair appeared to be sleeping, his head lolling to one side. Late-season pansies decorated the urns outside the entrance.

"How can they be outside alone if they have dementia?"

"Not everyone has that diagnosis," replied Henry. "There's an unlocked area for residents who are still mentally competent but unable to look after themselves. Some, like me, might have Parkinson's and need help with the medication schedule or bathing and dressing."

"What about that couple?" asked Jake.

"They may be one spouse in the secure area and another who's visiting. It's not a jail. Residents are free to come and go on their own if they're able, or more likely, with their spouses or children or friends. Okay, let's see what we can learn."

Getting up the curb cut was easy in the chair and the automatic doors swung open to admit them. Jake was beginning to appreciate disability accommodations.

A woman of ample proportions at the reception desk greeted them cheerfully. "Hi there, I'm Savannah. Are you Mr. Horton and Mr. Jordan? Could you sign in, please, while I tell Ms. Reynolds you're here?"

Picking up the phone, Savannah said, "Darlin', your guests are here in the lobby. Okay, I'll tell them." She put down the phone and said, "Ms. Reynolds will be here in about five minutes. Can I get you a cup of coffee? We just brewed a fresh pot in the activities room."

"Thank you," replied Henry, "but we've already had our coffee allotment for today." As Jake wheeled him toward the chairs grouped in conversational areas, Henry confided, "And I don't want to have to maneuver into the bathroom. It looks nice here, doesn't it?"

A shiny player piano tinkled a golden oldie. An elderly woman sat on the bench, hands in her lap, watching the keys go up and down. Several other residents were in a library area, many in wheelchairs and some sitting in comfortable upholstered chairs. Most had their heads down and appeared to be sleeping. A few wore loose sweatpants and shirts, but some were dressed up as if they were going somewhere.

Jake and Henry settled themselves as the bright green Dale Meadows bus pulled up to the front entrance and two employees stepped off. One had a clipboard and began calling names in a musical Caribbean lilt. Her male cohort grasped a wheelchair or helped a resident stand and escorted the person to the bus, using an elevator on the side of the bus to load most of them.

The man carefully strapped each resident into a seat on the bus while the woman checked each off on her clipboard. The two attendants chattered brightly as they worked: "Now, Miz Jeanie, let's get you onto the bus and we'll see the sights of the nation's capital today. Yes sir, Mr. Ken, we'll drive by a golf course just for you." Most of the conversation was by the attendants, but a few residents glanced up and smiled. All beeped as they went through the front doors so Jake surmised there was a security system. The caretakers were friendly in a way that he didn't think could be taught, so he assumed a warm personality was a requirement for hiring.

They could hear Savannah calling residents on the telephone with messages such as, "Miz Jenkins, breakfast is almost over and I haven't seen you this morning. Would you like me to ask the kitchen to send up a tray? How you feeling this morning, honey?"

A young stylishly dressed woman entered the room and held out her hand to Jake and Henry. In a British accent, she said, "Hi, I'm Gillian Reynolds. Thank you for coming to visit us. Let's go to my office."

Jake stood to shake her hand and Henry reached out from his wheelchair. Gillian led the way to the elevator and they ascended to the second floor. The foyer there opened into a lounge area with several residents sitting around a nurses' station. One corridor led to the administrative offices and another to residents' rooms.

All the residents seemed well groomed and dressed in daytime clothes, no bathrobes or pajamas in evidence. The two attendants at the nurses' station were doing paperwork and simultaneously holding conversations with those sitting nearby.

On first impression, Jake was favorably inclined. While the residents didn't look especially happy, neither did they appear neglected. Jake surmised that's what money bought, decent care and attention. One man complained furiously about his insurance company to an attendant who patiently listened and soothed him.

Gillian seated the three of them at a small conference table and handed Jake and Henry folders of information. Her approach was inviting and friendly. "Just what would you like to learn about us today?" she asked.

Henry began with, "My wife is in mid- to late-stage Alzheimer's and I have Parkinson's disease. At present, she can walk and feed herself but no longer speaks or dresses herself. I am mentally capable but my physical strength and control are waning rapidly. We live with our daughter and have a caretaker during the day."

"We can accommodate you both with those conditions. We have residents with those diseases." Turning to Jake, she said, "And are you the son-in-law or the son?"

"No, I'm a friend of the family, a journalist investigating the effects of the recently passed death law. Henry has been kind enough to include me in this interview," responded Jake.

Immediately Gillian's demeanor changed from warm to formal, almost chilly, as she said, "I'm not at liberty to talk about that. You can make an appointment and come back to speak with our administrator."

Facing Henry again, she turned the charm back on. "Let me tell you about our place." She described in detail the physical surroundings, the training of the staff and the activities for residents, pointing out the daily schedule of things to do and the menu included in the folder. "You saw people going out for a ride on the bus. Later today we'll have a trivia challenge. Yesterday we had church services, both Catholic and Protestant, and tomorrow we'll have Bible study."

"The food looks good," said Henry. "Would I be able to stay with Beatriz in the same room and would we take our meals together?"

"That's possible," said Gillian. "However, the cost of care in the 'cottage' – we call them 'cottages,' not wings or units – where Beatriz would be living is a bit more than in the non-secure cottage. We do have space available now, both in shared and private rooms. In fact, we've had a few vacancies in the past week."

"Really?" said Jake. "Have there been deaths?"

"Well, yes," hedged Gillian. "We had a death. But other vacancies have occurred, too." She appeared uncomfortable, making Jake think she'd dropped information unintentionally. "Some of our families have recently decided they'd rather care for their loved ones at home."

"So how many rooms do you have vacant now?" persisted Henry.

"There are several. I'm sure we could accommodate you and your wife," answered Gillian smoothly. "Would you like to see one of them?"

"Yes, thanks," answered Henry. Gillian grasped the wheelchair handles and trundled Henry down the hall, while Jake trailed, clearly uninvited. His presence made Gillian anxious, but she apparently needed the business too badly to risk offending Henry.

Jake saw several empty rooms on this floor. The rooms were spacious enough, each with a bathroom. Open doors allowed Jake to see that one or two contained twin beds but most had only one bed in the room. Large windows let in plenty of light and a view of the grounds. The furnishings were different in each room and a decorative placard with the resident's name hung beside each door.

"Could we bring our own furniture?" asked Henry.

"Yes," answered Gillian. "We want this to be as much like your home as possible. That's especially important for our residents in the memory care unit. We do require a hospital bed, which you can rent from a hospital supply store."

"Why is that?" Henry asked.

"There are times when a resident must have the rails up to prevent falling," explained Gillian. "We don't confine a resident to the bed, but there are times when some protection is needed. Also, it's a convenience for our housekeeping staff. We do all the cleaning and laundry for you, change the sheets, things like that."

"Okay, I've seen enough," declared Henry. "What about pets? We have a little cat that my wife is very attached to."

"That depends on the animal," Gillian responded. "We have one resident with a dog and we have a community parrot. We'd have to know more about the animal and its behavior."

"Sounds like a maybe. That might be a deal-breaker for us."

Gillian hastily replied with a big smile, "Oh, I'm sure we can work something out. Let's leave that until later."

They must really need the business, Jake thought. *Wonder what the room-and-board charge is for a cat? Bet there is one.*

"Fees – what would it cost us to live in this lovely place? Do you take Medicaid? What about long-term care insurance?" queried Henry.

"That's all spelled out in the folder I gave you. Why don't you read through that and call me if you have questions?" suggested Gillian.

"Where are you from, anyway?" asked Jake.

Gillian gave the most sincere smile of the morning as she said to Jake, "From England. I married an American military man I met when he was stationed at Lakenheath. I lived in the little town of Mildenhall. We moved to America when he left the Air Force."

"I thought you had a British accent. Thank you for showing us around," said Henry. "I'm ready to go now, Jake."

"Would you like to have lunch with us?" asked Gillian.

"No, we already have plans," said Henry.

We do? thought Jake. *News to me!*

"I'll see you out. May I call you in a few days?" asked Gillian.

"Yes, that'll give me time to read through this and discuss it with my daughter."

Gillian pushed Henry to the car and helped him into the

passenger seat as Jake held the door open. After Henry was inside the car, Gillian turned to Jake and said quietly, "As you Americans say, the death law sucks. And it's killing our business. But don't quote me, righto?"

"Agreed," said Jake. "Thank you for telling me that."

Jake turned on the heat full blast. Henry wasn't coughing much and Jake wanted to keep it that way. "So what's our plan for lunch?"

"Do you like fish and chips?" asked Henry. "There's a good little pub nearby. Gillian's accent made me fancy fish and chips."

"Great. I always like fried food."

"Down this street, then turn left," directed Henry. "They have fish fingers, easy to pick up and eat."

They found the Church Road Pub and quickly settled into a booth with high sides. Jake was not bothered by Henry's slightly messy meals but he knew the man was self-conscious about them. Jake wondered if that was why Henry chose this restaurant. A waitress in a very short kilt appeared to take their order; maybe the brief skirt was part of the appeal, too.

They both ordered fish and chips. Jake considered a British ale but decided he had too much work to do. "What's with the kilts?" Jake asked Henry.

"Culturally inaccurate but they sure are cute, aren't they?" chuckled Henry. Jake had to agree, fine dining for the eyes. His night with Julia had awakened some dormant senses.

"What did you think of Dale Meadows?" asked Jake.

"I was very impressed. For what you pay, though, you'd expect a lot. Everything looked clean, no odor. Some places you smell things and you just know folks aren't being properly looked after. Gillian was a pretty slick salesperson – kinda felt like I was being sold a timeshare at the beach.

"Everyone we saw looked well cared for and the staff seemed friendly and engaged with the residents. They were very patient while they were loading the bus, did you notice?"

"I did," said Jake. "I had trouble understanding what one of the nursing assistants on the second floor was saying. Obviously English was not his first language. Seems like that might be a problem for people with hearing and language deficits."

"Yes, I did notice. I'm interested to get into the costs and see if we really could afford to live there."

"They don't take Medicaid?"

"No, they don't. Would you be willing to visit a Medicaid-eligible facility with me so we could compare?" asked Henry.

"I wondered if you'd do that," replied Jake. "Would you be upset if it was markedly different?"

"No, it'd be reality. Do you know the lines from Psalms, I think it's Psalm 80, that goes something like 'God has fed them with the bread of tears and given them tears to drink...'? I feel like we've been eating and drinking tears but I fear there's worse to come."

Jake said nothing, just watched Henry steadily.

"We need to decide the next step for us, should it be required. I worry Hattie won't be able to provide enough care for us. Julia needs to keep working, both for financial reasons and for her own sanity, even though her job is insane." He said, "These fish fingers are really good, aren't they?"

Jake recognized the conversation change and asked, "Have you been following football lately?" This topic took them safely through lunch and the drive home.

After delivering Henry inside to Hattie, Jake said, "I need to go check in at the office. This thing on the death law is so huge, I'll need to devote all my time to that. I hope my editor sees it that way. I'll bring dinner. Any requests for take-out?"

"How about Chinese?" suggested Henry. "But don't go to the place we call Ptomaine Chow Mein!"

"There's a good place near my office. I'll see you about seven," replied Jake.

"Don't forget your toothbrush," said Henry with a clumsy attempt at a lascivious wink.

CHAPTER 14

Monday, November 14

Driving to his office, Jake marveled at how his life had changed in one week. He'd fallen in love, engaged himself in a family and started research for a book. Although a well published journalist, he'd never written a book. He dreamed of seeing his name on a book jacket, downloading it from Amazon onto his Kindle. He parked under the newspaper building and hiked up three floors to his office. He liked the exercise, but also disliked elevators.

His editor, Sam Wilkerson, popped into the hall as Jake appeared. "Nice to see you," said Sam sarcastically. "Would you have time to stroll into my office to chat?"

"I'll be right there," replied Jake. Sam was gruff but fair, and Jake wanted his support for a book. He reviewed his options: forget the book, retire and write it, or find a compromise to keep Sam happy and himself employed while he wrote the book. He couldn't resign before reviewing his finances, so he needed to stay cool if the discussion got heated. He definitely did not want to drop the book idea. Taking a deep breath, he entered Sam's office.

Sam shut the door, never a good sign. "Where've you been

lately? The staff is complaining you're never here and not pulling your weight these days."

"I'm onto something big," explained Jake, leaning forward in his chair. "I've been interviewing people about the death law, a bomb waiting to explode. I'll write a series of articles but I believe it's bigger than that. I want to write a book, ramifications of the death law for older folks and their families. There will be huge effects on the economy, good and bad. It's not as simple as the congressmen and senators who sponsored this believed."

"You expect us to support you through this? You know the business better than that. If you can't produce, clean out your desk," threatened Sam.

"I understand that but I need time to work on this. I'll keep on doing my column every Sunday and a short news story each week on the death law. I'll fold those into the book. I'll ask the paper to give me copyright on those by-lined stories and heavily cite the newspaper in my book. Should be good publicity."

Jake spread his hands. "You know as well as I do that more people read books than newspapers." He paused as he could see his boss thinking. Jake had bargaining chips from the faithful following for his weekly political column, but he didn't know how many.

"I'd have to take this upstairs," Sam said, steepling his fingers under his chin and rocking in his desk chair. "I see some merit in the idea. What will you do if they don't approve this?"

"Probably I'd resign," answered Jake. "I'm sixty-four so I can draw Social Security soon and I've got a decent pension coming. I own my apartment so I'd be okay. I'm not threatening, you understand, I'd rather stay here."

"That's what I thought you'd say. This gives me something

to take upstairs. I want you to stay, you're one of our best. But you have to contribute more than the past week."

"You gave me latitude to explore this, remember? I thought I was doing what you approved."

"Yeah, well, I thought so, too, until the 'where's Jake' question kept coming up," acknowledged Sam. "Do you have anything ready for print?"

"It'll be ready in the next few hours, plus my column for next Sunday's paper," promised Jake. He had plenty for his op-ed piece and a news article.

"Okay," said Sam. "Spend more time in the office. At worst, I'll hold off the dogs for another week. At best, I'll come back with whatever the boss lady agrees to. The managing editor is a tough old girl, but I think she'll see the advantage for the paper. You have a great idea and I'd like to read your book. Not promising anything, but I'll do what I can. And we may have some contacts with publishing houses."

Jake returned to his desk and quickly tapped out a column giving an overview of the death law and citing potential problems. For the news story, he focused on Representative Simms' rash repeal promise. He found what he needed to know about Marcus Simms on the internet. It wasn't his greatest story, but it would do.

Jake knew that he must keep his work and personal life separated. He could anticipate potential conflict between his interpretation and Julia's of events, just one more thing they'd have to work through.

Some human interest stories might be good news articles. Maybe Henry knew some people he could talk to. However, Jake decided not to write about Henry. That story was too close to home, as Henry's story was rapidly becoming Jake's story, too.

The social worker they were interviewing tomorrow might know someone. He'd look up hospice and see if there was an official attitude toward death, maybe find organizations that advocated death and suicide. Quality of assisted living facilities might make a good story, too. He had plenty to do this afternoon, but it would be an anxious wait until Sam got back to him with news from upstairs. He'd better work out his finances in case he decided to retire.

Julia noticed that things seemed to be calmer in congressional halls than the past few days. They needed another big crisis to divert attention from the death law so they could get to work on the repeal.

Her staff had a lot to report this morning. As predicted, Representative Simms had been swarmed by the media as he walked from his office. Walter reported that Simms had handled the encounter well, emphasizing the three points they'd crafted for him. Most important, he hadn't strayed from the script.

Their intern, Roberta, had copied reams of information for Julia to read on organizational positions on the web. Julia pushed that stack of papers to one side, waiting for the three-page summary she had asked Roberta to prepare.

Julia met with Sid, Carla and Juan about what was going on in the home district. She checked with her counterpart there, Tina Maria, and fervently hoped a visit there would not be necessary. She was reluctant to leave her parents, and besides, didn't want to be away from Jake right now. The district office staff was very competent so she hoped they could handle things there without her. They'd have to plan something for Simms' trip home at Thanksgiving, but it was too early to decide that something just yet.

It was hard to believe that Thanksgiving was only a few weeks away and Christmas just a month beyond that. *Wonder what Jake would like for Christmas...*

Telephones and e-mail brought the same message: Repeal the death law. Two other callers had threatened retribution if Simms went ahead with repeal, saying they represented taxpayers' associations that advocated savings from curtailing elders' care and the death law was the right first step.

Juan said several hysterical callers thought they had to make funeral plans right away. Carla reported that many of her phone calls came from feisty senior citizens saying, "Hell, no, we won't go." With nearly twenty per cent of the electorate in Simms' district over the age of sixty-five, the office couldn't ignore these callers. Alienating this part of the population was political suicide, especially in Florida.

"So the vast majority of callers oppose the death law and most are really upset for their personal situations?" asked Julia.

"Yes," affirmed Carla. "And we're getting a large number of callers who speak Spanish, right. Juan?"

"Si," replied Juan. "My people are *mucho* upset and mad. As hard as we've worked to get them to come out and vote, they will. Some of them want to know when the next election is."

"Thankfully, not for another couple of years," said Julia. "Okay, thanks, guys. Please keep me posted on anything you think I should know."

CHAPTER 15

Monday, November 14

Julia's phone buzzed as the other staff members exited. Sandy said, "I think you'd better take this call, boss."

"Oh, lord, not my parents," sighed Julia.

"No, it's a lobbyist," replied Sandy. "He said it's important he speak to you, right now."

"Okay, thanks," said Julia. "This is Julia Sanchez. How can I help you?"

"This is John Tilley. We met at a reception for Representative Simms a few months ago. I am chief partner of Tilley Associates."

"Yes, I recall. You represent firms in the drug industry," said Julia. She vaguely remembered a well-spoken fiftyish man, very low key compared to other lobbyists she knew. She had enjoyed conversing with him, something she couldn't say about most lobbyists.

"I'll be quick because I know how busy your office must be right now. I want to discuss a potential job offer."

"That wouldn't be appropriate," replied Julia. "I can't talk about Simms' professional future. You'd have to meet with him, but I can see what his schedule looks like."

"No, Ms. Sanchez, I mean an offer for you. We have a job

opening in our DC office due to an unexpected resignation. We need someone immediately who knows Congress inside and out. We expect the death law to have great effect on the industry we represent. We need to hire as quickly as possible, someone who can hit the ground running. You may be that person and we'd like to meet with you as soon as possible."

Julia was flabbergasted. A different job? From time to time – like every election year – she'd thought fleetingly about what she'd do if she lost this one.

Wow, my life has turned exactly upside down this week. A new boyfriend and now maybe a new job? "I... I really don't know," she stammered. "I need to think about this. Can I call you back in the morning?"

"That's reasonable, but we would want to talk with you no later than tomorrow morning. We can offer you a substantial increase in salary and some flexibility in working hours. I ... ah... understand that you have a potential health crisis in your family and we can offer you latitude of time and money. The companies we represent have connections with assisted living facilities so there's the possibility of negotiated fees for residents that might be... ah... favorable."

They've really done their homework, thought Julia. "I will call you by nine tomorrow morning." She ended the call and put her head in her hands. *Dear God, what do I do now?*

One imperative, regardless of further conversation with Tilley, was to talk to Marcus. Capitol Hill was one hotbed of gossip. Despite promises of confidentiality, word traveled fast. People sometimes labeled something confidential just so word would travel faster. Marcus had to hear about this phone call from her, not from anyone else.

Calling Jake's cell phone, she said, "Can you talk right now for a minute?"

"Sure, just thinking of you," he said warmly. "Everyone okay at home?"

"Yes, not that. I've just been offered a job – at least, I think so. At least an invitation to talk about an offer. Can we talk about this tonight? I'm not going to say anything to Henry yet."

"What kind of a job? Away from DC?" He realized that was a selfish question. Besides, he could move, write a book from anyplace. A wider perspective on the death law would actually improve his work. If Julia wanted him along, that is.

"No, here in DC, with the lobbying firm of Tilley and Associates. Do you know them?"

"Yes, by reputation, and I've met John Tilley a couple of times. It's a well-respected outfit, way better than most lobbying firms. Why did they pick you?" asked Jake. "Although you'd be anybody's first choice," he added hastily.

She laughed. "Thanks for the vote of confidence. They have an unexpected opening and need someone already up on congressional politics and health care issues. I can count on you to keep this confidential, right?"

Jake responded tartly, "No, I'm writing a front-page article as we speak. Of course you can count on me, so don't ever ask me that again. If we can't trust each other, who can we trust?"

"Sorry," said Julia softly. "I didn't mean it like it sounded. I'm so taken aback by the offer that I feel really off-kilter. I'm not used to discussing decisions with anyone else, but I called you as soon as I got off the phone with Tilley. My first instinct was to wonder what you thought."

"I'm glad to hear that," said Jake. "I've had a conversation with my editor I want to talk over with you, too. No sleep last night, sounds like no sleep again tonight for a different reason! So what'll you do?"

"I'm going to talk to Marcus this afternoon. I don't want him hearing rumors."

"Smart," agreed Jake. "I'll be in the office all afternoon if you want to call back. Henry requested Chinese, that okay with you?"

"Yes. I want to stay cool in front of Henry until we've had a chance to talk this out ourselves. Tilley offered me more money and a more flexible time schedule. He alluded to my parents' health and hinted at preferential payment for assisted living facilities."

"He's serious if he's done that much research on you. I'll be interested to hear more tonight. Keep cool and we'll talk it out. I miss you, Julia. I'll be glad to see you tonight."

"Me, too, you," she responded. Julia felt a little calmer after sharing the information with Jake.

Commotion in the outer office heralded Simms' return. *Might as well get this over with*, thought Julia. Emerging from her office, she said, "Could I speak with you, Congressman?"

"Yes, missy, and bring that speechwriter fella in, too. I don't want to look like a horse's petard when I talk to the press," Simms replied.

Then stay away from malapropisms, Julia thought. Her staff eyed her curiously as she replied, "I need a few minutes alone. Then I'll get Walter." She followed Marcus into his office and shut the door.

"Something happen to your parents?" he inquired.

Wow, Julia thought, *that's everyone's first guess – including my own. I must be a walking disaster these days.* "No, not that, and I want you to know this came completely out of the blue. Tilley and Associates wants to talk to me about coming to work for them," ventured Julia.

"What the Sam hell! You're looking for another job?"

"No, I just got the phone call not ten minutes ago and, as I said, it was entirely unexpected."

"So you're leaving?" asked Simms with a scowl. "Julia, that's going to put us in a pretty bad spot, you know."

"Marcus, I'm as caught off guard as you are. I don't know what I'm going to do. I love it here and we've been through a lot together. But John Tilley hinted there could be substantially more money involved and some latitude of time if I need it. You know about the precariousness of my parents' health and I have to think this through before I do something wrong, one way or the other."

"So when are you meeting with him?"

"I told Tilley I'd call back in the morning but I haven't planned a meeting with anybody. I talked to Tilley, called a friend, and then came in to talk to you, all within the last ten minutes."

"I suppose you called that reporter feller. What'd he have to say?" asked Simms gruffly.

Jeez, is there no privacy anywhere in this city? "We said we'd discuss it tonight. I told him I was going to talk to you and he agreed that was the right thing."

"Well, that's fair, I guess," grunted Simms. "We need you here – I need you and the American people need you here. We've got a humdinger of a job to get done and I can't think of anyone else who can help me do what needs to be done. I do understand your priorities with your parents. I appreciate your telling me first. But I don't like it one bit, somebody poaching in my office, and I intend to tell that SOB John Tilley just that."

"Thank you," said Julia, not sure what else to say.

"Anyone else, I'd think they were squeezing me for money but I know you've got more morals than that, and you're about the only person I can say that about. I can find a little more money for you and you know about time latitude better than I do since you're the chief. I'll do what I can to help you with your parents if and when the times get bad. That's all I can do but you understand that I do want and need you here. And I mean a little more money, not what that rat bastard lobbyist is going to offer you."

Overwhelmed by Simms' uncharacteristic recognition of anyone's personal circumstances but his own, Julia didn't know how to answer.

"Will you talk to me before you call that poacher back in the morning? And if you accept his offer, I want you gone from here immediately, is that clear?"

"Yes, I knew that. I've been as honest with you as I can. I've got to think it through and do what's best for my family. You're being very fair with me, and I'll be the same with you. I won't talk to anyone but Jake and maybe my dad. I'll talk to you early in the morning before I call John Tilley back," she promised.

"Okay, enough said. Get that speech writer in here and let's plan some strategy," barked Simms, "while I've still got some staff to plan strategy with!"

Julia opened the door, summoned Walter and hoped the staff hadn't overheard the conversation. Soon she, Walter and Simms were deep into planning strategy and sound bites on repealing the death law.

CHAPTER 16

Monday, November 14

Jake looked up from his computer to see his boss standing in the doorway. "Got a minute?" asked Sam

"Sure thing," said Jake as he hit save and followed his editor down the hall. Sam shut the door and Jake thought, *Uh oh, not a good sign.*

"I've got good news," began Sam. "The managing editor agreed to your request, mostly."

Jake asked warily, "What mostly?"

"Two news stories a week and in the office at least twice a week unless you're out of town doing research," replied Sam. "And six months."

"Six months isn't much time."

"You're right," agreed Sam. "But the work has to be done right now, so really, that's your timeline, too."

"Is there any give on that?" asked Jake anxiously, realizing what a daunting task he'd undertaken. "You're right. The story is now, not a year from now."

"That's your second book," suggested Sam. "Do this one right and they'll be panting for your sequel. I'm guessing there'd be some wiggle room, but don't ask for it now. Can you live with that?"

"I guess, though I'd be more comfortable with a longer time. Three articles a week is reasonable. On some aspect of the death law, right?" asked Jake.

"We didn't clarify that," said Sam, "but yes. And you can use anything bylined later in your book, as long as you attribute to the newspaper. She wants the first signed copy of the book."

"She'll have to get in line. Is this a contract or a handshake?"

"Handshake good enough for you? Something huge might come up that redirects us all. But I'll do my level best to get you the time you need."

"Thank you," said Jake. "I appreciate what you've negotiated."

"Then do I get the first signed copy?"

"Number five, maybe," threw back Jake with a grin.

Later that afternoon, the Chinese food filled Jake's car with a wonderful aroma. He arrived first so surmised Julia's day hadn't calmed any since they'd talked. Henry peeked out the living room window, evidently hungry for both food and conversation.

Henry opened the door as Jake carried the bags up the walk. He seemed fine after their morning outing. "I've been looking for you," hollered Henry. "Where you been?"

Laughing, Jake dumped his load on the dining room table.

"Julia called to say the traffic's horrible and we should go ahead and eat. But I'd rather wait, if that's okay with you."

"My preference, too," agreed Jake. "I'm sorry I was late and held you up, Hattie."

"No worries, I'm not doing nothing tonight," she replied. "But I'll go on and go now."

"Take some dinner home with you? There's plenty."

"No, sir, that wouldn't be proper," Hattie responded. "I'll offer it to Mist' Henry and Miz Beatriz tomorrow for their lunch."

"Not me," answered Henry. "Jake and I always eat lunch out."

"Un-huh, always," teased Hattie. "Y'all got a new lunch buddy, Mist' Jake."

Jake said, "We have an interview scheduled tomorrow, right, Henry? We'll get lunch after that. But my editor says I need to be in the office more."

"Oh, sure, didn't mean to assume," backtracked Henry. "Whenever is fine with me." Everyone realized that Henry's "whenevers" might be limited. "Here's Julia now! Traffic must have eased up."

"Let me get this dinner on the table, then I'm gone," said Hattie.

"You go on now," Jake said. "I'll set it out."

"Thanks, Mist' Jake. I don't like to be on the streets too late where I live."

Julia looked distracted as she greeted everyone. Jake gave her an extra good hug as she walked to the closet to hang up coat.

"Smells yummy," said Julia. "Bye, Hattie, see you tomorrow. Come on, Henry, let's get you and Mom fed and to bed."

"Not so fast," protested Henry. "Jake and I have a lot to talk about."

"Well, so do Jake and I. I'm pulling rank. You and Mom need to disappear so Jake and I can talk. I'll fill you in later."

"Later like when?" asked Henry petulantly, sounding like a child sent to bed early.

"Tomorrow, I promise," soothed Julia. She had already seated her mother at the table, complete with Calvin in her mother's lap. "Can we keep that cat off the table? Has anyone fed him?"

"Yes, Hattie did that and cleaned his box. I've had my meds and so has your mom. Anything else, Miss Bossy-Boots?"

They all laughed and passed around the cartons of an outstanding Cantonese meal. Desultory conversation carried them from egg rolls through main dishes to fortune cookies.

Henry opened his and read, "'You will have good luck tonight.' Oops, that's an *f*, not an *l*. Obviously I got the wrong cookie. Jake, are these dirty fortune cookies?"

Mortified, Jake answered, "The lady asked if I wanted the special cookies and I said yes but I didn't know what she was asking. I'm so sorry if I offended anyone." He could tell by the chuckles around the table that nobody else was embarrassed. Even Beatriz, seized by the group mood, laughed a little.

"Okay, let's get you all off to bed. Jake, I hate to ask but…"

"I'm on it," he said, gathering cartons of leftover food. "I'll stow these and load the dishwasher. Anything else I can do to help?" A grateful smile from Julia was plenty of thanks. He silently vowed to clear the table every night of their lives and to eschew "special" cookies.

Jake figured out how the gas logs worked and had the fire going when Julia got back to the living room. She poured two glasses of wine and handed one to Jake.

"Henry said he's read the material from Dale Meadows and was about right in estimating the cost. I told him you'd talk with him in the morning. He reminded you about the interview at ten. He's really exhausted so I feel better about insisting that they go to bed so early. I can't wait any longer to talk this thing out with you."

"Yes, I'm having trouble focusing on anything else. Except you, of course." He pulled her close for a long kiss. Her smile said she was a little more relaxed after that. "I have news from my work, too."

"Oh, I'm so self-centered, I forgot to ask how your day went. You first."

"You're the least self-centered person I know. Here's the deal. My editor agreed to give me six months for a book about the death law. I have to write my column and two other articles a week on the death law, and show up at the office a couple of times a week. I think that's fair, though I wanted more time for the book."

"Oh, Jake, that's wonderful!" exclaimed Julia, rewarding him with a brief kiss that turned into another long one. "Okay," she said breathlessly as she pulled away, "no more of that until we've finished talking."

"Maybe." Jake grinned, enjoying feeling his sixty-four-year-old hormones. "Tell me about your conversation with Tilley. Did you talk to Simms?"

Taking a deep breath, Julia plunged in. "I did, and he was more understanding than I anticipated. He even offered me a small – and he reiterated 'small' – raise and indicated I could take time off as I needed to. He made it clear that he wants me to stay – called Tilley a 'poaching rat bastard' – but equally clear that if I decide to change jobs, I leave immediately. Oh, Jake, what am I going to do?"

"For sure this is a dilemma – there's good and bad on both sides. But a decision either way should be okay. So in a way the stakes are lower. You're worried that a bad decision might affect your parents' care, right?"

"That's about it."

"Well, there are so many things we haven't talked about yet, like where we want to end up in our careers. Do you have career aspirations you haven't achieved?"

"Truthfully, I don't. I have enough status to satisfy my ego and job security hasn't been much of an issue because Simms gets re-elected. I like my work, feel productive and make enough money that we live well. Materially, I don't want for anything. What worries me is what if I have to pay for assisted-living care for my parents? It looks like that day may be getting closer. How about you?"

"I'm like you," said Jake. "I've achieved a lot more than I ever thought I would. Some things I'd do differently if I had a do-over, but mostly I believe I've contributed. I cringe when I think of how I went after stories and invaded people's privacy when I was a cub reporter, but mostly I'm proud of my work. I want to write this book, though. I think I could retire happy if I accomplished that."

"One thing I keep thinking about from my conversation with Tilley this morning is his hint of financial considerations if my parents go into a facility. He implied that the lobbying firm's connections through drug companies could ease the financial burden there. He wasn't specific, but it smacks of cronyism at best and illegal dealings at worst. How far would I go to be sure Henry and Beatriz got the best possible care? It bothers me – is it ethical?"

"A professor once told me, 'If you have to ask me, you already know the answer,' when I posed an ethical question. I'm not sure that's always right, but I learned if it niggles at your conscience, you'd better pay attention."

"In general I don't have the highest regard for lobbyists so it's hard for me to think of myself as one," Julia said. "But Tilley might be the exception to that, a reputable lobbyist. Is that an oxymoron? I don't want to compromise my own values for money, but I don't want to compromise my parents' care for lack of money. I hope you know how much it means to be able to talk this through with you."

Jake decided to forge ahead. "Sweetheart, you are one of the most moral and ethical people I know. It's one of the many things I love about you. And it's time for me to say that: I love you and will support your decision, whatever it is."

"Oh, Jake, I love you, too. That makes it seem like any decision about careers is secondary to everything else right now. Marcus told me this morning he thinks I'm a moral person, too. I'm not sure what that means, but thanks again."

"But he didn't say he loves you, right? That makes me trump."

Julia actually giggled. "No, he didn't come close to that! We have a good working relationship but that's all. I've got better sense than that and he does, too. Besides, I was waiting for you. Okay, back to the question at hand. Could we talk finances for a minute?"

"I wondered about that," said Jake, "but didn't want to bring it up. Seems like our time is being compressed by present circumstances. Yes, let's talk about both our financial situations. How much of a factor does higher salary need to be in your situation?"

"It's hard to tell. Right now we're fine. Our house is paid for and other than Hattie's salary, we don't spend a lot.

"We have good health insurance. There's a lot of talk about cutting Medicare but I doubt any cuts would affect those now receiving benefits. We pay a lot for health insurance, but, goodness knows, we use the benefits often."

"That's huge," said Jake.

"What worries me is the next step. Henry told me the place you visited is about ten thousand a month, plus other expenses. I know Medicare or their supplemental insurance won't pay much of anything. Henry has long-term care insurance but I don't know how that works."

"He told me in the car today. You'd be looking at something like thirteen thousand a month for the two of them, maybe a little less if they were in the same room, so something like ten thousand a month out of pocket if Henry's long-term care policy pays."

"Wow, that's a huge amount of money! That's about triple what we're paying Hattie."

"Can't Congress do something about these health care costs?" Jake asked.

"Yeah, right," deadpanned Julia. "Why don't you write to your Congressman and see what that gets you? Oh, I forgot, you live in DC. You don't have a Congressman, do you?"

Turning serious, she said, "So we'd have to come up with several thousand dollars more a month if they were both at Dale Meadows. I've got something like three hundred thousand dollars saved and we could draw that down, but that's less than three years of fees. Mom or Henry either one could live longer than that, and I hope they do. I'd hate to touch my 401(k) but I guess I could if I absolutely had to.

"Oh, Jake, what am I going to do?" wailed Julia softly, pressing her face into his shoulder. "This almost makes the death law seem sensible."

"That kind of arithmetic got the death law passed," said Jake. "Your dad's worried about leaving you destitute because of their care. Let's think a little more here."

Sitting up again, Julia said, "Okay, what else?"

"You own your house and I own my apartment. Neither of

us owes anything on a mortgage, right? I'm sticking my neck out, but I hope one day soon we need only one home, not two."

"Oh, Jake, I've been thinking that, too. I know we haven't been together long enough to say so. Let's hope that's never an economic decision, though."

"I agree, living together should never be an economic decision," said Jake. "But it might be a way of finding additional money. If we lived in my place, you could either sell or rent this house. I have only two bedrooms and two baths – I can't believe you haven't even seen my place – but it would be plenty for the two of us. It might be a little cramped for the four of us, but that could work, too."

"We'd save some money if we lived in DC," agreed Julia.

"I have one parking place but if we lived in DC, we could dispense with one car and use public transportation to save some money."

"Jake, I've never known anyone like you before. You make me feel so cared for. But my parents are not your worry."

"Julia, if we commit to each other, we're not going to have his-and-her worries, we're going to have *our* worries. And plenty of them, I'm sure, given our ages. If we were younger and one of us had children, they'd come with the package. Your parents and the cat are part of our deal."

He continued, "I never planned to be involved with anyone again, so our being together is a miracle to me. Let's figure out this job thing and then get on with our lives. Bottom line, where do you want to work?"

"Cut to the chase?" asked Julia. "You know, I don't even know anything about the other job. I don't know the salary, whether I'd be working pro-death-law or anti-death-law, or anything like that.

"But this much I do know. I want to stay just where I am. My job's not perfect, but I know its imperfections and I believe we're doing important work in the Congress. I like being a part of that, crazy as it is sometimes."

"I get that," Jake said.

"I'd rather introduce myself to someone as a congressional chief of staff than as a lobbyist. Part of me says take the money and run, lobby for a few years and swallow my feelings about the job. I guess I could go have an interview and see what's what."

"I'm guessing you couldn't suppress your feelings for long in that job. You'd be trading doing something you believe in for something you don't believe in, right?"

Julia laughed shakily. "Yeah, Mr. Wordsmith, that's exactly what I'm saying. What, you have a degree in counseling, too? Or mind-reading?"

"I'm imagining what I'd feel in your place. I know a representative who worked awhile as a lobbyist after he left office. He hated every minute of it and felt he'd sold out for the money. He said he was giddy with relief when they fired him. Of course, you would be good at lobbying, or anything else you did."

"Okay, so we have the beginning of a life plan. I stay in my job. You write a book. We move in together and live happily ever after. Is that about it?" asked Julia playfully.

"Yep, that's about it. Anything else we need to settle right now?"

"No, we've covered it all. I feel very good about this decision, and even better about the rest of our discussion. Let's watch the fire a little longer, and talk about other things… or nothing. Are you spending the night?"

Jake laughed and said, "I brought my toothbrush."

CHAPTER 17

Tuesday, November 15

Julia was surprised to find Marcus at work when she arrived. He lived only a short walk away, but preferred to work in the quiet of his home early in the morning. "I figured you'd be in first thing, missy, one way or another. I don't see any carry bags. That mean you're staying?"

"Yes, I'm staying. This is where I want to be."

"Good, that's settled. Find ten thousand dollars somewhere in the budget and give yourself a raise. Give me whatever I need to sign. I don't want to talk about this anymore and no word to the staff. Understood?"

"Yes, Marcus, thank you very much. I wasn't asking for more money."

"Everything's about money, bottom line. Especially here in DC. Let's get to work. You got facts for me to memorize? I better sound like an expert on old people."

As Julia moved to her computer to print out summaries, she thought gratefully, *That's one more month of Dale Meadows for Mom.* She called John Tilley and declined his offer as gracefully as possible.

Jake was glad he didn't have to drive to DC to change clothes that morning. Waking up with Julia felt even more special today. With difficulty Jake dragged his mind to the present and asked Henry about their day's interview.

"We see Anna Malotti, a wonderful hospice social worker at Fairfax Central Hospital. We met when I was hospitalized to get my meds straight. She now works with hospice care. She keeps in touch with us even though we're not hospice patients – yet. If we go for tests or something, we sometimes have a cup of coffee. I used to volunteer at the hospital, back when I could be useful."

Jake assured Henry that he was still useful, invaluable help on this investigation. "Okay, let's go meet this angel of mercy."

Henry laughed. "She wouldn't agree with that description, but I would."

In the hospital lobby, a uniformed security officer bid them good morning and offered directions. Henry replied, "We're going to Anna Malotti's office and I know the way, thanks."

"Have a good day, gentlemen," said the officer as she turned to greet the next visitors.

"I hate they have armed guards in buildings these days," commented Jake.

"Yeah, 9/11 changed everything," replied Henry.

They rode silently in the elevator to the fourth floor.

"We go left down this hallway," said Henry.

Jake noticed a sign that said Palliative Care and decided to find out just what that term meant.

"Here's her office. Hey, sweetheart, how're you? I brought a friend to meet you." A smiling woman dressed in slacks and sweater rose to meet them, stooping to give Henry a wheelchair hug. "This is Jake."

"I'm happy to meet a friend of Henry's. He's a special person to me."

"That's what Henry says about you, too," said Jake as he shook her hand. "Thank you for meeting with us."

"Henry says you're doing investigative work trying to overturn the death law. That legislation is so wrong."

Jake hedged, "The journalist in me would say I'm trying to determine the effects of the death law. Theoretically, I'm open to all sides of the issue. However, I'm becoming somewhat biased from what I'm hearing in my interviews."

"Good, let me bias you some more. Let's go down the hall to the conference room."

The Palliative Care Conference Room sign designated a small, comfortable space containing upholstered chairs and soft lighting. "What's palliative care?" Jake asked. "Is that the same as hospice?"

"They're similar," said Anna. "Palliative care may help people at any stage of an illness but hospice usually serves terminally ill patients. Patients come to this ward to have symptoms ameliorated rather than be cured. Henry, for example, might check into a palliative care ward while his physicians try different dosages and medicines. He's not terminally ill, but from time to time may need care. Unless the death law mandates his death, of course.

"Hospice is a concept rather than a place. Most people in hospice care have six months or less to live. Dementia patients may be in hospice care longer than that, since the progress of the disease is so difficult to predict."

Jake said. "I always thought hospice was where people went to die."

"A lot of people think that, but it has evolved differently in the US. It's a health care option for people with limited time left. They may be in the hospital, often in a palliative care ward, in their own homes or in an assisted living facility. Visiting nurses, health aides, social workers, chaplains, and/or counselors assist them. Many volunteers also assist and hospice also helps with respite care."

"What's 'respite care'?" asked Jake.

"The respite is usually for the caregiver, with someone else taking responsibility for a short while so the caregiver can have a break from the tremendous stress of daily caregiving."

"So how would the death law affect hospice care, respite care, palliative care?"

"Very negatively," responded Anna heatedly. "Older patients might not seek services, afraid of being labeled 'disposable' and discovered by the death law enforcers.

"One of our basic tenets in hospice is no one should feel pain. You'd have a whole lot of people unmedicated because they were afraid to seek assistance. Would the death law require that they be euthanized immediately? There's a whole lot of difference in three days and six months when you're considering how long you have left. You'd have people with unmitigated pain, fear, anger, afraid to get help."

"Sounds awful," said Jake.

"Many people don't believe they should take their own lives. Some don't know how or don't have the strength. I'm Catholic and my church says suicide's a sin. However, I'd readily take hospice help alleviating pain, living in God's time, waiting for Him to decide when it's right for me to die. Hospice people usually don't espouse physician-assisted suicide, much less government-mandated euthanasia."

"How is hospice paid for?" asked Jake.

"Insurance, Medicare, sometimes Medicaid, often fundraisers and donations. Not having hospice care for people over seventy would save a lot of government money, no doubt about that," explained Anna. "Why not euthanize hospice patients under seventy? That would save a lot more money. Officials might think, what the hell, if you're going to die in six months, what's the difference if it's next week instead? I fear we're opening terrible avenues of government intervention."

Henry had been quiet as he listened to Anna's torrent of emotional words. Now he asked cautiously, "But what if someone actually wants to die, Anna, if life isn't worth living anymore?"

"Yes, I understand that," she agreed. "You've probably thought a good bit about that, right? Not meaning to pry..."

"You're too good a friend to pry, Anna. I just wish I could see some end without bankrupting Julia in the process, making her life miserable. Jake's one of the family, Anna, I should have told you. He and Julia are an 'item.' He knows our future may affect his, too."

"Now hold on, Henry. Don't be making assumptions about what I may be thinking," protested Jake.

Anna intervened, "I understand, Henry. You'd like the right to decide, but not based on government mandate."

"Absolutely," verified Henry emotionally. "When I look at Bea and me, I just don't see a good end. Sometimes I'd like to quit before it gets worse."

"I wish I had answers to offer. Maybe there aren't any. Jake, I have another appointment. With the holiday coming up, we're really busy."

"Yes, fine," said Jake, ready to end the interview, given Henry's obvious distress. "Can I call you if I have more questions?"

"Certainly. Anything I can do to help. You're writing a news article, right?"

"Yes, along with my Sunday column and hopefully a book. May I use your name and some direct quotes?"

"Oh my God, you're *that* Jake Jordan! I read your column all the time! I didn't realize you're Henry's friend!" exclaimed Anna. "What an honor to meet you! You can quote me. I trust you'll do that accurately."

At the door, Anna touched Henry on the shoulder. "Are you and Beatriz doing okay at the moment?"

"We're always one disaster away from the next step, but we're all right. We visited Dale Meadows last week. We're making an alternative plan in case we need one."

"Oh, yes, they're about the best around. They cost an arm and a leg, though. Of course, if Beatriz is in hospice care, that would pick up some of the costs for services."

"Really? I didn't know that."

"I'll be glad to look at everything with you, Henry," replied Anna. "You're smart to plan. Have you looked any place else?"

"Could you recommend some place that takes Medicaid, if we have to go that route?"

With a bit of a grimace, Anna said, "I hope that's not necessary. Talk with the people at Hampton House. I'll warn you, you're going to see a big difference. Call Megan Kirby."

"Thanks a lot. We appreciate your time and may need you professionally sooner than we'd like."

"My thanks, too," said Jake. "I'll talk with you later."

With a hug for Henry and for Jake, too, Anna walked them to the elevator. Jake said to Henry, "I've lost track of time. What holiday was she talking about?"

"Thanksgiving, of course," said Henry. "Wait till you taste Julia's stuffing. Where's lunch today? My turn to buy."

CHAPTER 18

Saturday, November 19

The rest of the week flew by. Jake had moved clothes into space Julia cleared out for him. He'd spent more time at the office and produced the required amount of work.

They decided all of them would visit Hampton House Saturday morning, the Medicaid-eligible ALF mentioned by Anna. They wanted to see how Beatriz reacted and Hampton House personnel's response to her.

The hardest part was separating Beatriz from the cat. Finally everyone except Calvin drove away.

"What do you know about this place, Henry?" asked Julia.

"Not a lot. They've been in business for thirty years and describe themselves as a 'clean, caring Christian facility,' whatever that means. There really wasn't much on their web site."

Jake asked, "How shall we proceed? Ask questions and introduce myself as a reporter, or just tag along as a pseudo-family member and observe?"

"Drop the pseudo part. Let's introduce you as a friend and a journalist."

"Good," said Jake. "When we said my job at the last place, they clammed up. I won't ask anything today, just listen. If you drop the death law into the conversation, though, that wouldn't bend my ethics."

On approach they saw a two-story brick building surrounded by shrubs. It looked clean and tidy but not particularly welcoming. There were no sitting benches or flowerbeds. Inside they found a small foyer with four folding chairs along one wall. A woman seated at a desk greeted them pleasantly and asked them to sign in.

Henry said, "We have a ten o'clock appointment with Megan Kirby."

"Make yourselves comfortable," said the receptionist. "There's some instant coffee and hot water, if you'd like to help yourselves. I'll call her... No answer. I'll use the intercom."

"Ms. Kirby, Ms. Kirby, your ten o'clock appointment is in the lobby" sounded through the building.

Julia held one of her mother's hands and Henry held the other. Jake held Julia's other hand to make them a human chain. They sat for a long fifteen minutes with an increasingly restless Beatriz.

An apologetic Ms. Kirby rushed in just as Henry was about to suggest they leave. All five trundled down the hall: a flustered Ms. Kirby, an agitated Beatriz, and a disgruntled Henry, Julia and Jake. "I wear so many hats around here, it's hard to keep on schedule. Please call me Megan."

"Thank you for meeting with us," Henry said. "We realize it's a Saturday and you're short-staffed."

"I wish that was it," lamented Megan," but we've had some resignations and due to patient vacancies, haven't filled the positions. We're all doing double or triple duty."

"I didn't realize it was that hard to hire people in this field," said Julia.

"It's budget for us. The death law has everyone scared and ALFs everywhere are losing clients as families take their loved ones home, safe from the government. However," she continued with a professional smile, "we currently have space, something we haven't always had on short notice."

Jake glanced into rooms and saw many beds unmade and residents sitting in their sleeping clothes. Henry took in the scene as well, and Jake was glad Anna had forewarned them what to expect. Megan guided them into her small, cluttered office. "Oh, dear, I have only two chairs. I'll go find another one."

"Let me help you," offered Jake. He followed her down the hall where she plucked a folding chair from an office, protesting that she could do it alone. Jake wanted every opportunity to see this place.

A few residents moved around on walkers, dressed in sweatshirts and sweatpants and house slippers or socks. These mobile residents looked clean with their hair brushed. One or two staff members in nursing scrubs were visible but didn't appear to be interacting much with the residents. One old woman called plaintively, "Momma, Momma," to everyone passing by. Another shuffled along oblivious with his head down. Jake carried the chair back to Megan's office and looked for but did not see her job title on her office door.

With all of them seated in the cramped office, Megan began, "What would you like to know?"

Henry said, "Can you tell us what it's like here?"

"Sure," said Megan. "We have three very good meals every day and a snack. We have church services on Sunday mornings and Wednesday evenings. The doctor sees people who get sick, or we take them to the hospital in an emergency. People with a family member here are happy, because we are loving, Christian people."

"Do you have many activities?"

"Like what? We have some books and puzzles and you can walk around outside. Oh, sorry, or ride your chair outside. The nurses bring in their old magazines. Your own family should provide what you need for entertainment. And we have the TV."

"Do you take people out on rides or have community folks come in to do activities?" asked Henry.

"We wish we could. But we don't have a bus and can't use our own cars… the insurance, you know. We don't have an activity room so we can't have people coming in. Most of our folks have family nearby that visit a lot, so we're a cheery place."

Yeah, right, thought Jake, not yet having seen any cheer at Hampton House.

"We squeeze in a Christmas tree in the foyer in December. Last year the cutest little Brownies came and sang. Oh, and we have a candle thing we put out for our Jewish friends."

"Really!" said Julia. Jake wished she could have seen the difference at Dale Meadows. "How much does it cost here?"

"Most of our residents qualify for Medicaid payments," said Megan, "so you don't have to think about the money. You just let us worry about that."

Beatriz had sat fairly quietly so far but began waving her hands and talking gibberish loudly.

"What's she saying? What's wrong with her?" asked Megan.

"She's missing her cat," said Julia.

"She'd get used to being without it. You could get her one of those realistic toy cats. We don't allow pets here."

No cat, no Beatriz, thought Jake.

A distressed Henry said, "I think we need to take Beatriz home. She's upset."

"One more thing," said Megan. "She doesn't wander, does

she? No wanderers here. We can handle the not talking part, but she'll need to be able to stay put in her room, and take the meds our doctor gives her."

"What kind of meds?" asked Julia. "She doesn't take much now."

"Oh, all our people take meds to make them feel better," said Megan. "The doctor will tell you all about that later. That is, if the death law doesn't get you first," she added in an apparent attempt at humor.

Henry had begun clumsily wheeling himself out, saying over his shoulder, "Thank you, Megan. Come on, Julia, Jake, we need to get Beatriz home now."

Striding ahead, Jake said, "I'll get the car. Can you get them out front, Julia?"

She responded, looking shell-shocked, "Yes, thanks."

They quickly loaded the agitated Beatriz and an extremely distressed Henry. "If you ever put me in a place like that, I will haunt you the rest of your days," he stormed. "We are *not* going there. I don't know how we'll manage, but we are *not* going there." He shook his head back and forth in despair, further agitating Beatriz.

"Calm down, Henry," said Julia, reaching into the back seat to take his hand. "I promise you we'll figure something else out. A lot different than the other place, huh?"

"Calm down, how can I calm down? You're not the one who might live there."

"Henry, get a grip. Look at Mom," ordered Julia. "I promise you, you won't be there."

At that, Henry got a grip, including a grip on Beatriz's hand, calming her.

Jake felt shaken and couldn't imagine what Henry must be feeling. "Julia, even though we were warned, you wouldn't believe the difference in the two places. Let's go home and regroup."

"Could we pick up some barbecue from that place across the street first?" asked Henry hopefully, showing a remarkable recovery in view of good food.

Julia and Jake laughed and wheeled into the restaurant's parking lot.

PART TWO
Florida

CHAPTER 19

Sunday, November 20

The phone rang while Jake and Julia lazed in bed with the Sunday papers. Beatriz and Henry had yet to stir. Julia said, "Who would call this early?" She saw Simms' name and should have guessed.

"Missy, I'm sorry to call you early on Sunday, but Tina-Maria in the home office says I'd better get down there. The natives, especially the older ones, are restless. She thinks we should hold some town meetings, since I was coming home for Thanksgiving, anyway. I hate like hell to ask, but I really need you there. Congress is adjourning for the winter break, so it's a good time to go."

"Oh, God, let me think," replied Julia. "I'll have to see what – if – I can work out. Can I call you in an hour or so?"

"Yeah, but make it as quick as you can. I'm leaving later this morning on a Southwest flight to Tampa. Tina'll meet me there to plan the meetings. I'll need the research you've done and I want you there for the unexpected. Shouldn't be any important votes I'll miss on the floor. Nothing much goes on between now and the New Year."

Julia hung up and pulled the pillow over her head, wailing, "*Not* what I need this morning!"

Jake had overheard the conversation. He pulled the pillow off her head, cradled her in his arms, and said, "I have an idea. Hear me out before you say no."

"I'm open to anything, but I've got to phone Hattie right now."

"Listen to me first. How about a road trip with all of us? A change of scene will be good for Henry and I can't see how it would hurt your mother."

"That's crazy talk! If you think that would work, you really don't understand our situation."

"Listen a minute, hear me out. We'd drive down in your van, plenty of room. Let's take Hattie with us to look after your parents. A condo wouldn't cost much this time of the year. Hattie could cook and watch Beatriz, you accompany the congressman, and I'll do interviews. Henry could go with me. The drive down might be a pain, but I bet we could make it work. What do you think?"

"Oh, lord, Jake, could we pull this off? It sounds too much to me."

"Call Hattie. Your parents aren't going to be any sicker in Florida and a change of scene might help."

"It would certainly be easier if they were along. And travel with you would be fun. Could you take the time?"

"I just got leeway from my editor, remember? I'd like to get the Florida perspective."

"It all depends on Hattie. Let me call her before we talk to Henry."

"I'll figure driving time – Tampa, right?" asked Jake.

"Sarasota," said Julia, warming to the idea. "Oh, Hattie, I'm glad I caught you before church."

"What's wrong, Miss Julia? I can be there in half an hour."

"We're fine, Hattie. We have an idea. The congressman needs me to go to Florida, and—"

Hattie interrupted, "How long you need me to stay?"

"Thanks, Hattie, but we have an idea. Could you go with us and take care of my parents while Jake and I work? Jake has this wild idea we could all drive down."

After a moment of shocked silence, Hattie gasped out, "Miss Julia, you talking serious here? I never been nowhere and I always wanted to see Florida. You'd really take me? I'd not cost y'all anything. I got some savings so I can pay my own way."

"Of course we'd pay you and your expenses. Could you put up with us night and day? You'd miss Thanksgiving with your family."

"Huh," snorted Hattie. "Thanksgiving here means I cook and they eat. I'm not missing nothing!"

"We'll get a place with a kitchen and fix most of our meals at home rather than go to restaurants."

"So we carry pans and such along?"

"The beach place will come equipped with all that."

"Beach!" yelped Hattie. "I never been to a beach! I could take Miz Beatriz walking on the beach. She'd like that."

"Yes, I expect she would," replied Julia. She thought of the great economic divide in America: those who go to the beach, figuratively and literally, and those who don't.

Hattie said, "I'll be ready in an hour."

Julia laughed. "Go on to church, Hattie. We're not in that big a hurry."

"I can pray and read my Bible driving to Florida. The Lord'll let me miss church today. Florida, oh my! Wait'll I tell my folks!"

"We'll talk to Henry and see what he thinks. I'll call you

back soon, okay?" Jake's and Hattie's enthusiasm were catching Julia up, too.

"Talk to Henry about what?" Julia heard from the hallway.

"Are you eavesdropping, Henry?" she yelled.

"Your mother wants to get up. I heard my name and Hattie's and naturally, I'm curious. I don't eavesdrop – usually."

Julia went to her mother, saying to Henry, "I'll tell you while I get Mom up. I need to go to Florida with Marcus."

"And Hattie's coming to stay with us?"

"No, Jake suggests we all drive down. What do you think?"

"And take Hattie with us? I think that's a fantastic idea! Yay, Jake!"

"So you agree?"

Henry almost shouted, "You bet I do," then added, "but I wouldn't want us to be a hindrance." He turned exuberant again. "Thanksgiving in Florida? Hot damn!"

"Okay, it's a done deal. You'll stay healthy and help Hattie with Mom. Could you get online and find us a condo in the Sarasota area?"

"I'm on it!"

Julia got her mother up, dressed and settled on the couch. "Jake, when could we leave? Would we start out today?"

"I'd need to go home and pack. Hattie's probably already ready. I could pick her up and be back around noon. Would that give you enough time to get ready? We could drive a ways, then get there late afternoon tomorrow."

"That's good for me. Stay maybe two weeks?"

"Sure. I went in the office three times this week so that should keep Sam happy. I'll call him in the morning. Worst case scenario, I'd fly home early and you'd drive back."

"Okay, let's start packing. No space for my golf clubs, though," she lamented.

"You play golf? Why didn't I know this? I love golf."

"I love to play but haven't had time or energy lately. That's one more thing for our future."

"Great! Let's plan a golf trip," Jake said. "I wish we could take our clubs to Florida but not this time."

Hattie answered Julia's call on the first ring with, "We truly gonna go?"

"Yep. Can Jake pick you up in an hour?"

"Yes'm, I'll be ready in ten minutes! I'm just bringing the working clothes I wear every day. Maybe a church dress."

"Sounds perfect. A swimsuit'd be good or you can walk on the beach with Mom and Henry in your scrubs. Here's Jake."

"Can I pick you up about eleven? Where do you live?"

"Oh, Mist' Jake, don't come to my 'hood in that fancy car. I take the bus someplace near where y'all live, maybe front of Union station."

"Union Station at eleven? You know my blue Prius, right?"

"Yessir. Tell Miss Julia I'm gonna fix us some lunch to eat in the car when I get there and I'll clean out the fridge. We need one'a them thermal bags to take cheese and stuff in," directed Hattie. "Gimme your cell phone number, in case we can't spy each other."

"I'll bring my cooler. My phone number is 202-689-9041."

"Bye, gotta go pack and see can I borrow a swimmin' suit from my sister."

Jake laughed as he handed the phone back to Julia. "She's excited. I'm on my way." He gave her a quick kiss. "See you in a couple of hours."

Jake left and Julia yelled, "Henry, have you—"

"Found and booked."

"Really?! Are you going to tell us about it or let us vote or anything?"

"Nope, this is my treat. I found a three-bedroom condo, two baths and a powder room on the beach with an elevator. This is an economical time to go to Florida."

"Not your treat," said Julia. "The office will pay for it. That's really sweet of you to offer."

"I found our suitcases. There's a washer and dryer so Hattie can do our laundry, just like here," said Henry.

"Will you be all right for a few minutes while I run to the bank and get gas? Do you want me to get you any cash?"

"We're fine and I've got money. I'll find our summer clothes and maybe you could pack them. Do we have enough cat food?"

"Oh, damn," sighed Julia. "I forgot the cat. We'll have to find a boarding place."

"No, let's take his cat box in the CR-V. He'll be a good traveler and keep Beatriz calm. The condo will accept a cat, I checked."

"All right," said Julia. "Jake picks Hattie up at eleven and we want to be driving by noon. I need to call the congressman."

"Leave today?" shouted Henry. "Hot damn!" He pumped his fist like a teenager. "I'll make us a hotel reservation for about dinner time tonight, all right? One room, all of us?" he deadpanned.

"Yeah, right. Either two or three rooms, whatever you can get. Thanks." Julia called Marcus and affirmed she would be arriving in the home district Monday afternoon.

"Good," replied Simms. "I knew you'd work it out."

They headed out at noon. Julia had packed clothes, medications, Depends, and medical appliances for Henry and Beatriz. She threw a few things for herself into a bag, found the cat carrier, freshened the litter box and packed some cat food. She added her computer, iPad, charging cords and a briefcase of things she'd need. She looked longingly at her golf clubs, but no way this trip.

She loaded the suitcases, cat stuff and Henry's wheelchair where it would be easy to get out, leaving space for Jake's and Hattie's suitcases and Henry's walker. They decided to let Calvin sit on Beatriz's lap instead of crating him and just hang on to him when they opened the car doors. Julia felt tired already and dreaded the several-hour road trip ahead.

Hattie bustled into the kitchen after stowing her '60s-era borrowed suitcase in the CR-V. She quickly packed a lunch in Jake's cooler bag and dumped items from the refrigerator. "Mist' Henry, you forgot your eye drops," chided Hattie. "I'll just put them in the cool bag, okay?"

Oh jeez, what else have we forgotten? wondered Julia.

Jake saw her expression and said, "There's nothing here that can't be replaced in Florida. They have urgent care clinics and hospitals and stores. Do you have a list of Henry's medications?"

"Yes, he carries that in his wallet with his insurance cards. Oh, wallets... Henry, you have yours? I've got mine, plus medications, how about you, Jake?"

"I'm good; how about computers? Everyone got phones, cords, computers, stuff like that?" asked Jake, longing for earlier times when you took a few clothes, some money and a book to read on the plane.

Finally everyone was toileted, soothed and belted into the car. Hattie sat in the back with the lunch under her feet. Beatriz was in the middle holding Calvin in her lap, the only calm members of the expedition. Henry rode shotgun.

After a brief exchange, they decided Julia would drive first, then Jake, changing drivers whenever they made bathroom stops.

"Let's go," said Henry. "We've got rooms in South Carolina just before we get into Georgia, about a seven-hour drive."

They sailed south on I-95. The group was in high spirits, on the road together headed somewhere interesting.

Hattie handed out sandwiches and bottles of water, even a straw for Henry, for lunch. She'd brought fruit for dessert, along with brownies.

"Where in the world did you get brownies?" asked Julia.

"Had 'em in the freezer at home. They the special ones Mist' Henry likes where you put mint patties on top and smear them around when they're melted. Would you mind if I asked a short blessing, seeing it's Sunday?"

Receiving nods of agreement, Hattie fulfilled her promise to God that she'd pray in the car since she'd skipped church. She got them all blessed, fed and cleaned up in short order.

Julia knew the caregiver's presence would make this trip the best it could be for everyone and added Hattie yet one more time to her private blessing list.

The drive was predictably tiresome but pleasantly uneventful. The back occupants dozed. In the front seat whoever was passenger made notes for work. Each occasionally reached over and squeezed the other's hand or patted a knee.

As they approached the Georgia state line, Julia asked Henry, "Where's our hotel?"

"Two rooms at the Comfort Suites in Walterboro, South

Carolina. I figured you and Jake could have one suite and Hattie, Beatriz and I could have the other – okay with you, Hattie?"

"That's the best. I'd sleep easier was I where I could hear if y'all call out. I can sleep on the floor if there's an extra quilt."

"No, no, there's a bed for each of us, actually a pull-out couch in another part of the room so you'll have a little privacy. They don't mind if Calvin is there, to the tune of twenty-five dollars extra fee. But I figured we didn't want to smuggle him in, right, Julia?"

Gritting her teeth, Julia replied, "Right, Henry," though the twenty-five-dollar pet fee might have challenged her ethics. "Shall we stop for dinner now or find a place after we check in?"

"Miss Julia, we got enough left from lunch if y'all not too picky."

"Great," said Julia. "Pass around some supper." They found their hotel, piled into their rooms, and agreed to meet in the breakfast room and be on the road at seven-thirty.

Monday morning, Hattie seated Beatriz and Henry in the hotel breakfast room and brought them coffee while she organized their breakfast food. She smiled and greeted the black women tending the food and drinks, glad that for once she was a traveler and not the server. Well, technically she was serving others, but they made her feel like family, not hired help. As she assembled their breakfasts, a man with a Northern accent said to her, "Hon, run get me some wheat toast, lots of butter, and make it snappy because I've got to go."

Hattie realized he assumed she was a hotel worker. Restraining the impulse to set him straight emphatically, she pointed to the servers in the room, saying, "Sir, y'all can ask them. Or make it yourself in this here toaster." Scowling, the man stomped off with no apology. Hattie continued to fix Beatriz's and Henry's plates, a little shaken at the encounter.

"What was that all about?" asked Henry when she returned to the table.

"Nothing, just a case of asking the wrong person."

"Why would he think you work here?"

"I expect 'cause I'm black."

As she spoke, one of the servers stopped by their table, asking loudly, "Can I get you any more coffee or somethin', honey?" adding quietly to Hattie, "Sorry, he didn't mean no harm, he just thought you one of us."

"No offense taken," Hattie assured her. "He didn't know no better. And I am one of y'all."

"Yes, but you're one of us, too," declared Henry stoutly, trying to rise. "I'm gonna go poke him with my walker."

"Let's just eat up and be ready when Mist' Jake and Miss Julia gets here. If they not here soon, I'm gonna wrap up some food for the car."

At that moment, Julia and Jake entered the breakfast room. "Let's get this show on the road," said Julia briskly.

Henry snorted. "We've eaten, Hattie's been insulted by a Yankee, and we'd already be loaded if we had a car key. Calvin's had breakfast and a clean box."

"Oops," said Jake sheepishly, "guess we're the slow ones. We... uh... slept a little late. Julia, if you'll get me a large coffee and something to eat, I'll go load their stuff and Calvin. What about a Yankee?"

Seeing Julia hesitate at the coffee urn, Hattie offered,

"Nothing about a Yankee. Mist' Jake likes his coffee black. We ready in ten minutes."

"Great," Julia laughed. "Now I know how Jake drinks his coffee."

The caravan trundled down the road with high spirits. As they passed Hilton Head Island signs, Jake and Julia promised each other a golfing trip there. The Marshes of Glynn surrounded them as they neared the Georgia line, and Jake recited Sidney Lanier's poetry. "How'd you know that?" asked Julia.

"I took an elective in Southern literature and liked his work."

"Have you played the courses at St. Simon's and Jekyll Island? They're beautiful and a bargain in the winter. I love this area, especially the Jekyll Island Club Hotel. I've heard they have a great New Year's Eve celebration there. Maybe sometime…"

They crossed the Florida line, stopping at the Welcome Center for a free sample of Florida juice. "Aw, tastes just like regular juice," observed Hattie.

"That's because 'regular juice' probably *is* Florida orange juice. It tastes better actually standing in Florida sunshine, though," said Henry.

"Truly," agreed Hattie. "I wanna see oranges on their trees."

"In about a hundred miles," promised Julia.

They connected with US301 and traversed the horse country of Florida, seeing many small lakes and fruit tree groves. "Are those oranges?" asked Hattie.

"They look like grapefruits to me," replied Henry. "Might see some lemons, too."

"And limes. We'll get some of that famous Florida key lime

pie when we stop for lunch," said Julia, "and groceries after we get in tonight. Calvin is the only one who has any food. How's he doing?"

"Happy as a cat can be. I'm getting hungry. Can we stop for lunch?" asked Henry.

"How about it, Julia? You're the one with the time constraints here," said Jake.

"I'm not expected until this evening. But maybe we'd better find a McDonald's or Wendy's and just keep driving," replied Julia.

"You said key lime pie. They don't have that, do they?" asked Henry petulantly.

Julia and Jake laughed. "No, sorry, but they're quick and have clean bathrooms," responded Julia. "I promise pie for dinner."

"I guess it'll have to be," grumbled Henry, then quickly corrected his attitude. "I mean, sounds great. Let's get there and get settled."

"We gonna see the ocean soon? Seems like we moving in a different direction."

"We're heading toward the Gulf of Mexico right now. We'll see it when we get across the state," explained Jake.

"Mexico!" yelped the caregiver. "We going to Mexico?"

"No," laughed Julia. "But we're going to that part of the Atlantic bordering Mexico, I guess. Henry, you look it up and we'll all learn a little geography."

Everyone was in a kind of a fast-food after-lunch haze when Julia's phone rang. "Where you at, missy?" asked Simms.

"Hello, Marcus," replied Julia. "We're near Ocala, so a couple of hours from Sarasota. Do we need to meet tonight?"

"Not if you can have me a page of figures on the death law

for tomorrow. Our first stop is at the State College of Florida, in Bradenton," said Simms. "It's a gerontology nursing class but they're inviting other students and faculty, too. Tina-Maria thought we should start with something easy, get our act together before the town meetings. You okay with that?"

"That's a very good idea. The facts for tomorrow will be heavy on the effect on the medical community."

"Let's go over stuff at breakfast," said Simms. "I'll call you when Tina-Maria tells me where."

"Yes, fine, Jake can drop me off there and then I'll ride with you, okay?"

"Who's Jake? Oh, that newspaper feller. Why's he with you?"

"Maybe I forgot to tell you yesterday, but we're all here – my parents, their caregiver and Jake. We're staying in a condo at Bradenton Beach."

"What the Sam hell... do you know what that costs over there? On the taxpayer's dollar? I can see the headlines now!"

"Yes, I do know the cost, very reasonable this time of the year. If there's any blowback on this, I'll pay for it myself."

"No, no, that's not what I meant," he said, reconsidering. "Actually, I'm glad you brought them. Your mind'll be more at ease and you can concentrate on work better. Not that you don't already," he added hastily. "See you at breakfast. I'm gonna go find some key lime pie."

Hanging up, Julia chuckled, "The bad news is I have to work tonight. The good news, I already have that briefing paper ready for him."

The closer they got to the Gulf, the happier everyone seemed. They enjoyed the warmth every time they crawled out of the car. The rivers grew wider and the lakes more numerous. Hattie had stopped asking "That it?", wide-eyed at the tropical scenery even if she hadn't yet seen the Gulf.

They drove through Bradenton and cruised the long causeway to the islands, finally arriving in Bradenton Beach. They ooh-ed at the blue water and beautiful palm-tree-lined beach. Hattie breathed reverently, "Oh, Lawdy, didn't know it got this fine in this world!"

Henry held Beatriz's hand and smiled his widest. Jake and Julia were more focused looking for their condo address, but they too held hands.

Calvin purred.

At the realtor's office they collected keys and instructions. The nearby condo was as advertised, beachfront with an elevator. Hattie helped Beatriz, Calvin and Henry into the elevator and escorted them to the third floor.

Julia said, "I'm not wild about elevators but I'll try this rather than carrying up the luggage."

"Not my preference, either, but I don't want to trundle all this stuff up the stairs. At least we'll be safe in a hurricane on the third floor," said Jake.

"Don't say that! Hurricane season is officially over but I'd hate to sit through one this week, wouldn't you?"

"We could have our own hurricane party. There's no one I'd rather hurricane with than you," he said, giving Julia a quick smooch. As they stepped off on the third floor, they were rendered speechless by the vista of sand, palm trees and blue water.

Henry yelled, "Come and see!" The condo was plenty spacious for the five of them with a large balcony running all along the living room. "You take the front room and we'll take the other two," suggested Henry. "Hattie says she'll sleep in the bottom bunk of the kids' room and Beatriz and I'll be in the room next to her. You two can take the bridal suite with the wall of windows on the Gulf."

After a perfunctory protest, Julia and Jake began distributing luggage to the right rooms. "Let's set up Calvin's box in the powder room. You share this bathroom and we have the en suite."

They explored the condo and Hattie declared it almost clean enough, saying she'd take care of the rest. The carpet was dark bluish green, the color of the Gulf water. The condo was a bit dated and showed the effects of wear, but the walls were a lovely shade of pale green and the white trim looked fresh. Overhead fans moved the air around and the small kitchen looked perfectly adequate. The rattan furniture held cushions in a palm leaf design and the whole place felt delightfully tropical.

Henry announced, "Nap first, then beach, then dinner. How's that sound?"

"Plus get some groceries and do some work," added Julia.

Hattie said, "I'll get these folks and the kitty settled and y'all get groceries. I can cook fish. Reckon you could find some for dinner?"

"And key lime pie," chimed in Henry.

"Done. Any other requests?" asked Jake. Julia and Jake headed to the nearby Publix. Finally alone after two days of family travel, they relaxed into the quiet car. "Our first grocery trip together," said Jake.

"We're having lots of firsts in a very short time," agreed Julia. "I like it."

"I couldn't be happier." Jake said as he reached for her hand again.

CHAPTER 20

After Hattie's delicious fried grouper and key lime pie on their deck overlooking the Gulf, everyone slept soundly. Tuesday morning dawned Florida-beautiful. Jake and Julia had a brief snuggle looking out their picture window at the Gulf.

"When and where do you meet Simms?" asked Jake.

"Eight o'clock, the Peaches café, near our first speaking engagement. You can drop me off and I'll call later you about picking me up. What are you doing today?"

"Looking for senior centers, hospices, other places where I might interview people. There's an Elderstudy program at USF-Sarasota and many volunteers around here. I'll look for a volunteer coordinator. I also want to talk to people in the Latino community. Could you break away long enough to translate for me?"

"Better yet," said Julia, "let's schedule a town meeting with the Latino population. Tina-Maria and I can translate. My Spanish is rusty, though."

Hattie had everyone up so Jake and Julia hugged her parents, patted Calvin, and left. It was great to begin a day with everyone happy.

Jake walked Julia into Peaches so he could get coffee and a muffin to go. Julia said, "There's Marcus, Tina-Maria's here, too. Come meet them."

The congressman stood and introduced himself to Jake. "Sit down if you have time. Tina-Maria and I have hatched an idea. Can you have breakfast with us?"

Julia gave Jake an I-have-no-idea shrug. Jake said, "Sure, my day's unscheduled."

"Excellent. This is Tina-Maria. She helps Julia out."

The women laughed and Julia said, "No, Marcus, we both try to keep you out of trouble!"

"Whatever," rumbled Simms. "Jake, you work for the DC papers, right?"

"I work in the Kidd-Rudman newspaper syndicate there. Essentially, I work for the Washington paper, although my Sunday column also goes out across the country."

"Even better," said Simms. "Here's my idea – maybe it was Tina-Maria's idea." as Tina-Maria and Julia exchanged an eye-roll, knowing Simms owned all the ideas regardless of the origin.

"Could you go with us to our meetings and report on them? Kind of a house journalist. Unpaid, of course," Simms added hastily.

House journalist? Like a house dog or a house boy? That wouldn't fulfill his journalistic responsibilities to either his employer or his profession. Jake said, "That might help us both. *But* – this is a big thing – I'd have to have journalistic freedom, nobody editing what I'm writing." Jake glanced at Julia, ready to leave if they were on colliding turf. She nodded agreement.

The congressman ruminated over sips of coffee, waving to the waitress for a refill. "Okay, if you wouldn't write negatively about me."

Jake hedged, "That shouldn't be an issue. You're mostly listening to constituents? You're taking the same position you announced on television? I'd be reporting what your constituents say, not you."

"I'd sure as Sam hell want my name in there."

"Of course. I never know what my editor will print so I can't guarantee anything. Your name would be in my Sunday column as the organizer of the meetings where I gathered information."

"A national audience, you said? Excellent! We've got a deal. What you think, missy?"

"I think it's a little late for my opinion," said Julia. "Yes, could be mutually helpful."

Tina-Maria asked, "How are your parents, Julia? They came with you?"

"They're at the condo at Bradenton Beach with their caregiver, happy slurping Florida orange juice when we left. Jake convinced me this would work and so far it has."

"Keep it that way," said the congressman. "Let's get to work. What's outside the public meetings is off the record, agreed, Jake?"

"Agreed."

Tina explained that the town meetings around the district were scheduled for one hour with the expectation they would last two. Today Simms would talk to a nurses' class, a high school civics class, and a drop-in at a social club. A black church had requested that he share the pulpit on Sunday and a Latino community center wanted him to drop in. *Wow*, thought Jake, *at least three scheduled meetings a day. Book fodder galore!*

"Okay with me," said Simms and Julia nodded, hoping her family's health held up. "About preaching, can I just say a few words and pray?"

Tina-Maria nodded. "That's what they're expecting."

"Missy, find me some Bible quotes on old people."

"You can use facts on this area, too, percent of black population that are seniors, stuff like that." Julia assumed she was "missy."

"What I'd like to do," said Simms, "is drop in at a Thanksgiving dinner for the homeless."

Oops, forgot about Thanksgiving, thought Julia. *Gotta talk to Hattie.* "Great idea, boss. Lots of affluence here, but also many homeless and poor."

"Resurrection House will know about Thanksgiving dinners," Tina-Maria said and jotted notes.

"Now what do I need to know, Julia?"

"Here's a briefing sheet, but basically, Florida has the largest percentage of population over sixty-five and our district is even older. Four other states have a higher median age. California has the highest number of older people, with Florida second. Just say Florida has the largest percentage of population over sixty-five and don't confuse people."

"Confuses me," snarled Simms. "Can't the government just make a simple statement?" He laughed. "I *am* the government, aren't I? What else?"

"The Latino population in your district is slightly higher than the national average."

"We're all getting old, aren't we?" commented Simms.

"America isn't the only aging nation. People live longer in some other countries, some say because of our obesity. Your talking point is that we need to pass laws to care for seniors, not to eliminate them."

Simms said, "You have a page of facts for me?"

"You can refer questioners to this book by Ted Fishman,

Shock of Gray. One chapter is 'Greetings from Florida, God's Waiting Room.' Forty percent of the households in our district have someone sixty-five years of age or older. You can also refer to Margaret Cruikshank's *Learning to Be Old.*

"You can mention the wealth disparity here. Having less-well-off people helps our wealthy because they can hire help. We have upper-end senior communities and the income they generate, plus the seasonal arrival of the older 'snowbirds.'"

Simms scribbled notes. "Anything else, Tina-Maria?"

"No, Julia's got it. We have many mixed-generation households because lower income generations often live together. People will vent about the death law and then demand that you do something. This morning's meeting was not advertised, so you shouldn't have any strident reporters – uh, sorry, Jake," Tina-Maria said sheepishly.

"I'm never strident and I'll ask my questions after the meeting. Don't introduce me. When journalists attend, I'll introduce myself, probably'll already know some. You'll get some good journalists. This is a big story if Congressman Simms is headed for higher office."

"Sounds good," said Simms, "let's roll. Tina-Maria, you pay the checks. Julia, give me Fishman's and Cruikshank's books for a prop. Ride with us or follow?"

"We'll follow, since Tina-Maria knows where we're going," said Julia. *Or if we get an emergency call from Hattie.*

At the college they lined up for posed pictures with the president and a dean or two. A large classroom filled up with nursing students and faculty in a rainbow of scrubs. Julia arranged the room for the speaker, put water on the dais and tested the microphone. Tina-Maria schmoozed the nursing faculty and verified who'd be introducing the congressman. Jake watched the two women organize everything while Simms chatted up the bigwigs in the room.

The president waded through opening remarks and introduced the congressman. After polite applause, Simms thanked the officials by name and the students and faculty as a group. He delivered the speech his communications director Walter had prepared, outlining the main points of the death law, briefly acknowledging his error in voting for it, and vowing to get it repealed.

Simms peppered his remarks with Julia's facts. He ended his speech with the quote: "In *Lonesome Dove* by Larry McMurtry, a character says, 'It ain't dying I'm talking about, it's living.' We need to talk about living, not dying, in Congress. I'll do my best to head the conversation in that direction."

After enthusiastic applause, he asked for questions. Predictably, the first question was how could Congress be so dumb. Simms repeated his earlier statement on culpability and his intent to work for repeal. He was candid, succinct and non-defensive.

Most of the questions fell into two categories: "Will I have a job when I finish my degree?" and "What will happen to me / my spouse / my parents / my grandparents under the death law as we get older?" Simms held up the books on aging as recommended reading to understand the economic and social dimensions of aging. He saw professors writing down the titles and figured they'd show up on somebody's required reading list soon.

After an hour of questions, the president thanked Simms, who walked to the side of the room to more appreciative applause. Julia and Tina-Maria were relieved with the successful dress rehearsal. Simms said to his staff members in a low tone, "How'd I do?"

Julia replied, "Magnificent, Marcus. Where'd you get that quote from *Lonesome Dove*?"

Simms laughed. "I read it in a *Southern Living* magazine I found in the bathroom this morning. Keep it in?"

"Definitely."

He turned back to the audience to shake hands and receive thanks. The president approached and said, "Can I take you to lunch?"

Julia shook her head slightly so Simms looked at his watch and said, "This has been great but we have another appointment." They exited after hearty handshakes, back-slaps, and see-you-later's.

In their own car, Jake laughed and gave Julia a quick hug. "Wow," he said, "I knew you were important but I didn't know you ran the show!"

"Not really. We always know who really runs the show. What did you think of his performance?"

"I thought it was masterful. Where'd he get that quote at the end?"

Julia laughed and explained the bathroom origin of that gem. "Did you hear anything you can use?"

"The main new wrinkle was students wondering if there'll be jobs when they graduate. Senior citizens make up so much of the population, those aspiring nurses might have a valid fear," replied Jake. "I read about eighty percent of senior citizens have at least one chronic condition. If you eliminate most people over seventy, that would sharply decrease the number of medical jobs."

"True, but some people argue that eliminating the

over-seventy population would alleviate the current shortage of medical personnel, so there'd be better medical care for children and adults of a younger age. You could argue that point either way."

"Medicare and Medicaid costs would go down sharply if every sick person over the age of seventy dies. But some say those programs aren't really what's driving the high cost of medical care. It's a convoluted topic, isn't it?" said Jake.

They followed Tina-Maria's car to their next speaking engagement. As they pulled up to a park-like area adjacent to the Sarasota Bay, Jake asked, "What is this place with the beautiful view?"

"It's a lawn bowling club. This is a drop-in because their president is a big donor. No press at this one, mostly their own members. We planned low-key meetings today until we get a feel for the public and Marcus is zeroed in with his presentation."

"I've never been to a lawn bowling club. What do they do?" asked Jake.

"Kind of like indoor bowling except it's outdoors on grass. They wear white, like a croquet club, or team colors when they compete."

"Judging by the cars in the parking lot, it's a pretty affluent group."

"Much of our district is, although those in the poor parts are in dire straits. But they're all potential voters."

Handshakes and introductions abounded. Jake watched the bowling, fascinated with the concentration and accuracy of the bowlers, older men and women dressed in conservative white clothing. It looked to be an ideal seniors' sport.

The members' comments centered on whether or not the

death law would affect them if they had plenty of money to hire help. One man thundered he'd return to his native Scotland. A couple of Canadians quietly voiced the same. Everyone appeared to be displeased with the death law but not overly worried. Having money apparently gave people confidence they could determine their own future.

An hour later, Julia said, "Okay, on to today's last stop, a high school government class. Students also take economics so we'll get good questions here."

"It'll be interesting to see if these kids realize what the death law might mean to their families. I didn't worry about life-and-death issues when I was their age, not until I got into the Air Force contemplating 'Nam," said Jake.

"I have no idea what young people today think, but most high school seniors are old enough to vote. This will be an interesting stop. And I want to hear more about your college and military days."

The high school visit began with the inevitable picture-posing with the principal and her minions. The visitors were impressed with the alert, attentive young people in the classroom. Some of the questions they asked sounded rehearsed, so the teacher had coached the students well.

However, students had concerns of their own, especially regarding grandparents and other older relatives. These kids believed everyone had the right to live as long as they wanted. One mentioned an elderly relative with dementia and perceptively suggested maybe everyone didn't want to stay alive.

One bright young woman quoted the Declaration of Independence regarding life, liberty, and the pursuit of happiness, and declared passionately, "We have a right to live, even if we are old and sick. Our government says so!"

Not anymore, thought Julia. Simms' sincerity and forthright manner made a connection with the students and Julia decided to find some big youth conference for him to keynote, maybe Boys' or Girls' Nation. She reflected, *Okay, if we can get the old people, the medical community, the young voters...* a daunting task with such varied groups. This next campaign could be quite a ride.

They exited the school and rendezvoused briefly to get their next day's directions from Tina-Maria: three town meetings and a luncheon. "Oh, and a Thanksgiving dinner for homeless on Thursday. Can you come, Julia?"

"Yes, we can make that. I want to get my parents out some. Could they come with us? We won't be there long, right?"

"No problem," responded Tina-Maria. "We'll see you tomorrow at our first town meeting at the Senior Companionship Center downtown at nine-thirty. That's going to be a different group, older, poorer, more disgruntled and frightened. You'll get some good material, Jake."

"Okay, we're forewarned," said Julia.

"Yay," said Jake.

CHAPTER 21

Tuesday, November 22

Julia called Henry to ask what they should get for dinner on the way home.

"You don't need to stop, everything's taken care of. We're chilling pinot grigio for you."

Julia didn't remember buying any pinot but it would be welcome after the long day of meetings. "We'll see you soon. You're sure there's nothing..."

"Positive. Just come on home. We had a wonderful day."

Jake said, "Henry's calling a beach condo 'home.' He was really upbeat."

"Isn't that great? I don't remember getting that wine yesterday. Did you pick it up?"

"Nope, I thought you did. Our memories are as bad as your mom's. Oops, I shouldn't have said that, nothing to joke about. I just meant..."

"I know, and it's okay. Obviously one of us had a memory lapse."

Their condo was brightly lit up in the early evening dusk. The last remnants of the sunset over the Gulf painted the sky with deep scarlet and purple wispy clouds.

Henry waved, obviously watching for them. They parked in their space under the building and ascended the stairs to their condo. Julia sniffed appreciatively. "What's that aroma? Smells wonderful!"

"Gumbo," explained Henry as Hattie came from the kitchen carrying a wooden spoon, trailed by Beatriz followed by Calvin II. Everyone looked happy and slightly flushed as if they'd been in the sun, wind, or wine bottle. "Hattie's making a recipe she remembers from her childhood. We've been on the beach and we're starving."

Gumbo? wondered Julia, pretty sure they hadn't bought shrimp and file powder and rice yesterday. "How'd you go to the store without a car? Did you find a delivery service? Doesn't that cost a lot?"

Henry and Hattie laughed as Beatriz joined them with a smile. "Hattie's got an admirer and he took us."

"You went with a strange man? And 'us' – who went?" Julia demanded.

"No'm, he ain't strange, he's real nice. Mist' Nate works here doin' the lawn and flowers. He's too old to do any damage to us! He took us all to the Publix. We met him when we at the beach and he's jus' nice."

"Really nice," added Henry.

"He's a widower and a lonely old man. Kinda like I am, except my kids' pa just took off a long time ago. I asked him 'bout a church for Sundays, because he looks like a church-going man. He offered to take us to the store and we thought some dinner be welcoming to y'all. So we all went, except not Calvin. And we did just fine."

Henry chimed in, "Julia, I feel more normal here. Lots of people have wheelchairs and walkers and the stores have wide aisles and little beeper carts you can ride. A few other shoppers looked just as vacant as your mom. Some had a helper with them. Oh, and Publix has snacks. What fun! Then we napped while Hattie cooked."

"What'd you do for money? Hattie, don't you spend your money on things for us."

"I'm not deaf and I'm not broke," snapped Henry. "I'm still good for some things, you know."

Oops, thought Julia, *stepped on a nerve.* "Thank you, Henry. Can I pay you back?"

"No, you cannot. Dinner tonight is my treat. And Beatriz's."

And treat it was. Henry had arranged hummus and pita chips to go with the wine. Hattie spooned the gumbo over steaming basmati rice and had set the table with large spoons for easy eating.

"Sit down, Hattie," said Henry. "I fixed five places."

"They told us at the agency to take our meals separate. I'll eat my gumbo in the kitchen."

"You're not at the agency now. Tell her, Julia, she sits or we don't eat."

"Henry's right," said Julia. "Please join us, Hattie. In fact, I wish you'd asked your chauffeur, too. We wouldn't have this feast if he hadn't driven you."

"Well, I guess," said Hattie reluctantly. "But I return thanks before I eat."

"Please, for all of us," said Henry. "Make it short because this food smells great." He reached for Beatriz's and Hattie's hands. Jake and Julia followed suit as they joined around the table.

"Bless this food to our bodies and our lives to Your use," intoned Hattie.

"Amen," chorused the others as all dug into the fine seafood and sausage stew.

"This is the best gumbo I ever ate," said Julia between mouthfuls. "And you just remembered the recipe?"

Hattie admitted, "Well, most of it. Mist' Henry looked it up on the computer, too."

"Lots of gumbo recipes on the web. Hattie peeled the shrimp so it'd be easier for me to eat."

"Very thoughtful," said Jake. "This is way the best I've ever eaten. Where'd you find the okra in winter?"

"At Publix but Nate says he take me to a little stand where he buys his greens and such. We three go one day, okay with y'all?"

"Fine, but when would he take you?" asked Julia. "He works."

"Today he took us on his lunch time and we just kinda' snacked through the store. He seemed happy for the company."

"Well, good for all of us," said Julia. "This is just delicious, and there's key lime pie, too, I bet."

"How'd you guess?" deadpanned Henry. "Julia, this is the best day I've spent in a long time. I wish we could just stay here."

"Oh, Henry, I'm so glad. I wish we could, too, but you know my job's in DC."

"I know. Just sayin'…"

"That was a wonderful dinner, Hattie," said Julia. "Thank you so much for coming with us."

"Oh, Miss Julia, thank y'all for bringing me. I'll get dinner cleaned up and help Miz Beatriz and Mist' Henry to bed."

"I'll clean up dinner," offered Jake. "You and Julia go ahead."

"I'll help, Jake," said Henry. "I'm not tired yet."

They ferried the dishes to the kitchen and Henry loaded the dishwasher, supporting himself on his walker as he bent over.

"Is this kitchen easier to manage? Seems like I can reach things here."

"I think it is," said Jake, looking around. "Things might be arranged just a little better. The doors are wider and there's no doorsill between rooms. Is your bathroom any different?"

"The shower is larger, no bathtub. I can walk in but you could roll a chair into it. There's a seat at the back so I can sit and hose off. It's easier for Beatriz and me to be in there together, too. Wonder where that'll lead?" he joked with an attempt at a leer.

"Cleaner bodies, if not cleaner thoughts. Okay, bud, we're done. I'll say goodnight so you can get to bed."

"You don't want a chaperone, right?"

"Boy, you really are in a good mood tonight!"

"Seriously, how could I not be happy here? It's beautiful, no heavy coat, and we get out more. This will be a wonderful two weeks. I wish it could be forever. We have all the comforts of home plus warm weather, the Gulf, shrimp and key lime pie. The Buddhists say the best way to prepare for death is to experience every minute today, and I intend to do just that."

"I'll try to practice that myself," seconded Jake.

With everyone else in their rooms, Jake said to Julia, "Let's take our wine and sit on the balcony. Isn't there a door to the deck from our bedroom?"

"Yes, let's. It's been a good day."

"It has. I'd like to talk about tomorrow."

"We'd better figure out Thanksgiving, too," replied Julia."

Settled in rockers, they counted their blessings in the quiet Gulf Coast dark. "Coming here was a great idea, Jake. And if we have a crisis, it's no different than at home. Those three sure looked happy."

"I'm happy, too," agreed Jake, taking her hand. "How about you?"

"More than I can remember, maybe ever. I like the pace here. People are busy, they just seem to be friendly instead of frenzied. Have you noticed that?"

"Yes, I have," said Jake. "But there's no place as frenzied as Capitol Hill. I like not being in heavy clothes and that makes life easier for Henry. He's using his walker more than his chair."

"I worried Mom might be more agitated here, but seems like as long as she's with Henry and the cat, it doesn't make much difference."

"And you. And Hattie. Her world's really about the same, I guess."

At breakfast everyone seemed eager for the day. So far Beatriz hadn't exhibited the "sundown" syndrome and hadn't wandered at night so they'd all slept well

"Hattie, about Thanksgiving, have you given it any thought?" asked Julia.

"Yes'm, there's a turkey thawing in the fridge. We got it yesterday when we shopped. But that's all we got. I didn't know y'all's plans."

"A step ahead of us, as usual. One thing, we're going with the congressman to a dinner for the homeless around noon. Dinner in the evening or mid-afternoon here, maybe?"

"Tell her what your guy said," Henry prompted Hattie.

"My *friend*," emphasized Hattie, "said their church does dinner for the needy and he asked if I wanted to help. I didn't say, because I feared it'd bother what y'all planned. But I like to do that, help some folks and meet some church-goers, if that fits y'all's plans. But who'd stay with Mist' Henry and Miz Beatriz while y'all gone?"

"We don't need a babysitter every minute," growled Henry. "Couldn't we go with you, Julia? We could just sit in the car. I think Beatriz would like the ride."

"Yes, we thought you'd come, too. We won't be long, just a drop-in. We could ride around Sarasota afterward, maybe come home the beachfront road through the keys."

That word "home" again, noticed Jake.

"Okay, our dinner about five? We'll pick up everything else this afternoon. Unless you've going shopping again?" she teased.

"No'm, but we did offer to fix a bite for a picnic with Nate, you don't mind."

"I suggested it," said Henry, "to thank him for taking us to the store yesterday."

"Of course I don't mind. I don't need to approve everything. Be sure to take a phone so we can find you, and leave us a note if you're out. Anything else, Hattie, Henry?"

"We're getting low on key lime pie. Just sayin'."

With a laugh, they were out the door.

"Wanna go for a walk, Mist' Henry? Some air might suit Miz Beatriz this fine mornin'."

"I sure do. Let me get my phone. Can you write a note?"

"Uh, Mist' Henry, my spelling not too good. Could you write and then we use it every time?"

"We need the whiteboard and marking pen in that drawer over there. Then we'll just change the time each day."

"Here 'tis, can you write on it?"

With some difficulty he managed to scratch out "Gone to

walk" and Hattie put the time down. "Chair or walker, Mist' Henry?"

"Neither one, I wish! Chair, we can go farther. I'm just happy to be out, not gonna worry about how I get there this morning," Henry finished with a smile. "We should get a leash so Calvin can go, too."

They separated the cat from Beatriz with difficulty and strolled and rolled to the elevator. A portly gray-haired man in a loud Hawaiian shirt stepped out to hold the door for them. "Are you visiting here or new owners?" he asked. "Glad to see some life around the place in November."

"We're visitors, here for a couple of weeks. I'm Henry, my wife Beatriz, and our friend Hattie. We're here with our daughter and her, er, guy. They're working and we're enjoying."

"I'm Mac. Me and the wife's got a place here. Sure beats the winters in Pittsburgh – they got snow today. We all call our friends back home when they get snow to tell them how warm it is here. Gets 'em every time! Say, some of us men are playing bocce ball in a few minutes. Want to join us?"

"That'd be good, Mist' Henry. Miz Beatriz and me manage just fine. Mist' Mac, can you push his chair back on the elevator later?"

Henry scowled and muttered, "I can do it myself, Hattie. I'll handle this."

"Mist' Henry," Hattie said gently, "I just want to be sure you okay."

"Of course I will," said Mac. "Good to have you with us, Henry."

Hattie and Beatriz trailed slowly down the sidewalk while Henry rolled off with Mac. Hattie admired the view and chatted to Beatriz who shuffled along with her head down. Hattie pointed out things on the sidewalk – a palm frond, a huge palmetto bug, and a little green anole lizard. Beatriz followed it with her eyes as it skittered away, her first interest in anything lately. Hattie wondered if the others saw Beatriz's decline as much as she did, but she hesitated to broach the subject. Nothing could be done, so maybe no use talking about it.

Mac and Henry headed for a shaded sandy space with balls lying on it and several men gathered on the sidelines. Henry shook hands all around, not getting many names but feeling the welcome. "Can I keep score or something?" asked Henry. "You could just park me along the side."

"No, no," protested Melvin, one of the group members. "We need you to make up the teams. You can throw underhand from your chair, right? We had a guy in a chair who used to play with us."

"Well, I don't know. Gimme a ball." Henry hefted the ball and flung it more or less down the court. The group clapped and somebody commented that was better than most of them did. Henry sat up a little straighter and thought he was going to like this game and these men. He'd hated losing the company of pals, especially giving up his bowling league. Maybe this would be a decent replacement for the next few days.

The town meetings that morning were a far cry from yesterday's speeches. Waiting for the meeting to begin, Tina-Maria said to Julia, "Could I talk to you privately for a couple of minutes?"

"Sure thing," said Julia, bracing herself to hear office intrigue.

"I hate to tell you, but I'm going to have to leave my job. I broke up with my boyfriend awhile back and my family is just killing me over it. They love him and my parents foresaw a whole string of grandchildren. They're driving me crazy. He's trying to get me back and it's just more than I can take. The only solution is to get out of town and leave them all to each other."

Tina-Maria spoke matter-of-factly but she was holding back tears. "The stress is so bad, I can't sleep and I'm not doing a very good job at work, either. The staff is covering for me but that can't continue. I need a new start somewhere else."

"Is he stalking you?" asked Julia anxiously. "Are you in danger?"

"No, he doesn't have to stalk me. My parents have him at the house all the time! I feel pushed out of my own home," sobbed Tina-Maria, finally breaking down.

Julia gave her a hug. "Life gets tough. Couldn't you just move out of your parents' house without having to leave the area?"

"You know how it is in our kind of family, Julia. They expect me to live there until I get married and take care of them in their old age. I need my own life! I will take care of them, just as you do with your parents, but they're still young and healthy and they're smothering me! I've never lived on my own, not even while I went to USF. My advisor, Dr. Robinson, helped me get this job. I want to be on my own and I have to move somewhere else.

"Oh, Julia," Tina-Maria wailed, "I wish I could just trade places with you!"

"Well, that's not going to happen. My life is pretty well anchored in DC."

Julia hated to think about the chaos of having no chief in the district home office right now. Tina-Maria's degree in social work was perfect for all the suffering that walked through their office door. What would they do without her?

"Can you hold out a little longer? It's a really bad time for change. Who in the office could replace you?"

"I wouldn't do anything until after the holidays. I'm thinking January, to set out fresh somewhere else. I'll have to find a new job first. Thanks for listening, Julia. My co-workers are great, but no one's ready to head up the office yet. Especially not now with everyone so worked up over the death law."

"Let's not say anything to Marcus yet. There's so much on his mind, I'd hate to add one more thing," said Julia. "He might fire us both on the spot!"

"I haven't said anything to anyone else and I don't intend to. But I thought it only fair to give you warning."

Everyone got a bird's-eye view of misery as the speakers tolled out a story of inadequate, unresponsive and prohibitively expensive health care for themselves and their senior relatives. Many detailed how their lives had changed by caring for an infirm elder. Jake did not hear resentment toward the person being cared for but rather toward the system that provided inadequate help. Assisted living facilities and caregivers were far too expensive. Medicaid-eligible places had long waiting lists, as did respite and day care facilities. Veterans eligible for VA hospitals were on waiting lists. Families had to figure out how to provide round-the-clock care themselves, at great cost to their own finances, not to mention their own health.

And those were the legal residents. Spokespersons for the undocumented segment voiced even more woeful tales of people who'd come to America looking for a better life but living a marginal existence as they cared for elderly relatives. America was not the Promised Land for the elderly and sick or their caretakers.

Listening to the litany of woe, the congressman formed ideas to begin to fix the broken health care system. Some said Obamacare had helped the nation's uninsured, but others said it hurt business owners forced to provide insurance. Simms was not so egotistical to think he could correct all the ills, no pun intended, but he had some ideas of what might help. "Simms-care" sounded pretty catchy for a campaign. *Hmm, "correct the ills," how would that play in a speech?*

Jake followed an articulate young woman out of the meeting hall and asked a few questions about what she had just recounted to the congressman. He could feel his next column coming on. For a news article, he'd report the essence of the meeting today. In his Sunday column, he'd give personal accounts that conveyed the hopelessness of the situation.

No one spoke in support of the death law. Most specifically condemned it, asking for better care, not cessation of their responsibility. Jake caught both the desperation and the commitment he was hearing from these caregivers and determined to reflect both in his columns.

Two speakers in particular got Jake's attention. One man dressed in a business suit, director of the local veterans' hospital, spoke eloquently about the need to improve VA services. He reiterated the high quality, but lamented the long waiting time for so many former servicepersons. He emphasized that many veterans returning from battle were grievously wounded both physically and mentally, with visible and invisible scars. Applause from the audience indicated this was a popular stance.

The other interesting speaker was a pony-tailed, bearded man in cargo pants who identified himself as a licensed counselor, director of a substance abuse clinic. He said to Simms, "I waved signs for you and will again." He echoed the VA representative, deploring underfunding and the need for more professionals to provide mental health services to a needy growing population. "Do you know how the death law is affecting those already suicidal? Depression is an issue with six million older Americans. We can treat this with sufficient professionals and access to clinics for our older adults." He pounded on the podium, saying, "We do not want a wave of suicide to decimate a generation that can be helped to a functional life style."

Julia made notes to add these facts to Simms' future speeches. *Six million... what would it take to turn out depressed voters?*

The therapist concluded with, "And what do you see as the solution, Congressman?"

Simms shot back, "Not the death law, that's for sure. The medical system in general and Medicare in particular seem to be broken, so somewhere between where we are now and what the death law mandates, that's what I see as the solution.

"Did you know that an internist discussing an elderly patient's choices, end-of-life decisions, receives far less compensation from Medicare than a surgeon who implants a device that might prolong life but not necessarily quality of life? And the number of geriatrists is decreasing, while the elderly population is increasing? About twenty percent of our elders die in the hospital, most of them in intensive care. I ask you, do you want your life or your loved ones' lives to end that way?" he asked.

"Overtreatment is costing American taxpayers billions annually. So who gets to decide who needs what? Why can't we pay physicians for taking the time to talk those things through with a family?"

Someone in the audience yelled out, "Just because you can't wipe your own butt anymore shouldn't mean you have to die!"

"That's what I'm trying to fix," Simms shot back. To rousing applause, the congressman exited the stage.

All three town meetings were much the same and everyone was glad when the workday was over. Tina-Maria gave directions to the homeless dinner they would attend the following day. All went home, except Tina-Maria, who stopped off at a friend's house to postpone the barrage she'd get from her parents.

As they drove back to Bradenton Beach, Jake asked Julia, "What was that about waving signs for Simms?"

She explained, "That's a Florida tradition. Volunteers stand on busy street corners and wave their candidates' signs to encourage people to vote. A lot of volunteers love to do it."

"Including our pony-tailed therapist, apparently," laughed Jake.

Thursday morning, they made some preparation for their family holiday dinner and set out mid-morning for the Thanksgiving dinner for the homeless. Hattie had already left with Nate. Henry said, "I love not wearing a coat, hat, gloves, scarf, boots, all that stuff. And I don't have to worry about slipping on ice."

The dinner for the less fortunate community members was as extravagant as for any family Thanksgiving. Carving stations offered slabs of sliced turkey on serving platters and a huge table held beautiful desserts. Servers ladled potatoes, stuffing, sweet potatoes, green beans and gravy onto plates.

Everyone was in a festive mood, and Simms, laughing in his shirtsleeves and tie, carved turkey. Tina-Maria and her camera took full advantage of the photo op. The press were taking pictures, too, so the stop was well worth their time.

They seated Beatriz and Henry at a table near the door and approached the serving area.

"Not yet," said one of the volunteers. "Find a seat and we'll bring you a plate soon."

"We're with Congressman Simms," explained Julia, wondering if her casual outfit rendered her homeless-looking.

"Oh my God, I didn't mean to offend," apologized the woman. "We're busy here and I just reacted to seeing people standing there. So sorry."

"No offense taken," said Julia. "This is really impressive. Where'd you get the food?"

"Churches and businesses pitch in. Some people bring food, some send money and some come work. Did you notice those desserts? Publix always gives us their day-old bread and pastries. Those little key lime tarts are from Chart House restaurant."

"Looks like everything's good here," said Julia to Jake. "Let's leave before Henry spots the key lime tarts."

The family drove back to Bradenton Beach on the beach road. As they drove through St. Armand's Circle, Julia said, "I'd like to shop here. Look at those neat boutiques! Probably no time, though."

The roadway paralleled the Gulf and they reveled in the view of aquamarine water and white sand at New Pass, the palm trees, the beautiful beaches, the egrets and pelicans, all of it. There was little conversation in the car as they drank in the coastal beauty.

Glancing into the back seat, Jake saw Henry enthralled with

the scenery and Beatriz deep in slumber. Taking Julia's hand he said, "I've never had so much to be thankful for."

Her smile assured him she agreed.

As Julia's phone rang, she remarked, "It's not about my parents this time. We know where they are."

"Miss Julia, y'all home?"

"No, we're on the way. What's wrong?"

"Nothing. We all too uptight when the phone rings. The folks here are having their own Thanksgiving dinner and I was thinking about staying and eating if y'all don't need me for awhile. Nate can bring me back in time to help Mist' Henry and Miz Beatriz to bed. Would that put y'all out any, if I stayed awhile longer?"

"Goodness, no, Hattie, we're glad you've found some friends here. You do too much for us, anyway. One request, though, would you bring Nate in to meet us when you get back?"

"Sure thing, Miss Julia. Y'all like him, I promise. We'll be back by seven this evening."

"See you then," Julia said as she rang off. "Hattie's making a place for herself in the community here. I was worried about her being away from her church people and family in DC. Yet one more thing to be thankful for."

Thanksgiving was the first holiday Jake had spent with others in several years and he thoroughly enjoyed it. Julia made turkey and trimmings and Jake whipped up his fancy sweet potato casserole, which was actually quite healthy – mashed sweet potatoes, orange juice, cinnamon and nutmeg, no added sugar or butter – and declared delicious by all. Even Henry, after a mild protest, agreed to pumpkin instead of key lime pie for a change.

Julia and Jake enjoyed their first cooking venture together, with Henry kibitzing from the sidelines and Beatriz in her own quiet world. It was a tranquil scene, one they'd all treasure in the months to come. At the last minute yesterday, Jake had dashed out to get a centerpiece of flowers. Despite grumblings about late requests, the florist produced a lovely arrangement, earning Jake a really big hug from Julia, worth every penny he'd paid to soothe the shop owner.

Nate proved to be as nice as Hattie had said. Unpretentious, neatly dressed in a checked shirt and khaki pants, he chatted easily with Jake, Julia and Henry while Hattie made them all coffee. He knew a lot about plants and other wild things and Henry was delighted to hear about birds in the area. After Nate left, everyone bedded down for a good turkey-tryptophan-induced sleep.

It was the best Thanksgiving anyone could remember in years, even with the unspoken realization it might be the last one they'd all spend together.

CHAPTER 22

Friday, November 25

At breakfast, Julia asked, "Are you getting good stuff at the meetings, Jake?"

"I sure am. I need to file a story that I'll write today. My main goal today is avoiding Black Friday frenzy!"

"Mac's coming to get me about ten and I'll eat lunch with the guys, if everything's okay here," said Henry.

"Mac? Who's Mac? And who are the guys?" Julia questioned in surprise.

"Am I a teenager getting grilled?" Henry laughed as he explained his new friends and the bocce ball group. "They'll take good care of me."

"That's great," said Julia. "Just don't overdo, remember your pills–"

Henry held up his hand. "Okay, Mom, I've got it."

Julia laughed and stopped mothering. "Hattie, does that fit your plans?"

"Yes'm, I'm taking Miz Beatriz walking on the beach again. Okay if I fix Nate a turkey sandwich to eat lunch with us? He doesn't have any turkey since he ate at the church."

"Certainly. Everyone's getting their own life going here. Except Mom, of course," Julia said somberly.

"Your mom's enjoyin' every minute she's outdoors. The time's comin' right soon when she won't be noticin' nothing."

"You're right," Henry said. "We really appreciate what you're doing for her, some quality of life. As is Calvin. Julia, I can't thank you and Jake enough for bringing us. My quality of life's better, too. I intend to enjoy every second of this two weeks."

"I'm glad, Henry. There's a meet-the-candidate social thing after the town meetings. Will you all be okay if Jake and I stay? I should greet our big donors."

"Why not dinner, too?" asked Henry. "Okay with you, Hattie? Julia, did you tell Jake Sunday's your birthday?"

"Why, I hadn't even thought about it. Is that the 27th? Let's see, I'll be…"

"Thirty-nine?" ventured Jake. "Thanks for the tip, Henry. I'll break away for a few minutes today."

"Can I speak to you in private?" asked Henry.

Julia laughed. "I'll give you two conspirators five minutes."

Henry asked Jake to pick up some cash and a card. "I noticed Julia looking around St. Armand's Circle yesterday and thought she could go shop there before we leave."

"I think I'll look for jewelry, maybe a ring. Not engagement," he added hastily.

"You absolutely have my blessing. You are the person we always hoped Julia would find. I hope you know that."

"'Excuse me for interrupting but I was wondering about making a cake."

"Hattie, that'd be wonderful! We haven't done much for Julia's birthday lately. Let's make up for that on Sunday."

Julia came back into the kitchen. "We really need to go, Jake. Everything good here?"

"Yes'm, we're fine."

"See you later today, or maybe in the morning if you kids stay out late," said Henry.

Jake and Julia exited laughing. It'd been quite awhile since they'd been called kids – long time since they'd felt that way, too.

The day passed quickly. Jake pushed his way through Black Friday shoppers and found a lovely blue topaz ring and matching earrings, Julia's birthstone. He chose cards, one funny for them all to sign and one sentimental for him to give her, and got Henry's cash.

He got a bottle of good chardonnay, plus a bottle stopper made of blown glass in a heart shape. Okay, enough mushy.

He caught up with Julia late afternoon for the social at the Ringling mansion, Ca d'Zan, overlooking beautiful Sarasota Bay. They joined others sipping drinks on the terrace, keeping an eye on Simms as he back-slapped and cheek-kissed his way through the well-heeled Floridians.

Jake drifted from group to group while Julia greeted the big donors. No chitchat here about the death law, he noticed. Conversation was about defense spending and tourism, economic enterprises still effective after the slump in the real estate market. Jake heard astounding accounts of the low price of real estate in Florida. It would be a good time to buy, if one were in the buying mood.

Tina-Maria appeared, slurping what was obviously not her first drink. "Oh, God, Julia, I've just got to get out of here."

Julia took her by the elbow and steered her to one side, saying, "Let's talk in the corner so Marcus won't notice."

"I've got to get away. My family's driving me nuts. And I have to tell you something else, Julia." Looking around, she whispered, "I've been seeing someone from another congressional office. We met at a briefing awhile back and something just clicked."

"Can't you tell your family that?"

"Well, he's, um, not exactly free at the moment."

"You mean like married?"

"He's separated but he's technically still married. His wife's a real bitch and we're afraid to be seen together. He'll be divorced in a few months and he's moving to their office in DC. Maybe I'll go to DC and see if I can find a job, too. I've gotta get out of here. My family's trying to make my decisions for me."

"I hear you."

"By the way, he's Jewish and will be divorced and I'm Catholic, so that's another reason I can't take him home to my family."

"Wow, you really know how to engender some drama. At least you're not pregnant, too," joked Julia.

Tina-Maria hesitated a moment and replied, "I'm pretty sure I'm not."

Oh, Lord help us, thought Julia. "You'll get a job on Capitol Hill with your credentials. I'll ask around when I get home, okay? This is still just between us?"

"Oh, thank you, Julia," gushed Tina-Maria. "I feel better than I have in a long time."

"Just between us right now, okay?" cautioned Julia. She saw Marcus' eyes boring into them from across the room and realized a conversation with him wasn't far off.

"Right." Tina-Maria laughed. "Let me go back to work and you and Jake slip out. I don't want to go home, anyway."

Julia tugged at Jake's sleeve and asked quietly if he was ready to leave. "Let's do a little wave and a hasty exit." She gave Marcus a wave and a surreptitious shake of her head to Tina-Maria to remind her to be quiet.

"Someone told me about a restaurant named Mar Vista over on the keys that has great food. Maybe we could run by the condo, change into something more casual, check on the folks and grab a jacket. How's that sound?" asked Jake. "And no politics tonight? I'd like to just hold your hand and watch the water."

Julia gave him a brilliant smile and said, "Perfect. One thing, though – I'm thinking about something I want to talk over with you. Not exactly politics but sorta."

"If it includes me, I'm all for it."

Julia giggled. "Everything includes you. But you'd better not agree until you hear my idea."

Jake looked at her and said, "Julia, I'm so in love with you, I'd agree to most anything right now. But," he added more seriously, "I'll listen."

CHAPTER 23

Jake and Julia returned to the condo and found Henry comforting Hattie.

"What happened?" cried Julia.

"She got a phone call from her sister. A little girl in her neighborhood got caught in gang crossfire and is in the hospital."

"Walking home from Thanksgiving dinner at church! Miss Julia, y'all ever hear such a thing? I gotta get outta there before they kill me, too."

"Oh, Hattie, that's awful. Jake, we'd better stay here tonight."

"No," said Henry. "You go on. We'll take care of Hattie as she takes care of us. Right, Hattie?"

"Truly, Mist' Henry," pulling herself together. "I'm fine, just can't go on living there. But I'll pray on it and God'll tell me what to do."

Jake and Julia were charmed with the Mar Vista's Key West feel. The water visible through the palm trees glowed pink in the setting sun. "Inside or out?" asked the waiter. "I recommend out."

"Isn't it too cool in November?" asked Julia.

"Honey," replied the bearded waiter in t-shirt and baggy shorts, "it's Florida November. We've got these heater thingies, too. Follow me." He advised, "Try the fresh grouper. And the margaritas are always special."

"Thanks, but I think we'll want a wine list instead. Right, Julia?"

"I only drink margaritas in Key West. We said no politics – but did you hear the guy today say he was moving to Key West? The Conch Republic is telling people they won't enforce the death law. He said real estate prices are skyrocketing there."

"Ah, the wine list. Okay, let's splurge a little," Jake said, pointing to a fifty-dollar bottle. The waiter answered, typically, "Very good choice, sir."

"We can split this bill," said Julia. "Can we afford that bottle?"

"This is your early birthday dinner. Let's enjoy, and I can afford it," said Jake, approving the wine the waiter presented. "Tell me your idea."

"Ooh, good wine. What if we left DC?" asked Julia.

"Like retire in a few years?"

"No, sooner. Move here," replied Julia, glancing at him uncertainly.

"Why would we do that? I thought you were settled in DC."

At Jake's dismayed face, Julia said quickly, "Okay, hear me out. It just popped into my head this afternoon so it's still fuzzy thinking."

Julia held up fingers as she itemized. "One, Tina-Maria wants to relocate in DC and we like it here. We could trade jobs. She jokingly already mentioned it. Two, the real estate market's high in DC and low here. I could sell my house, buy here, and bank something toward health care for my parents. We could stay at your apartment in DC when we need to. Three, there's better elder care in Florida. Four—"

"Whoa, woman, that's enough for now. That's a huge idea. I'd live in DC and you here and we'd visit occasionally? I don't like that one bit."

Taking his hand, Julia replied, "No, no, we'd all live here, keep your place in DC and sell mine. We'd live in mine here, yours when we need to go to DC. Could you write your book here?"

"I thought you were handing me my walking papers. I'd have to talk to my editor but it'd probably speed up the book writing. But what about your parents?"

"We'd have to find a Hattie-clone here in Florida, scary thought. Henry keeps saying he's happy here, but I don't know how he'd feel about moving. I don't think Mom'd even notice.

"Right now we have a workable situation and it might be hard to replicate that here," she continued. "This idea sounds totally off the wall but the pieces seem to be coming together almost magically. The Sisters who taught me would say God's leading us to a better place."

"Would you all be leaving friends behind?"

"I don't think Henry's or Mom's ties are very strong anymore," said Julia. "I'd have to find them good doctors. Dr. Robinson at USF is a gerontologist and would know the geriatric physicians."

"And your friends?"

"You, first and foremost. My limited social life is at work, and I'd still be within that team. I'd enjoy a change myself, and we can ill afford to lose Tina-Maria, which we'll do if this plan won't work. What about you? Who'd you be leaving behind?"

"I'm really not attached to anyone. My niece and nephew

both live far away. I have occasional golfing and bar buddies, but no one close. I was leading a pretty solitary life before you came along."

He squeezed her hand. "So I'm saying – hypothetically – this'd probably work for me."

"It's a really big step. Would you want to? We haven't been together very long."

"The death law seems to compress time. It's made me realize life is short. Your parents don't have much time left, but we may not have, either. I'm becoming a 'seize-the-day' guy."

Looking at the view, he said, "How could anyone not want to live here? The traffic, the people, even the poverty seem a little less intense than DC. The beaches are sure a lot better than on the Potomac, and Florida libraries are great!"

Julia agreed. "Life for us will be good wherever and it might be better for Henry here. Financially, for me, too. You and I will *be* Henry before many more years. This idea just makes crazy sense – admittedly, not my usual cautious self talking."

They quieted as the waiter delivered their grilled grouper, black beans and rice. Julia said, "Mmm, I could eat grouper every day!"

After a few minutes, Jake picked up their conversation. "Finding a new house, selling yours, moving would be a major headache."

"That's a real downside. I'd hire a relocation service to pack it all up there and unpack it all here. My house should bring considerably more than something here would cost, giving me some cushion in case Mom or Henry needs an ALF. The only kicker is Hattie. She's so important to us, it almost makes me want to forget the idea. Maybe it's not such a hot plan, after all."

"Wait, don't dump it yet. Far-fetched though it sounds,

Hattie's talked about moving out of her neighborhood. Suppose we could talk her into coming with us, find a place with four bedrooms, one for us, for Hattie, for your parents, and an office for me? I can work anywhere on this book and after that I might just retire and join the bocce-ball boys. Honey, I think this has huge potential."

"Jake," said Julia with a big smile, "my life has turned upside down in such a short while. First I fall in love with you. Then we go on a family vacation, which I thought a thing of the past. Now we're contemplating moving. I feel like I'm on a roller coaster that mostly goes up, but I'm afraid of a long down swoop coming," She took some more sips of her wine thoughtfully.

"Okay, let's go one step at a time," suggested Jake. "What will Simms say?"

"Who knows? He may see it as a way to keep me on staff and let me take care of my family better. Tina-Maria is at least as good a manager as I am, though she'd have to learn Capitol Hill. She'd be so far ahead of anyone else who'd come in, and we're going to lose her if we don't help her get out of Florida.

"Day to day, he'd see little difference. In months to come, the more important work may be in the home district when he runs for bigger office. It might be advantageous for me to be in Florida. I have to talk with him before we can go any further, even before I take the idea back to Tina-Maria – or anybody else."

"Not even Hattie or Henry?"

"I'd hate to get their hopes up if it didn't work out."

"Maybe you should just see how it plays out after you talk to Simms," said Jake. "Do you think this thing with Hattie and Nate is serious?"

"She's only known him a week. It took the two of us, what, two weeks, ten days? We can't condemn hasty romance! I really don't know her that well. She has family in DC but from what she's saying lately, she might not mind leaving."

"And your mother?" asked Jake gently. "She seems the same here as she was in Virginia. The cat seems to be her comfort right now. What about leaving her doctor and familiar surroundings?"

With tears in her eyes, Julia reached for Jake's hand again. "I don't think Mom's going to be with us much longer. Does she seem that way to you?"

"She does seem less responsive now than she did even two weeks ago. Her head is down most of the time and she sleeps a lot."

"That's what I've seen," said Julia sadly. "From what I've read, it looks like she's entering late-stage dementia. I wonder how long Hattie can handle them."

"That's probably a question for Hattie. Couldn't we hire a little more help if necessary? I know you're worried about money, but we could manage a little more. I know we could if you'd let me help."

"You are a very generous person to say that. I don't deserve you."

Jake laughed appreciatively. "I hope you never change your mind on that. We mostly need to keep your mom comfortable and safe and I think we could do that as well here as we can in northern Virginia.

"One other thing, though," he cautioned. "Yours is a two-year job. What if Simms isn't re-elected to another term?"

"Most people don't have even a two-year guarantee. I have good degrees and experience so would find something else. I'm pretty sure Simms is moving on to something bigger, so the question may be whether or not I can stay here. Sadly, Mom and Henry won't be a consideration for where we live after the next few years."

As they enjoyed their fish and beans, Jake said, "We have some latitude of time to think this over."

As if on cue, Julia's phone sounded and she feared the worst as always. Checking the display, she said, "Hello, Congressman, how did the rest of the party go?"

"Missy, you and me need to talk. Something's going on and I want to know what. Breakfast, eight o'clock, that little place where you sit outside and walk out onto the beach. Know which one?"

"Yes," Julia replied, wishing for the umpteenth time the congressman had some family of his own to keep him occupied. Long-divorced with adult children scattered around the country, he had little regard for his staff's time. "I know which one. But don't worry, there's no crisis that'll interfere with your plans."

"Best there not be," he growled as he hung up.

"I guess you heard that," said Julia ruefully. "There went our latitude of time. No sleeping-in tomorrow. I hope Hattie can handle things."

"Hattie and *I* can handle things," Jake emphasized. "Hopefully we can have the rest of the weekend, especially with Sunday your birthday."

"Oh lord, I'd forgotten that again! I'm getting too old for birthdays. But since you said this is an early birthday dinner, could we have an after-dinner drink? I'd just like to sit here a little longer."

"Certainly, sweetheart. I'll just have a little more wine while you have a...?"

"Drambuie, please. That's my after-dinner drink of choice, up, in a snifter. But only one!"

"It's your birthday dinner, plus it fits my philosophy of grab whatever time there is," said Jake as he signaled their waiter. "But I'll drive home, okay?"

"Thanks. How much time would you need to be in DC?"

"I've got a few months' leeway right now. I could affiliate with Kidd-Rudman here, maybe Tampa or Orlando. I'd have to be able to work in a home office here in Florida."

"That shouldn't be a problem. Hattie or someone else will care for Mom and Henry, or else we'll have to find an ALF. You'd have to lay down some ground rules for Henry, though."

"Maybe not. He seems pretty well socialized here. Who knows, he might even find a girlfriend. Oops, didn't mean to bring up a bad subject."

"I've thought about that," mused Julia. "It'd be hard in a way, but he's been a wonderful husband to Mom. If there's some happiness left for him, he's sure earned it. Whatever the case, I'm committed to taking care of Henry."

"How's your Drambuie? Can I taste?" Julia's big smile gave him his answer. "Oh, that's good. Let's get a bottle for deck-sipping later. Do you know how cost of living compares between here and DC?"

"It's cheaper to live here. Plus we'd eliminate the cost of commuting. Not to sound too independent, but I'd buy our place here and be sole owner, or owner with Henry. You and I'd each have our place and it's nice and tidy that way."

Jake wondered if there was a hidden message, but it did make sense to keep things simpler.

"I'd want you to help decide what, where, all those details, of course," she said. "The way I see it, the DC one would be both of ours and the FL one would be, too, just not in both our names. Actually, I know married people who keep their property that way, too."

"That makes sense," agreed Jake. "I think food is slightly cheaper here because so much of it is produced locally. I know eating out can be more economical because so many retirees live here on a fixed income. Do you know what the state bird of Florida is?"

"Egret? Flamingo? Pelican?" guessed Julia.

Jake deadpanned, "No, the Early Bird. Haven't you seen all those signs about Early Bird specials?"

"Ha! I love shopping in thrift shops and second-hand stores. Or we could buy something already furnished and sell the furniture in my house."

"Some people at the town meetings tell me health care for seniors is almost an assembly line thing, with medical and insurance procedures streamlined for people who have trouble keeping up with details. You'd have medical personnel who know how to handle an aging population and take care of the paperwork."

"We'd have cost of travel back to DC," said Julia. "We could take the autotrain and have our car when we get there. Those little roomettes are pretty cozy."

"Yeah, right," said Jake drily. "Have you ever slept in one? Course it'd be a lot better with you. There's good plane service between Tampa and DC, and from Sarasota too. Your office might cover some of your travel and with a place to stay, the cost wouldn't be too bad. The time may come when there's just us two and we want to move back to DC."

"I'd thought of that. I hope I wouldn't take a financial bath here, but hopefully the market will come back enough by then. And maybe we have a few years left with Henry. Actually, you know, we still have Henry's car so we could leave one car in DC if we wanted to."

"Big decisions looming," offered Jake as he paid the check and helped Julia off her tall stool.

They were surprised to see living room lights ablaze as they pulled into the condo parking lot. "Oh, God, I hope everything's okay," said Julia.

Henry greeted them as they walked through the door with, "How was your dinner? Both our leftovers and Jeopardy were good." Speaking loudly, he said, "Can we sit on the deck a few minutes before we go to bed?"

"Sure," replied Julia, mystified as he put a finger to his lips to indicate silence, gestured toward the deck and waved at Hattie's room. "Let's do that. Anybody want coffee?" There were no takers as they all exited to the deck. Julia slid the glass door shut. "What's up, Henry?"

"I want to talk to you about something without Hattie."

"Not trouble between you two, I hope," ventured Jake.

Henry laughed. "Of course not. But I talked some more to Hattie about where she lives. She's been burglarized twice lately. Nothing much was taken because she has very little of value, but it's scared her a lot. Her neighborhood is terrorized by drug dealers and their clients."

"Yeah, tough area of DC," affirmed Jake.

"She helps us," Henry said, "and we should help her. I think she should move in with us. That would be an advantage for everyone, don't you see?"

Jake and Julia exchanged a glance and Jake nodded at her to go ahead. "Well, that dovetails with what Jake and I have been talking about at dinner. Now don't get too excited until I talk to the congressman about this. What if we all, maybe including Hattie, moved to Florida, sold our house in Virginia, and Jake and I worked between here and DC, keeping his apartment there?"

"Whoa, Nellie, am I hearing you right?" asked Henry. He

almost shouted, "I vote yes! And I got your mom's proxy, so she votes yes, too! Let's go talk to Hattie right now!"

"Let's not," said Jake and Julia in unison.

Jake continued, "Quiet down, Henry. Julia talks to Simms tomorrow morning so we'll know what to say to Hattie, either moving to your – our–house in Falls Church or moving to Florida. That might make a big difference in her decision."

"Yes, of course." Henry subsided. "I'm going to breakfast with the guys tomorrow, a diner where they go Saturdays. They'd know about property values. I'll pick up some of those little real estate magazines."

"Good idea," said Julia.

"I plan to walk down the street tomorrow and just take in the general atmosphere of this place in the winter," Jake said. "Maybe I can talk with an older resident or two for background on the effect of the death law. Julia, can we leave Beatriz and Hattie here alone?"

"Sure. You could drop me off and keep the car. I'm sure Marcus would bring me back."

"No, I'd rather you could make your own getaway. I'll enjoy the walk."

"Okay," said Julia. "We've got a plan. I feel like we're leaving Mom out of this discussion."

"Julia, honey, she *is* out of this discussion," said Henry, shaking his head sadly. "We're losing her, we all know that. The woman we know and love is already gone. I'm going to bed, excuse me," and he shuffled off, wiping his eyes.

Nobody got much sleep that night. Beatriz took an uncharacteristic midnight stroll to the refrigerator, at which Calvin set up a yowl, a cry of alarm to the sleepers. Everyone converged on the kitchen where Beatriz sat, head down, munching on turkey.

They let her finish her mini-meal and shepherded her back to bed, so everyone could settle down to their own private insomnia as they contemplated changes in their lives.

CHAPTER 24

Saturday, November 26

Anna Maria Island Beach Café was Julia's favorite breakfast place anywhere. The food was good and the view spectacular. Twice she'd seen a flock of parakeets on the beach and several times she'd observed people grouped in a circle of chairs on the sand. Her waiter told her it was an early-morning Alcoholics Anonymous meeting and she thought the setting would enhance one's serenity.

She liked sitting outside under the umbrella eating and watching the waves. After meeting Marcus, maybe she'd step through the gate in the low wall and walk on the wide white beach. A solitary stroll might help her think things through before she got back to her family.

Driving into the sparsely populated parking lot, she wondered how crowded it got during the high season. *If everything aligns, I might know that answer myself.* Marcus' car was already there.

"'Bout time, missy, where you been?" Simms asked as he contemplated his first stack of all-you-can eat pancakes. "I didn't get you anything because I didn't know what you'd want."

"Hi, Marcus," responded Julia. "I'll get some coffee and a sausage biscuit and be right back."

"Good," grunted Simms around a mouthful of pancakes and syrup, "'cause we got stuff to talk about."

Julia hoped the coffee was strong because she knew she'd need the fortification – too early for a beer for Dutch courage, or she'd be joining the early-morning AA group. Waiting for her biscuit to be delivered from the kitchen, she began, "It's really beautiful here, isn't it, Marcus?"

"Yeah," he allowed, "but we're not here to look at the view. Tell me what the Sam hell's going on."

"Tina-Maria's having some problems—"

Simms interrupted with, "Tina-Maria's always got problems. Her life's a soap opera. I don't need to hear about personal problems. That just complicates a working relationship."

"Let me explain, okay? You need to hear this because if something doesn't work out, we'll lose her. She wants to move to DC and get away from her family. They and her wanna-be-fiancé are driving her crazy." Julia decided to omit Tina-Maria's current romantic reason to be in DC.

"That'd be a loss. Can we make a place for her in our office on Capitol Hill? Last week I thought I'd lost you – now her. What's going on?"

"I'm proposing that Tina-Maria and I switch places. Let me head up the home office and Tina-Maria, Capitol Hill. We don't have budget for an additional person there and I don't think we've got time to train anyone new here. Her assistants are not ready.

"If you run for another office, I might be more valuable here than in DC. You know how my parents' care is a huge factor in my life right now. I think I can take better care of them here.

But I may be able to do you more good here, too." Taking a deep breath, she asked, "So what do you think, Marcus?"

Fixing her with a hard stare, he said, "Eat your biscuit, missy, while I consider this."

Better than an explosion. "I'm getting more coffee. Want some pancakes while I'm up?" Simms absent-mindedly handed her his plate while he gazed over the Gulf, deep in thought.

When she returned, he said, "Missy, that could work. I do know you're trying to do what's best for your family. I didn't mean you when I said that about personal problems. Let's finish our breakfast and then chat on the beach where no one can hear us."

Julia felt as if a load had just been lifted from her shoulders. Now it was all just details, although admittedly some pretty daunting ones. "Thanks, Marcus. I really believe this will be win-win for everyone."

"Win-win, that's what I'm after, especially in the next election. Okay, tell me what you and Tina-Maria have cooked up."

"We haven't talked specifics yet. We're talking maybe the end of January, something like that."

Simms nodded as she continued. "We plan to ask our caregiver to move here with us. She lives in a desperate DC neighborhood and needs to leave. We'd sell my house in Falls Church and keep Jake's apartment on Capitol Hill. With a live-in caregiver, I can come to DC as you need me there."

Simms grunted, which Julia took as approval.

"I think my house will sell well and now's a good time to buy here. I'd bank enough money so I could pay awhile for my mother's care if she has to go into a facility. The logistics are pretty monumental but I don't foresee any big roadblocks."

Simms mopped up the syrup with the last of his pancakes and asked, "What about the two offices?"

"Tina-Maria knows her way around DC. I'll need to get up to speed on things here in the district office but that won't take long. I'd rather deal with constituents than lobbyists for awhile."

"Less chance the lobbyists will steal you here, too. That feller Jake would move with you? Do you have any qualms about Tina-Maria handling things in DC?"

"Yes, Jake and I'll be together, and no, I don't anticipate any problems with Tina-Maria." She was hoping Tina-Maria could keep her love life secret until her sweetie was divorced. "And you could transfer some responsibilities to me here, if you wanted."

"Like what?" asked Simms. "Budget?"

Wishing she'd thought this through first, Julia hedged with, "We'd have to look at that. But budget would seem to be fine to handle here. We could make this office the first-line point of constituent contact, too."

"Would we transfer any other staff?" asked Simms. "This might be a good time to look at reorganizing everything."

"Interesting thought. Let Tina-Maria and me talk about that. We might get some interest, especially if we ask them when they're freezing in DC in January!"

"I didn't say 'invite.' I said 'transfer,'" Simms shot back. "If we're gonna do this, let's do it right. Finished with your biscuit? Let's get more coffee and walk, look for those little green birds."

The November wind whipped in off the Gulf but the morning was beautiful, the hard-packed sand was easy to walk on, and it was warm by Virginia standards. The beach was nearly deserted and the old guy scouring the beach with a metal detector seemed unlikely to eavesdrop on anyone's political plans.

"I know I don't have to tell you this is in strictest confidence, missy. The Senate seat in Florida vacates in two years. I think I've got a decent chance at it if this law thing works out right. If I got elected, we'd have six or maybe twelve years to figure what's next. There's a lot more national coverage for a senator than a representative. People at that bash last night were talking to me about running. We'd have to gear up pretty fast. It could be very good to have you here running things backstage before the whole campaign went public. You up for that?"

"I don't think I'd be the best campaign manager."

"No, I mean run the office here, talk to the constituents, keep the big boys in the party happy, make contacts for contributions, stay out of the limelight until the campaign gets underway. We both know an election isn't won once the campaign goes public, it's the background stuff. That'd be asking a lot of you when you've got problems at home, so tell me now if you think that won't work."

"You do know that people in DC are already talking about your run for Senate?" asked Julia.

"Really?! Of course I know that!" he snorted. "You even briefed me on what to say, remember? But I've got to put my mind on repealing this law or I'll have no political future. I'm gonna ask to be appointed to a committee the repeal could come from. When I go back to DC, I want to hole up with some of the Democratic Caucus leaders and see if they'll agree. I don't want to give up my Armed Services Committee membership, though. That's too important to the Florida economy."

"Not repealing the death law is going to be pretty damn hard on the Florida economy, too."

"When I talk with the caucus leaders, I'll see what their support might be if I run for Senator," Simms said. "Someone has to lead the charge on this death law thing and I'm hoping they'll agree it's me."

A half-hour's walk produced a plan of action they thought would work. His parting words were, "Okay, missy, keep me posted. See you Monday at the office. And happy birthday," he threw back as he sped off.

Julia was astonished that Marcus knew it was her birthday. She wondered who'd briefed him.

Julia returned to the rental condo to find high excitement. Hattie met her at the door with, "Mist' Henry told me what y'all thinkin' and I'm so ready to move outta that hellhole, excuse the cussing. I'm gonna call Sister Green at church here and ask her does anybody have a room to rent. I'm hoping this will work out for y'all the way Mist' Henry says. Uh-oh, he told me not to say anything yet."

Henry came in from the other room, laughing. "Yes, but I figured you'd talk to Julia and I'm pretty sure Julia'd know I couldn't wait to talk to you. What'd the congressman say, Julia?"

"Yeah, you talked to Hattie like I guessed you would. The congressman agreed the plan has merits. I'm going to call Tina-Maria and see what she thinks. Actually, I think I'll meet her for lunch if everything's good here. And Hattie – we want you to live with us if you're willing and be our housekeeper and Henry-and-Bea-keeper. So you don't need to find a room unless you don't like that plan."

"Miss Julia, this like a dream come true. For sure I'll live with y'all. Suits me best, too. Y'all don't have to pay me hardly anything because it won't cost me much to live if I'm here with y'all."

"Of course we'll continue to pay you, Hattie. But let's slow down a little and see where this all goes," cautioned Julia. "Lots of details to work out."

Jake entered the condo and said, "What kind of details? Simms said yes?" He hugged Julia and smiled at the others. "I can see from your face he did. So what's our plan?"

"Hopefully lunch with Tina-Maria," said Julia. "You want to go, too, so we can talk through some details?"

"Certainly. We need to get going on house-hunting while we're here, too."

Henry waved a sheaf of papers and said, "Here's a beginning."

"Didn't you go to breakfast with your buddies?" Julia asked. "When did you do that? Where's Mom?"

"She won't get up," replied Henry. "My friends were very helpful. They told me which realtor is best and good places to live. Actually, one of them wants to sell his place, four bedrooms, three baths, right here in this complex. What do you think of that?!"

"What do you mean Mom won't get up?"

"I guess she's sleepy from her late-night snacking last night. She just kind of rolls over when I nudge her and tell her it's time to get up, and she wouldn't get up for Hattie, either."

"It's mid-morning," said Julia. "I don't like this. I'm going to get her up. Hattie, can you help her shower and dress?"

"Yes'm. It'll be lunchtime when I get her presentable, so I'll fix lunch for anybody here. Y'all go ahead and go."

"Henry, keep doing research, but for goodness' sake, don't call any realtors or make any promises, you hear me?" warned Julia. "We're a long way from buying any property yet. Tina-Maria's still got to agree."

Jake and Julia met Tina-Maria at the Anna Maria Oyster Bar, a bright, sunny place filled with customers but not so noisy they couldn't converse. Tina-Maria jumped at the chance to exchange positions, as Julia had predicted. They hashed out details and agreed to make the change by February 1. Jake invited Tina-Maria to stay at his apartment while she hunted for a place of her own. Glancing around to be sure no one else heard, she confided, "I hope to move in with my guy when his divorce is settled. His wife has investigators snooping around so we have to be discreet."

"It's there if you need it. I plan to be at Julia's most of the time from now on, right, Julia?"

"Absolutely," she replied with a big smile. They polished off their seafood pizza, sharing advice on housing areas in their respective new domains.

Tina-Maria advised them to look for a condo in an established building with a solid resident base. She explained that a brand-new building might offer enticing prices but not have enough owners to carry the expenses of upkeep in the depressed market.

Julia and Jake encouraged Tina-Maria to seek housing in the Capitol Hill area, trading a higher price for significantly less transportation hassle and a safer neighborhood.

They agreed not to say anything to the collective staff until late December. Tina-Maria wanted to get through the holidays before breaking the news to her family.

"What a great beginning to a new year," said Jake as they left. "We have a more pressing issue, though. We have a birthday girl here and I need to know what she wants for her birthday dinner tomorrow."

Julia laughed and said, "Shrimp, of course!"

"Any other requests?"

"Nope, I'll just be surprised. This'll be the best birthday I've spent in awhile."

"Uh-oh, the pressure's on! I'll do my best."

The birthday Sunday dawned clear and sunny and everyone enjoyed coffee on the deck. Henry declared, "Time to get this birthday started. What do you say, Jake?"

"Good idea. I'll get the good stuff." He went inside and brought back the small packages and envelopes. He noticed an extra package and wondered if Henry had shopped while he was out with his friends yesterday.

"Open the one from your mom and me first," urged Henry. "It affects the rest of your day."

"Oh, how generous and thoughtful!" said Julia, removing the cash from the card. Henry's labored handwriting said she was to shop at St. Armand's Circle. "Henry, what a sweet thought. You saw me drooling as we drove through, didn't you?"

"Yes, I did. You deserve something special, Julia. You do so much for us."

Julia kissed the top of his head and hugged her mother, who sat oblivious with her head down, not reacting to Julia's touch. Julia determined to be thankful they were all together and not dwell on unpleasant thoughts today.

Opening Jake's package, she exclaimed, "Oh, Jake, how beautiful! Now I know what color clothes to shop for. Look at this ring!"

"That's your birthstone, blue topaz," he pointed out.

"I've seen brown and smoky topaz but never blue before.

This is just gorgeous. I feel very loved," she said with a big kiss for Jake. "Thanks for what you said in the card, too."

"I won't even ask," said Henry. "Open your other package. Jake, I didn't know you'd gotten something else."

"I didn't," said Jake. "I thought it was from you. It must be from you, Hattie."

"You shouldn't have done that, Hattie," said Julia. "But thank you so much."

"Y'all done so much for me, I want you to know my thanks," said Hattie. "Your mama and I walked to a little shop yesterday while y'all was out."

Julia found a lovely bracelet made of small shells strung on elastic. She slid it onto her wrist and paraded it around for all to see, with a hug for Hattie on the way by. "My first Florida jewelry, Hattie. It'll always remind me of this day. Okay, guys, I'm ready to shop! Hattie, you're not in this. It's your day off."

"Yes'm, Nate's picking me up for church but I can be back after that to tend your folks."

"Indeed not," announced Henry. "Beatriz and I are going shopping, too. That is, if it's okay with you, Julia. I saw benches on the street when we passed through. I'm buying lunch, maybe some carry-out and sit on the beach or a bench."

"I'd love it. This is a wonderful birthday. Hattie, you come back whenever you're ready. It's your day – and evening – off."

"I'll be back in time to help y'all get your bedtime stuff done," said Hattie. "Me and Nate would enjoy doing something and there's an evening service, too. He said he might cook me a little dinner. Now that'd be something, a cooking man! I didn't tell him yet we may be coming back to live. I hope he'll be happy at that."

The birthday was the best one Julia could ever remember.

She was a quick shopper in the boutiques, mindful of her parents resting on the bench outside. At Jake's urging, she bought Florida-casual Tommy Bahama and Fresh Produce clothes for when they returned permanently in a few months. She was accustomed to conservative dressy business attire and it was a pure treat to shop here. And the colors were perfect with her new jewelry.

The birthday dinner was served on the deck, prepared by Jake, who was also a cooking man. Hattie looked happy when she returned later in the evening, reporting that Nate was very glad to hear of their impending residence. Everyone was as contented as they could be, Beatriz' withdrawal notwithstanding. Julia knew tough times were coming but was so thankful she'd had this day.

CHAPTER 25

Wednesday, November 30

Their remaining time in Florida flew by. Julia and Jake attended town meetings where they heard more consternation about the death law and the health care system in general. Jake had one more interview he hoped to conduct, someone he'd heard about when he cruised the coffee shops.

A couple of cups of coffee had accompanied a sad but fascinating conversation with a man named George Witten about how the death law affected a forgotten population. George, in his late seventies, told him about his brother Jeremy, a prisoner in a federal penitentiary who had been convicted of molesting a student in his fifth-grade class. Jeremy had been a beloved teacher in the community where he lived in upstate New York, a somewhat eccentric bachelor who had taught generations of children in the town.

After the trial and conviction, George had relocated to Florida where he wouldn't keep meeting people who knew of his brother's troubles. He thought Jeremy would talk to Jake about prison life and his wish to die. George had promised to call if Jeremy agreed to an interview. Jake had forgotten the conversation in the excitement of Julia's birthday and was surprised to receive a phone call from George, saying his brother had written Jake a letter. They arranged to meet at the same coffee shop on Bradenton Beach where they had met earlier.

Enjoying their coffee, George explained that his younger brother Jeremy had been an inspiring teacher. He took kids on field trips, hosted summer activities, entered their projects into competitions, and inspired hundreds of children to learn. However, there'd always been rumors of unhealthy interest in young boys.

Finally there was a criminal charge, and Jeremy was now in prison for the rest of his life. George had e-mailed Jeremy about Jake's research on the death law and Jeremy had replied in a letter for his brother to give Jake. George handed it over. "Here, I'll get a bagel while you read it."

Jake was astounded that this material had fallen into his lap. He read:

> Dear Jake, My brother thought I should tell you what the prison population thinks of the death law. There are two groups who are concerned: those near 70 who fear they will be executed by the government before they finish their sentences and will never be free again. For some, their attorney saved them from a death and now they are sentenced all over again. They are very hopeless in the face of this law.
>
> The second group includes me: people so heartsick over the crimes they have committed, they want to be put to death. We actually feel hope at maybe escaping the everyday misery of being incarcerated, thinking about things we've done we can never atone for. The death law would shorten my prison sentence. A prayer

in my church asks forgiveness for things done and undone. I can't forgive myself and I don't believe God will forgive me, either. I know those children never will.

I tried to commit suicide before I was taken into custody but a friend found me before the pills had taken effect. Every day I wish she had not checked on me so I could have died then. So I am in a hellhole for the rest of my life. I tried to kill myself here, banging my head on a metal sink, but all I got was one hellacious headache. I won't do that again. God's punishment for me is to keep me alive in this awful place until He calls me home. If the government can speed up God, so much the better.

I went from being a respected teacher to the lowest of the low – I did that to myself and I take full responsibility. Other prisoners hate pedophiles – there, I've named myself properly. I have to protect myself constantly, not always easy for an old man to do among young angry men. I wish someone would just kill me but they don't – they intimidate, harass, and physically hurt me.

The guards turn their backs whenever someone is assaulting me. The chaplain has been no help, either. So here I am, a Vietnam veteran – and you know about the black dog of depression for us vets – a teacher deprived of anything meaningful to do with my life. Thank God my brother has not abandoned me and a few friends write me letters. That's all that keeps me sane – if you can call this sanity. I was used to reading, roaming in nature, doing productive work. Now I have nothing to do and I am nothing. I long for the final nothing of death.

If you can use any of this information in your book, please do. Just don't identify me in any way that will further humiliate my brother.

I am no longer a person. I am a number.

God's peace to you,

#693421, formerly known as Jeremy

Jake looked up from his second reading of the letter to see George regarding him with tears in his eyes. Jake had no idea of what to say and reached over and patted George on the shoulder wordlessly.

George cleared his throat and said huskily, "I hate what he did but I love my brother. Every day I wish him dead, to get him out of that misery. But as far as the death law is concerned... I'm over seventy with my own health problems and I don't personally want to die. If the death law kills my brother, it takes me, too."

Jake sat silently as George continued.

"Couldn't there be some kind of 'hold up your hand if you want to be offed' system? I wish Jeremy could die but I don't want to go with him just yet. What a moral quagmire!"

"I think you just named my book, George, *A Moral Quagmire*. I can't tell you how helpful this has been to me. May I write to your brother?"

"He'd appreciate that. He left his address off the letter because he didn't want you to feel obligated, but I'll give it to you. I'd be much obliged if you'd take the time to write to him."

As he walked back to the condo, Jake could feel this week's Sunday column composing itself in his mind.

CHAPTER 26

Julia and Jake extended their stay in Florida a week, to the delight of Henry and Hattie. Julia observed procedures in the district office, planning revisions for both offices. Clearly one person had to be overall chief of staff for both offices and Marcus appointed Julia.

Julia knew Walter and his wife planned to move to Florida when he retired in a couple of years. Maybe he'd be interested in relocating sooner. Having the communications director in Florida could be advantageous in a campaign.

Real estate was a huge item on Julia's agenda and she and Jake scoured the neighborhoods Henry turned up online. A realtor showed them condos, bungalows and newer homes in subdivisions. Each night the family conferred on neighborhoods, prices and possibilities.

They learned about hurricane-proof construction, flood zones, difficulty getting property insurance, condo fees, and homeowner association solvency. Henry researched properties in Falls Church and estimated their home would sell for about three hundred thousand dollars more than a spacious place in

Florida would cost them. That would give them a comfortable cushion and considerable peace of mind.

The more they searched, the more they appreciated the condo community where they were renting. Henry had talked more with his bocce buddy who wanted to sell. A widower with grown children, the man believed a new, smaller place would improve his outlook on life – if the death law didn't get him first.

The unit was open, airy and in reasonable shape, close to the elevator with a great view of the Gulf. Julia put a contract on the property, contingent on selling their place in Falls Church.

Hattie called it a dream come true, Henry claimed it a new lease on life, and Jake and Julia were too busy to make philosophical pronouncements.

Beatriz slept and Calvin purred.

Julia called Dr. Janet Robinson, the USF gerontologist, to find a physician for her parents. The professor suggested they meet for lunch at a restaurant across the street from her campus. Upon meeting Julia, the professor held out her hand and said, "Call me Janet."

They immediately liked each other, getting acquainted over shrimp po'boys.

"I was at a function at Ca' d'Zan for the congressman recently," said Julia, "beautiful place. We'll enjoy living here but I need to find a doctor for my parents." She briefly described their ailments.

The professor said sympathetically, "No wonder you're so interested in the death law. You're looking for a geriatrist?"

"And probably hospice care for my mother. She's deteriorating rapidly."

"Yes, that's how it happens with dementia sometimes. I'll suggest a doctor with strong ties to hospice. Dr. Trinh is a most compassionate and knowledgeable practitioner. She doesn't over-medicate, but she doesn't let people suffer, either."

"She takes Medicare?"

"Yes, almost everyone does except for a few 'boutique' doctors. Sometimes physicians limit the number of new Medicare patients because Medicare reimbursements are so low, especially for the doctors who practice 'slow medicine.' Did we talk about that when you called me?"

"I'm not sure. Could you define that again, Janet?"

"Just because you *can* do a procedure, doesn't mean you *should*. Dr. Trinh cares for the patient, doesn't just do a procedure just because it's available, if it's not the best thing for the patient," explained Dr. Robinson.

"My partner's doing a book on the death law and that's where I heard that term."

"Oh, I'd love to meet her," said Dr. Robinson. "When you move here, let's all get together."

"Yes, but it's a 'he' partner, not a 'she,'" Julia said, laughing.

"Sorry, how stereotypic of me! I'd love to meet *him*. And the congressman has that keynote date on his calendar, right?"

Julia assured her the date was reserved. When she got in the car she called Dr. Trinh's office and set up an introductory appointment.

The next morning as Julia, Jake, Henry and Beatriz set out for their doctor's appointment, Henry grumbled a little at missing bocce ball and his friends but agreed they needed to complete this task. Dr. Trinh's office was in a doctors' strip mall near the Manatee Memorial Hospital. They were called in just a few minutes.

"Would you come in, too, Jake?" asked Julia.

"Sure," he replied.

The nurse said, "Hello, I'm Angie. We have the whole family here, great! Who's who?"

Henry replied, "We're the modern American family. My wife, her mother," pointing to each. "Julia's my stepdaughter. He's Julia's partner. We are a family, living together and our caregiver lives with us."

"Okay, got it," said the nurse, typing information into the computer.

"And this is an introductory visit? Is anyone actually sick?" asked Angie.

"That's correct, it's an introductory visit, although my mom has dementia, as you can see," said Julia. "We're moving here and need to establish a doctor. You're taking new Medicare patients?"

"Yes, thanks to the death law," said Angie.

"How's that?" asked Julia. "I thought you'd have more patients, trying to keep healthy."

"We thought so, too, but it's just the opposite. Some call to cancel, others just don't show up. We think seniors are reluctant to be on anyone's patient roster. Yes, we're definitely taking new patients."

As the nurse bustled out, Jake said, "I'm afraid this will reinforce those who tout the death law as money-saving. There'd be a whopping savings in tax dollars if the majority of seniors didn't use Medicare."

"Yes," agreed Julia, "if everyone stopped going to the doctor and taking their medicine, it'd be manslaughter on a large scale."

His head down, Henry said, "Maybe everyone would be better off if I stopped going to the doctor and taking my meds. My life is pretty useless."

Julia snapped, "Get a grip, Henry. I know things are tough for you but this is no time for self-pity. You know how much you mean to us. If we have to, we'll smuggle you to Cuba, and we must have relatives in Mexico. But I just can't bear to hear any more talk like that."

Ouch, thought Jake. *The stress of all this is really getting to Julia. I've never heard her talk like that before. Well, maybe the day of the cat...*

Henry straightened in his chair and, to Jake's surprise, turned a beaming smile on Julia. "Thanks, daughter, I guess that's what I needed. Besides, the bocce ball group would miss me."

Julia was near tears as she apologized. "That came out harsher than I meant, Dad. I'm just so worried about Mom. Look at her."

Beatriz sat slumped on her chair, eyes open, head down, oblivious. She hadn't reacted to Julia's outburst or Henry's sadness.

A slim middle-aged Asian woman walked in, holding out her hand with a big smile. "Hello, I am Dr. Trinh." Sitting down at the computer, she said, "Let me see who's here. You are Henry and this is your wife Beatriz, right? And Julia. And you are who, sir?"

Jake said, "I'm Julia's partner. Also I'm a journalist doing an investigative study of the death law."

"Oh, good, somebody needs to!" exclaimed Dr. Trinh. Turning to Henry, she said, "Tell me about your medical history and your situation right now."

Dr. Trinh listened intently and typed notes into the computer as Henry related his story. After he had detailed symptoms and medications, she appraised him a minute or two and asked, "Are you fairly stable right now?"

"Yes, I am. The idea of moving to Florida feels like a new life for me."

Facing Beatriz, Dr. Trinh said gently to Henry, "Tell me about your wife." Dr. Trinh noted that Beatriz did not respond as Henry took her hand, though she did not seem asleep.

"My wife has left us, as you can see." He detailed Beatriz's worsening condition, concluding with, "Lately she is like you see her, a pretty sudden decline in the past few weeks."

Julia struggled with composure as Henry described her mother's recent changes. Listening to Henry, she was forced to admit just how deeply her mother had sunk into dementia.

Dr. Trinh reached over and patted Julia's hand. "This is so hard. My own mother died recently of this disease. Would you add anything to what Henry has described?"

Swallowing hard, gripping Jake's hand, Julia replied, "No, Henry said it all. Will you take us as patients?"

"Of course I will," Dr. Trinh responded. "Your move may be very well timed. We in Florida know how to take care of our seniors."

Turning to Jake, she added, "Do you know what effect the death law will have on Florida? Everyone thinks of Mickey Mouse, but all of Florida is Disneyworld to senior citizens. Our health care is among the best in America at providing quality of life for elders. Now we may no longer have that opportunity. We who work here would lose a lot, but those who moved here to enjoy their quiet years would lose everything."

The doctor asked Julia, "Are you living here now? Or when will you relocate?"

"We live in Virginia. We plan to be here in a month or two."

Dr. Trinh weighed her words before saying, "From what you tell me, I think you should enjoy the holidays with your mother but be thinking about her care in Florida. Your description indicates deep dementia. When you get here, we must discuss options for care right away. That is, if she comes back with you.

"We will be with you every step of the way." Rising, the doctor once again shook hands with everyone, including taking Beatriz's limp hand. "I am pleased to be your physician when you move here. All of you," she emphasized.

A subdued group exited the doctor's office. Henry finally broke the silence with, "Let's go home and talk about what the doctor just said. We can't put off that discussion any longer."

When they returned to the condo, Hattie saw no one was happy. "That doctor not gonna work out, huh?"

"No, Dr. Trinh was great. We had a distressing talk about what may be happening next," explained Henry. "Could you take Beatriz in our bedroom for a little while? We'll fill you in later."

"Sure," replied Hattie. "Come on, Miz Beatriz, let's us go find that kitty."

As they shuffled off, Henry said, "I don't think Beatriz can understand what we're talking about, but just seems wrong to discuss it with her sitting here."

"I agree," said Julia. "That's most perceptive and kind of you, Dad."

Jake said, "I'll excuse myself now, too."

"Please stay," pleaded Julia. "I think we have to look at all our plans. I don't see how we can move when Mom's in such an indefinite state."

"Honey, that was my first thought, too," Henry said, "just put everything on hold and see what happens. But she could be this way for years. Do we just wait? I don't think so. And I'm not just saying that because I want to move to Florida. I mean it for all of us."

"Things are so precarious, though, Henry. What if we're in the middle of selling the house and moving and Mom dies?"

"Yes, what if?" asked Henry. "We'd postpone everything for a week, have a funeral, and get on with it."

"That sounds so callous. Would we be able to – or should we – do that?"

Jake offered, "Want to talk through different scenarios?"

"Yes," replied both Henry and Julia.

"One is Beatriz continues as she is now, we move here, and get her settled with a new doctor. Then you decide whether she stays at home or goes to an ALF," Jake said.

"Another scenario would be that she is 'actively dying,' as they say, somewhere between how she is now and having actually passed. In that case, we could bring her here, a medical transport maybe, or someone could stay behind in my apartment with her. Or we could let others handle the move and just all stay in DC."

"I guess that could work," said Julia.

"The third possibility is she passes in the next month or two before we move. As Henry suggested, we change our timeline, pay our respects to Beatriz, and move on, quite literally."

"I'm not sure I could handle that," said Julia. "Everything would change at once: losing my mother, moving to a new place, starting a new job. I just don't know if I have that much emotional stamina."

Henry took Julia's hand. "Honey, we've already lost her. We've grieved for years now. One thing we'll feel is relief. We won't have to worry about the death law taking her from us and she won't be living the way she is now. Any way you look at it, her death'll be hard. But you'll still have Jake and me."

Jake said, "This seems the time to discuss something else.

When Beatriz no longer needs Hattie, will Hattie still live with you?"

"I guess that's my question to answer," said Henry. "I'm not sure how much longer I can stay on my own all day. It's a real comfort to have Hattie around if I fall or get sick or just get hungry. I think she should be with us as long as there are at least three of us in the family."

Hattie came back into the living room. "Miz Beatriz asleep in the bed, holding onto the kitty."

"Okay, Hattie, thanks. Please sit down and let us fill you in," said Julia. "The doctor thinks Mom is declining quickly, something we've all observed, too. Dr. Trinh suggested we prepare ourselves for Mom's death, probably sooner rather than later. We're talking about how that affects us as a family."

"Miss Julia, I'm so sorry to hear that. Don't give me a thought. If y'all don't need me, I can find other work here with no trouble. There's a lot of other old folks around here, 'scuse me for calling y'all old, Mist' Henry."

"I *am* old. What we're saying is I'd need you, even if Beatriz is gone," said Henry. "Would you stay on with us, to take care of me?"

"Course I would, y'all know that, Mist' Henry. You and Mist' Jake be going back to DC some, that right, Miss Julia?"

"Yes, fairly often," replied Julia. "So that's settled, then. I guess we have the beginnings of a plan. I always feel better when I've got a plan."

"Miss Julia, sometimes God got the plan and we here on earth don't rightly see it," murmured Hattie softly.

Julia and Jake looked down at the floor and Henry somberly nodded.

"One more thing," said Henry. "I think I should call Anna

and ask about hospice services. Maybe we should enroll Beatriz when we get home."

"Excellent idea," said Julia, rising to her feet. "Well, hard as it is, I've got to pull myself together and go to work for awhile. What about you, Jake?"

"If you don't mind, I'd like to go, too, and visit that volunteer center near your office. I hate for you to be alone right now, and Henry's got his friends and Hattie, so he'll have company."

"Thank you, Jake," said Julia.

Hattie added, "Miss Julia, y'all go on to the office while I gather up things here and clean for our leaving tomorrow."

"Thanks, Hattie. I'll pack my clothes when I get back. Do we have food for dinner, or should we pick something up on the way back?"

"We're good. Not sure just what, but I know there's plenty for tonight and a lunch for on the road."

Henry appeared to be holding himself together reasonably well. "I'm going to lunch to say goodbye to the guys."

"Good idea," said Julia.

Julia surveyed the district office, soon to become her own domain. She liked parking right outside the spacious suite of offices located in a small strip mall in Sarasota. She liked the palm trees swaying in the breeze and the more casual clothing for warmer weather. She wore a pair of beige slacks and a turquoise tank top with a long-sleeved flowered shirt over it, nothing like her DC apparel. Her new blue topaz jewelry added sophistication to the chic Florida look.

At least twice the size of the suite on Capitol Hill, this office had fewer employees. Most staff members shared workspace but the whole place was quieter and less frenetic than DC. Julia and Jake entered Tina-Maria's private office, greeting her as Julia appraised the room to see how she would personalize it. An interior door connected the chief aide's office with the congressman's, which doubled as a conference room.

Jake said hello to Tina-Maria and kissed Julia goodbye as he left, agreeing to meet the two of them for lunch.

Julia said, "This feels almost overwhelming to plan, doesn't it, Tina-Maria? I wish I knew more about what goes on here and you were more familiar with the DC routine."

Noting Julia's drawn look, Tina-Maria said, "That's not your usual optimism. Are your folks okay?"

"No, they're not," said Julia, and with uncharacteristic tears, explained her mother's situation to Tina-Maria. Afterwards she wiped her eyes and felt better for having unburdened herself. With Henry, she tried to keep a stiff upper lip.

They discussed what they needed to do, their timeline, and who they needed in each office. Julia did not betray Simms' confidential aspirations, but the savvy Tina-Maria understood the subtext of their conversation. They discussed possible staff member swaps.

As they worked through the morning, both women became excited about their new opportunities. Julia's natural optimism resurfaced as she realized the opportunities spreading out before her.

Jake found the volunteer center alive with activity.

"Sign in right here and we'll be with you shortly. We're

swamped this morning," the chunky, blue-haired, brightly clad none-too-young receptionist apologized. "Every senior in Florida has decided the easiest way to be useful is to volunteer."

"Really," exclaimed Jake. "That's wonderful, so many people wanting to help."

"Not sure if it's wanting to help or wanting to live. The death law, you know," confided the woman. "Look around. Do all these geezers look like they're capable of helping others?"

Jake glanced around. There were many robust, animated seniors in the room while others were on walkers or in wheelchairs. Some sat immobile with their heads down, reminiscent of Beatriz. A few had attendants sitting beside them.

Sitting in a corner of the waiting room for half an hour was most instructive for Jake. People chatted amiably as they waited their turn to be interviewed for volunteer postings. The coffee pot and a big box of cookies contributed to everyone's good nature.

The man sitting in the next chair leaned over and said, "Lots of old farts here, aren't there?"

Jake replied, "It's wonderful so many people want to volunteer."

The man snorted. "Well, some of us want to help and some of us just want to be on the books if anyone ever asks."

"On the books?" asked Jake.

"If the government comes poking around wondering if you're still productive, it'd be good to show that we volunteer. Just puttering around the house all day might not be good enough for them government fellers who come sniffing around."

"Sniffing around," echoed Jake.

"Yeah, you know. The death law says you gotta be useful,

and sooner or later they'll send somebody sniffing around. Like the FBI or the welfare people."

Well, thought Jake, *here's some black humor for my column. The social-worker-FBI-sniffer agency.*

"So you're here to get on the books? Kind of like looking for a job with the employment service if you're getting unemployment payments?"

"No, not me," said the man. "I've been planning to do something useful for awhile. Like the death law kinda kicked my butt, know what I mean? Mostly I just sit around and watch ESPN and I could still be doing something useful. A lot of folks need help. I ain't got much money, but I got plenty of time. So it kinda made me think maybe I should get my ass in gear and do something to help somebody, ya know?"

"Everybody seems pretty patient here," observed Jake, looking around.

"Well, why not?" asked his new friend. "We ain't got a whole lot else to do and they're giving us cookies and coffee. You want to see this room empty out, let 'em run out of cookies. I was at a bank meeting one time down here in Florida and they run out of cookies and everybody just got up and left, while the bank man was still talking. No cookies, no audience, that's the Florida way! Say, ain't you a little young to be here?"

As Jake was deciding how to answer, the man said, "Hey, they just called my name. Nice talking with you. You'd better get you a cookie before they're all gone."

Jake found plenty to take notes on as he sat in the convivial waiting room. Finally he heard "Mr. Jordan?" and he followed the woman with the clipboard.

"I'm Geraldine Linkous," she said as they entered her cubicle. "What brings you here today?"

Jake quickly explained his line of research and Geraldine relaxed as she realized she had a breather between actual clients.

Geraldine summarized the work of the volunteer center, run on grant money shared by several cooperating agencies. Three paid employees and many volunteers served as receptionists, interviewers, fund-raisers, outreach workers, and clerical assistants.

Geraldine said she was a paid employee with a degree in counseling. "Florida has a wealth of well educated, financially secure, bored retirees who do very high-level service as volunteers. This agency's mission is to match people with appropriate volunteer sites."

"And you're able to place everyone?" asked Jake.

"Used to be 'yes.' We're now getting people who have trouble taking care of themselves, much less helping others. It's this law thing, trying to show they're productive. Most people really want to help others. They just hadn't taken action without the push of the death law. So we're swamped right now, but it's a good problem. We'll have better staffed libraries, schools, feeding kitchens, hospitals, museums, and assisted living facilities because volunteers provide so much unpaid manpower here."

"So the death law has had a good effect on volunteerism?"

"You bet." Geraldine nodded enthusiastically. "Anything else I can tell you? I need to keep on interviewing – or else throw out the cookies so they'll all go home!"

PART THREE

A New Beginning

CHAPTER 27

Tuesday, December 6

Everyone and everything got packed into the car early Tuesday morning. A much more subdued group journeyed home than had driven down.

Julia kept thinking about her time with her mother ending. Beatriz was physically present but recognized no one and sometimes appeared not even to notice Calvin on her lap. Julia thought, *In many ways my life is a new beginning. But in this most basic way, it's ending.* She felt the excitement of a new job in a new place and most of all, a new love in her life, but also a profound sadness at the loss of her mother. She feared Henry's time with them was limited, too. She worried about how their intended move would affect Jake's work and his tentative balance with his editor.

Wednesday, December 7

Pearl Harbor Day, thought Henry as Julia pulled into their driveway in Falls Church. *Wonder if we're headed toward catastrophe, too.*

Once everybody was in the house, Hattie said, "When y'all

okay, I'm going home and start talking to the people I need to plan with."

"I need to get some groceries, but Beatriz and Henry can stay alone that long," said Julia. "We're good."

"I'll stay while y'all do that, get Miz Beatrice and Mist' Henry settled, unpack their stuff and start some laundry. By then y'all be back and I'll head home and be here in the morning, as usual."

"Jake, are you staying here or going on into DC?" asked Julia.

"I'll stay tonight and go in tomorrow. Are you going to work in the morning?"

"Good, I'd hoped you'd stay. I'll go to work later in the morning, depending on when we can see the social worker and maybe the doctor. We have to figure out next steps with Mom."

Henry shuffled back into the living room. "I called Anna and she's meeting with me at ten in the morning. She's coming here. Those hospice workers are unbelievable. Who else wants to meet with her?"

"Of course I'll be here, Henry. We've got to figure this out together," snapped the road-weary Julia.

"No offense intended," answered Henry hastily. "I think we need to make some plans fast, though. Hattie's putting Beatriz to bed, even though it's only late afternoon. We can't get her to wake up." Henry shook his head sadly and repressed tears.

"Oh, Henry, you never mean to give offense. I'm so sorry I snapped at you. I'm just tired and frustrated. Jake, let's get some groceries and I'll come back in a better mood."

"Bring back a pizza?" asked Henry hopefully.

"Sure, but you order it and have it delivered," replied Jake, reaching for his billfold.

"I don't want your money," growled Henry. "I can still do that much!"

Jake said, "Come on, honey. Let's get a few things done and maybe a pizza will put us all in a little better mood. I'll drive and you rest. No anchovies, Henry!"

Anna Malotti pulled up in her little red Fiat just before ten o'clock Thursday morning. She had guessed this conversation was coming soon, after talking with Henry a few weeks ago. Feeling the December chill, Anna wished she knew friends in Florida to visit.

Julia opened the door and greeted her. "We met when I was with Mom and Henry at the hospital. I really appreciate your meeting with us so soon."

With a hug for Henry who had rolled into the living room, Anna answered, "Henry's phone call yesterday sounded like this meeting needed to be a priority. Where's Beatriz this morning?"

"We couldn't get her up," said Henry. "She opened her eyes but wouldn't sit up. It just didn't seem worth the effort to haul her out of bed. Hattie, our caregiver, will be here later this morning and we'll try again then. Our other family member, Jake – you met him the other day – has already gone to work."

"Please tell me as much as you can about Beatriz's current condition," said Anna.

Julia and Henry alternately gave information about Beatriz's past few weeks. Julia found it easier to talk about her mother than she had thought it would be. She was already beginning to distance herself a little from her emotions, knowing that the end was near.

Henry, however, was a basket case. He finally broke down and wept openly as they described their situation.

Tactfully giving him a few minutes to compose himself, Anna turned to Julia and said, "Could we go see your mother?"

Julia led the way down the hall to her parents' bedroom. Beatriz appeared to be in deep slumber, not responding to Anna's gentle calls to her. Calvin glared fiercely from his guard position beside his mistress.

They returned to the living room to a moderately composed Henry. Anna asked, "Do you plan for Beatriz to remain at home if her condition continues as it is now?"

Looking to Henry for agreement, Julia said, "As long as we can manage. Jake and I are here at night and Hattie, during the day. Henry rarely leaves Mom."

"And you think your caregiver can manage the personal care required for a patient who's entirely confined to her bed?"

Henry and Julia answered almost in unison an emphatic, "Yes."

Henry said, "Hattie is the kindest, most competent person we could possibly have. I believe she would do a better job than anyone in an assisted living facility, don't you, Julia?"

"Beatriz would have twenty-four-hour attendants in an ALF. How about the hours when Hattie's not here?" Anna reminded them.

"We're here and I don't anticipate that being a problem," answered Julia. "And we've talked to Hattie about moving in with us full-time."

That conversation led to more talk about future plans and the impending move to Florida, including Hattie.

"Okay," said Anna. "You've obviously thought a lot about this. I fear Beatriz won't be going with you to Florida in two months."

Henry nodded his head sadly. "That's what our new doctor in Florida implied, too. So, what do we need to do?"

Anna explained the procedures for acceptance into hospice care and offered to contact Dr. Singh and take care of the paperwork. She explained the services of hospice and they scheduled a visit for a hospice nurse the following Monday.

"And how about you, Henry, my friend?" asked Anna gently. "And you, Julia? Hospice cares for families, too, you know."

Julia and Henry looked at each other, each willing the other to speak first.

"I'm together enough right now," said Julia. "There's so much else going on that I can distract myself from time to time as I need to. Congress is in recess so that gives me some latitude of time at work. I worry about you, though, Henry."

Henry replied steadily, "Julia, I knew this was coming and I think I'm as mentally prepared for it as possible. I'm sad but okay."

Placing her hand on his arm, Anna asked gently, "Henry, have you talked to your priest?"

"No, but I'll call her," he answered, wiping tears from his face.

"And Julia," said Anna," you said you were going to put your house on the market. How will having your mother bed-ridden affect showing the house?"

"Oh, God, I hadn't even thought about that. I haven't talked to a realtor yet – we just got home yesterday. I don't see how we can show a house with a person dying in it."

They heard a key in the lock and the front door opened to admit Hattie.

"Excuse me, folks, I didn't mean to barge in. I can take a little walk and come back later."

"You are absolutely not barging in," said Henry. "We should include you in this conversation, anyway. Anna, Hattie."

The two women shook hands and Hattie took off her coat and hat and sat down with them.

"You brought a suitcase, Hattie?" asked Julia.

"Yes'm, figured I might need to be staying here some. Miz Beatriz didn't look good at all when I left yesterday and I thought y'all might need me here for longer. If you don't, I'll just leave the case and go on back home tonight."

Anna had just learned all she needed to know about Hattie.

As Julia drove to work at noon, she admitted to herself that she was not nearly as calm about her mother's dying as she had professed to Henry and Anna. She decided the office could wait until after she had talked to Jake. Grateful to hear his voice when she called, she asked, "Would you have time for lunch? I'm a little shaken after our visit with the hospice social worker this morning and just need to be with you for a little while."

"Oh, honey, I wish I'd stayed until after the meeting. I'm at home, and I was thinking this morning, you've not yet been to my condo. Why don't you come here and I'll pick us up a sandwich for lunch before you get here?"

"Thanks, that's just what I need." Julia sniffled. "I didn't know I'd be this upset."

Jake flew into a whirlwind readying his apartment for her visit. He picked up newspapers, cleaned up the remains of his breakfast, and gave the bathrooms a quick swish. He quickly hung up the clothes he'd unpacked and tidied the mail stack. He looked around, decided that would have to do for short notice, and hoped it looked okay for a bachelor's place.

When Julia called again, he met her at the visitors' parking to escort her upstairs to his condo. "I am so glad to see you," she said as she stepped into his embrace. She recounted the morning's conversation as they walked up the stairs.

Looking around as they entered the apartment, she said in surprise, "This place is beautiful! I thought you'd have some leather furniture, a velvet painting or two, and a huge TV, a typical bachelor pad."

She surveyed his tasteful décor, understated beige walls with a darker painted accent wall. The furniture was modern and minimal in design. Bright oil and acrylic original paintings glowed against their neutral background. A few small artifacts contributed to the overall impression of refined comfort. Floor-to-ceiling bookcases held hundreds of books and CD's and large windows offered a view of the Capitol and other city landmarks.

"I like flea markets and second-hand stores, too," explained Jake. "Decorating is kind of a hobby of mine. Most of the paintings are by local artists, mostly from the Eastern Market here on Capitol Hill. I buy too many books, though."

"The more I learn about you, the more I love you," declared Julia. "I knew you were well read, darling, but had no idea that you lived in such a beautiful place. And you did this all yourself?"

"Yep, just me. Of course, you can change it any way you want."

"I'll love living here part of the time. We may look for reasons to be in DC."

"I doubt we'll have to look very hard," said Jake ruefully. "I'm pretty sure our bosses will provide plenty of reasons."

"Seeing this lifts my spirits, knowing we're going to have part of our future here, too," said Julia.

As they ate their sandwiches, they discussed contingencies for the immediate future. As they talked about putting the house in Falls Church on the real estate market, Julia despaired of selling it while the house sheltered her dying mother. And they couldn't buy the new Florida condo until they had sold the property in Falls Church.

Holding her hand, Jake asked, "Are you worried about your mom or just about the whole thing?"

"I'm focusing on the house," Julia said tearfully, "but actually, I guess it's the whole situation with Mom, the move, all of it. You know, for a journalist you're a pretty good counselor, Mr. Jordan."

"And us," Jake added quietly. "We're pretty new, too."

At that, Julia smiled through her sadness and said, "That's the one part I'm not worried about."

"Good," he answered, pulling her in for a long kiss.

Separating finally, Julia said shakily, "If that's an invitation, the answer is yes, but I really have to get to the office now. They were expecting me an hour or so ago. Can we resume this mood later?"

Jake drew back reluctantly. "Yes, definitely. I need to go to the office, too.

CHAPTER 28

Friday, December 9

At breakfast, Henry said to Jake, "I have a huge favor to ask. Could you take me to meet with our priest this morning? I could get a taxi, but I thought you might get some information you could use for your book."

"I'm going to the office later today, but sure, I'd like to hear what he has to say about the death law."

"Actually, it's a she. Unfortunately, death is what this conversation will be about. The death law fits right in. I'll be ready as soon as Hattie gets here. You two lovebirds say goodbye while I give Beatriz a kiss."

Julia said sadly after Henry left, "It doesn't seem fair. Their life together is ending just as ours is starting."

"If anyone guaranteed us the years they've had, I'd grab it in a heartbeat, sweetheart. All we have is today and we'd better enjoy it."

Julia gave him a heartfelt kiss and began the morning rat-race to her office, waving to Hattie who was walking up the street.

As they drove, Henry said, "Let me tell you about our church. Beatriz was Roman Catholic and I was Presbyterian.

We wanted to be married in a religious ceremony, but neither of those churches seemed to fit."

"How'd you find this church?"

"We tried the Episcopal church and just loved it – enough ritual to satisfy Beatriz and I like the litany and the music. Most of the sermons are on social action issues. We were married by an Episcopal priest and found St. Luke's when we moved here."

"Is Julia a church-goer?" asked Jake.

"Sometimes but usually she's so wrapped up in her work, she doesn't do much else. She used to take us to church or somebody picked us up. Lately they bring communion to us at home sometimes."

He continued, "We love our church. Kind of ironic, St. Luke is the patron saint of doctors and healing. We need all the healing we can get."

"Don't we all," agreed Jake.

"Beatriz finally got up the nerve to join the women's book group. She's the best-read person you ever met who's had very little formal schooling. She'd always take little Julia to the library. I don't think she ever said much and she never led a book discussion, but she probably got more out of it than most."

"Do they still keep in touch with her?"

"Oh, yes, they remember her with an Easter basket, stuff like that. They used to take her on their outings. Sometimes they bring us a special dinner, and our pastoral care volunteer visits us, too. We still feel very much a part of the church. We've left them a little something in our wills, if anything's left when we 'shuffle off this mortal coil.' Our ashes will be scattered in the church memorial garden."

"Wow, some church," said Jake.

"Do you have a church home? If not, join us. Oops, I forgot, we're moving."

"Don't start proselytizing me, or I'll throw away your walker," joked Jake. "I was raised in the Methodist Church but it's easier just to read the Sunday papers and laze around. My late wife and I worshipped at the temple of Starbucks with the *New York Times* for a prayer book."

"You'd always be welcome," said Henry. "Reverend Parks is a little tiny lady, comes up to about my shoulder, but a powerful presence. She looks like a little bird in her priest's robe. She understands what we're going through because her husband died a few years ago after a lengthy illness. Deborah's the real stuff. You'll like her."

"I know you have a lot to talk to her about, but I'd like to ask her a few questions, if you wouldn't mind," said Jake.

"Oh, yes. Getting Deborah to talk has never been a problem! She seems to have a pipeline to God."

An elderly black man weeding the flower garden straightened up slowly and yelled, "Y'all need any help?" as they got out of the car.

"Thanks, Raymond, we can manage," Henry called back. To Jake he said, "Raymond's our assistant sexton and keeps our grounds looking beautiful. He's recently lost his girlfriend of many years to cancer and he's eighty himself. Wouldn't be surprised if he saw the death law as an end to his woes."

As they entered the church building, a sparrow of a woman in a clerical collar greeted them. She bent to kiss Henry's cheek and shook Jake's hand. "Hello, Jake. Henry's told me about the story you're investigating. Come in. We'll get you coffee, if you'd like," she said as they passed the administrative assistant's desk.

As they settled into their chairs, coffee arrived in steaming mugs bearing the church's crest. Deborah said, "Welcome to St. Luke's. Henry's a treasured member here and anyone he brings, most welcome."

"I appreciate your meeting with me," said Henry.

"You said on the phone that Beatriz is largely unresponsive. Tell me how I can assist right now."

Henry teared up as he explained. "Hard decisions are coming. She has eaten hardly anything for the past few days. I need help with all this."

Deborah cried a little, too, as she took his hand. "Henry, I am so sorry. Yes, hard decisions are coming. As you know, I made them for my wonderful husband a few years ago. Know that God is with you and so is your family here at St. Luke's."

"How do we know when to give up trying to get her to eat and drink?" asked a distraught Henry.

"We pray God gives you the answer to that question, Henry. The hospice people will help you. Would you like me to come and see Beatriz?"

"Yes, please. Beatriz was Roman Catholic. Can you do the last rites thing for her?"

"Yes, the Episcopal Church has a similar prayer."

"What if you do and then she doesn't die yet?"

"It's a prayer, Henry, not a funeral rite. It's okay if we pray for her and she doesn't die."

"Could you talk to Jake while I read it in the prayer book?"

"Of course, Henry. It's called 'A Prayer for a Person Near Death.' Read the next part, too."

Turning to Jake, she asked, "Jake, how'd you meet Beatriz and Henry?"

"Maybe Henry didn't tell you that Julia and I are a couple. I got to know her when I was looking for congressional response to the death law. She led me to Henry for an interview."

Deborah sputtered, "I'm so spitting mad about this whole thing. I'm glad to talk to anyone who might be able to change it. This law is so wrong in so many ways. It's against everything I believe."

"Could I quote you on that?"

"Yes, and anything else I say. Are you taping this? I want you to get exactly what I say."

"Thanks, I am," said Jake, fumbling to get his digital recorder going before she started her next tirade. "How does it violate your beliefs?"

"I'm speaking for myself and not the Church as a whole, or even for St. Luke's, though most parishioners probably agree with me."

"Okay, got that recorded. I can quote you by name and affiliation, right?"

"Oh, yes, I'll stand behind my words. I'd go picket Congress if I thought the idiots there would pay attention. Oh, hell, sorry, heck, don't quote that."

"Right, deleted. How does the death law offend you, specifically?" asked Jake.

"Let me start with practical aspects. It's often the over-sixties who perform almost all of the service work. At St. Luke's, altar guild, food pantry, office volunteer work, lay pastoral care, other charitable work – the over-sixties have it hands down. Many of our volunteers are in their seventies and beyond. Younger people don't have the time, and older people often feel a reawakening of their spirituality. Churches will suffer dramatically from the death law because most larger financial contributions come from older members of any parish."

"And the moral implications?" asked Jake.

"I believe God, and only God, gives and withdraws life. A surgeon or physician gives new life, but as an instrument of God. Only God should decide when someone's life comes to an end, not the government," said Deborah, pounding her small fist on the desk for emphasis as she spoke.

"Your next question is going to be where I stand on assisted suicide, right?"

Jake nodded as she plunged ahead. "I think assisted suicide – physician-assisted suicide – is a decision to be made between physician and patient, hopefully with prayerful consideration.

"I also believe a person has the right to make such decisions beforehand in a legal document. Where's the line between refusing treatment and having a little too much morphine in your next shot?"

Jake noticed Henry listening closely and nodding in agreement.

"There's a whale of a lot of difference in the ICU and the palliative care unit. What I emphatically *do not believe*," again Deborah pounded the desk, "is that the government can make that decision for us. They already make enough death decisions related to war and capital punishment, which, by the way, I'm also against. But for individuals based on age and infirmity? That's just not right."

As she paused for a sip of coffee, Jake hazarded, "So you would support physician-assisted suicide but not legal mandate for death?"

"That's exactly what I'm saying. I can't believe in a merciful higher power without believing God doesn't want us to live in torment. While God required Jesus to be crucified, She didn't require Him to linger on the cross forever. If it's hard for me with my seminary study to deal with these issues, how much harder is it for people when it's suddenly slapped in their face? Although apparently it's not hard for many members of Congress."

Struggling for a moment for composure, she continued, "I lost my husband to cancer a few years ago. It was excruciating to watch his last weeks, and I'd have done anything to spare him. It was all I could do not to pull out his IV and put a pillow over his face, bugger the consequences. At the end, I'm pretty sure we were both praying for death. I believe that one should be able to choose the time of one's own death without putting anyone else in jeopardy for assisting the process."

"I can see your point, that's for sure," said Jake. "My wife died in a car accident many years ago and that was hard enough. I can't imagine watching someone you love suffer as you describe."

Henry had been pensively quiet. He said, "I have to talk to Julia on behalf of her mother and me. I must be sure she knows our wishes so she doesn't have to agonize through decisions herself. This has helped me clarify what I myself must do."

Jake said, "Deborah, I can't thank you enough. You have really opened my eyes to some issues. Can I call you if I need to clarify anything?"

"Of course," she said. "Or how about dropping by on a Sunday morning sometime? Do you have a church home?"

"I already tried that," Henry said, "and he pretty much told me to mind my own business."

"Yes, but that *is* my business," Deborah said, smiling. "Seriously, I'd be honored if you ever wanted to join us some Sunday. No pressure, no pressure!"

Turning back to Henry, she asked gently, "Could I come by about seven tomorrow evening? You keep the prayer book and decide with Julia if you want just the prayer or if you want to say together the litany following it."

With his face in his hands, Henry managed a barely audible, "Okay. I'm ready to go home, Jake."

Physically or metaphorically? Jake wondered.

CHAPTER 29

Friday, December 9

Julia had two big items on her agenda today. She'd get things back under control in her office and contact a realtor to get her house on the market.

Everyone swarmed her as she entered the office suite. She scheduled a staff meeting for ten so everyone scurried back to their own cubicles to get ready. As she paged through things on her desk, Julia saw that most items had been taken care of in her absence. She debated announcing her move to Florida but decided to wait. She called her secretary and the communications director into her office and shut the door.

"This is in strictest confidence," she began. "And I don't mean Capitol Hill confidence, I mean keep it absolutely to yourself."

"Oh, no, you're takin' that lobbyist job," moaned Sandy.

"How'd you know about that?" asked a surprised Julia.

"Capitol Hill confidence, absolutely none," replied Sandy. "Oh, I hate to hear this, Julia."

Julia laughed and said, "No, no lobbyist job. I'm going to switch places with Tina-Maria and move my family to Florida to run the home office. Tina-Maria will head up things here and I'll be overall chief, but from Florida."

"I wish you'd take me with you," joked Walter.

"That's partly why I'm talking to you now. I want to take you, too. And Sandy–"

Sandy interrupted, "Darlin', I can't move. My children are in school and their daddy's got a good job here."

"No, I'm asking you to think how to make the transition work. I'll still be in this office often. Jake and I'll be back here every month or two."

Sandy crowed, "Jake's goin', too, fantastic! Okay, girl, we'll make this work. Tina-Maria'll be fine here, once we get to know her a little better."

Walter said, "Julia, this could be great for me. If we move to Florida, I wouldn't retire like I planned. I'd work another few years and we could move sooner."

"So much is done electronically these days, it doesn't make much difference where we live," said Julia.

"He announces for senator, we're already there," Walter said.

"Walt, nobody said that," cautioned Julia. "We're dealing with the present and job one is to get the death law repealed."

"So you're announcin' this switcheroo at the meetin'?"

"No, not today. Tina-Maria wants to wait until after the holidays. I'm talking to only you two now. Understood?"

"Yes, but I want to call my wife right away."

"Of course," replied Julia, "but caution her–"

"Yeah, I know. We've been on Capitol Hill a long time."

"Remember, absolute secrecy."

The staff looked curiously at Sandy and Walter as they exited Julia's office and returned to their desks. Walter said, "I'm stepping out for a few minutes to check some facts. I'll be back before the staff meeting."

"I just bet you are, Walter," drawled Sandy. "Hope you find what you're lookin' for."

Julia dialed the realtor she'd bought her house from several years ago. She'd referred others to Holly Carson through the years but Julia hadn't thought she'd be using Holly's services herself again so soon.

She heard a cheery, "Hello, Holly here. It's a beautiful day in northern Virginia. How can I help you?"

"Hey, Holly, this is Julia Sanchez, remember me? I want to sell my house in Falls Church. You helped us buy it a few years ago so I thought I'd call you first."

"Julia! Great to hear from you!" squealed Holly. "I'm the woman to help you! Will we look for property, too? Can I come over right now?"

Holding the phone out from her ear to muffle the irrepressible Holly, Julia laughed. "We're not in *that* big a hurry, Holly. No, I'm moving away and I'll explain. Could we meet in the morning?"

"Of *course*," chirped Holly. "Eight o'clock okay?"

"Um, nine might be better."

"Ab-so-lutely!" trilled Holly. "I'll pull some comps in your area to help us with pricing."

"Thanks," said Julia, hanging up and shaking her head to get the sound of Holly out of her ear.

The staff meeting produced no surprises for Julia. The most pressing matter was deciding a course of action on the death law. Among Julia's phone messages was one from her buddy Max, chief of staff to another congressman, inviting someone from Simms' office to a meeting regarding repeal planning.

Julia delegated Georgia and Sid to attend but to make no

commitments for Simms to join any coalition. To get a repeal bill drafted and reported out for a vote was a monumental task, best accomplished by bi-partisan action.

Jake entered his editor's office with some trepidation to explain his intended move. He carried with him two Sunday columns and two news articles based on his interviews in Florida.

"Good to see you again, Jake."

Jake couldn't tell if Sam was being sarcastic or not.

"Here are four more pieces, in addition to what I've already sent you online," explained Jake. "I found an interesting perspective on the death law in Florida. People I talked to there have a very grim outlook under this legislation. Interviews with elderly poor also turned up a desperate feeling toward health care in general. These columns may be the best I've ever written."

Somewhat mollified, Sam asked, "And now you're here for awhile?"

"Yes and no." Jake explained his future plans, then sat quietly while his editor took in that news.

"Every time you come in here, you give me a headache," sighed Sam, fixing his steely glare on Jake. "Okay, I'm not gonna take this upstairs this time. Whenever you're in town, spend a little time with us. We'll say you're on location. I'm putting myself on the line, but what else is new? We'll want to claim you as a staff member when this book takes off. But dammit, I better see a book, is that clear?"

"Yes, it is," said Jake. "There's a book in this and I'm confident that I can write it."

"Then get out of my office and write!"

Julia and Jake met at home after their long, grueling work-day. She'd tried not to think about the visit from the priest that evening, but could no longer evade that thought. Henry had shown her the prayer and litany in the prayer book the previous night. She was especially glad Jake would be there this evening – actually, she felt that every evening.

Hattie had sandwiches ready when they arrived home, though no one had an appetite. She said, "I appreciate y'all including me in this prayerful evening."

"How's Mom doing today?" Julia asked.

"She's sleeping and hasn't had a thing to eat. I wetted a cloth and put a little water in her mouth."

All steeled themselves when the doorbell rang. Deborah hugged and shook hands all around and declined refreshment.

They gathered in the bedroom where Beatriz lay motionless with her eyes closed. Julia led Jake by the hand so he didn't ask if he was included.

The priest distributed *The Book of Common Prayer* to everyone and grouped them around the bed. "You can touch Beatriz as we pray, or you may want to hold hands with each other. Henry, shall we do the prayer or the litany?"

"The whole thing," Henry choked out.

Deborah donned her clerical stole and stood near Beatriz's head, directing them to the page in their prayer books. Jake noticed she had something in her hand. He held Julia's hand and tilted the book so she could read, as Julia reached for her mother's left hand. Henry positioned his chair and held Beatriz' right hand. Hattie stood at the foot of the bed, smoothing down the covers. Calvin jumped up on the bed next to Beatriz, and no one removed him.

Deborah led them in prayer. With many sniffles, they haltingly read the litany. Deborah anointed Beatriz's forehead with oil. They hoped Beatriz was with them in spirit, because she was achingly absent in the present.

Declining their invitation to linger, Deborah removed her stole, hugged everyone goodbye, and quietly let herself out of the house.

"I'll sit with Beatriz a few minutes," said a weeping Henry.

The others mopped their faces as they exited the bedroom. Julia hugged Hattie. "Thank you for staying, Hattie. We ask too much of you."

"Wouldn't have been proper not being here, Miss Julia. I'll clean up the kitchen and then I'm going to read my Bible a little."

Julia turned into Jake's arms and wept piteously as he stroked her hair and held her until she calmed. Muffled into his shirtfront, she cried, "You didn't know what you were getting into, did you, darling?"

With his cheek on her hair, he tightened his embrace and said softly, "I've never felt more a part of a family than I did just now."

Pulling away, Julia said, "I'm so grateful to Henry for asking Deborah to come. I feel like I've said goodbye now and I can get through the rest of what's coming."

Henry shuffled into the room as she spoke and said, "I feel the same way, Julia. Now we can get on with it. Seems like the rest is just details."

Saturday morning Holly hustled in, her car and briefcase emblazoned with her picture and company affiliation. She embraced Julia and gushed, "It's great to see you again! You look wonderful!"

Julia moved beyond Holly's reach and led her into the living room. She'd decided to be strictly businesslike and not offer coffee. "This is confidential, but I'm moving to Florida and want to sell this house. I'd like you to list it and tell me how to get it ready for sale."

Holly turned off the gush, drew a contract from her brief-case, and immediately was all business. "This is the standard contract we ask people to sign when we represent them." She explained the fees and services and became the brisk, efficient professional Julia remembered.

"Are you the sole owner of the home?" asked Holly.

"I am now," said Julia. "My parents and I bought it together, but when they both got sick, our lawyer had us change the deed to my name alone."

"Let's tour and see what needs to be done," Holly said after Julia had clarified a few points and signed the contract.

"I need to explain something," said Julia. "My mother is in late-stage dementia, in bed and unable to get up. The hospice people tell us this is probably her permanent state until death."

"Oh, Julia, I am so sorry," said Holly. "Let me think how we're going to show the house. Let's look around and I'll come up with something."

They toured the house, with Holly ooh-ing and ah-ing over the attractive house and its stylish furnishings. They peeked into Henry and Beatriz's room and saw Henry sitting beside the bed, holding Beatriz's hand. Julia introduced Henry to the realtor.

Henry said, "Julia, I'm sorry to be leaving you alone but the decisions are yours and I'd like to sit with Beatriz."

"Jake is checking his email but he'll join me in a minute."

Julia led Holly into the den and found a very frustrated Jake trying to get his e-mail. "What's wrong?" asked Julia after doing introductions.

"I don't know … oh, God, what's this mess? It stinks."

Julia exclaimed, "Oh, damn, I think Calvin threw up on the router. I swear, I'm gonna kill that cat!"

"Let me clean up this mess and I'll come talk with you. Sorry, Holly," Jake said.

"I'm glad I know there's a cat," said Holly, struggling not to laugh at the cat crisis.

"Just one more frustration." Julia sighed. "Hey, would you like a cup of coffee or something while we talk?"

"Sure," said Holly. "We need to see the kitchen, anyway."

Hattie was cleaning up breakfast and starting a load of laundry. She served them coffee as Holly said to Julia, "Very little needs to be done. Mostly you need to de-clutter and stage things a little but we have someone who'll do that. It looks in good repair. This house is going to sell quickly and fetch you a really good price. I wouldn't be surprised to see a little bidding war erupt and get you more than the asking price."

"That would be welcome," said Julia. "It makes me tired to think of doing the work to get this ready, though."

"'Excuse me for butting in, Miss Julia, but I can do that. I helped with that before when folks I stayed with died. If Miss Holly tells me what, I can do that during the day while y'all at work."

"We might as well sort what we want to take with us to Florida while we're at it," sighed Julia. "There's so much to do."

"Mist' Henry could help with that. That poor man needs a project right now, get his mind off things some."

"Great idea," agreed the businesslike Holly. "Store the boxes in the garage or basement, though. And closets need to be neat and orderly."

"I get on that today, if that's all right with you, Miss Julia. I can work while I look in on your momma."

Holly went on, "Julia, could you get your mom out of the house for a day or a weekend? We could have an open house and I believe it would sell quickly. That way we wouldn't be doing constant showings."

Jake walked in with his hands full of smelly rags. "The internet's working. I heard what you said, Holly. Julia, could we take your parents to my place for a weekend?"

"Great idea," said Holly.

"How would we get Mom there?" asked Julia. "She can't walk."

"We could lift her into Henry's chair, take her to the car, strap her in, then come back for Henry. There's an elevator at my place."

"Take the cat, too," added Holly.

"What if it doesn't sell by the end of the weekend?"

"Then we stay longer or we think of a new plan," said Jake. "Holly says it'll sell fast."

"I'm not promising anything. But that's my prediction, especially if we don't price it too high. The holidays are traditionally a slow time, but I have a good feeling about this." She named a figure that seemed outrageous to Julia but would give them a comfortable financial cushion.

"Okay, let's try it," said Julia, taking a deep breath. "Everything seems to be happening too quickly, but let's go for it. When would you do this open house, Holly?"

"Is next weekend too soon?" asked Holly.

"Oh, God, that fast? I guess we could be ready but I'd like to delay leaving here until about the end of January, at least."

"Understood. It'll take that long to work through the financing on this, anyway, once it's sold. Could we have a home inspection with your mother here?"

"That'd be okay," said Julia.

"I can get us ready in that time," said Hattie. "I'd kinda like to go home to church in the morning, if that suits, but otherwise I be here working. We can get it done. Not saying anything bad, but it might be better to get this over with while Miz Beatriz like she is now, instead of waiting longer."

"I thought of that, too," said Jake.

Julia echoed, "Yeah, me too. Then we've got a plan. Let's move Mom Friday night, okay, Jake?"

CHAPTER 30

Saturday, December 10

Everybody pitched in to get ready for the open house and the move. Jake went in search of packing boxes. Henry investigated moving companies online, then called a few to discuss rates and procedures.

Poking through boxes in the attic, Hattie exclaimed, "Miss Julia, here's the Christmas stuff. Reckon we should put it up?"

"Oh, jeez, I hadn't even thought about Christmas. Holly said de-clutter but maybe we could do Christmasy clutter."

"Seems like it'd make the house mighty pretty."

Holly gave phone approval for a few secular, simple, sparse holiday decorations.

Memories flooded through Julia as she opened the Christmas stuff. She unwrapped small crèches she and Beatriz had bought, one each year for the past several years. *No nativity scenes until after the open house.* She dug around for tasteful tree decorations and found some glass candleholders to cluster on the dining table.

Jake returned with packing boxes, bubble wrap, and large plastic boxes. "I thought we could just shove some stuff under the beds to get it out of sight," he explained.

"Great idea. The movers will pack everything so anything

we do ourselves will probably save a few dollars. Could you go get us a small Christmas tree and a wreath? Maybe some greens for the mantle?"

"I'll do that, but, honey, how about coming with me? This is our first Christmas together."

"There's just so much to do…"

"Go on, Miss Julia. I can see to your folks."

Julia had been so preoccupied she'd hardly noticed the community preparations for the holiday season. Now she saw Christmas banners hanging from light posts and decorated trees in windows and yards.

At a Boy Scout tree lot they argued good-naturedly over a spruce or a white pine, finally agreeing on a beautiful little balsam. They chose a wreath resplendent with a maroon bow and lots of pine cones. Julia gathered an armload of Virginia creeper for the mantle and Jake added a small sprig of mistletoe.

Accepting cups of spiced cider from the Scout moms, the couple wandered through a small merchandise area. "We have a tree stand and skirt," said Julia. "Let's get some of this spray stuff that makes your house smell like baking. Maybe Hattie could bake some cookies and put them out for the open house. How are we going to get all this done and be gone by Friday night?"

"Hattie'll be a huge help," he replied, putting an arm around her. "We'll get it done. More cider?"

They strolled around the lot with the other tree-seekers, listening to the Christmas music and warming themselves at the small open fire. Scouts and dads lashed huge trees to the tops of customers' cars or muscled them into the backs of SUVs.

"Use your Scout knots!" yelled one dad.

"Were you a Boy Scout?" asked Julia.

"Yes, Eagle Scout, actually."

"Really!" exclaimed Julia. "I'm impressed! Wonder what else we don't know about each other."

"It's about the only thing my dad and I did together. Were you a Girl Scout?"

"No, after school I'd go with Mom to the houses where she worked. I asked once but she said the uniforms cost money we didn't have. But I enjoyed singing in my school's chapel choir, like a good little Catholic girl. Christmas music makes me think of midnight Christmas Eve mass. We'd put on little red robes and sing carols during the season."

"I can just picture you, a beautiful little black-haired girl singing your heart out." He punctuated that with a quick kiss.

They entered the house with their Christmas greenery and inhaled the smell of cookies baking. Hattie explained, "Mist' Henry says we need cookies."

"He's right," said Julia. "We thought maybe you'd make some for the open house next weekend. Feels funny to host a Christmas social we won't attend."

Henry had unearthed some Christmas CDs so they put aside their packing chores to beautify the house. Calvin paw-tested their progress and they hung some bells low on the tree for him to bat around. The afternoon of decoration had a subdued feeling of contentment, as long as they pretended Beatriz was just napping in the other room.

The rest of the weekend was consumed with cleaning, discarding, packing, and hiding things. Hattie washed windows, floors and bathrooms. Henry dusted the blinds and baseboards with a long-handled feather duster. Julia neatened closets, ending up with bags of clothing, shoes and purses to take to Salvation Army. Jake rearranged the volumes in the bookcases and the

CDs and DVDs in their racks. Calvin guarded the tree and the sleeping beauty Beatriz.

Julia considered all that needed to be done in the office as she drove her Monday morning commute. The death law repeal was the biggest task, though in the flurry of everything else, it was almost getting lost. She and her staff would have to figure out the details of the job switch and anticipate complications and problems. Looming was Simms' Senatorial bid and a political campaign. Personally, her list was even longer: selling and buying a house, moving to another state, planning for the death of her mother, taking care of an ailing father...

And there was Jake, the one thought that made her smile this morning.

As Julia entered her office, someone greeted her with, "Hey, Julia, why's your house listed in the real estate ads?"

Oops. Didn't think anyone in the office would notice the open house advertisement. "I'll talk about that at the nine o'clock staff meeting," she answered. "Send a memo on a meeting, okay, Sandy?" Julia called Tina-Maria and warned her that staff changes were about to be revealed in a meeting.

Tina-Maria responded, "I'm so ready to be out of here, I don't care. I'll wait until after the holidays, but if my parents hear earlier and kick me out of the house, so much the better!"

After an initially uneasy discussion, Julia believed all were on board. She invited anyone who wanted to discuss a transfer to the Florida office to let her know immediately, avoiding looking at Walter.

Julia worked a short day and went home early to meet Bonnie, the hospice nurse. The house looked Christmas-y, even if the tired, sad occupants didn't feel very spirited. It was surreal to be packing for a move, decorating for Christmas, and monitoring Beatriz's last days. Julia felt like she was living a modern-day version of William Faulkner's novel *As I Lay Dying*.

The nurse's visit produced no surprises. Julia, Henry and Hattie learned specifics about caring for Beatriz and heard that a hospice aide would come twice a week to bathe and shampoo her. They gave the nurse a copy of Beatriz's living will and DNR order. All agreed on enforcing the previous decisions of no medication other than palliative care, no feeding tubes, no IVs with life-sustaining fluids.

Julia said to the nurse, "I feel like we're starving her to death and depriving her of water."

"I won't sugar-coat the fact, yes, that's what's happening. But she has told us that's what she wants, right?"

Both Julia and Henry nodded in agreement.

"So we're following her wishes?"

"Yes, I know," said Julia softly. "But it feels inhumane, like we're playing God."

"Look at your mom. Who put her in this condition? Not her family."

"Thank you, that helps." Julia sighed as she spoke. "Any kind of time frame?"

"Now you are talking God's decisions," replied the nurse. "I've seen people pass in a week or maybe not for a month or two. Sometimes they rally a bit and take a little water or food by mouth. We'll know more as we visit over the next weeks and perhaps months. I can tell you this: she won't be a victim of the death law in six months."

Henry and Julia both caught the nuance of probably weeks, not months. Henry voiced both their thoughts, "I don't know what to hope for, more or less time for Beatriz."

The experienced hospice nurse recognized the feelings of a distraught family and did not give her opinion that less time was better for everybody.

They moved Beatriz, Henry and Calvin to Jake's apartment on Friday night and Beatriz seemed no different after the journey.

Julia was touched that Jake had gone to the trouble of putting up a small Christmas tree to welcome them. Henry was delighted with the snarl of train tracks around the tree.

Jake apologized, "I hoped to get the train set up but it took me awhile to find it and I ran out of time."

"We had one around our Christmas tree when I was a boy," exclaimed Henry.

"This came from my childhood," said Jake. "I don't know why I've kept it. Let me put the track together and you can run the control box, Henry."

Hattie checked to be sure all were properly settled and said, "I'm going on home now, Miss Julia. Y'all call me if y'all need me, hear?"

"I hear. You'll be the first person I call if we need help. Thanks!"

The weekend passed uneventfully but the tension mounted as they waited for Holly's promised Sunday night phone call. Finally Julia's cell phone signaled her call.

""What's the news?" asked Julia.

"All good," gushed Holly. "Three offers on the table, and two of them are over the asking price. When can we discuss them? The sooner the better. I'd like to get a signed contract and nail this down tomorrow."

"You suggest a time and I'll be there."

"You're bringing your parents home tomorrow, right? Could I meet you at nine at your house?"

"Yes, that's good. You've got a key. If you get there first, let yourself in. This sounds like great news. Thanks, Holly."

"It went just as I hoped. I'm happy to make a sale this time of the year. Your Christmas decorations and cookies set the mood." She laughed. "You must have me on speaker phone. Is that cheering in the background?"

"Yes, indeed! I'm going to hang up and cheer, too. Thanks again."

She ended the call and danced Henry's wheelchair around the living room, giving Jake a big smooch on the way by.

"Now everything really is just details," exclaimed Henry. "I was so worried this wouldn't work."

"Half that profit is yours, Henry. We bought that house together."

"And your mom and I transferred it to you, remember? That money is yours, daughter. I need to stay poor in case I need Medicaid help."

"Henry, we promised you we'd take care of you after we visited that awful place. This extra cash from the house sale is a cushion, a huge relief to me."

Jake reminded them, "There's still a ways between offer and closing, you know."

"Spoilsport," retorted Julia. "But you're right."

CHAPTER 31

Monday, December 19

Hattie arrived at Jake's apartment Monday morning at eight and helped ready Beatriz for the trip back to Falls Church. She was delighted that the house had sold.

"Me and my daughter made us some plans, too. She and my grandkids are gonna move in my place when I'm gone. She's not happy with my leaving but things be better for her if she doesn't have to pay rent. So she's some happier with the plan since she's gettin' a home out of it."

"That's good, Hattie. Things do seem to be falling into place."

"When the Lord leads, good things happen," Hattie said.

"But won't your daughter have to pay rent on your place?"

"Oh, no, I paid it off. I lived with different folks I was taking care of and didn't need much of the money they gave me. My preacher told me, 'Give half that money to God and put ten per cent into your house.' Well, I just kinda reversed that and gave the preacher ten per cent and put half into that little house. I paid it off and now my daughter and them can live in it for free. Maybe it'll give her the boost she needs. She's gonna get it when I pass, anyway. My other kids already got their houses and they live in other parts of the US of A. She's the onliest one left in DC."

"I knew you were smart, Hattie," said Henry. "Good for you for not listening to that preacher."

Hattie laughed. "Sometimes what the preacher says and what God says to me not exactly the same!"

Julia wasn't surprised to see Holly sitting in her BMW in their driveway.

"Let me get Mom settled and I'll be ready to meet," said Julia by way of greeting.

"No hurry, I've got paperwork to do and calls to make," chirped Holly.

Julia and Jake lifted Beatriz while Hattie held the wheelchair steady. Her once-robust mother had become very light, making her easier to lift but punctuating her physical decline. They carefully laid Beatriz in her bed, and Jake and Julia returned to the car to ferry Henry in.

Julia waved Holly to the kitchen table and was glad to smell Hattie's good coffee brewing. "I wasn't sure this weekend would work. I'm glad it sold that quickly. Three offers, imagine that!"

"I'm sorry to tell you that one of them was withdrawn," said Holly.

"Oh, no!" said Julia, throwing up her hands in alarm.

"Not to worry. We still have the other two and I'm expecting a third today. This is going to work out, Julia. Have patience."

"I'm pretty short on that right now, but I'll do my best to trust you on this, Holly,"

The two women went over the offers in detail with Jake and Henry interjecting an occasional question. The four of them selected the next-to-highest offer since it was a cash sale and the new owners were willing to wait a bit to take possession.

"They're a retired couple and they understand your situation because they went through something similar with one of their parents a few years ago. They're in their sixties and want to move near family before they face the consequences of the death law. They've already sold their house in New England and are staying with their children here temporarily. So they have the cash and they really want this house."

"I'd rather have the extra time than a few more thousand dollars," said Julia. "You agree, Henry, Jake?"

The men nodded and Henry said, "It sounds too good to be true."

"Hattie would say it's what the Lord intended," said Julia.

"Yes'm, that what she say," said a grinning Hattie, entering the kitchen.

"All right, I'll get back to them this morning."

The doorbell rang and Holly gathered her papers. "That's my cue to exit. I'll call you later today, Julia."

A man from a medical supply company truck parked in their driveway said, "We have a hospital bed for this address."

"Oh," said Julia. "I forgot the hospice nurse said that'd be delivered this morning. Bring it in."

The two workers manhandled the bulky bed down the hallway as Jake and Hattie shoved the bed containing Beatriz closer to the wall. Beatriz never stirred during the shifting of the furniture.

When they had the bed in place, one of the men removed his cap, held out the paperwork to Julia to sign, and said, "Sorry for your troubles, ma'am. My mama looked just like that a little while ago. She's gone to God now, rest her soul."

Julia choked up at the unexpected empathy as she thanked the men and showed them out. It seemed like everybody had somebody with Alzheimer's these days.

"Lemme get this here bed ready," said Hattie. "I hope we got sheets."

"Here's a bag they left," said Jake. "There's a mattress cover, sheets, blanket and pillowcase."

"I probably just signed to buy them," said Julia. "They're a pretty yellow color. That won't help Mom any but it might make the room a little more cheerful for Henry."

"Okay, y'all give me space and I'll ready the bed and call y'all when it's time to lift Miz Beatriz."

Henry was visibly upset as they settled Beatriz in her new accommodation a few minutes later. "I'm sad about no longer sharing our bed but glad caring for her is easier," he said. "At least we're still together, not miles apart with her in a home and me stuck here unable to drive." He wheeled over to Beatriz and took his accustomed place by her side, holding her limp hand.

Julia hated to leave Henry but really needed to get to her office. She knew missed days of work were looming as her mother's condition worsened. She and Jake treasured their conversation time as they drove together into DC. "The morning commute is actually pleasant when we're together," she commented. "How's your research going? I feel like we haven't talked much lately. It's going to a relief when we're settled in Florida and back to some kind of normal life."

"I'm making good progress. My columns are getting attention and will become chapter headings in the book. I've got a lot of back-up material, too. Today I plan to see if I can determine what changes have occurred in the six weeks since the death law, if it's making a difference in people's behavior. What's happening with the repeal?"

"That's my first question today," replied Julia. "I sent someone to a meeting last week so I'll know more later today."

Julia found a businesslike calm in the congressional office as she entered.

Walter approached as soon as she arrived. "Julia, can I have a minute?"

Knowing a "minute" was probably fifteen or thirty minutes, she preceded him into her own space and sat down. Hanging up her coat and stowing her purse, she asked him, "What's new, Walter?"

"My wife and I want the transfer to Florida," he said. "We were planning to move there but unsure of our finances. If I keep working, it's a sure thing for us."

"Sure thing for two years," Julia reminded him. "It'd be easy for you to get another job in DC but maybe not quite so simple in Sarasota."

"In two years, our finances will make better sense," replied Walter. "Besides, I expect Simms to be re-elected to something, if this law thing plays out like we plan."

"Yes," agreed Julia. "I think – hope – you're right, just wanted to be sure you'd thought of that."

"Actually, I'm energized to be a part of something this big," confided Walter. "I was feeling kind of stale and we're about to get excitement again. I might not want to retire. That is, if the Congressman wants me to stay on."

"I'd be really surprised if he didn't. You're the best communications director around – he knows it and so do I. He'll be happy you're moving, and I'll be glad to have your familiar face there."

Okay, check one item off, thought Julia. She called in Georgia and Sid to find out what had happened at the meeting of legislative aides. She knew Simms was in an ideal position to head up a bi-partisan coalition to repeal the death law but also knew timing was crucial.

Georgia, their assistant for health areas, was the most knowledgeable about the implications of the death law. "Everybody's getting pressure to repeal," she reported. "The surprise is that everyone's so cautious about taking a stand. There's a void in leadership our guy can step into. I didn't commit us to anything, of course, but I find it curious others aren't leaping into the breach."

Sid added, "I think the stakes are so high, other congressmen haven't figured out how to play this. They know the death law has to be repealed but they're also sitting ducks if the vote fails. There's a big difference between voting for something and sticking your neck out to sponsor it. Once it gets written, others will sign on. Besides, a lot of congressional leaders are over seventy so maybe they're just keeping their heads down."

"That's about what I figured," surmised Julia. "Simms is ready to lead. He announced his position weeks ago and nobody else has jumped into the fray with him yet. Can we draft something for him to look at and decide if we're ready to look for co-signers?"

"Got it right here, boss," replied Georgia. "It's an early version, but it's ready for him to see."

Julia scanned the document. "One or two minor things I'd change, but looks good to me. I don't see anything here other than repeal, though. Are we going to propose anything in its place?"

"Like physician-assisted suicide – PAS – you mean?" asked Sid. "We didn't put that in the draft, in case it fell into the wrong hands too early. We decided you and the congressman had to make that call."

Julia asked, "Did that come up at the meeting the other day?"

"Yeah," said Georgia, "but nobody wanted to commit. Everyone wants it in but nobody wants to put their name on it."

"I know," said Julia. "That's my feeling, too. But somebody's going to have to own it. Good work, guys. I'll talk to you again in a day or two after I've discussed it with the congressman."

As her day wore on, Julia dealt with various other staff projects and advised her staff on answers to constituent questions. She caught up on her own voluminous e-mail.

She met with high school students from their home district who were visiting the nation's capital. Their questions about the legislative process were perceptive and Julia congratulated the teachers. She answered their questions about what it was like to live and work in Washington, DC.

Then she turned the tables on the group and said, "I'm moving to Florida. What's it like to live there?"

The students' answers ranged from praise for their area to typical teenaged comments of it sucks, can't wait to leave. One young woman in a thin sweater said, "Here it's cold! You'll be warmer in Florida." On that note, the laughing students filed out, toting leftover campaign pens, coffee mugs, and signed pictures of the congressman. Julia wished more of her duties were this much fun.

Sandy buzzed Julia and said, "Your caregiver is on the line. She's upset."

Oh God, this is it, Mom's dead, please keep me strong. "Hattie, what's wrong? Did Mom die?"

"No'm, it's Mist' Henry what's upset. He's crying his eyes out and I can't get him to stop."

"What happened?"

"The cat crawled up right up next to your Mom. Her hand moved just the teeniest bit and she started petting on him real slow. Mist' Henry was holding her other hand and saw it. Now he thinks she's coming back to life. Or he knows she's not, I can't tell which. He won't stop crying and talk to me."

"Can you get him to come to the phone?"

"No'm, don't reckon I can. He doesn't say nothing when I talk to him, just sits there and cries. I'm so sorry to bother you, Miss Julia, but I never seen him this way."

"Okay, I'm on my way. I want you to stay right there with them and pat his back or something so he knows he's not alone. I'll be there in about thirty minutes."

"Yes'm, that's what I been doing and I'll just sit right here with him."

"Oh, and call Dr. Singh and see if they can see us this afternoon, please. And the hospice people. I'm on my way right now. If anything changes, call me, okay? Hattie, thanks."

As she rushed out, Julia told Sandy, "My dad finally broke under all the stress. I hope I see you tomorrow morning."

She called Jake as she walked, explaining that she was taking the Metro so she could get home as quickly as possible.

"Oh, honey, he's been so brave so long. Do you need me to come right now? Would that be faster?"

"No, I'm just about to step onto the train. Can you bring the car and meet me at home later?"

"Of course I can. Call me as soon as you get a minute, okay? I love you, Julia. I'll be there just a little behind you."

Julia exited the Falls Church metro station and flagged down a passing taxi. She flew into the house a few minutes later and found a subdued, exhausted-looking Henry, a comatose Beatriz, and a worried Hattie.

"Miss Julia, so glad y'all home. Mist' Henry's feeling some better but still really sad."

Henry sat with his head down and did not react to Hattie's statement or Julia's presence.

Julia knelt down and put her arms around him. He leaned forward in his chair and put his hands over his face. He sobbed, "I thought she was waking up. But she didn't. And she's not going to. Not now, not tomorrow, not ever again."

Julia and Hattie cried with him. Words were pointless.

Julia asked Hattie, "Did you get the doctor's office?"

"Yes'm, they're calling in a prescription for Mist' Henry, something to help him calm and sleep a little. They asked did you need one, too. I said you seemed strong but we'd call back if you did. I can sit here with them if you wanna go get it."

"That might be a good idea. Do we need anything else?"

"I could use me some aspirin."

After explaining to a slightly calmer Henry that she would be back soon and brushing away his teary apology, Julia drove to the local pharmacy. It was the last non-chain drugstore in their area, and the sympathetic pharmacist who owned the store had the prescription ready when she arrived. His wife was working the cash register and said, "We knew things must be bad when the call came from the doctor. We hope your worries ease soon." Julia thanked them, grateful for the caring touch these two people provided their customers, and added a big bottle of aspirin to her purchases.

She called Jake as she drove home and told him things seemed calmer than they had been earlier.

"I'll be leaving here very shortly," he said. "Please call me if I can get anything on the way home. And, honey, remember you're not in this alone."

As he was gathering his things to leave, Jake's phone rang. *Oh, not now. Shall I ignore it?* he dithered. He picked it up and heard his editor's voice on the line.

"Jake, have you seen the news?" asked Sam.

"No, I was just leaving. What's up?"

"Russia has filed a resolution in the UN Security Council accusing the US of genocide for killing senior citizens. It just came across the screen on CNN."

"You're shitting me," Jake exclaimed. "How can they do that?"

"According to CNN's Foxx Donder, the UN passed a resolution in 1948 making genocide an international crime. They're accusing us of genocide for enacting a law for 'mass slaughter of innocent senior citizens.'"

"Yep, here it is, I've got it up on the computer. It's called 'The Convention on the Prevention and Punishment of the Crime of Genocide,'" affirmed Jake. "Let's see, they define genocide as 'intent to destroy a national, ethnical, racial, or religious group.' How does that fit seniors?"

"I guess the Russians extrapolated that to include seniors," replied Sam. "We'll want a story on this for tomorrow."

"I'll get something to you by ten p.m."

Jake settled back into his chair and called the US Ambassador to the United Nations, Virgil Whiting. He was relieved to get an answer, knowing every other journalist in the country was probably dialing the same number. Jake was glad he and the Ambassador had played in a charity golf foursome a few years ago, and hoped the Ambassador recognized his name.

"Hey, Jake, good to hear from you. You calling about that resolution those Commie bastards introduced? Don't print that. How'd you hear about it? I just got the word a few minutes ago."

"It's on CNN, Mr. Ambassador."

"How the hell did they get it?"

"According to Foxx on CNN, some nameless diplomat leaked it to the media."

"Yeah, like the SOB Russian ambassador, probably. Anyway, everybody's piling on. North Korea, Iran, Venezuela, all those boys are jumping right in against us. Not to mention statements from ISIS, Al Qaeda, those terrorist groups. And here we've been filing complaints about Rwanda, Iraq, Darfur, Somalia – we're the laughingstock of the world right now over that stupid death law. Do you think any of our allies are going to stick their necks out for us? Not a chance. We're fu... screwed on this and it's all the fault of Congress! Gotta go, let's golf sometime."

With that, Jake packed up again and headed home, figuring he could get background information from the internet. And Julia needed him at home.

CHAPTER 32

Sunday, December 18

Everything virtually shut down on Capitol Hill near Christmas, so Julia could spend her time at home instead of in the office. She cared for her mother and saw to it that Henry got some rest and food every now and then.

Hattie stayed in Falls Church most nights, going home for Christmas programs at church and her grandchildren's Christmas concerts at school. She slept on the daybed in the den and tended the whole family as best she could. The visiting hospice personnel showed her what needed to be done both for Beatriz and for family members.

Jake moved his computer into Julia's and his bedroom and worked on stories and columns. The UN resolution filed against the US for genocide gave him plenty for this week's publications. He kept the household stocked with groceries and rubbed Julia's tired back every time she came close to him.

Henry and Calvin kept vigil. Henry now prayed for Beatriz to have a peaceful passage to the next world.

The Christmas decorations they'd put up for the real estate open house were a sad reminder of a season they were not celebrating this year. They tacitly ignored the holiday for now as they focused on Beatriz's impending death.

Thursday, December 22

Three days before Christmas Julia and Jake cleaned up the kitchen after dinner since Hattie had gone home for the night. Henry called to them in a broken voice, "Can you come here? Right now?"

Oh God, breathed Julia in prayer, *help us through this last part.*

They entered the bedroom to find Henry holding Beatriz's hand. "She's breathing funny," he whimpered.

As her mother took long, slow, occasional breaths, Julia recognized the symptoms the hospice nurse had told her to expect. She gripped Jake's hand as he pulled out his phone.

Letting go momentarily of her hand, Jake said, "I'm calling the hospice nurse and the priest."

Julia nodded but could not speak as she began crying. She reached for Henry's and her mother's hands. They made an odd trinity: one person leaving life, one struggling to remain in this one, and the third full of vitality. Yet they were united as a family is only at moments of great emotion.

A team of hospice nurses arrived within the hour and performed the formalities of pronouncing Beatriz dead. Julia and Henry sat with her body for a short while. Then Julia withdrew and left Henry with his private thoughts.

One of the nurses asked gently, "Is there a funeral home we can call for you?"

"Oh, no," said Julia, despairingly. "We didn't pick one. I have no idea."

The phone rang and Jake relayed, "It's Deborah. She's on her way and will be here in about fifteen minutes. She'll know how to proceed with a funeral home. Let's just wait until she gets here. Shall I call Hattie?"

"Oh, yes. Jake, I thought I was ready for this but I'm not," she cried as she laid her head on his chest. "What else do I need to do?"

"Nothing right now, honey," he soothed her. "Should we check on Henry?"

"I just did," the nurse said. "There's nothing anyone can do for him right now. No matter how much you've thought about it, when death actually happens, you're never really prepared."

Jake dialed Hattie's number and relayed the news.

Hattie responded, "She's with the Lord, now, Mist' Jake. It's as it should be. I'm on my way."

Julia took the phone and said, "Hattie, we are okay right now. You can't miss the holidays with your family."

"You're my family, too, Miss Julia. I'll come now and go on back home later to be with my grandies Christmas morning. People be coming over to your house beginning in the morning and I'll be sure we're ready. God know what He's doing, taking Miz Beatriz home just as the little Baby Jesus born into the world. Don't despair, Miss Julia."

"Thank you, Hattie," Julia managed as she handed the phone back to Jake.

Deborah arrived in her priest's collar and hugged both Julia and Jake. "Peace be with you," she said.

"And also with you," Julia responded automatically. "Thanks

for coming, Deborah. Wait a moment, please, before you go to Henry – can you recommend a funeral home?"

"There are several good ones but many parishioners at St. Luke's use McCoy Funeral Home. They're reliable and compassionate."

The hospice nurse said, "I'll call them for you. They'll come tonight to collect your mother's body."

"So soon?" said Julia. "Is that the right thing to do?"

"Yes," replied the nurse and the priest in unison.

"Thank you," said Julia. "Tell them to wait an hour or so until Hattie gets here."

Deborah sat with them and they reminisced about Beatriz's life, bringing more tears but also some laughter. The priest's prayers were short but heartfelt, giving them some comfort.

Hattie arrived and brushed Beatriz's hair and washed her face before the men from McCoy Funeral home claimed the body. She sat with the family and kept a watchful eye on Henry as Deborah led them through memories and prayers. She helped Henry prepare for bed, then tidied the house for the friends and neighbors she knew would come in the morning.

Fortified by his medication and soothed by his priest, Henry fell into an exhausted sleep. Calvin kept him company.

Jake was not sure how much to discuss with Julia right then, but the people from the funeral home had drawn him aside and explained the decisions needed. He said to Julia, "McCoy expects us at ten tomorrow. Do you want to talk now or wait until in the morning?"

Rubbing her pounding headache, Julia said, "Let's get it out of the way now. Do you think Henry needs to be involved?"

"I'm guessing he'd just as soon we handled things."

"Maybe Mist' Henry pick out her burying dress in the morning?" asked Hattie. "He knows her favorites."

"Good idea," said Julia. "How can we have a funeral this close to Christmas? I'd hate to ruin people's holidays and Mom would have hated it even worse. She never liked being in the limelight."

"You don't have to have a funeral, you know," Jake reminded her. "What about a memorial service after the holidays? Deborah sort of hinted at something like that before she left. The McCoy folks can do the cremation, but the memorial service can be any time. I assumed you planned a cremation, based on something Henry had said the other day. I told them you'd let them know in the morning."

"Oh, Jake, how are we going to get through this?"

"Together, that's how," he assured her as he gathered her close.

Friday morning when Jake woke, he went quietly to the kitchen to start some coffee, glad to leave Julia sleeping since he knew she had been awake much of the night. He was surprised to find Henry sitting at the table.

"You're up early," said Jake. "How're you doing? Did you sleep any?"

"About like you'd think. I took one of the pills so I did sleep. Hattie already made coffee. I'm going with you to the funeral home, Jake."

"Henry, you don't need to do that. Why don't you stay here and rest?"

"I said, I am going to the funeral home," emphasized Henry. "Beatriz was my wife and I'll do my duty toward her. Besides,

I'm the one who knows what she wanted. If you won't take me, I'll call a taxi."

"No, no, I didn't mean that. Of course you'll go." He hoped he was speaking Julia's mind, also. "Let me take Julia some coffee."

"And you can tell her what I said, too."

A disheveled Julia entered the kitchen. "Tell me what, Henry? Oh, thanks, Jake," she said as he handed her coffee. "That's what I need."

Henry sat mute so Jake said, "Henry plans to go to the funeral home with us."

"Oh, no, Henry, we can take care of this," Julia said. "You stay here and rest."

"I *am going to the funeral home*," howled Henry, his face contorted in anguish and anger. "*Don't treat me like a child.*"

Julia retreated hastily. "Of course you are, Henry. We are only trying to spare you."

Jake said, "This is such a hard time—"

Both Julia and Henry turned to him and Julia snapped, "Stay out of this, Jake."

Jake set down his coffee cup and awkwardly embraced them both as they all clung together and wept.

"I'm sorry," whimpered Julia. "This is just so hard."

That's what I just said, thought Jake, wisely remaining silent.

Hattie stepped into the kitchen carrying a colorful dress. "This the one you mean, Mist' Henry?"

"Yes, her favorite. I gave it to Beatriz for her birthday a few years ago. I want her to leave this world in a happy dress. All right with you, Julia?"

"It's a beautiful dress, Henry, and I remember Mom being happy in it, too. I'm glad one decision's made."

Julia and her coffee retreated to the bedroom to prepare for the long day ahead.

Hattie urged gently, "Mist' Henry, could you eat you a little piece of toast or something? Or some applesauce to make your pills go down better?"

His point won, Henry seemed to retreat into himself. "Whatever," he muttered.

Jake found Julia crying in the bathroom.

"Oh, God, why'd I do such a dumb thing to start this awful day?" she wept. "The last thing I want to do is antagonize Henry or make him suffer more."

Jake enfolded her "Honey, put it out of your mind. Henry already has. Let's make sure we don't treat him like a child. He may be the clearest thinker of us all."

"Thanks, love. Let me call my office and get that over with. Then I'm ready to go."

Hattie stayed at home to finish preparing for expected drop-by visitors. She'd already answered a few phone calls from neighbors who had seen the funeral home vehicle in the driveway. She would honor Beatriz's memory by having the house pristine.

At McCoy Funeral Home Jake shuddered at the whole funeral home atmosphere, the muted music, hushed tones, the deep carpet that masked the sound of footfalls. This visit brought back memories of his wife's death and he thought, *Uh, oh, might not be as easy as I thought for me, either.* He sensed Julia's and Henry's tension and vowed to pre-plan his own last rites so no one else had to.

A dark-haired man in a suit to match his hair, of middle age and generous girth, introduced himself in a warm Southern accent. "I'm Donnie Freeman. So sorry for your loss. Come right this way. Can I get you coffee, tea, water?"

They declined refreshment and entered a small room furnished with comfortable chairs upholstered in a subdued floral print. He spread out some papers and brochures on a little glass-topped table and murmured, "Our job is to make this as easy as possible for you. Let me get some information about your beloved."

Julia and Henry provided the facts that reduced Beatriz's life to a one-page form.

"Have you made some decisions about final rituals?" asked Donnie.

Henry fumbled forward the bag he was carrying and said, "Yes, this is her favorite dress. I mean, was..." and broke down crying.

Julia took his hand and said, "Donnie, we want to have a memorial service next week, after Christmas, at our church. Can that be scheduled?"

"Certainly we can on our end, and the church is probably available. Who is the minister?" Donnie asked as he made notes on a pad of paper. "Are you planning a cremation?"

"Yes, that's what Mom wanted," said Julia as she, too, broke down.

Guess I'm up, thought Jake. "St. Luke's, the Reverend Deborah, uh, what is her last name?"

"I know her, a wonderful priest. We have the number."

"Just how does all this work, Donnie? The timelines?"

"I'll call your priest in a few minutes and then we'll schedule with you. We'll likely cremate tomorrow and place the cremains in whatever container you suggest, with the container at the memorial service or not, as you choose. Let me step out and call the rector right now. I'll be right back."

Jake wondered if *cremains* was an actual word, passed around the box of tissues, and hugged everybody. Everyone took a deep breath as Donnie re-entered the room a few minutes later.

"I talked to Reverend Parks and she suggested Tuesday or Wednesday of next week."

"Let's do Tuesday and get it done," Henry said.

"I agree," said Julia. "I think there'll be only a few people attending. Can we do Tuesday morning?"

"Yes. So we prepare the deceased tomorrow—"

Henry interrupted with, "Do you mean cremate?"

"Yes," said Donnie. "Do you want to be here during that process?"

Henry broke down again but managed, "No, I don't think so. You, Julia?"

In tears again at the thought, Julia agreed with Henry. "I don't think our presence is necessary."

"As you wish," said Donnie. "The memorial service will be Tuesday morning. Do you plan to receive people or hold a wake beforehand?"

"Oh, God, I don't know. What do you think, Jake, Henry?"

"Wouldn't it be easier for you all to do it all at one time?" asked Jake.

"Your priest indicated the church would have a reception afterwards. Many people have a memorial service and then gather afterward, especially if there's no viewing," explained Donnie.

"Oh, I hate that they'll ask people at church to fix stuff for a reception at a holiday time like this," Julia said.

"People at that church, especially her book group, loved your mother," Henry reminded her. "We'd be cheating them not to let them do something to honor her."

"I'd expect some leftover Christmas cookies," advised Donnie. "I have a price list for you to review. You've brought a dress for your beloved. Do you want to purchase a coffin for the cremation or use our standard container?"

"A coffin to burn up?" asked Julia incredulously. "I think not! That money should go to a memorial or something."

"Let's get back to that memorial idea in a moment," said Donnie smoothly. "About a container for the ashes…" He slid a brochure across the little table for them to look at.

All three were open-mouthed at the plethora and price range of the containers. Henry broke the silence. "I don't think we need Beatriz's ashes at the service. Her spirit will be with us. I'd like to take her ashes with us to Florida and decide later what to do with them."

"I absolutely agree," said Julia. "How are they returned to us?" she asked Donnie.

"In a simple box," explained Donnie, "perfectly adequate for storage but not what you'd want for display."

"Okay, that's settled," declared Henry. "My wife was not a 'display' kind of person."

Donnie made a note and said, "How about an obituary? Have you thought about what newspapers and what you'd like to say?"

Jake said, "I want to do that. Like most cub reporters, I started out on the obituary desk. I'll get that to you, with a list of newspapers, in a few hours."

Julia gave his hand a squeeze and said through tears, "Thanks, love."

"Fine," concurred Donnie, seeing everyone's nods. "Will you want flowers or a memorial or a combination of the two?"

"Flowers on the altar, as with any church service, but I think that's all," said Julia. "What do you think, Dad?"

"Yes. I've been thinking about a memorial. What about a donation to the church, maybe to the book group to use for books for children at the church? Or maybe a lecture in her honor? Couldn't the book group decide?"

"Oh, Henry, that's a wonderful idea," agreed Julia. "Mom would have loved that. Can you imagine, from an illegal immigrant to having a lecture named for her?"

"All right, those are the decisions. We'll consult with the church and order the flowers," said Donnie. "Do you want to select some hymns or favorite Bible passages? You can think about that for a few minutes. Let me go run up some figures and I'll be right back and we can finish. Oh, and death certificates; will five be enough? We'll take care of Social Security notification," he said as he left the room.

Julia said, "Henry, that is such a great idea for a memorial. And, Jake, I'm touched that you'll write the obituary."

Henry said, "Could we just leave the service up to Deborah?"

"Absolutely," said a relieved Julia.

A few minutes later Donnie re-entered the room and presented them with an itemized list and a contract.

Julia commented, "If I hadn't been looking at assisted care costs, this would probably look high to me but as it is, it's fine, if it's all right with you, Henry."

"Whatever," quavered Henry. "Just do it right for my wonderful Beatriz."

"Thank you for seeing us so early this morning," said Jake as they rose after Julia and Henry had signed the documents.

"No problem, we had the time," said Donnie. Shaking his

head, he continued, "Until this death law thing kicks in. I don't know how we're going to keep up with the funerals after that."

Donnie said, "There's one last thing. We ask the family to confirm the identity of the deceased."

Henry and Julia responded together, "I will," each hoping to spare the other. "We both will," confirmed Julia.

Jake added, "We all will."

Clutching each other's hands, the three followed as Donnie opened the door into a nearby room where a peaceful-looking Beatriz lay. Henry walked over to Beatriz's body and smoothed her hair while Julia clung to Jake. Sobbing, Julia asked, "Do you want a moment alone, Henry?"

A remarkably composed Henry responded quietly, "No, I've already said my goodbyes. Let's go."

CHAPTER 33

Christmas week

Jake, Julia, and Henry returned home to find a florist's van. Hattie was placing beautiful Christmas arrangements of greenery, pine cones, gold ribbons, and candles to complement their other holiday decorations.

Julia read the cards and discovered that one was from her office, the other from Marcus Simms. The thoughtful notes moved her to tears once again. *Oh, I wish I could just quit crying for awhile,* she thought. She was surprised to see cookies and breakfast foods sitting on the table. She was ravenous, though horrified that food could be enticing at this time.

"Oh, good, food. We all need to eat," observed Henry as he shrugged off his coat and lumbered toward the food. He picked up a plate, filled it with Hattie's help, and sat down at the table to eat.

Julia and Jake looked at each other. Something was normal around here – Henry's appetite. They joined Henry at the table.

"There's a list of phone calls wrote down. I hope I spelled the names right. Nobody's expecting you to call back, just wanted you to know they thinking of you. Miz Francine coming over directly. Hope that's okay. She didn't exactly ask, just said she was coming."

"She's probably going to give me a piece of her mind after I ratted her out to her daughter." Turning to Jake, Julia wailed softly, "How are we going to get through the next few days?"

"I've been thinking," said Jake. "Could we just postpone Christmas until we get to Florida? You can mourn without worrying about that."

"It feels so empty here without Mom."

"We could go to my place. You don't want to be rude to anyone, but you may not want to answer the phone and doorbell constantly, either. If people don't see your car, they won't feel like they have to run over and check on you."

"Jake, nobody'll be coming or calling. A change of place might be helpful, though, without so many reminders around. What do you think, Henry?"

"Whatever," mumbled Henry around a mouthful of somebody's special pecan rolls. "It's a time to get through, no easier one place or another."

Hattie interjected, "I'm plannin' to go home tomorrow, if it's okay with y'all, and be home on Christmas morning. I can answer the phone and door today and then maybe we could go back to the city in the morning. Y'all can see people today, then get peace and quiet for a couple of days, pray to the Lord, and be ready for the funeral on Tuesday."

"You need to go on to your family, Hattie," agreed Julia. "We could all come back Monday evening."

"If y'all don't mind to bring me back, I can help y'all and Mist' Henry through the funeral. I'm worried 'bout him doing too much on Tuesday."

"Quit talking about me like I'm not here," growled Henry. "That sounds like a good plan, though."

Hattie went to answer the doorbell. "Hello, Miz Francine. Yes'm, they eating some breakfast. No, you not interrupting. They be glad to see you. Come right this way."

Julia braced for a tirade but was amazed to see how vibrant and alert their neighbor looked, compared to a month earlier.

Francine hugged Henry first, then Julia, and greeted Jake with, "You're still here, I see."

Jake thought, *Yeah, honey, I'm here to stay. Get used to it.* "Good to see you, Francine. Thank you for coming."

"Would you help us eat this food?" asked Henry. "Maybe you brought some of it."

"Don't mind if I do," said Francine, choosing several delicacies. "I brought those pecan thingies you're eating."

"Some coffee, Miz Francine?" asked Hattie, hovering with the pot.

"Don't mind if I do. I'm glad I can eat and drink again."

"You surely look well today," ventured Julia.

"I am well, and I have you to thank for it, I guess. My daughter made me go to the doctor after you called her. Turned out I just had a little inner ear thing and the doctor fixed me right up with some silly exercises. But they worked. I was real mad at you at first but not now. That law's not getting me for awhile yet!"

Turning to Henry, Francine touched his hand and said, "Henry, dear, can you eat another one of my pecan buns?"

Ye gods, thought Jake. *Beatriz's body is not yet cold and the widows are descending.*

Neighbors and phone calls poured in all day. Hattie acted as hostess, shuttling some people toward the family and others to the door. Francine appointed herself as Henry's guardian and Henry didn't seem to mind, or even notice. They survived the first day and night of their new family structure.

As planned, they closed up the house to drive to Jake's for the next couple of days. "We can just leave food and water for Calvin. He'll be okay for two days," said Julia.

"No, he's going with us. He reminds me of Beatriz," Henry sobbed, leaning against Julia.

Julia and Jake exchanged a glance over Henry's head as Jake said, "I'll get the cat carrier."

Henry declared, "He'll sit on my lap."

"He'll like that," Julia said soothingly.

They loaded lots of funeral food into the car. Against Hattie's protests, they drove her to her house and helped her unload the food they insisted she take. Hattie suggested Henry and Calvin remain in the car to remind neighborhood thugs the little Prius was under someone's watchful eye. Julia fervently hoped Calvin would turn into an attack cat if needed. The neighborhood was grim.

They agreed to pick Hattie up early afternoon on Monday, after Christmas. They'd have plenty of time to get ready for the service on Tuesday.

Jake was surprised to see a beautiful beribboned poinsettia sitting outside his apartment. He was touched to see it was from his fellow condo residents George, Jeff and Dreama. The message read, "So sorry to hear of your friend's loss."

"How in the world did they know we were connected?"

"Just one more reminder of how small this city really is," Jake said, smiling. "The obituary was in the paper and I suppose they realized you were the person I've been seeing."

Their two days in the city passed in relative tranquility. Julia,

Jake and Henry joined other city-dwellers in a neighborhood restaurant for dinner on Christmas Eve. They sat around Jake's place crying through feel-good Christmas movies on TV and nibbling the funeral goodies their Virginia neighbors had provided. They were almost able to pretend that these were ordinary days. Time felt almost suspended as they talked about Beatriz, cried a little, and hugged each other a lot. No one suggested Christmas Eve service, no one mentioned gifts, and they got through it.

When they arrived at their home in Falls Church Monday afternoon, Hattie settled Henry and organized the neighbors' food into a semblance of dinner as Julia plowed through telephone messages. Jake tried to do a little work on his next column, using a death in the family to illustrate the potential effects of the death law on next year's holiday season. Calvin prowled and howled, looking for Beatriz. Henry just sat.

CHAPTER 34

Tuesday, December 27

An early-morning knock on the door surprised them all as they sat morosely at the kitchen table drinking coffee. The blustery, cold day seemed to mirror their collective mood.

"Who could that be?" asked Julia. "All the neighbors have already been here. I'm not even dressed yet. Somebody's got a nerve, coming this early on a funeral day."

"The preacher-lady come by, check on y'all," explained Hattie as she led Reverend Deborah into the kitchen. "Here, sit here, Miz Preacher, and I get y'all some coffee."

A flustered Julia said, "I'm sorry I'm not dressed in something other than my robe."

"Thanks," said Deborah, sipping the hot coffee. "Henry asked if I'd stop by if I had a minute and I have all the minutes you need today."

Julia glared at Henry, who said, "I knew you'd say no, Julia, so I didn't mention it. I thought we needed a private word of prayer before the service."

Julia sighed. "You're probably right, Henry. Thanks for coming, Deborah. I do apologize for not being dressed, though."

Deborah said, "There are no rules on this, Julia."

They chatted a few minutes about the schedule for the day. Then Deborah asked, "Would you join me in prayer?"

They sought each other's hands, with Henry motioning Hattie into the group.

"The Lord be with you," said the priest.

"And also with you," responded the family.

Deborah offered a short prayer asking for guidance for all of them through the day, concluding with thanks for peace at last for Beatriz. All were in tears yet again by her final amen. Deborah rose, hugged everyone, and followed Hattie to the door.

Mopping her eyes, Julia said, "Thank you, Henry. That was the right way to start this awful day."

As everyone scattered to don their darkest suits, Hattie asked, "Okay with y'all if I wear church clothes instead of my working suit? Seems like it'd be more respectful to Miz Beatriz."

"Of course, Hattie. You're family."

As they arrived at St. Luke's, they were surprised to see the lot filling up with cars as the funeral assistants directed people to parking. They flagged the family into a reserved space in front of the church.

""There must be a meeting of some kind," said Julia. "There wouldn't be this many people at Mom's service."

"Guess we'll see when we get inside," said Jake.

Dark-suited men helped them from the car and guided them into a small room adjacent to the nave. Hattie helped Henry position himself comfortably in his chair and said, "I'll just slip in the back and get me a seat. I'll see y'all after the service."

Henry grabbed her arm and said, "You go in with us, right, Julia?"

"Absolutely," said Julia. "If you're uncomfortable, just assume you need to be here with Henry."

"That's not far from the truth," said Henry. "I do feel better if Hattie's here."

"Whatever y'all think best."

"Do you want to walk up or will Hattie roll you to the altar rail for communion?"

"Let Hattie bring me. I'd hate to fall and mess up the service."

"I stand behind you, Mist' Henry, then roll you back."

"Anyone baptized is welcome to communion in this church. Jake, if you don't want to go forward, just stay in the pew. Hattie, you can do like Henry does or if you don't want to partake, just keep your hands on the chair," Julia explained.

The priest entered, taking Julia's and Henry's hands. "Is there anything you want to ask me about the service before we begin? I will make a short statement about Beatriz's life, based on what I know and what I read in the beautiful obituary someone wrote. Your work, Jake?"

"Yes, I wrote that."

"When everyone's seated, someone will come and escort you to the front pew. After the service, we'll process out as usual, and I'd like you four to fall in line behind us as we leave. We'll take a moment privately in my office before we go down to the reception together. Okay?" At their nods, she added, "God be with you and provide you with comfort," and rustled out in her vestments.

The door opened and a man beckoned them to follow. Julia entered the nave first, followed by Jake. Hattie guided Henry last so his chair could stay in the aisle after he stood and slid into the pew.

Julia was overwhelmed again by emotion as a quick glance showed her the church was full, including the balcony. She was surprised to see Congressman Simms, Tina-Maria, and the rest of her office staff. She was comforted that so many people had turned out to honor her mother, as she grabbed Jake's hand and hung on for dear life.

The organ music swelled and everyone stood as the crucifer moved down the center aisle carrying the tall golden cross, followed by acolytes and the white-robed communion assistants with Deborah last in solemn vestments. The congregation's voices rose in the words of the opening hymn. Julia stared at the stained glass window above the altar and willed this to be to over with. *Please, God, let me keep my composure through this.*

The words of the funeral liturgy were comforting in their familiar phrases. Henry remained seated when others stood or knelt during the service. Julia slipped easily into the familiar rituals, though she rarely attended services anymore.

Jake was trying to decide whether or not he would participate in communion. He didn't consider himself much of a believer, yet he supposed there was Something behind the creation of the world. *Okay,* he concluded, *I'm in.*

Hattie was having similar thoughts, though not about the sanctity of her beliefs. The ornate cross, furnishings, and clothing were foreign to her. But the real bugaboo was she was pretty sure what was in that silver cup wasn't grape juice. *Oh, Lord, help me here,* she prayed. *I don't wanna go against my belief about alcohol. But Jesus drank wine, didn't He?*

Her head bowed, Hattie heard a voice in her head say, *Drink it.* With a private *Thank you, Jesus,* she maneuvered Henry into his chair and joined Julia, Jake and Henry at the altar rail with hands outstretched to receive the host.

After communion, the final hymn began and those at the

front of the church assembled for the recessional. As Deborah passed their pew, she gestured for them to follow her.

Julia gripped Jake's hand and kept her eyes lowered as she walked down the aisle.

Henry had remained in his chair after communion and rolled after them with Hattie maneuvering the chair. He noticed many of their friends from church and was surprised to see their physician, Dr. Singh, as well as his social worker friend, Anna.

At the rear of the church Deborah gestured for the family to assemble near her and raised her hands as she pronounced the benediction: "Go in peace to love and serve the Lord," to which the congregation responded a quiet "Amen."

Deborah led the family down the hall. The four family members plus the priest made a crowd in Deborah's small office, but the closeness was a comfort to all of them.

Jake wiped tears from Julia's face. "Hang in there, babe. You're doing great."

"I'm sure I look a mess," she sniffled.

"You look beautiful to me," he assured her. "Henry, anything I can do for you?"

"Could you push me into the men's room?"

Julia turned to Hattie. "Thank you so much for being here, Hattie. We all appreciate it."

"I expect this where the Lord wanted me today."

Deborah removed her vestments and shrugged into her suit jacket to attend the reception. "All set?" she asked. "Anyone want the bathroom here off my office?"

"I'll just wash my face," said Julia. "I'm sure my makeup is all smeared."

When Julia stepped back in, Deborah asked, "Do you want to stand in a receiving line or would you rather just circulate?"

"I'll move around the room, if that's okay."

"Just relax as much as you can and listen to the stories people tell you about your mother. We'll make sure you get some food afterward."

Jake returned Henry to Hattie's care and they entered the reception area. The family members were surprised at the large crowd of people there.

People stood in small groups talking while women of the church fairly trotted between the amply provisioned reception tables and the kitchen. Julia said, "Oh, I didn't know Mom had so many friends. What'll I say to people?"

Putting her arm around Julia, Deborah replied, "Your mom's friends, Henry's, yours... your family is important to a lot of people, Julia. About the only good part of a funeral is realizing how many lives you and your family members have touched. When you've absolutely had enough, signal me and we'll leave."

Drawing a deep breath, Julia steadied herself, reached for Henry's hand, and said, "Ready, Henry?"

"I'm with you," he replied as they entered the reception holding hands.

Immediately people began greeting Julia and Henry, embracing them and relating an anecdote or expressing their sorrow at Beatriz's passing. A sort of impromptu reception line formed, despite their intentions to circulate. Before they knew it, an hour had passed and the crowd had thinned considerably. They had greeted neighbors, parishioners, bird club members, friends from their old neighborhood, and most of Julia's office staff. The congressman held court in a corner of the room as only a charismatic politician can do.

The anecdotes reminded Julia that Beatriz had been a vibrant member of the community, not the dysfunctional woman of the last couple of years. She was also amazed at the preparations for the reception with food fanned out in a beautiful array. A bouquet of white roses interspersed with Christmas greenery anchored the table. Julia wondered who knew roses were her mother's favorite flower.

After most people had left, a stooped, frail elderly woman, assisted by a helper in nurse's garb, approached. The woman was dressed in 1960s style in a well-tailored blue wool suit with a matching pillbox hat. The woman looked ready for an afternoon with Jackie Kennedy, except for her clunky orthopedic shoes.

She approached Julia and held out a trembling hand. "You won't remember me. I'm Elsa Brockhurst. Your mother worked in my home for many years. I wanted to pay my respects to her."

"I do remember you, Mrs. Brockhurst," said Julia, taking the woman's shaky claw in both her own hands. "You always let me read the books in your home. Sometimes you gave me milk and cookies."

"You liked animal crackers best, if I remember," reminisced the woman.

Julia replied, "You sat down and talked to me about my books. I have thanked you many times in my heart for your kindness."

"I wanted to see how my investment has paid off," said the old woman.

"Your investment in books and cookies? You made me feel like someone cared about what I learned."

Looking around, Julia noticed Hattie helping a pale Henry to a chair and realized they needed to get him home for some rest very soon. She'd wrap up this condolence conversation quickly and get him out of here.

"No, the rest of the investment," said Mrs. Brockhurst.

"What do you mean?" asked Julia, turning back to the old woman.

"Since Beatriz has passed, I don't see any harm in telling you the story now."

Julia wondered what secret her mother had kept all these years. "Would you like to sit down, Mrs. Brockhurst?"

"No, I'd just have to struggle up again so I'd best stand."

"I'm eager to hear the story," said Julia.

"When you were just a little girl, Beatriz told me how much you wanted to start school. I gave you books to read to see what you'd do with them. You see, Mr. Brockhurst and I hadn't any children of our own but we always took a keen interest in little ones."

"So some of those books I thought were from your library were actually gifts to me?" asked Julia. "How wonderful! They meant so much to me."

Leaning on her cane and her attendant, Mrs. Brockhurst took a deep, shaky breath and continued, "I saw for myself how bright and inquisitive you were. I was very active at my church and on the board of Sacred Heart Academy. So I approached them about offering you a scholarship."

Julia put her hand over her heart and exclaimed, "Really! So that's how I ended up at that wonderful school. I can't thank you enough, Mrs. Brockhurst. All of the teachers were so good to me there."

"I guess they were," Mrs. Brockhurst said with a chuckle. "I was looking over their shoulders all the time and receiving progress reports on you."

Many thoughts flitted through Julia's head. Tears welled up as she said, "I'm just overwhelmed to hear this. I wondered how

Mom paid tuition to that school. I guess it was all she could do to pay for uniforms and books."

"Well, that was part of my investment. Your mother couldn't afford that expense either, so I provided your uniforms, books, your little school shoes, things like that. I guess it's okay to reveal our secret now."

Julia could hardly believe what she was hearing, but she knew it had to be true. "Mom always said it was her job to worry about how to pay for it and mine to get good grades. I never dreamed I was such a charity case but I'm so grateful to you. I wouldn't be here now if it weren't for you."

Glancing toward the door, Julia saw the congressman shaking hands with everyone in sight as he exited. You never knew who might become a constituent, especially if you had your sights set on national office.

Simms caught Julia's eye and waved her away as she took a step toward him. He made the universal finger-and-thumb sign by his ear and mouthed, "Call me," as he walked out the door with Tina-Maria, who gave Julia a little wave. Julia turned her full attention back to the conversation at hand.

Mrs. Brockhurst continued, "You were never a charity case, dear. Your mother earned every cent of your education with her hard work and loyalty to me. It was a bond between us that we were caring for you together. I assure you, she more than deserved what I spent on you. In those days, people didn't pay their help nearly enough – they still don't. Helping you was my way of giving Beatriz more of what she deserved."

She tottered a minute, then righted herself with the help of the aide at her side. "Your mother was a wonderful woman and did so much beyond what she was paid to do. Believe me, we all benefitted from the arrangement. You were never a little matchstick girl! And look how it's paid off. I am so proud of you."

Julia wiped away tears of gratitude both for Mrs. Brockhurst and for her mother. "I never knew all that. Thank you so much for telling me. How will I ever repay you for what you've given me?"

Mrs. Brockhurst reached out and took Julia's sleeve in her hand. "Now stop crying, Julia. You're worth every penny I spent. If you want to repay me, get that boss of yours to repeal the death law," said Mrs. Brockhurst tartly.

"I've kept up with your career, you know. I've watched your congressman on television but I didn't get a chance to talk to him today. I know I'm old but I'm nowhere near ready to die. I've committed no crime except to get old, and I don't deserve a death sentence."

"We're working on that and I'll do everything in my power to make the repeal happen. Would you mind if I shared the story you've just told me with the congressman? No names, of course. I wish I could have introduced you before he left," said Julia.

"You feel free to use the story and my name, too. In fact, I'll stand beside the congressman and talk if you think that would help," declared Mrs. Brockhurst. "This nonsense has got to stop!"

Julia was already thinking along those very lines. What a media coup that could be, to prop up this articulate, appealing old lady in her dated blue suit next to the congressman. That could make a fantastic ad for the next campaign. Julia was counting senior citizen votes already.

"Please tell me how to get in touch with you," said Julia. "I am overwhelmed at all you are telling me, including your offer to help us in the campaign... uh, the effort to overturn the death law."

Mrs. Brockhurst laughed and said, "I hear you about the

campaign. I follow the news, you know, dear. Whatever I can do, I will. It would add a little excitement to my life."

Turning to her caregiver, she said, "Give this young lady my card and make arrangements for us all to go to lunch. And, Julia, don't wait too long. I am old, you know."

Julia hugged Mrs. Brockhurst, gave her business card to the aide, and promised to call very soon. As Mrs. Brockhurst tottered off leaning on her companion and her cane, Julia stood shaking her head in wonder at the revelations of the last few minutes. She was bursting to tell Jake about her benefactor and the congressman about his newest campaign volunteer.

But first, they had to get Henry home before he collapsed. A funeral attendant approached Julia and said, "Would you like us to take your father home? He looks pretty tired."

"Oh, that would be such a help. Then I can stay and thank others for this wonderful reception."

"Consider it done," said the man as he moved toward Hattie and Henry.

Julia could see the relief on Hattie's face from across the room as she nodded gratefully at the man's offer. Henry was slumped forward in his chair, emotionally and physically exhausted, and didn't react as Hattie wheeled him across the room.

She turned to the church ladies standing behind the laden food tables. Politeness dictated that she sample the offerings, but she was surprised to find she was also hungry.

"This looks wonderful," Julia exclaimed.

"People really went all out," said a woman who appeared to be in charge. "We all loved your mother, you know, especially those of us in the book group. Jane is famous for deviled eggs, Josie for cold salmon, others for cookies or dips, and we all brought our specialties. We miss what your mother used to contribute."

"I didn't even know she brought food to receptions," admitted Julia.

"Oh, my, yes, before she got, um, sick, Beatriz brought the most wonderful little chicken enchiladas. We were just saying earlier this morning, we wish we'd gotten the recipe from her before she couldn't, um, before she got sick."

Jake joined Julia and they enjoyed the wonderful array of foods. One of the women said, "We've fixed some boxes for you to take home, so let us know when you're ready to go. Take the flowers, too."

"Oh, thanks so much," replied Julia. "I've been admiring the roses."

Jake said, "Most everyone's gone, and you look beat, sweetheart. Could we say goodbye to Deborah and go? Might be good to check on Henry, too."

"Yes," said Julia gratefully, "I'm ready. I'm blown away by how much my mother meant to people. And do I ever have a story to tell you about my own childhood."

Julia hugged her way out of the church reception hall. She could see trees swaying in the wind and thought the sky looked like imminent snow. She said, "I don't know how I would have done this without you, darling. I'm almost giddy with relief. I hope that's not disrespectful to Mom."

"You held up beautifully, but I knew you would. After all, there's really no alternative, is there, but to just get through it."

Julia leaned her head on his shoulder for a moment and said, "Did all this bring back memories for you of your wife's death? We've really never talked about that."

"Not really. Today I was so busy thinking about you and Henry during the ceremony, plus trying to keep my place in the prayer book, I didn't even think of that."

As they entered the driveway, they saw Francine flouncing off their porch, stiff-backed with fists pumping as she walked. She didn't even stop to greet Jake and Julia, just glared at them as she swept by.

As she entered the front door, Julia saw Hattie with her hands twisting nervously in her apron and asked, "What was that all about?"

"Miss Julia, I hope I didn't do nothing wrong, but Miz Francine came knocking on the door, say she had to see Mist' Henry right away. I told her he sleeping and she say she just sit and wait until Mist' Henry woke up. I told her we wasn't receiving visitors right now and didn't ask her in. I hope I didn't make trouble but Mist' Henry done had about all he can take today and he doesn't need no widow woman hanging 'round."

Julia and Jake laughed at the memory of Francine bristling her way back across the street. "Right on, Hattie. That's what Henry needs, a protector," said Jake.

Julia added, "You did exactly the right thing, Hattie. I guess Dad's going to be a hot commodity now, a widower. This may not be the last widow-woman you have to protect him from."

"Yes'm, I'm thinking that same thing."

Julia was glad to change out of the dressy gray wool jacket and skirt she'd worn to the funeral. She kicked off her heels and told Jake, "Henry's life might get really interesting when we get to Florida."

"If he can escape Francine, you mean," joked Jake. He took Julia in his arms for a quick kiss that turned into something longer.

"How can I think about sex at a time like this?" she asked, drawing away. "Not now, but soon, okay?"

"I think a counselor'd say you are reaffirming the life force," he said. "How else can we feel but very alive after a funeral? I agree, not now… but soon."

Dressed in jeans, sweatshirt, warm socks and fuzzy slippers, Julia said, "I'd better call Marcus. He told me to as he was leaving the reception."

"I thought it was really nice of him and your other staff to be at the funeral, then stay for the reception. Tina-Maria told me she almost brought her boyfriend but decided against it."

"Thank God," responded Julia, "since he's not divorced yet. I'm going to check on Henry – if Hattie will let me! Then I'll call Marcus."

Jake was pulling a sweater over his head to go with his faded jeans and answered in muffled tones, "I'll get the fireplace going and find some music. Maybe you can doze a little, too."

Henry was sleeping deeply under an old, colorful afghan Julia hadn't seen in years and she hoped it brought him comfort. She remembered her mother knitting it in bright wool many years ago. Calvin raised his head from his place beside Henry and glared at Julia as she backed quietly out of the room, shutting the door softly.

Hattie reported, "Mist' Henry been sleeping ever since we come home. Best thing for him right now, Miss Julia. He too old and sick to be this tired. He's taken his medicines, though. I brought them with me to the church."

Julia settled on the couch in the living room where Jake had the gas logs blazing and Mozart streaming from the Bose. She opened her iPad to be ready to take notes and scrambled through her purse for her cell phone.

"I'll be in the den, if you don't mind, for a few minutes," said Jake. "A couple of things occurred to me for my book during the funeral and reception. I want to get them down before I forget."

The congressman answered immediately, as if he'd been waiting for her call. "Thank you so much for taking the time to be with us this morning," she began.

"Where else would I have been?" he asked gruffly, cutting off any further personal conversation. "Listen, I have some news."

"Okay, I'm ready," said Julia, shifting her mind to work mode.

"I talked to the party leaders about the Senate seat, and they agreed I'd be a good candidate, if I don't screw up this repeal thing. Of course, if it fails, they'd drop me like a hot apple, but if that happens, we're all going to be in such deep sh... uh, stuff, it won't matter anyway."

Hot apple? Oh, another one of his mix-ups. Hot potato. Hot dog. Gotta be sure those are right in his speeches.

"We figured they'd support you, but that's good news."

"Yeah, I didn't want to bother you with it when you were tied up with your mother's thing."

My mother's thing? That seems a little callous.

"They want me to do the rebuttal after the President gives the State of the Union speech in January. I'll be the party spokesperson, with twelve minutes of free television time."

"Marcus, that's wonderful! That's a great honor."

He snorted. "Honor, horseshit! I'm just the only fool who's stuck my neck out so far on this death law thing. I can get the party message across and then if things mess up, they can just dump me. I'll be either the hero or the donkey. Uh-oh," he laughed, "wrong word. I already *am* the donkey, that's why I get to speak."

"Well, stay a donkey and not an ass," Julia agreed. "So when do we get a copy of the President's speech?"

"Why'd we need that? We know what we're going to say, regardless of what he says."

"Don't you need to react to his points, at least a little?"

"Well, yeah," said Marcus dismissively, "maybe. But the party leaders just want me to come out swinging on this law thing. Hey, are you coming to work tomorrow? Or do you need another day?"

Or another week or another month? Sighing, she said, "Yeah, I'll be there. Assuming Henry is doing all right, of course."

"He'll be fine. He's a tough old bird. Just let the widows take care of him."

"They're swarming already," said Julia. "At least, one is."

"Okay, see you tomorrow. Wear your boots and dress warm, missy, it's gonna snow, you know."

Snow was indeed forecast, and a lot of it, Julia learned after checking her weather app. She was very thankful they'd finished her mother's funeral without having to delay it due to weather.

"Jake," she called into the next room, "have you seen the forecast? Are you going to DC tomorrow? The congressman requests my presence at the office."

"Yeah, I'd better check in and leave some columns with my editor. Is it going to snow? Sure looks like it?"

"That's what they say. I'll talk to Hattie about her plans. Maybe we'd better pack to spend a day or two if necessary."

Hattie affirmed that she had no need to return to her home for a few days. However, she had a question. "What y'all want me to do if Miz Francine comes calling again?"

Julia bit her lower lip and pondered the question. "I think Henry can decide that for himself. Maybe he'll want some company. What do you think?"

"Indeed, makes no never-mind to me. Just wanta know how much to protect him."

"All right, we're going to assume we may be snowbound in DC for a day or two. You sure you'd be okay here alone?"

"Yes'm, we be fine. We got lots to eat and I help Mist' Henry decide what he gonna move to Florida. Then I'll go home for the weekend and do the same for myself."

CHAPTER 35

Wednesday, December 28

Jake brushed snow off Julia's Honda CR-V, happy for an all-wheel-drive vehicle for this morning's commute. The flakes falling lazily from the slate sky were beautiful but portended traffic nightmares. He yearned for the coming days in Florida. He was wrapped up in his puffy down coat with one of Henry's scarves. He also looked forward to having all his clothes under one roof. *God, I hate to be cold*, he thought grumpily.

Julia traded last-minute instructions with Hattie. She carried a small suitcase and a large briefcase, anticipating she'd need both for the maelstrom of office tempest and the near-blizzard predicted for later that day. She was glad Henry was still asleep and she didn't have to listen to his weather-fretting this morning, also.

Jake asked, "Do you want to drive?"

"No, you, and I'll watch the GPS app on my iPad to see where the traffic is snarled."

"All right, I think we're ready. Who's that looking out the window across the street?"

Julia laughed. "That's Francine. I bet she's been up early baking for Henry. Well, he may welcome that diversion today." The curtain snapped shut as Julia gave a cheery wave to her neighbor. "She's probably dialing all the neighbors about how heartless I am to be going to work and leaving Henry."

"Does that bother you?"

"Not a whit! Drive on, dear one."

As they neared their destination, Jake observed, "Traffic's not too bad."

"It's the weather. You know how DC shuts down in a storm. I'm surprised to be looking forward to going to the office, getting back to normal. I'm ready for Florida, especially today. You?"

"Exactly what I was thinking, but I didn't want to sound insensitive. The sooner, the better to get moved farther south. This snow is really coming down and the usual Southern idiots are out driving in it."

Julia nodded in agreement.

"Shall I drop you off near your office and then park the car at my office? Oh, hell, I don't have a sticker on this car. I'll either pick you up or we'll both ride public transportation to my condo this afternoon. We'll just hole up here for a couple of days, right?"

"Yes, I'm looking forward to that quiet time together," said Julia, reaching over to give his hand a squeeze. "Would you want to walk over to my office and we'll go together to the condo, maybe get some dinner on the way?"

"Better idea," he agreed. "On foot will be the easiest way to get around this afternoon." Peering down at her feet, he noted, "Good, you have your boots. I left mine at my condo."

"Father Marcus reminded me to wear my boots today." With a quick kiss, she exited near her office with her briefcase, leaving her suitcase for him to ferry upstairs to the condo. "Be careful. See you later," she said and added, "I love you, Jake."

"Me, too, you," he shouted out the window as he pulled away into the storm-snarled traffic.

Inconvenience notwithstanding, Julia always thought the city looked its best twice a year, cherry blossom time in the spring and a good snowstorm in the winter. The snow covered the grittiness and muffled the traffic screeches and sirens. Pedestrians were more likely to greet each other with bonhomie in the shared beauty and tribulations of a snowstorm.

Julia schussed her way into her office building and hiked the stairs to their third-floor office suite. She was not looking forward to everyone's condolences, but wanted to get it over with.

Many of the staff members were at their desks when she entered. Most cast their eyes downward, not knowing how to greet her the day after her mother's funeral. By the subdued murmurs in the room, she surmised that the congressman was already in his office.

"Good morning, everybody," said Julia.

Heads snapped up and then quickly back down as the staff chorused, "Morning, Julia."

Tina-Maria came forward and grasped both of Julia's hands as Julia thought, *Please, God, no Latina histrionics from Tina-Maria this morning.*

"Your hands are cold," Tina-Maria said. "We're all glad you're here. The congressman's been asking–"

At that moment, Simms yelled from his inner office, ""Bout time you got here, missy. Come in and let's get to work."

Tina-Maria released Julia's hands as both women gave a rueful laugh. *Back to normal, just like that,* thought Julia. *Okay, that's done.*

"It's really messy out there," observed Julia to the group at large as she removed her outerwear and hung it on the back of her desk chair to dry. She gathered her notepad and pen and entered Marcus' office.

"Shut the door," he said. "You okay, Julia? Thanks for coming in but we really do need to get to work. I can't afford to screw up this thing or all of our jobs will be in jeopardy."

Julia steeled herself not to react to his unaccustomed kindness, caught off guard as always when he dropped his normal gruffness and revealed a heart underneath. Steadying herself with a deep breath, she replied, "I'm okay. Let's get started. What did the National Committee actually say to you when you met with them?"

An hour later, they had mapped out the dimensions of the short speech Simms was to deliver, focusing on calling for the repeal of the death law. Julia settled in her own office and shut her door to do some research before her staff forgot she was in mourning and mobbed her.

Jake was shrugging off his wet coat and unpacking his laptop in his office when Sam Wilkerson leaned against the doorframe.

"So nice of you to stop in today," said the editor sarcastically. "What's new with you?"

"Hey, Sam. Happy holidays. I've been pretty tied up with Julia's mother's funeral," replied Jake evenly.

"Oh, damn, I forgot that was what you were doing," apologized Sam. "I thought you were lounging on the Gulf while the rest of us poor bastards are shivering in DC. I'm sorry for my remark. How'd that go?"

"We're just glad it's over." Jake dismissed the topic. "I've done some good work on the book. I wrote up the town meetings and interviews from Florida, 'God's Waiting Room.' And you've been receiving my columns and articles, just like we agreed, right?"

"Yes, and they're good. Very good. We've gotten lots of positive responses from your fans, as well as some static from the crazies out there. People are reading them."

"I'll have another couple of things to you today," said Jake defensively. "I know I've got a few more pieces due."

"That's not what I stopped by for," said Sam. "The Boss Lady wants you upstairs. Today, she said, if you came in."

"Oh, hell, what've I done now?"

"Probably nothing because she suggested lunch. She wouldn't feed you and then eat you. If she was going to fire you, she wouldn't waste money on lunch."

"Oh, Lord," sighed Jake. "I dressed at Julia's this morning and here I am in old cords and a sweater. I think I have a tie in a desk drawer." He began opening drawers and rummaging around.

"Calm down, fella." Sam laughed. "She said upstairs in her conference room at noon, so you got deli coming in. She wouldn't want to go out and ruin her shiny high-heeled devil-lady boots she's sporting this morning, anyway. Most useless snow boots you ever saw!"

"You got any idea what this is about?"

"She said there's somebody she wants you to meet and bring your notes on your book, plus a couple of your recent columns."

"I better call her secretary and confirm."

"I already did that when I saw you coming down the hall."

"How'd you know I didn't have other lunch plans?" huffed Jake.

"Because when the top dog at the news bureau calls a reporter to come to lunch, he doesn't have other plans," said Sam acidly. "Let me know what's going on," he threw back as he walked back to his own office.

Yeah, right, thought Jake, *as if everybody won't know soon whatever it is. This is one big gossip pile. I better find that tie, though.*

Julia discovered some interesting tidbits on the death law as she fact-searched for the congressman's rebuttal speech. She found information on a young newlywed who became a celebrity in 2014 when she ended her own life after being diagnosed with a terminal brain tumor. The former teacher, according to *People* magazine, became "the unexpected face of the right-to-die movement."

Hmm, thought Julia, reading further. *That'd make a great sound bite. Oh, damn, she's already dead.* The woman had moved to Oregon, where physician-assisted suicide was legal, and ended her own life. Julia jotted a note about contacting one of her family to support the congressman's stance.

She investigated the website of Compassion and Choices, an organization advocating options including physician-assisted suicide. She read anti-suicide messages at TheFederalist.com. She learned about a nurse in Pennsylvania who was tried, acquitted, and interviewed on *60 Minutes* for assisted suicide when she handed her dying father his prescribed dose of morphine that allegedly led to his death. She read that Oregon, Vermont and Washington permitted physician-assisted suicide under very stringent safeguards. She discovered that Montana and New Mexico had had court decisions related to physicians' culpability in such cases, and other states, including California, New Jersey and Colorado, were debating legislation on the topic. Julia concluded that this was a viable – no irony intended – and timely topic for Marcus to explore and probably champion. It was the ultimate opposite of the death law.

She was surprised to learn that the first movement to legalize assisted suicide began in the U.S. in 1906. More recently, the work in the '90s of Dr. Jack Kevorkian was highly publicized. Many other states, including their own Florida, had had ballot initiatives or relevant court cases through the years – Massachusetts, Alaska and New York among them. *Oops, better read up on that Florida case ASAP.* She was convinced there was plenty of factual material to back up their position.

She assembled her notes and called Walter into her office. The speech construction had begun, the most important speech of Simms' career.

Jake quickly printed off some columns to carry upstairs to the Boss Lady. He worried that he might be losing his journalist's objectivity on this subject. The experience with Julia's mother had solidified his own belief regarding the rightness of death by choice, with dignity. *Sounds like a good column title*, he thought.

He scrounged his tie from a bottom drawer and decided it was hopelessly wrinkled. Then again, he could tuck it into his sweater, so he put it on. Better to be disheveled-respectful than blatantly-casual. He found enough reflective surface in his computer screen to tie the knot and smooth down his hair. He tried to shake creases into his rumpled brown cords, shined his shoes on the back of his pants, and pulled his wool v-neck sweater over his head. *Probably good I don't have a mirror in here.*

Grabbing his laptop and the columns he'd just printed, he

set off up the stairs. As he walked down the hall, he saw Sam peering out of his office. *Is he bird-dogging me?* Jake wondered. *Jeez, did he think I'd forget this meeting? I can't wait to be a long mile away in Florida!*

Jake received a warm greeting from his big boss's secretary, which he viewed as positive. She directed him to the conference room and said the others would be in shortly. Jake could hear voices behind the closed office door but couldn't identify them.

He brought up the outline of his proposed book on his laptop. He wasn't ready to share it with others yet, especially others who deal in print media. He set out the folders of columns he had brought along. He idly watched the snow beautify the city outside the wall of windows and rubbed his chest where he felt a little heartburn beginning.

Jake heard the inner office door opening. He stood as his boss ushered a middle-aged man into the conference room. He noticed she was still wearing the silly high-heeled boots Sam had mentioned.

Jake's first impression of the managing editor was always her imposing stance. A tall, slender, ebony-skinned woman in her early forties with a short afro, she intimidated anyone she chose. She dressed better, thought faster and talked louder than anyone else in any meeting. People either loved her or hated her – more the latter – but almost everyone respected her and most were scared of her. If Jake wasn't so close to retirement age, he'd be more scared, too. She'd always treated him fairly, though. She used to be called "Black Thunder" behind her back, but everybody was too politically correct to do that these days. At least while they were sober.

The Boss Lady held out her hand to Jake and said, "Thanks for coming in, especially with the snow and the death in your friend's family. I wanted you to meet Harrison Billingsley and he's in town just for today. He has to catch a plane later this afternoon – if they're flying."

Jake was surprised that she knew about the death of Julia's mother. Or even Julia, for that matter. Obviously she'd done her homework before today's meeting. Jake shook hands with the man, relieved to see he was in slacks and sweater, also.

As they seated themselves at the table, she said, "I have been very impressed with your columns of late, and you know I don't say that often, Jake. Sam says you're making good progress on your book on the death law."

The secretary poked her head in, distributed three boxed lunches, and handed out bottled water. *So much for coffee,* thought Jake. *Probably don't need that with this heartburn, anyway.*

The Boss Lady ignored the secretary and continued, "Harrison is one of the best literary agents in the business. I've known him since we were undergrads together and have the highest regard for him. The publication of your book would be a real boost to our bureau. I think your columns and articles on the death law are Pulitzer-worthy, too. Did Sam tell you we intend to nominate you for that?"

Jake was untying the string on his box of lunch but was speechless and appetite-less at her words. He managed a "thank you."

"Now I want you to tell us just what you propose in that book and let Harrison take it from there. Do you have an outline?"

She sat back and relinquished the floor to her companions.

Jake knew his chance to talk would be brief so he quickly described his idea for a book and his progress to date.

Harrison swallowed the potato chip he'd just put in his mouth, swigged his water and asked in a bored tone, "You have anything I can look at?"

Jake got the distinct impression that the Boss Lady was more interested in this meeting than the agent was.

"These columns illustrate the tack I'll be taking. The outline isn't ready to hand over yet."

Harrison quit chewing and glanced up at Jake after scanning the first column. "This is good, Jake. It's interesting, well written, and has real substance. Let me read the other one."

The agent's voice showed more interest. The managing editor seemed to be smiling into her box lunch, having apparently anticipated both of Harrison's reactions.

After reading the second column more attentively, the agent asked, "Is that your outline on your screen? Can I take a look?"

"Sure," said Jake, angling the laptop so the other two could see it. The Boss Lady continued to eat and watch the snow pile up over the city. Her job had been to bring the two together, not to participate in the proceedings.

Harrison nodded at the words on the screen and said, "Get me a copy of this and a chapter or two ASAP. Maybe next week? This topic is ready to take off and I want to sell this book right away. It's bound to come up at the State of the Union speech in a couple of weeks and I'd like to be ahead of that, if possible."

Oh, yeah, it'll come up. Jake inwardly laughed, thinking of the speech Julia was probably composing right that moment. "Sure, I already have a few chapters written. By next Friday?"

"Earlier, if possible. I want to hit the big publishers right at the first of the year. This may be the topic of the year. If we're first, this could be a real blockbuster. As much as any nonfiction is, I mean."

Jake gulped and said slowly, "Okay, I'll shoot for Wednesday. Not promising, though."

"Skip New Year's and write," advised the boss. "New Year's will be around next year but a book contract might not be."

Yeah, but will Henry? Jake thought.

"Good, I'll let you guys do the paperwork," said the managing editor as she crammed her lunch debris back into the white box. "Harrison, stop by my office before you leave. Jake, don't screw this up. And help Sam write up the Pulitzer thing."

Jeez, no wonder he's testy, if she's making him do the nomination, thought Jake. *I don't think Sam's ever been nominated himself.*

Harrison had pulled some documents from his briefcase and said, "Can we go over some papers about my representing you, Jake? Or shall we finish our lunch first?"

I always heard getting an agent was impossible, Jake thought. *My life is out of control again, spinning so fast, wish I could talk to Julia. But I'm not going out the door without signing these papers.*

Jake shook his head and said, "Not hungry. Let's do this," as Harrison spread the papers across the table.

Thirty minutes and several signatures later, Jake and Harrison had discussed content, strategy and procedures as well as money and representation. Jake felt, as they say, gob-smacked as he and Harrison shook hands goodbye. He carried his untouched lunch with him down the stairs to his own office.

Sam was trolling the halls outside Jake's office.

"So what happened?" the editor asked impatiently.

"Come in and share my lunch," invited Jake. "I haven't touched it yet."

"I want to share your news, not your lunch," said Sam. "What did the Boss Lady say?"

"Not much, actually. She introduced me to a literary agent and made it pretty clear we were to sign a contract. I liked him and it's a huge load off my mind."

"And?" prompted Sam.

"She said you'd be writing up a nomination for the Pulitzer for the work on the death law."

"Yeah, that's what I thought she wanted," said Sam. "I'm a little jealous, to be writing up yours instead of you writing up mine. But you've earned it. You're ahead of the pack on the death law. You deserve the nomination, more than those turkeys who usually win it," he added grudgingly. "It'll be good for us to get that lift, especially for some of our struggling papers."

"And what newspaper isn't struggling these days?" offered Jake. "Except for the Gray Lady in New York, we're all in pretty deep shit together."

After Sam left, Jake called Julia to share the news. He left a "call-me" message on her unanswered phone. He picked up his sandwich and realized he didn't feel so good. His chest was tight and he was a touch light-headed. *Too much excitement this morning.* Shaking it off, he dumped his lunch in the trash. His life was good: Julia, his career, the move to Florida, all of it.

CHAPTER 36

Wednesday, December 28

Julia called Jake back an hour or so later and congratulated him on his phenomenal news. She asked, "Honey, are you okay? You sound a little funny."

Jake hesitated and said, "Actually, I don't feel very well. I just don't feel right."

"What's wrong? What hurts? Why didn't you call me?" Julia asked in a panic.

"Well, I did call you. A little hard to breathe, a small pain in my chest–"

"Jake, you've got to get help right away! That sounds like a heart attack or a stroke. What's the nearest hospital?"

"Julia, calm down. Memorial Hospital, I guess. Let's wait and see if I feel better in a little bit. Ooh," he groaned involuntarily.

"Hang up, Jake. I'm calling an ambulance and somebody in your office. Hang on, honey, I love you," she finished with a sob.

"Might not be a bad idea," Jake whispered.

Sam walked by and saw Jake slumped over. "Jake, what's the matter? Jake? *Jake?* Somebody call an ambulance! STAT!"

Chaos reigned for the next half hour. EMTs rushed into the

office in a matter of minutes, though it seemed like hours to Sam and to the semi-conscious Jake.

"Can you hear me, sir? Stay with us now," said one EMT loudly as he inserted an IV needle into Jake's arm. He asked Sam, "What's his name?"

"I'm Jake," slurred the fading man.

"Okay, Jake, buddy, you keep talking to us and we'll have you in the ER right away. How you feeling, Jake?"

"Not... so... good..."

"Do you have a wife, children, someone these folks here should call?" asked the EMT. He attached other equipment and began speaking into what looked like a microphone on the shoulder of his uniform.

"He's a widower, no children," supplied Sam, amazed at the efficiency of the technicians as they worked to stabilize Jake.

"Julia... on her... way...here," Jake managed.

"You're doing great, buddy. Keep talking to us," said the EMT. "We'll get you to the hospital in just a minute."

"Am... I..." began Jake.

"Dying? No, not now. We'll get you to the hospital alive and then they'll keep you that way. That's our job and we're good at it."

To Sam, the EMT said, "Who's Julia? Somebody better call her."

"Julia's his girlfriend," said Sam. "I don't even know her last name. She works for a Congressman."

"Sanchez," managed Jake. "My phone."

Sam scrolled through the names until he located Julia's, and punched in the call.

"Jake, is that you?" asked a breathless Julia.

"No, it's Sam, his editor. Where are you?"

Julia looked up through the blinding snow and recited land-marks. "How's Jake?" she asked frantically.

"The EMTs are working on him right now. He's conscious and told me how to call you on his phone. I think – hope – that's a good sign. You're almost here. I'll call the front desk and tell them to admit you. Government security badge, right?"

"I see your building. Oh, God, tell me this isn't happening," she whimpered as she trotted along.

"He's conscious, Julia. Let's hope for the best, okay?"

"Yes," she managed shakily. "Okay, I see the flashing lights and there's a crowd gathering."

"We're on the third floor. Security'll meet you at the door and escort you in."

"Thanks, Sam."

Julia could see a uniformed man hovering inside the door of the news building. She flashed her security badge at the guard. He took her arm and ushered her in, pointing at the elevator, and said, "Third floor, ma'am."

A small crowd of concerned employees stood outside a door so Julia had no trouble finding Jake's office. They gave her a curious once-over as she ran down the hall, briefcase bouncing over her shoulder.

She lunged forward to take Jake's hand. "Oh, Jake, what's happening to you?"

"I sure hope you're Julia," said a man standing nearby. "I'm Sam."

She glanced up and said, "Of course I'm Julia. Jake, honey, are you okay?" realizing what a foolish question that was.

He opened his eyes and said, "Not sure... better... now... you're... here."

The EMT apparently in charge turned to Julia and said,

"Lady, we're going now. You can meet us in the ER waiting room."

"I'm going with you," she said, moving down the hall with the gurney.

"No room, meet us there. Regulations—"

"I'm going," said Julia firmly. "You both rode over in the front seat so there's space for me. Don't tell me regulations and don't make me have to call a congressman."

"No, ma'am," said the EMT, more respectfully this time. "No time for a congressman. Come on."

Jake thought, *That's my girl*, as he drifted into unconsciousness.

They loaded Jake into the back of the ambulance. One of the EMTs jumped in beside him while the driver said, "Hurry up, lady. We need to get there."

Siren wailing, they wove through the snow-snarled traffic and arrived at the hospital in a very short time. As they unloaded Jake, one of the EMTs said quietly to Julia, "Ma'am, if they tell you to leave the ER, you really do have to go, okay?"

"I understand," said Julia, as she trotted along beside the gurney, clutching Jake's hand. "I didn't mean to give offense back there."

"None taken, ma'am. Good luck to both of you. And God be with you."

"Thank you," whispered Julia, as she sent up her own prayer.

The next several hours were a blur that Julia could never quite remember. She made herself as small as possible in the corner of Jake's cubicle and no one threw her out. She answered all the intake questions she could, listing herself as "next of kin, fiancé" and left blank the parts about whether he had a do not resuscitate order or a living will. *We haven't gotten to this conversation yet,* she realized. They could straighten it out later, if necessary.

Jake got a lot of attention, but nobody was pounding on his chest or shouting "code" and no beepers were going off so she hoped those were good signs. Mostly they were drawing blood, taking his vital signs and watching his heartbeat on a monitor, blips that looked reassuringly steady to Julia. Jake was unconscious but appeared to be in no pain and his color looked normal.

Julia listened to all the conversations among the hospital workers in the welter of activity surrounding Jake. She asked no questions until they decided to move Jake to a room upstairs in the Coronary Care Unit. She asked Dr. Ahmed Kahn, a cardiologist according to his name tag, what his diagnosis and prognosis were.

"And you are?" he asked courteously in a Middle Eastern accent, focusing his attention on the computer screen above Jake's head.

"His fiancé. He is a widower and has no children. I will be taking care of him after he's discharged."

"Yes, thank you. We do not think he has had a heart attack but we are going to monitor him overnight to track his heartbeats. We are not sure what has happened but sometimes there can be a momentary spasm that mimics a heart attack. We will x-ray for other causes later in the evening. We want to watch him, keep him sedated and comfortable. Has he had unusual stress lately?"

"Yes," explained Julia. "He's writing a book, we've sold a house and will move to Florida, and my mother's funeral was just yesterday. So yes."

Dr. Kahn sighed and spread his hands. "We believe the heart just gets overloaded sometimes and takes a blip, you might say, until it readjusts itself. We watch such patients carefully until we are sure the blip is corrected."

"You mean, we may never know what caused this?" asked Julia.

"There is much about the body we do not understand. Right now your Jake is not in pain and his heart appears to be functioning normally. We gave him some medicine and he is sleeping. We will see how he feels when he wakes. I suggest you stay with him, if possible."

"That's a relief," said Julia, exhaling breath she didn't know she'd been holding. "I want to be here."

"He will be more content if you are here, if you bring comfort to one another."

"Yes, we do," she said. "Thank you, Dr. Kahn."

A large, cheerful man in green scrubs, showing a gold tooth when he smiled, entered the cubicle. He said in a Caribbean lilt, "We goin' upstairs. I take you dere."

"How can I help?"

"Just stay outta my path and I'll handle dis, ma'am," he responded with a golden smile. Julia trailed along carrying Jake's wallet and her own purse, coat and briefcase.

They rolled down the hall of the fourth floor to a room where a nurse waited to receive Jake. When they efficiently scooted him onto the bed, he murmured something incoherent but did not wake up.

The nurse began taking his vital signs, arranging his IV tubing, and hooking him up to a machine or two. Julia saw similar small rooms grouped around a central command post with workers looking at computer screens.

The nurse draped a contraption around Jake's neck and explained to Julia how a Holter monitor worked to record his heartbeats. "We'll watch him carefully here for twenty-four hours and then Dr. Kahn will decide what's next."

"Can I stay with him?"

"Yes, that chair actually folds out into a sort of cot," said the nurse. "Not the best, but beats sitting up all night. We'll get you a blanket and a pillow. There's a cafeteria open twenty-four hours a day and a Starbucks in the lobby."

"I have to make some phone calls. Can I do that here?"

"No long or emotional ones in the room. There's a waiting room and also a conference room right outside the door. Just ring when you're finished and we'll buzz you back in. You're Jake's fiancé, right? Would you know anything about a DNR or living will here or medical power of attorney?"

"No, I don't," said Julia. "We haven't talked about that yet."

"When he wakes up, if you have the chance without upsetting him…"

"I'll ask him if the time seems right," agreed Julia.

"We're taking him for some x-rays shortly. He'll probably be awake after that."

"Thank you so much. I appreciate all everyone is doing for Jake, and your kindness to me."

"No problem, that's our job."

Through the wall she could hear an alarm going off in another cubicle and was thankful that all Jake's machines seemed happy. She sank down in the chair, scooting close so she could hold his hand. The adrenaline propelling her subsided and she felt a profound weariness. She nodded off in her chair, firmly anchored to Jake.

When she awoke, she saw a drowsy Jake regarding her. "You're beautiful. Have I ever told you that?" he slurred.

Julia laughed shakily, pushed her hair out of her eyes, "You must have some good meds, if you think that! How are you feeling, love?"

"Okay, I guess. Where am I? What happened?"

"You slumped over on your desk, scared everyone half to death, rode in an ambulance, got lots of attention in the ER, and now you're in the CCU being observed."

"What's this thing around my neck?"

"That's measuring your heartbeat. Don't pull it loose."

Jake fell back with his eyes closed. "I'm hungry. Now I remember, no lunch."

"Well, you may not get dinner, either," warned Julia. "They want to run some more tests and do more blood work. Your IV may be dinner."

"IV? Oh, yeah, I see it. Jesus, Julia, I'm hooked up all over. What's going on?"

"They're trying to figure out why you had the chest pain. So far it's not looking like a heart attack."

"If not that, then what?" He was becoming more alert. "I guess that's good news. I gotta get out of here. I need to get back to my book and we're getting ready to move and..."

He shifted around, an alarm went off, and the nurse hurried in. "What's happening? Oh, I see, you came unhooked. Looks like your blood pressure went up, too." Glancing at Julia, she asked, "Were you talking about something important?"

"I can't stay here, I have too much to do," protested Jake, struggling upright and disarranging another tube or two.

"Here," the nurse handed Jake a small device. "Instead of sitting up, just stay still and push the button and let the bed move. That way you stay connected. Try to relax," she said as she exited.

Julia squeezed Jake's hand and said, "Let's just get through this, Jake. We can adjust our timetable. With your place here in DC, we don't have to move right away. And you can work on your book when you feel like it. That'll wait."

"Actually, I didn't get to tell you all the details about the contract I signed with an agent today. He wants the book ASAP."

"Oh, Jake, that's wonderful news! Now you can just concentrate on the writing."

"Yeah, I guess you're right. Okay, I'll do my best to be patient. Actually, I feel fine now, just stupid to be here."

"Jake, we have so much, but it all rests on good health. Just get well." She broke down for the first time that day as awareness of what she'd almost lost washed over her. She laid her head on the side of the bed and sobbed quietly.

Jake patted her head awkwardly and said, "If you'd just climb in beside me, I could reassure you better."

Julia lifted her head and laughed shakily. "If you can think about 'that,' you must be feeling better."

"I always think about making love to you, Julia," he said softly. "It's the most beautiful, most unexpected thing in my life. If I think about it, I'll set off my alarms again!"

Another orderly who looked a lot like the first one, but with a gold ring in his ear, appeared at the door of the room and said, "Hey, mon, we be goin' to X-ray. Miss, back in about an hour but dey busy down dere so not to worry if it be longer, okey-dokey?"

After Jake was rolled out, Julia began to make phone calls. She called Sam, reporting that Jake was feeling much better, and perhaps had not had a heart attack. She relayed the same news to Tina-Maria, who said even the congressman seemed worried. Then Julia called Hattie to say they wouldn't be home for a day or two.

"That'll be fine, Miss Julia. We already made those arrangements. Mist' Henry and me getting' a lot done, sorting and packing his things. He wanna throw out everything heavy but I tell him he gotta keep some clothes for visits back to DC. He says he never leaving Florida once he get there!"

Julia briefly explained Jake's predicament and Hattie moaned, "Oh, no, Miss Julia. I'll commence to praying and call my church circle, too. Don't you worry a bit about us. I call you if anything goes awry. Mist' Henry fine, except he's clamoring to talk to you."

"Is Jake okay? Where are you?" Henry said. "I can get a cab. You give it to me straight, now."

"Settle down, Henry. We don't need you in the hospital, too," warned Julia. "This is what I know. Jake's in the cardiac care unit in Memorial Hospital and seems to be doing okay."

Henry calmed down some. "Call us again tonight, okay? Have you had anything to eat? You sound puny, too. I'll contact Deborah and get the book club prayer thing going."

"Sounds good. I'll call tonight and now I'll go get something to eat while Jake's getting x-rays."

"Good idea, daughter. I love you both, tell Jake I said so."

Jake looked exhausted as the attendant rolled him back into the CCU a couple of hours later. The nurse had promised him broth and Jello. He told Julia their car was still at his office, good news since she could retrieve her suitcase with a change of clothes. She left to collect the car while public transportation was still running in the snow.

The day of hurting, testing and worrying had worn them out. Both were grateful to settle down for the night under the watchful eyes of the CCU nurses. Comfortable or not, they slept holding hands, with intermittent attention from the nursing staff.

Morning brought achy bodies and cranky minds. Jake was ready to go home while Julia wanted some solid information. Breakfast arrived so they assumed the testing was over.

Dr. Kahn arrived mid-morning. Julia was attempting to do some work on her laptop and Jake was watching mindless television to distract himself. "Mr. Jordan, you look much better than you did yesterday. How are you feeling?"

"Much better, thank you, and I'd be even better with a shower."

"I have mostly good news. You did not have a heart attack. However, we are not sure what exactly did happen to cause your chest pain. We have detected some irregularities in your heartbeat, so that could have been a contributing cause, along with stress, being over-tired, other factors."

"I guess that makes sense," responded Jake. "I really feel fine now. Can I go home?"

"The city is virtually shut down with snow," said Dr. Kahn. "I would feel much better if you would remain with us most of the day. I'll see you late this afternoon. By then I hope to have more data."

The day passed slowly. Julia helped Jake and his IV shuffle to a waiting area with windows that afforded a view of the snowy city.

Jake worried about the lack of his laptop, confirming for Julia that he was feeling much better. He called Sam, who offered to bring it to the hospital. Jake didn't want a visitor but figured it was a decent trade-off, and Sam sounded relieved to hear Jake's voice on the phone.

After Sam's visit, Jake was more content to sit out his sentence in his hospital room.

He was startled to see how much time had passed when Dr. Kahn entered the hospital room about four p.m. "I see you are feeling better, if you are working," said the doctor. "Let's remove your monitor."

"Yes, I feel fine now," answered Jake. "Can I go home?"

"Let me tell you what we have learned. We find no evidence of disease of the gall bladder, lungs or other organs from our x-rays and tests. We want to treat your irregular heartbeat. This may have caused you to lose partial consciousness yesterday and with some indigestion or heartburn, you had the chest pain."

"Treat it how?"

"Medication, at least initially. Atrial fibrillation will not kill you, but it could cause a stroke." The doctor explained in some detail what he wanted to prevent.

"Oh, yes, that's the A-fib thing I've seen on TV commercials," Jake said.

"Exactly. We will give you medication and I will want to see you in my office again in a month and then probably every three months for awhile."

Julia said, "Dr. Kahn, we are moving to Florida in about a month. Do we need to postpone that? We can if we need to."

"Congratulations on escaping this winter," said the doctor ruefully. "No, I will refer you to a colleague there."

"Does he need to limit his activity?" asked Julia, earning a scowl from Jake.

"No, more exercise is always good. You will likely be more

active in Florida sunshine. It will be easy to eat a good diet of fish and vegetables and fruits there."

Glancing at Jake's laptop, he said conversationally, "Your fiancé said you are writing a book."

Fiancé? thought Jake. *That sounds good!* "Yes, I'm writing a book on the effects of the death law."

"Fiction or nonfiction?" asked the doctor. "That whole thing is like a horror story. At least to us doctors and especially those of us in specialties where most of our patients are elderly and frail."

"Nonfiction. Most are against it, though I've encountered a few people who think it's a good thing because they want to die."

"That is something physicians and their patients can handle together if the government and the media will stay out of it," Dr. Kahn snorted. "And the church. Sorry, I do not mean to give offense if you are of a different mind.

"And the death lawyers," added the doctor. "Doctors and patients and their families can take care of this by themselves, without help from others. We need to have more conversations about end-of-life and fewer about surgery."

"The AMA wants Medicare to begin to cover such conversations," Jake added. "I read that somewhere."

"I fear too much publicity on the death law may actually inhibit such conversation, because people may not trust their physicians not to put them on some list somewhere. There's a book, *No Good Deed,* by a Dr. Cohen that might give you some perspective from the medical profession. And also *Being Mortal* by Atul Gawande.

"However," he said as he moved toward the door, "the good news is that you and I don't need to have such conversation today. You are doing very well. You can go home. Please call my office and make an appointment for a month from now, if you will still be in town."

After the doctor left, Julia turned to Jake, gave him a hug, and said, "Let's get out of here."

"Shower together at home?" he leered.

"Now I know you're feeling better," Julia said, laughing. "Let me figure out how to get us out of here."

The city had come to a standstill with the first significant snowfall of the year. Snow glistened under streetlights as Julia slowly drove them home. There was very little traffic, though they heard an occasional siren as an intrepid emergency vehicle plowed toward the hospital.

When they and their suitcases and Jake's new medication were in the apartment, Jake embraced Julia and said, "You are beautiful, you know. I was groggy when I said it earlier, but you are beautiful in spirit, too."

She looked up and smiled at him. "Thanks. What brought that on?"

"I was just thinking how you introduced yourself as my fiancé. I like that."

Julia paused before speaking and chose her words carefully. "I hoped you wouldn't think I was being presumptuous. But I was afraid they wouldn't let me stay if they thought I was only casually connected."

"I like the way it sounds," he said.

"I do, too," said Julia, reaching over to squeeze his hand.

Julia had walked only about a block toward her office Thursday morning, full of misgivings about leaving Jake, though he seemed fine, when her phone rang. *Oh, God, he's sick again,* she feared.

"Missy, you coming in today?" rasped a familiar voice.

"Yes, Marcus, I should be there in about fifteen minutes. Why, has something come up?"

"Nothing new, just we got a lot of work piled up. Oh, how's Jake?" he asked as an afterthought.

"He seems okay. He's at the condo working, though I kind of hate to leave him alone."

"Just let him be a potato couch today. Let's get some work done and we'll all leave early before the traffic gets snarled and everything re-freezes, ok?"

Potato couch? wondered Julia. *Oh, couch potato.* With a laugh, she strode on through the sloppy sidewalks, enjoying the fresh air after the confinement of the hospital.

The minute she entered the office, Julia faced a barrage of questions of "How's Jake?" followed by "Can you spare a minute to help me with this?" Settling herself into her office, she worked her way through the many issues that confound a congressman's office, even in a holiday week.

She waded through insurance issues, pension errors, immigration plights, and various other requests to unsnarl bureaucratic snafus for constituents. She fended off lobbyists from the defense, pharmaceutical, and many other industries and organizations. She sifted through requests for the congressman to speak, endorse, co-sponsor, and write on various topics. She met with her staffers, spending the most time with Walter working on the upcoming rebuttal speech. There was no opportunity to plan transition with Tina-Maria, but that could wait a bit. Except for occasional check-ins and short conversations, the congressman left Julia on her own to restore order to the office, which she did with remarkable efficiency.

CHAPTER 37

Friday, December 30

To everyone's relief, Jake's health seemed restored. Other than taking medicine, little seemed changed in their lives. After a few days of work in their offices and welcome solitude in the evenings, they headed home to Julia's to spend a quiet New Year's Eve with Henry.

Julia had asked Hattie earlier if she wanted some time off to return home, but Hattie declared, "Not my home no more. My daughter and her kids done moved in already. No telling what kind of foolishness occur on New Year's Eve in the 'hood, people get all drugged and liquored up. If it's all-same to y'all, I druther just stay here. We got lots to do, but me and Mist' Henry done a lot while y'all in the city."

Henry was visibly happy to see them back. He gave Jake a man-hug and said, "Don't scare me again like that, boy!"

Boy? I'm not that far from Henry's age. But the loving welcome moved and pleased him. "I'll do my best not to. It scared me plenty, too. But I feel fine now."

"Julia, we found something you'll want to see right away," urged Henry.

"Really, what?" she asked as she hung up her hat and coat and tugged off her boots.

"We found – well, Hattie found," he amended, glancing at his helper, "a little trunk that belonged to your mother, buried in the corner of the basement. I guess your mother put it there when we moved here. I never saw it before."

"Huh," said Julia. "I don't remember anything like that, either. What's in it?"

"It's stuff from Beatriz's early life."

The little trunk, small enough to be carried on a strong back, was scratched, weathered tooled leather, bound with thin straps and buckles. As she gingerly unclasped the straps and opened the lid, Julia wondered if her mother had brought the little box when she illegally entered the US from Mexico many decades ago. Musty air with a hint of history wafted up.

An envelope, obviously of more recent vintage, lay on top with Julia's name on it. She opened it, saying, "What's this?"

Inside she found a letter from her mother, written in Spanish. The writing started off firmly on the page but sloped off into incomprehensible squiggles after a few sentences.

Julia translated it through tears as she read it aloud to the others. "'My darling girl, my mind is leaving me and I want you to have these things from our family. Never forget me or your father or our people in the old...' I can't make sense of the rest of it." Holding it out to Jake, she said, "Can you read any words there?"

Jake scanned the page and said, "I don't know Spanish, but it doesn't look coherent except this part here at the end." He read out, "Looks like a T and an E, maybe *amor*."

Julia smiled through her tears. "One last love message from my mom. Let's see what else is in here."

Old photographs depicted smiling dark-skinned people – her relatives? Turning the brittle paper over carefully, she found Spanish names but no clue as to who the people were. She wondered if genealogy searches could be done in other countries. Someday she would try to track down these people.

Other items included a small, much-handled homemade doll that Julia had never seen before that must have belonged to Beatriz. Next to it she found her favorite little threadbare stuffed elephant she barely remembered from her own childhood. There was a small turquoise ring she'd never seen her mother wear, wrapped in colorful woven cloth. She wondered it if might have been a gift from her father to her mother. She lifted out two little cellophane envelopes containing locks of hair. One was black and coarse. The other was the same color but baby-fine in texture.

"Maybe this is my father's and this other one is my baby hair?" she guessed. She barely remembered her father and felt awed to perhaps be holding something related to him. She placed the items back in the trunk and said, "These are definitely going with us to Florida. This is a wonderful find, Hattie, Henry."

Jake said, "Could we place the urn with your mother's ashes in there, too?"

"I think that's a wonderful idea. What do you think, Henry?"

Wiping his eyes, Henry nodded, "I agree. I want us to take Beatriz with us."

CHAPTER 38

Saturday, December 31

New Year's Eve came and went as a pleasant evening by the fire on a very cold night. Mid-evening Hattie's phone rang. She checked the display, her face lit up, and she said, "'Scuse me, y'all," and disappeared into her own room with the door closed. Quiet bursts of laughter emerged from the room, followed by periods of low conversation.

"Who in the world is she talking to?" wondered Julia.

Hattie returned with happy face and saw expectant faces. "What?" she asked.

"We wondered who that was. You sounded so happy."

"Oh, just Nate callin' to say Happy New Year. He wanna know when we getting back. I say about the end of the month. That about right?"

"How nice of him to call," said Julia.

"Oh, he calls most every day," Henry said.

"Not every day, Mist' Henry. But he says, if we not back soon, he's coming to get me," she said with a giggle.

"Well, let's discuss strategy here," said Julia. "We wouldn't want you kidnapped."

"Oh, he'll wait," she laughed, "but I'll be glad to be back."

"The movers are coming January 20, so we should be in Florida on January 21 or 22. Marcus gives his State of the Union rebuttal on January 26 and we can watch it from our new home."

"Will he want you here for that?" asked Jake.

"No, we already discussed that. I need to be available but not present. We'll have a few days to get organized in Florida before I hit the road running in the office there."

"How'll we get everything done here before January 20?" asked Henry. "That's just three weeks."

"Don't fret, Mist' Henry, we get it done," said Hattie.

Julia reminded them, "We just decide what to take. The movers'll pack for us. We can take things and gradually replace them there with Florida-style stuff. We don't really have time to sort here."

"Good idea. We begin with the familiar and then merge into a fresh start," said Henry.

He sounded optimistic, especially for a man in his seventies, newly widowed, with precarious health. She admired his optimism, courage and appreciation for life, limited though his was these days.

"If this death law holds up, I won't be needing stuff much longer," said Henry. "I'm giving most of my bird books away. Hattie and I figure to donate Beatriz's clothes and some of mine to Salvation Army. Okay, Julia?"

"Fine," she said. "I plan to leave a few winter things at your place, Jake."

"Me, too," said Jake. "I'll take some clothes and my golf clubs but that's about it. We'll be back here often enough, we can bring what we want later."

"Y'all gonna celebrate Christmas this year or just forget it?" asked Hattie.

They looked at each other blankly, not even remembering they'd skipped exchanging presents in their grief.

Henry suggested, "Let's exchange one gift each," to which they nodded.

"How about January 26? We'll be home to watch the congressman's speech that night. We can have a holiday dinner."

Everyone agreed enthusiastically, pleased to have something positive ahead in the maelstrom of moving. "No decorations, though," threw in Julia.

"I make dinner, that'll be my gift to you," offered Hattie.

"Shrimp, please," Henry replied promptly. "Happy New Year, dear ones. I'm going to bed." He picked up the cat dozing on his lap, stood and steadied himself.

Hattie moved to help him. "I'm going to bed, too. See y'all next year!" She grinned.

After the others were gone, Julia nestled closer to Jake and said, "Were they just being tactful and leaving us alone?"

"Yes, and I didn't even have to bribe Henry to get lost!" he laughed as he drew her close for a long kiss. "Happy New Year, my love."

They sorted, sifted and tossed for the next few weeks. How'd they ever get so much stuff? They kept things that reminded them of Beatriz, including many colorful Mexican artifacts. They donated Henry's car to an organization that helped homeless people get back to work.

Julia shed tears as she chose items from her mother's jewelry to keep. She regretted there was no one else in the line to pass it on to.

She and Jake wrapped up loose ends in their respective offices and readied their DC condo to leave for a few months. Her leave-taking from her staff wasn't hard, knowing she'd be seeing them often as she traveled between the offices. Walter would join her in Florida in a few weeks.

The movers arrived and boxed, wrapped, crated, draped, hefted and stuffed everything into a huge yellow moving van. Julia was surprised not to feel more emotion at leaving her home of many years. She had so much to look forward to in Florida. Her mother's spirit was moving with them to Florida, while the Falls Church house held the ache of absence.

They shoehorned the leftovers into Julia's CR-V. Two days later, a tired but happy family drove into their new driveway in Florida, a few hours ahead of their furniture. As they lowered the car windows to breathe in the warm Florida air, Henry waved to some of his bocce buddies.

"Hey," yelled Mac to others standing nearby, "It's Henry! He's back!"

Julia saw Henry's huge grin.

Inside the condo, Hattie said, "Mist' Henry, you make a list of things we need if I say them?"

"Sure," he said. "I've got a pad of paper in my man-bag here."

Julia rolled her eyes at Jake, wondering where Henry had learned about man-bags.

"Okay, spray cleaning stuff, food, TP, dustin' thingies, coffee, cat food..."

"TP? Oh, yeah, TP, got it."

Hattie looked around, shaking her head with her hands on her hips. "I gotta get this place clean!"

Julia ventured, "It looks clean to me already, Hattie."

"You never know," said Hattie ominously. "Might be them germs here."

"It's beautiful, isn't it, Jake? Just look at that Gulf view," said

Julia, linking her arm through his and drawing him onto the deck for a welcome kiss.

"Here's the list," Henry said, handing it to Julia. "I added wine, shrimp and key lime pie."

"You two want to wait for the movers while Jake and I make a quick run to Publix?"

"We'll get Mist' Henry's case empty. I brought some sheets and towels to start us before we get unpacked from the movers. Add laundry powder to that list. Mist' Henry, you may want you a nap whilst it's quiet."

"Quit bossing me, Hattie," grumbled Henry. "Might be a good idea, though."

CHAPTER 39

Friday, January 21

They quickly established a new daily routine of Julia going to her office, Jake working in his little office at the condo, Henry playing bocce ball and with his cronies, and Hattie waging war on the germs in the condo. Calvin prowled, looking for Beatriz.

Jake took it easy at first but quickly returned to his demanding work level. He could concentrate and write in his new office at home and the book manuscript was developing well. He kept the columns and articles flowing, so his editor left him alone. *Should have had a heart attack sooner, seems to have gotten Sam off my back.*

Late afternoons, they continued their unpacking and placing items around their new home. Evenings they collapsed in front of the television or sat on the deck while Hattie disappeared with Nate.

They tackled chores necessitated by the move: registering their car, getting a Florida driver's license for Julia, registering Julia, Henry and Hattie to vote, and doing the myriad other chores associated with a new address. Jake would retain his DC residency for the present.

They loved their new home. Mexican artifacts displayed well in the tropical atmosphere of Florida. The four of them settled into a pleasant hum of daily life. Their sadness at the loss of Beatriz remained but was mitigated by their pleasure in their new life.

Some days Jake took Julia to work and kept the car. Some days he walked down the beach and contemplated his writing or talked with other residents in the coffee shops. It was easy to focus on his writing, hearing all the anxiety surrounding the death law.

They had noticed billboards with messages such as "Save the GEMS" and "Long Life to GEMS." One afternoon Julia came home from work to find bright green t-shirts draped over the arm of the sofa. Emblazoned in orange letters on one shirt was "GEMS Rock." The other said "GEMS Roll."

"What in the world are these?" she asked Hattie.

"They're Mist' Henry's shirts. He's done joined the protest."

"What protest?"

Henry lumbered into the room, grabbed a shirt and waved it over his head like a flag. "The grassroots seniors' protest against the death law. I've never been in a protest before and it's fun!"

"What's a GEM?" Julia asked. "What are you protesting? Didn't you protest Vietnam?"

"Julia, honey, I was a Marine. Marines don't protest wars. Semper Fi. But I used to listen to Peter, Paul and Mary."

"GEMS stands for 'Gang of Exasperated Mad Seniors.' I wear the 'Rock' one when I'm on my walker and the 'Roll' one in my chair. I'll carry a sign, too. We plan to circle in front of the federal courthouse in a couple of days, chanting 'Save the GEMS' or 'Don't kill the GEMS.'"

Julia was already phoning Simms. She briefly explained the movement to him and said, "Can you get down here for that rally? What a photo op! Free, too!"

Ending the call, she turned back to Henry and fired off questions: "Where'd you get the shirts? Who's in charge?"

"It's a grassroots thing. Mac got me involved, all the bocce guys. Somebody sends us an e-mail and says where to show up in our shirts."

Jake walked out of his office and joined the conversation. "I've noticed signs in coffee shops and stores, 'Spare the GEMS,' 'GEMS Rule,' 'GEMS for Life.' I feel a column coming on. Henry, who can I interview?"

"Mac, I guess, or he'd know who. We hear it's spreading to other states. People are so mad about this death law thing. And we might stand on street corners and wave signs, too."

"I thought that was for elections," said Jake.

Henry looked him in the eye. "If this law isn't repealed, most GEMS will never see another election."

Julia and Jake both scribbled notes as fast as Henry talked, recognizing a political bonanza.

Henry continued, "We've got a gang sign, too. It's the time-out sign, right hand on top of left, perpendicular. It means wait on this law, don't put it into effect."

Hattie rolled her eyes and laughed. "Better'n sitting around slumped in front of the TV, I reckon."

Monday, January 23

Thousands of senior citizens rallied in their fluorescent green and orange GEMS t-shirts. As they clumped, shuffled, limped, rolled, sashayed and strutted in a ragged parade around the courthouse, they recited, "Free the GEMS," in quavering but enthusiastic voices. They waved their protest signs and the frail hung onto stronger friends as they marched. Every time they passed a camera, they made their gang sign.

Congressman Simms flew in for the courthouse rally and received great coverage on national television. Julia had planted a few "Simms loves GEMS" signs among the chanters.

The protesters availed themselves of the bottles of water and Florida oranges some volunteers handed out. They chatted like it was a party. Everyone had a great time, although one old geezer yelled, "Where's the cookies?"

CNN and other network cameras rolled as newscasters asked seniors, "What does the death law mean to you?"

"Well, young man," answered one blue-haired woman, "I won't shop for Christmas presents because I won't be here if this law thing isn't repealed."

Congressman Simms shook as many hands as he could reach, posed for photos, and made a few on-camera remarks for news people jockeying to interview him. "The message is clear. Seniors do not want their government to make their death decision. GEMS rule!"

One newscaster opened his nightly show with, "Call them gray, grizzled, gloomy or grave – no pun intended – the GEMS – Gang of Exasperated Mad Seniors – staged a protest today in Florida. They are not grasping, greedy or grumpy, they just want to live. And to do that, Congress has to repeal the death law." Some of the footage, Julia was happy to note, included Simms.

An exhausted but beaming Henry watched the evening news propped up on the couch, commenting, "Everyone feels good because they're doing something, even if it doesn't make a difference. Who knows, it might help. We do vote, you know."

"Oh, yeah, believe me, we do know that," said Julia.

CHAPTER 40

Thursday, January 26

Their designated Christmas approached and Julia decided on a new set of golf clubs for Jake. They still hadn't played together, but she had noticed that his clubs were pretty old. She planned to buy him state-of-the art clubs and her head was awhirl about hybrids, shaft composition, club head speed and other factors. She opted for a generous gift card, to be presented with a new golf glove and a dozen balls, along with a brochure on golf courses in the area.

A gift for Henry was simple – a couple of bright Hawaiian shirts and some new shorts and he was set. For Hattie, Julia chose a gift certificate from Beall's. Julia guessed the thrifty Hattie would go to one of the ubiquitous Beall's Outlets and really stretch her Christmas dollars. She added a gift card for Nate to a restaurant. There, one gift each – Julia was done. She thought maybe all their future Christmases should be this easy.

A few wrapped gifts showed up under a small, lighted Christmas tree. She'd decreed no decorations but had to admit the little tree was festive. She assumed Hattie and Henry had found it while unpacking. Julia wondered how Henry had managed to shop. She added her offerings to the assortment under the little tree. Poking around like an eager child, she saw presents with Hattie's and Henry's names on them in Jake's handwriting but nothing for herself. *Huh*, she thought, *wonder where mine is?"*

On Tuesday, the day dawned bright, sunny, and balmy in Florida but cold and snowy in most of the rest of the country. Julia and Walter put Simms through his paces one more time via computer camera, checked his wardrobe, and pronounced him ready for the big speech. Julia was worried about not doing an actual rebuttal to the President, but the congressman was adamant that everyone wanted to hear about only one topic: repeal of the death law. And he was ready to give it to them.

Hattie produced a marvelous dinner of red snapper, rice and black beans, her gift to the family. Nate had joined them for the festive evening and had grilled the fish to perfection.

Julia was so anxious over the speech, she'd thought she couldn't enjoy their delayed Christmas. But the food was so good, she found herself entering into the spirit.

Henry was like a kid and could hardly contain himself, waiting for his gifts. "Pass stuff out, somebody, anybody," he directed after the table had been cleared.

Jake knelt by the little tree and handed gifts to Julia, who gave them to the intended recipients. Soon a couple of gifts sat in front of everyone except for her. *Did everyone forget me? Where's mine?* she wondered. She had an envelope addressed to "Julia and Jake" in Henry's handwriting, but no packages in front of her.

Still on his knees, Jake crawled to her chair and pulled out a beautiful little box from his pocket, unwrapped but festive. "Julia, would you do me the honor of becoming my wife?"

She clasped both hands over her mouth and breathed, "Really, darling? Oh, yes!" as she threw her arms around him, toppling them both into the tree in a heap of tears and laughter. They sat up and sealed the deal with a kiss as she tried on the gorgeous sapphire encircled with tiny diamonds. "Oh, Jake, it's beautiful!"

Jake said shakily in a voice filled with emotion, "I thought maybe you'd like that better than the traditional diamond. But we can trade it in if you'd rather."

"This is the most beautiful ring I've ever seen! Of course we won't trade it in," she assured him. She saw from the beaming faces that everyone else had been in on the secret. "You knew!" she accused Henry teasingly.

"Of course I knew. He had to ask my permission. Now open my envelope, daughter."

Julie retrieved the envelope with their names on it and found a Christmas card inside with a folded brochure describing Guadalajara. In Henry's shaky hand was the message, "Your mother and I give you a honeymoon in Mexico. Perhaps you can find a cousin in Guadalajara."

Again, she covered her mouth with one hand and reached out to grasp Henry's hand with the other. She finally managed to get the words out, "There's nothing we would love better, right, Jake?"

Jake reached over to shake Henry's hand, ending up in a half-hug. "Why couldn't I have thought of such a great thing, Henry? You stole my thunder!"

Henry explained, "It's from Hattie, too. She actually got me thinking when she asked what we'd do with Beatriz's ashes. I thought maybe you could scatter a small amount in Guadalajara. Hattie's agreed we can manage just fine by ourselves while you're gone."

Julia reached out to embrace Hattie, too, who said, "Yes'm, this is a fitting thing. It's not usual to do a honeymoon and a funeral thing together, but this time, just seems right."

"It seems right to me, too," agreed Julia, as Jake nodded in agreement. "Wow, what a Christmas."

"Now can I open my presents?" asked Henry plaintively.

They all laughed and everyone else ooh-ed and ah-ed over their presents while Julia could hardly tear her eyes from the beautiful ring on her finger.

As they began gathering up their wrappings, Nate said, "Wait, I got one more thing, kinda like a gift. Y'all know I'm a deacon at my church. Well, they're knowing Miss Hattie's my lady and they wanna know if you're willing to be a deaconess, Hattie."

"Law, yes, I be honored," she said. "Now I feel like I truly belong here. Thank you, Jesus, and Nate," as she gave Nate a big hug.

"Oh, Lord, we're about to miss the speech. Somebody turn on the TV quick!" yelled Julia. Enthralled as she was with her ring, she was still a consummate professional.

Jake quickly found the channel and they all settled in around the TV.

Looking around the living room, Henry realized everyone was paired but himself. He was lonely, though he felt Beatriz's spirit near him. It felt like she'd been gone a long time before she actually died. He held Calvin on his lap, but a cat wasn't a mate.

Marcus Simms came on the screen, conservatively but fashionably dressed in a navy suit and bright red-striped tie. He was introduced by the party chair as "our party's rising star who was bold enough to speak out on the death law."

Yeah, or dumb enough, thought Julia. *Either this goes as planned or we're all screwed.* She knew they'd dump him in a heartbeat if their rising star turned into a flame-out.

"My fellow Americans," began Marcus, as he paid obligatory lip service to the "distinguished President" who had preceded him in speaking. "I have only one message for you tonight: We must repeal the death law and we must do so now. Our distinguished President didn't talk about the death law in his speech, so I will rectify that oversight."

The camera panned to a half-dozen gray-haired citizens wearing GEMS t-shirts, interrupting the congressman's speech with applause.

"Did you fly them up there?" asked Jake. "I didn't know there were GEMS in the DC area."

"No," Julia said, grinning, "we just mailed some t-shirts and told Tina-Maria to find some volunteers."

Simms continued, "We are only five months away from the time the death law is to take effect. People are working on the logistics of implementation, but I tell you, we need to work on the morality instead!" He pounded the podium for emphasis and glared into the camera lens.

Once again, he was interrupted by applause, which broke off quickly. It appeared the GEMS had missed a cue to sit quietly and had applauded spontaneously.

Briefly Simms detailed the havoc and heartache that would ensue if the death law took effect. He reminded the American public that "the world watches in horror and disgust as we prepared to slaughter our elders."

He waited until the applause stopped again and said, "But I have some heartening news. The repeal bill that we introduced into Congress, the Simms bill, has been reported out of committee and will come to the floor of the House for a vote next week. A similar bill is moving rapidly through the Senate committee structure and we are confident this bill will reach the Senate floor next week, also. I am sure that your congressmen," pointing his finger at the camera for emphasis, "and your senators will vote to repeal when these bills come up for a vote next week. I urge you to call, write, or e-mail your representatives and senators tonight to let them know how you feel. Time is short, and we must stop this nonsense now! Thank you for doing your duty as a citizen to stop this egregious act against our seniors. And God bless America!"

The fading camera shot was of the GEMS group standing and waving – except for the two in wheelchairs, and the two on walkers who were getting up more slowly. *Yea, Tina-Maria, good staging!* thought Julia. *Damn, she's good!*

Her phone rang immediately as she was reaching to dial Tina-Maria. Simms barked, "How'd I do?"

"Marcus, you were magnificent! I've never seen you better!" she said wholeheartedly. "Listen, I want to tell you about–"

"Gotta go, media fellers want to interview me, talk to you tomorrow." At that, he hung up.

"So much for sharing engagement news!" Julia laughed. "He really *was* magnificent, wasn't he?"

"He sure was," said Jake, as the others nodded agreement. A good journalist, he began flipping between channels, checking the coverage, and scrolling down websites on his laptop to gauge the immediate response. "What happened to physician-assisted suicide in the speech?"

"That comes later," said Julia. "We decided the first task is to repeal the death law. Then we'll work to replace it with something sensible. Someone else is going to introduce that part of it. We thought to keep the Congressman clean of that so we wouldn't give the opposition a murder-rap thing to hang around his neck when he runs for Senate."

"Good idea," Jake approved. "Pretty smart, when I think about it."

"Whew, too much in one day," said Henry. "I'm exhausted. No, Hattie," he waved her off, "I can get myself to bed tonight."

"Okay, if y'all don't need me, Nate and I going out for awhile. I'll be back directly."

Jake and Julia turned off the TV but lingered awhile. "Let's go sit on the deck," said Jake.

As they settled into their chairs, looking out over the Gulf in the moonlight, Jake took Julia's hand and said, "Are you happy, sweetheart? Did you really like the ring?"

She squeezed his hand, inched her chair closer, and hooked her legs over his knees. "I love it. Even more, I love you." She leaned in for a long kiss. Rubbing her hands over his back, she said, "Let's go inside and get comfortable."

"Oh, yes." He grinned as he took her hand to help her up and through the deck door into their bedroom.

CHAPTER 41

Monday, January 30

After his bocce ball game, Henry wandered along the beach sidewalk, moving slowly on his walker but enjoying the view and the warm weather. All the conversation he'd heard the last few days was on repeal of the death law and he was a little tired of the topic.

He spoke pleasantly to those sitting on the benches, riding their bikes, and strolling along the path. He felt a little tired and decided to sit a bit before he headed back home.

There was no vacant bench so he stopped at one occupied by a gray-haired woman holding a little fluffy white dog. Glad he was wearing one of the bright new shirts Julia had given him for Christmas, Henry hesitated and asked, "Is this seat reserved?"

She replied, "Please join us. Logan and I would enjoy your company."

The dog, smaller than Calvin-the-cat, immediately jumped toward Henry, licking his hands. Henry laughed and said, "Hey, boy. You're a friendly dog."

"Yes, too friendly sometimes," said the woman as she tried to pull the wriggling dog back away from Henry.

"Please, let him visit with me," said Henry as he continued to pat the little dog's head.

"Are you a dog-lover?" she asked.

"Yes, I like dogs, though I have a cat right now. My name's Henry and I just moved here a few weeks ago."

"I'm Beth," she answered. "I've been here a few years. I didn't think I'd seen you before. You get around well with your walker."

"I feel very lucky that I can still do that. My Parkinson's hasn't made me completely dependent yet. Where'd you move from?"

"Wisconsin," said Beth. "My late husband and I moved here about three years ago, to get out of the cold. He died a few months after we arrived, but I stayed and got Logan to keep me company. He was a rescue dog. Can you imagine anyone giving him up?"

"No, he's a charming little fellow." Logan settled himself on Henry's knees and looked blissful as Henry stroked his head.

"I'm a widower, too. My wife died only a month ago." Henry swallowed the lump in this throat. "She had Alzheimer's for a few years but we were able to keep her at home with the help of our daughter and a caregiver. Sorry for getting emotional. I thought I was prepared for her death, but I guess you never really are."

"Oh, that's so sad. That's a dreadful disease. My late husband showed a few signs of it but had a stroke and died before it became problematic. His death was very hard but I have to admit, I was grateful we were both spared his dementia."

"And you stayed here?"

"Yes, our kids are scattered all over the country. I'd already said goodbye to Wisconsin, so I decided to stay. The condo's paid for and I like being warm. I've made some good friends here. I can always move near my kids later if I have to. How about you?"

"My daughter and her fiancé – they just got engaged last night! – and our caregiver and I all moved here a couple of weeks ago. We love it and she can work for the congressman here as well as in DC."

"Congressman – do you mean Marcus Simms? He was so impressive last night! What a hero!"

Henry was pleased at the woman's astute recognition of Julia's boss. "Yes, and her fiancé Jake is writing a book on the death law. He's a journalist."

"You don't mean Jake Jordan? I read his columns every Sunday!"

Wow, thought Henry. *This lady's on the ball!*

"Yep, that's our Jake," he said. "And Hattie's our caregiver. Well, my caregiver now."

"Fascinating," said Beth. "You must have interesting dinner conversations."

"Yes, we do."

Beth rose and disengaged Logan from Henry. "Logan and I need to go. I'm meeting some friends for lunch. Logan and I usually walk about this time each day. Will I see you again?"

"Yes… yes, I believe you will," said Henry as he struggled to get to his feet. "Probably tomorrow."

"Good," said Beth, as she turned the little dog, straining toward Henry, in the direction of home.

Henry watched her leave, thinking, *That is one classy lady.* He looked out over the lovely blue waters of the Gulf, the white sand beach, and the green of the swaying palm trees. As he turned toward home, he suddenly thought, *Wonder if I can still whistle a tune?"*

Henry hadn't felt like whistling in a long, long time.

IDEAS FOR FURTHER READING

Butler, Katy. *Knocking on Heaven's Door: The Path to a Better Way of Death.* New York: Scribner, 2013.

Cruikshank, Margaret. *Learning to Be Old: Gender, Culture, and Aging, (3rd Edition).* Lanham, MD: Rowman and Littlefield Publishers, Inc., 2013.

De Grey, Aubrey & Rae, Michael. *Ending Aging: The Rejuvenation Breakthroughs that Could Reverse Human Aging in Our Lifetime..* New York: St. Martin's Press, 2007.

Evison, Jonathan. *The Revised Fundamentals of Caregiving: A Novel.* Chapel Hill, NC: Algonquin Books of Chapel Hill, 2013.

Fishman, Ted C. *Shock of Gray: The Aging of the World's Population and How it Pits Young Against Old, Child Against Parent, Worker Against Boss, Company Against Rival, and Nation Against Nation.* New York: Scribner, 2010.

Hauerwas, *God, Medicine, and Suffering.* Grand Rapids, MI: William B. Eerdmans Publishing Company, 1990.

Hurme, Sally Balch. *ABA/AARP Checklist for Family Caregivers: A Guide to Making it Manageable.* AARP.org/Caregiving Books, 2015.

Jacobs, Lawrence R. & Skocpol, Theda. *Health Care Reform and American Politics: What Everyone Needs to Know*. New York: Oxford University Press, 2010.

Mace, Nancy L. & Rabins, Peter V. *The 36-Hour Day: A Family Guide to Caring for People Who have Alzheimer Disease, Related Dementias, and Memory Loss*. (5th Edition). Baltimore: Johns Hopkins University Press, 2011.

Mittelman, Mary S. & Cynthia Epstein. *The Alzheimer's Health Care Handbook: How to Get the Best Medical Care for Your Relative with Alzheimer's Disease, In and Out of the Hospital*. New York: Marlowe and Company, 2003.

Moyes, Jo Jo. *Me Before You*. New York: Pamela Dorman Books/ Viking, 2013.

Rosofsky, Ira. *Nasty, Brutish, and Long: Adventures in Eldercare*. New York: Avery, 2009.

Theroux, Phyllis. *The Journal Keeper: A Memoir*. New York: Atlantic Monthly Press, 2010.

Volandes, Angelo E., MD. *The Conversation: A Revolutionary Plan for End-of-Life Care*. New York, Bloomsbury, 2015.

Willis, Claire B. *Lasting Words: A Guide to Finding Meaning Toward the Close of Life*. Brattleboro, Vermont: Green Writers press, 2013.

TEN QUESTIONS FOR BOOK DISCUSSION GROUPS

1. How plausible is the idea that Congress might pass such a law? What would be the benefits and losses with such legislation?

2. How would passage of such a law affect you or your family?

3. How does Hattie's life affect the others in the book? Do you know a Hattie?

4. Americans (and the world's population) are aging. What problems do you see ahead in America in caring for elders? What solutions would you suggest?

5. With which character in *The Death Law* did you most identify? Why?

6. Have you or someone you know well been faced with the situation of caring for a sick relative? How did that affect your or someone else's life? How did that caregiver cope with the stress associated with the caregiving?

7. What would you yourself choose if you had a degenerative disease you knew would end in death?

8. What would you suggest as end-of-life decisions for a loved one with dementia or other incurable illness?

9. Do others know your wishes about your death and the time preceding it? Have you put these wishes in writing? Are your legal documents in order?

10. Do you know what your parents/spouse/significant others in your family wish about prolonging their lives as they age, if you were to be involved in the decisions?

ABOUT THE AUTHOR

Dr. Claire Cole Curcio is Professor Emerita, Virginia Tech, Blacksburg, VA, and a former English and math teacher and school counselor. She is a Licensed Professional Counselor in Virginia. She and her partner Selby McCash, also a writer, live in Fredericksburg, VA, and Outer Banks, NC.

CPSIA information can be obtained at www.ICGtesting.com
Printed in the USA
BVOW04s1231231015

423615BV00001B/1/P